PRAISE FOR *THE CORAL BRIDE*

'A riveting story of old enmities, jealousies and friendships that come to light after a woman goes missing in a remote fishing village. It's beautifully atmospheric, with astutely drawn characters and a fascinating evocation of life on the edge of a wild ocean' Gill Paul

'After a gut-punch of an opener, the story takes on a wistful tone ... *The Coral Bride* is a haunting murder mystery about how human nature is every bit as dangerous and inscrutable as the sea' *Foreword Reviews*

'In this author's work, it is the journey, rather than the destination, that is important. Which is a joy – because it gives the reader a chance to revel in the sheer lyricality of the text, get to know the quirks and foibles of the characters and, ultimately, marvel at the clever plotting that creates such a satisfying finale' Crime Fiction Lover

'This isn't just a novel, it's a song. An ode to the sea and the fishing community. You will feel as if you're at the heart of this fascinating community and its dark side ... lyrical and mesmerising' The Book Trail

'Beautifully written and atmospheric police procedural that is centred around the sea and has a truly unique style' Rachel Hall

'Emotive and tragically beautiful in its execution, this is another wonderful story that will stay with me for some time to come' Jen Med's Book Reviews

'What enchanted me, once again, was Bouchard's lyrical prose, what held me captive was the people and their love interests, the sea first and foremost ... Beautiful, readable, unforgettable' From Belgium With Booklove

'I was hooked from the get go and I look forward to future instalments of this series. Yet again ... n impeccably and ... holds raw em roughout' Book (

'A thrilling take on life, love, jealousy, greed, revenge and family feuds in a close-knit fishing community' Goodreads

'The beauty of the writing creates a vivid picture and alongside this the entire story is full of subtle observations about those around DS Moralès, the people in his life and the awe-inspiring power of the sea' Amazon reviewer

'Beautifully written ... Kept me reading and certainly is a can't-put-it-down book' Amazon reviewer

'The captivating investigation also conjures up the tides and their mysteries, following the rhythm of the region, the icy course of its autumn tide' *Le Devoir*

PRAISE FOR ROXANNE BOUCHARD

'Lyrical and elegiac, full of quirks and twists – *We Were the Salt of the Sea* is an elegant crime novel that deserves to be a tremendous success' William Ryan

'A writer needs a distinct voice and Bouchard has that, she knows how to tell a story and captivate readers' *New Books Magazine*

'A tour de force of both writing and translation' Su Bristow

'A gripping thriller. I became utterly lost in this book, and when I briefly came up for air, I only wanted to dive straight back in' Louise Beech

'A tour de force of both writing and translation' Su Bristow

'A hypnotic read that manages to be by turns quirky, lyrical and insightful' Michael J. Malone

'An isolated Canadian fishing community, a missing mother, and some lovely prose' Eva Dolan

'This book is the definition of atmospheric ... Quiet characterisation, brooding secrets: I didn't actually care much about the whodunit part, but I was still absolutely unable to put the book down' Book Riot

'Dreamily poetic' *The Times*

'As a lover of the more naturalistic writing of authors such as Annie Proulx and Ron Rash, I loved the way that Bouchard showed such an incisive and lyrical edge to her writing in her depictions of the sea' Raven Crime Reads

'An engrossing look at the dark complexities of a close-knit community. This is a highly original, thoughtful and engaging story about love and loss that will appeal to anybody seeking more literary crime fiction' Hair Past a Freckle

'The whole story was like the sea. It was unpredictable, stormy and unforgiving but the beauty of it all was quite superb!'
Books from Dusk Till Dawn

'A stunning lyrical read, and I expect to be seeing Bouchard's name on award lists' Cheryl MM Book Blog

'A beautifully slow rhythm that captures the essence and atmosphere of this small fishing village with its distinctive and beautifully drawn characters that seduce Joaquin into a stupor of indecision' Live & Deadly

'A real treasure ... Enchanting, beguiling and I hope there are more of the same from this author' Mrs Blogg's Books

'A beautifully written tale that I think would appeal to lovers of literary fiction ... the crime element changed a story about a tight-knit community to a mystery that just begs to be solved'
Bibliobeth

'An absolutely beautiful book, both in its narrative and its setting ... A great investigation in a beautiful setting with the sea as much of a central character as Catherine and Joaquin' Have Books Will Read

'Atmospheric, but sometimes claustrophobic, *We Were The Salt of the Sea* is probably one of the most difficult stories that I've tried to write about. It's not one thing, it's a combination of many things, and that combination equals a book that truly is a joy to read. Bravo Roxanne Bouchard!'
Random Things through My Letterbox

ABOUT THE AUTHOR

Ten years or so ago, Roxanne Bouchard decided it was time she found her sea legs. So she learned to sail, first on the St Lawrence River, before taking to the open waters off the Gaspé Peninsula. The local fishermen soon invited her aboard to reel in their lobster nets, and Roxanne saw for herself that the sunrise over Bonaventure never lies. Her fifth novel (her first to be translated into English) *We Were the Salt of the Sea* was published in 2018 to resounding critical acclaim. She lives in Quebec. Follow Roxanne on Twitter @RBouchard72 and on her website: roxannebouchard.com.

ABOUT THE TRANSLATOR

David Warriner grew up in deepest Yorkshire, has lived in France and Quebec, and now calls British Columbia home. He translated Johana Gustawsson's *Blood Song* for Orenda Books, and his translation of Roxanne Bouchard's *We Were the Salt of the Sea* was runner-up for the 2019 Scott Moncrieff Prize for French-English translation. Follow David on Twitter @givemeawave and on his website: wtranslation.ca.

Also in the Detective Moralès series:
We Were the Salt of the Sea

The Coral Bride

ROXANNE BOUCHARD

Translated from the French by David Warriner

**ORENDA
BOOKS**

Orenda Books
16 Carson Road
West Dulwich
London SE21 8HU
www.orendabooks.co.uk

First published in the United Kingdom by Orenda Books 2020
Originally published in French as *La mariée de corail* by Éditions Libre
Expression 2020
Copyright © 2020, Roxanne Bouchard and Libre Expression,
Montreal, Canada
English translation © David Warriner 2020

A catalogue record for this book is available from the British Library.

ISBN 978-1-913193-32-4
eISBN 978-1-913193-33-1

Background vector created by brgfx – www.freepik.com

Typeset in Garamond by www.typesetter.org.uk
Printed and bound by CPI Group (UK) Ltd, Croydon CR0 4YY

*We would like to thank the Société de développement des entreprises culturelles
(SODEC) for its financial support*

SODEC
Québec ✚ ✚

For sales and distribution, please contact info@orendabooks.co.uk

For Catherine Asselin, SVN, counter of words and
dear friend though the highest of tides.

The Bridal Gown

Angel Roberts wakes with a start to the crash of a lobster trap tearing the water's surface in two. It's a lobster trap, she's sure it is. Thousands of times she's heard the whoosh of the sea surging into these things, swallowing them up and spitting them out again. It sounds like a sail being torn to shreds.

She smiles, satisfied with her deduction, and then tries to figure out what the heck could be making the other sound she can hear: a hammering. It almost sounds like her anchor chain, but it's not the regular clanking of the metal as it hurtles its way overboard. Truth be told, she barely ever uses the chain. Nor the anchor, for that matter.

The sound is curiously persistent. Little by little she comes to her senses and takes in her surroundings: the water lapping at the hull, the salty air filling her nostrils, the fabric of her dress clinging to her skin in the damp chill of the night. The pain of having her right arm twisted behind her back. Angel struggles to open her eyes. She's propped up against the wheelhouse of her lobster trawler. The tailgate is open, and a chain is clanking overboard. The swivel connecting the chain to the anchor rode thunks over the edge, and now that rope is being dragged down to the depths. It's attached to something, but what?

IDENTIFICATION OF DECEASED
Name: Angel Roberts
Age: 32
Place of residence: Cap-aux-Os
Cause of death: Drowning

Something yanks at her ankle and pulls her off her feet. Drags her body along the deck. She hits her head. Her dress is riding up, exposing her legs. The cold bites her thighs. Why is her right hand stuck behind her back? In a surge of panic, she spreads her left palm wide and presses it into the rubber deck matting, trying to slow her slide. Suddenly, the movement stops of its own accord. The counterweight of her body has halted the trap's descent to the depths. Or maybe it's already hit the seabed. The rope twitches tighter around her calves. Pulling herself together, Angel tries to wriggle her legs. What's happening?

She draws a sharp breath as it dawns on her that someone's trying to kill her. Yet she turns her gaze to the sky and exhales, and allows a sense of calm to wash over her.

The dainty face of the moon smiles softly on Angel. She's always loved the moon. But her mother said it was a liar. 'If it looks like a D, you think it's decreasing, and if it's shaped like a C, you'd swear it's curving bigger. But the moon is a liar, oh daughter of mine, you remember that. When it looks like it's shrinking, it's growing, and when it looks like it's getting bigger, the opposite is true.'

A sharp noise shatters the silence, Angel's dress tears, and, slowly, the line starts pulling her closer to the edge. Angel lets go. There's nothing she can do. She knows she had this coming.

CIRCUMSTANCES OF DEATH (excerpt)
At around 6.00 pm on Saturday 22nd September, Ms Roberts had dinner at her father's home with her husband, Clément Cyr, her father, Leeroy Roberts, and her older and younger brothers, Bruce and Jimmy. She and her husband were celebrating their tenth wedding anniversary, four days early. They chose that night because it was a Saturday.

At approximately 10.00 pm, Mr Cyr and Ms Roberts made

their way to Le Noroît, an auberge in Rivière-au-Renard known
by locals as Corine's, where the annual party to mark the end of
the fishing season was taking place. (See attached list of
individuals in attendance.)

At around 11.15 pm, Ms Roberts asked her husband to take
her home, claiming she was tired. Mr Cyr proceeded to drive his
wife home and returned to the party at around 1.00 am.

Angel's body pivots slightly as it slides, freeing her hand. She
feels sick, and now she's wide awake. Turning her head to one
side, she sees the watery shards of the moon lighting a path on
the swell. The shimmering film of splinters around her trawler
grows thicker as it reaches for the horizon.

Landlubbers rattle on about the moon on the water being a
glimmering silver road or a rolling carpet bejewelled with
thousands of sequins. 'They're a bunch of romantics,' her mother
scoffed. 'There's no road and no silver in the reflections the moon
casts on the sea. Try to touch them and they'll slip right through
your fingers, you'll see. The moon is a liar, and the sea is a lure.'

Angel's slide continues sternward, inching her feet closer to
the watery threshold rocking the hull. A cold wave kisses her
feet, licks at her legs. She could try to shake herself free, untie
the rope, cling on to the boat, cheat fate and stay on board, but
she won't. Soon Angel's lobster trawler will drift out to sea as
she sinks like a stone.

MISSING-PERSON REPORT (excerpt)
Mr Cyr returned home around 10.00 am on Sunday 23rd
September to find his wife absent. Despite multiple calls to her
phone, Ms Roberts failed to answer. Concerned for his wife's
well-being, Mr Cyr drove to the Grande-Grave wharf, where
he observed Ms Roberts' vehicle and noticed that her lobster

trawler was not tied up at the dock. Mr Cyr then called Jean-Paul Babin, one of his wife's deckhands, who told him he was not on board the boat. Mr Babin called Ms Roberts' brother Jimmy, who then called their father. Establishing that no one had seen Ms Roberts, the fishermen began to look for her in places she liked to sail to when she went to sea alone. Around three that afternoon, Mr Cyr alerted the local police and reported his wife and her trawler missing. Coast-guard vessels were then scrambled to join the search. (See attached report.)

The boat sways from side to side as Angel stretches out her left hand to touch the cold metal gunwale. She smiles. She's one of only two women on the Gaspé Peninsula to own her own lobster trawler. Later, that statement will be repeated in the past tense.

'Only two women skippers in all the Gaspé, there were!' people will say.

Mariners will add that one of them died at sea.

That it wasn't even a stormy night.

The sea is no place for a woman, they'll say. Fishing is a man's job. Obviously, they'll infer, because it's hard work and men like to prove how tough they are.

She was the daughter of an old cod fisherman with a grudge to bear, they'll remind people. The big sister of a poacher and the baby sister of a man suspected of murdering his rival. And her husband, he lost his own father at sea too, before he lost his wife. He's a man with a waterlogged past, they'll say. The swell always consumes those who open their hearts to the ocean.

AUTOPSY REPORT (excerpt from findings)
There is no observable evidence of physical violence inflicted ante-mortem. No evidence of self-defence against a possible assailant was detected on the deceased's arms or hands, or under her

fingernails. The rope wrapped around the deceased's calves was tied firmly, though not tightly enough to impede blood circulation. The high alcohol level and traces of sedative detected in the deceased's blood suggest she was unconscious at the time of death. If she had been conscious, one might assume that she would have attempted to untie the cord around her ankles or scratched her nails on the rubber matting as she slid along the deck. However, no fibres or rubber were found under her fingernails.

Now her dress is saturated with seawater, her thighs dripping wet. This current, the swell that's rolling at just the right height, has been coldly calculated, she thinks. A well-planned death, that's what this is. Whoever has done this has thought of everything. The wedding dress, the lobster trawler, the elusive moonlit path she's following like a fish fixated on a coppery lure.

'The wretched of the sea and their dreamers' souls are easily hooked by enchanted bait, oh daughter of mine.' Her mother was right, but Angel regrets nothing.

WITNESS STATEMENTS (excerpt)
There are no direct witnesses to this incident.

Suddenly, the boat lurches forward. For a fraction of a second, and in midair, Angel resists the fall the way a cormorant spreads its wings. Then she surrenders to her fate. Her trawler glides out to sea without her as the water sinks its icy jaws into her. For a moment, her dress billows out, suspending her at the surface. Angel takes her final breath and spreads her arms wide in acquiescence to the sky, not resistance to the sea. She opens her eyes wide, turns one last time to the moon and never closes them again.

Sunday 23rd September

Before the midnight hour, people are still trying to wrap their head around their day. After midnight, they're usually sleeping like logs. So to speak. They're at ease. Lost in their dreams. When an officer of the peace rings at the door of a citizen who's fast asleep, there's always something serious to report. The worst kind of drama or bereavement. A car crash, a stabbing, a stray bullet. You press the doorbell, hear the chime ring out in the hall and wait, standing in the dark like a messenger of the apocalypse. You think about the people inside, looking at the time, worried to be woken like this, pulling on their clothes in a daze, hushing the barking dog, turning on a light in the hall, peering through the window to make sure they haven't imagined the ring at the door, seeing there really is someone standing on the porch, petrified by the thoughts that cross their mind when they see the uniform. When there's good news to deliver, no one needs a police officer to do it. And it can always wait until morning.

No, that's not why anyone becomes a police officer, thought Joaquin Moralès, when the four symphonic notes of his door chime rang out around six that morning. The pale light of the dawning day filtered through the curtainless windows as he stepped out of bed and into a pair of jeans, pulling a sweater over his head as he shuffled downstairs.

He wasn't too concerned by the early wake-up, because he knew the duty officer that night was the young rookie, Robichaud. She spent her time flitting around him, fishing for advice, begging an opinion, fluttering her eyelashes so he'd recommend her for a transfer to Montreal. She wasn't a bad cop, just a bit wet behind the ears. Reckless for no reason, too easily influenced. As erratic as a chickadee chirping in an evergreen forest.

Constable Joannie Robichaud followed the chimes with a few discreet knocks at the door. That was the protocol for all Sûreté du Québec officers when they couldn't hear any noise inside or see a light come on. There was always a possibility the doorbell might not be working.

Moralès rubbed his eyes and gave his neck a stretch as he stumbled through the living room. It wasn't that he cared that much about sleep. He had already been awake, anyway, and had planned to get up soon and go fishing. But this Sunday was his day off and he'd rather the rookie had waited until Monday. With her though, everything was urgent. A matter of life or death. Justice prevails, everyone is equal before the law and all that.

Moralès flipped a light switch in the hall before he opened up, not wanting to take her by surprise. A jumpy young constable who's armed to the teeth can easily pump you full of lead.

Sure enough, there Joannie Robichaud was, standing stern as a bailiff on the doorstep in the early-morning sun. She had pulled her hair into a ponytail so tight, it was slanting her eyes. Her coat fell open to reveal a uniform bursting at the seams with outrageous cleavage. Every inch of her hips was loaded, as if she were patrolling the Bronx: cuffs, baton, pepper spray, the works. Her trousers were so figure-hugging, they looked like they had been sprayed on, her boots shined to military standards.

'I'm sorry to wake you, but it's urgent,' she said.

Rookies like these were ten a penny in cop shops everywhere, even in the darkest depths of the Gaspé Peninsula.

She stepped inside, and Moralès edged forward to close the door behind her. There was a chill in the air, and he was standing there in bare feet. He tried to shuffle around her, but in the narrow hallway, with her encumbered by all her gear, they bumped awkwardly into one another. They both recoiled. She blushed, walked towards the dining room and stopped, turned on her heels and planted her feet like she meant business, thumbs hooked in her belt loops, elbows wide, ready to serve and protect.

Moralès closed the door and reluctantly followed.

'Would you like a cup of coffee, constable?'

She declined with a curt shake of the chin. She should be doing her military service, he thought.

'It would be better if you were sitting down, Mr Moralès.'

No. 'Mr Moralès' would not be sitting down. Talk about trying his patience. He resented her ruining his morning with her trivial rookie concerns. Especially since it was the time of year when the remnants of summer slipped through your fingers like the sands of time. She'd cornered him, and she hadn't even called him 'sergeant'. Had she forgotten she was speaking to her superior?

'Listen, constable, I don't mind helping you, but I'm not at your beck and call around the clock…'

'It's your son,' she interrupted.

'My son?'

'A thirty-year-old man answering to the name of Sébastien Moralès.'

'Sébastien?'

It suddenly dawned on him what the constable's morning call must mean. She had followed the night-response protocol to the letter.

'I received a call about four this morning, but I waited until my night duty was over to come. I didn't want to wake you too early.'

'A call from who?'

'A friend who works at the New Richmond station.'

'I don't understand.'

Joannie Robichaud pretended to refer to her notes. She had memorised the details, but she had also seen a lot of crime movies and she liked to play things up. She might come across all formal, but she secretly dreamed that a seductive criminal would draw her into a passionate affair and tease her away from the straight and narrow. Yes, a rich drug baron who'd be so infatuated by her, he'd kidnap her and make love to her in a water bed. A heartbreaking tragedy of crime and desire.

'Sébastien Moralès was stopped shortly before two this morning by patrol officers in Carleton-sur-Mer. People were partying in town to celebrate the autumn equinox. The officers asked him to stop singing outside houses whose residents had gone to sleep for the night. Er … and to refrain from urinating in front of the town hall. They told him if he didn't stop, they'd bring him in for disturbing the peace and gross indecency. He said he could find his way behind bars by himself, because his father was down at the station in Bonaventure. The officers thought he meant his father was in a holding cell.'

'That's not possible…'

Moralès wouldn't be surprised if this were his youngest son, Manu, but Sébastien? No way. His eldest was as straight-laced as you'd expect a son from a good family to be: he never got drunk, took ballroom-dancing classes, drank alcohol-free beer and only bought toilet paper when it was on special.

'He resurfaced a little later down by the water, dancing on the wharf with the last of the revellers. That was the last they saw of him. They weren't exactly keeping him in their sights.

But then, around quarter to four, your son showed up at the station in New Richmond.'

She looked down at her notes again.

'Apparently he rolled up there by car, but no one saw him at the wheel. He waltzed in and announced – and I quote – "Tell Detective Moralès his *chiquito* is here!" When he realised he was at the wrong police station, he wanted to get back in his car, but the duty officers stopped him. Well, Constable Leroux, he likes to write as many tickets as he can, so he wanted to let him go and then pull him over for drink-driving, but my friend insisted on calling me instead. I've told her all about you and she remembered.'

She blushed, but Moralès didn't notice. His gaze was wandering, searching in vain for an answer that might miraculously have latched itself on to something in this silent room.

'Maybe it's a different person. My Sébastien wouldn't have driven all the way from Montreal without telling me…'

'My friend sent me a photo.'

Joannie Robichaud reached for her phone, scrolled until she found the photo and turned the screen to Moralès.

'Is this him?'

'Not really.' His son was barely recognisable. It was partly the unruly beard, lazy moustache and tousled hair, but mostly the drunken air of bravado, voracious smile and wicked glint in his eye. Still, he nodded. 'If you say so.'

Joannie couldn't help biting her lip as she ogled the image on her phone. In Moralès's son she saw all the sex appeal of a moneyed rogue. 'That's why I came,' she said. 'I thought … I might drive there with you. He's still too drunk to drive, and my friend wants him out of there before the day shift takes over. Otherwise, her boss is going to rap her knuckles and say it's a police station, not a hotel. You know what a pain bosses can be, when you…'

She stopped short and blushed again, but Moralès said nothing. Joannie and her friend in New Richmond had done him a favour this morning, and there was no need to crack the whip on a Sunday. Strutting around like that, she'd scare the living daylights out of anyone, but he couldn't bring himself to make her change into civvies before they went to collect Sébastien. Besides, he figured she must be keen to show off the allure and authority of her new uniform to her colleague in New Richmond. So Moralès let it slide, but he insisted they take his car. Driving would take his mind off the embarrassment.

'I mean, it's not a big deal to have one drink too many, but your son shouldn't have been driving,' Joannie said.

Moralès turned to his left and gazed at the sun rising over the sea, before getting in the car and driving away. He couldn't help but wonder what Sébastien was doing here on the Gaspé Peninsula.

'If this is a problem, you'll have to get him one of those devices to test his blood alcohol level before he gets behind the wheel,' said Joannie.

Why didn't Sébastien call to say he was coming? And what about Maude? Was he here without her?

'My uncle's in Alcoholics Anonymous, so he can help. I'll have a word if you like,' the young constable rattled on.

What about his work?

'But sometimes only a proper detox will do, you know. Because often it's not just the drink. Maybe it's drugs too.'

Moralès lost any patience he still had.

'Constable Robichaud, my son does not have a drinking problem.'

'You're his father. Obviously, he's not going to tell you everything.'

'We're very open with one another.'

'Not to contradict you, but you didn't even know he was here in the Gaspé…'

'He's a decent man. This must be some kind of misunderstanding.'

Joannie nodded, somewhat disheartened. So much for Sébastien Moralès being a lovable rogue. To think she'd kept her uniform on so he'd see what an irresistible figure of authority she was. If she'd known he was a 'decent man', he'd be forking out for a taxi ride instead. 'That's all right. If he needs help, he'll know I'm here, Mr Moralès. He can count on me.'

Moralès sighed. Right now, he'd rather be working a crime scene.

He steered into the car park at the New Richmond police station without a word. As his colleague took the lead, Moralès stood for a moment looking at Sébastien's car, which was straddling two spaces. Joannie held the front door of the station open for a few seconds, cast a disapproving look at Moralès, who didn't seem to be in much of a hurry to see his son, and crossed the threshold alone.

Joaquin's heart skipped a beat when he saw the disaster area inside his son's car. It was full of boxes, bags, suitcases, clothes, and pots and pans, all thrown in as if during a hasty getaway. A life turned upside down; a relationship gone up in smoke. Sébastien had to be in distress, he thought. That would explain the drunkenness. And who else would he turn to, when it all hit the fan, other than his father? Moralès drew a deep breath to ready himself for the drama ahead, and entered the station.

There was no one on the front desk. He knocked on the reinforced door, heard something behind it. Something loud. He couldn't quite make out what it was. Eventually, the duty officer threw the door open. The music surged over Joaquin like a tidal wave. 'La Vida Es Un Carnaval', by Celia Cruz. Sébastien used to play this song to death in his younger years.

The duty officer motioned for Moralès to come inside.

Yes, this was his son all right. Sébastien was down on one knee, reading the future written in the palm of Joannie's hand. 'I see you on a looong and wiiiinding rrrroad by the sea, with a teepsy Mexican vagabond at your side,' he slurred. 'And, I see your beauuuty.'

Joannie was lapping this up.

'*Papà!*' In a brusque yet no less graceful manner, Sébastien Moralès let go of the young officer's hand and strutted over to his father. '*Como estas? Señor*, you're my saviour!'

Wrapping his arms around his father and pulling him close, he turned to Joannie and her colleague, both of them rosy-cheeked. '*Con las señorrrritas…*'

Time for a word in his son's ear, Joaquin thought. 'What are you doing here? And drop the cheesy Don Juan accent, will you?' He made sure to keep his voice lower than the music, which was blaring from a tinny Bluetooth speaker he assumed belonged to Sébastien. It was a wonder it hadn't been confiscated.

Sébastien flashed him an inebriated smile. 'I've come to see you!' he gushed, planting a kiss on Joaquin's lips. 'Shall we go?'

Out in the car park, Sébastien tossed the rookie his keys. 'I'll ride with *Señorita*.'

'Only if you behave yourself, Sébastien,' she said, averting her eyes from her boss's.

'Oh, I promise, you'll have nothing to complain about…' He got into the passenger seat and Celia Cruz started singing through his portable speaker again. At the top of her voice.

That was how Moralès found **him**self on Highway 132, following his son's car, with Joannie **Robi**chaud driving – if that's what you could call speeding up, slowing down and swerving from one side of the lane to the other. Even blind drunk, it'd be hard for anyone to drive more dangerously. As soon as they got to Caplan, the car veered to the right without warning, towards the public beach. Following on autopilot, Moralès pulled up behind as the youngsters bounded out of the car and onto the beach.

Sébastien had cranked the music high and left his door open. Moralès stood in disbelief as his son took the rookie constable by the hand and twirled her around on sand packed firm by the outgoing tide. She'd ditched her gun and her baton, left her belt full of model officer's gear in the car. What the hell was his son doing, courting his father's subordinate right under his nose? Moralès was fuming at his son's shamelessness, and was torn between paternal love and the value he placed on fidelity in relationships. He himself had been married to Sarah for more than thirty years and…

And what?

Out beyond the dancers, the sea was dumping its waves on the sand. Three months ago, a woman tied his heart in knots. Catherine. Then she sailed off into the sunrise, and Joaquin hadn't heard a word about her since.

How, God only knew, but in one pirouette Sébastien managed to pluck the elastic loose from the spunky young constable's painful ponytail, setting her golden locks free, so they spilled out like a wave of honey, and unleashing a flaxen-haired Medusa who frolicked in the damp morning air. Transfixed, Joaquin watched his son – somehow still standing despite his long drive, drunken antics and sleepless night – turn this insufferable rookie into a graceful dancing queen. Was he really in any position to lecture him? Joaquin's gaze drifted back to the sea, searching for that sailboat of Catherine's he longed to see return, before settling on the young couple once more. How did he know things were rocky between Maude and Sébastien, anyway? Maybe he'd got the week off work, and Maude was away at a conference abroad. It wouldn't be the first time. His son loved to dance, so maybe all this was completely innocent. Joaquin's eyes wandered out to the Baie-des-Chaleurs, deserted in the morning light. He looked away, put his car in gear and headed back to the road.

It was about time he set the fishing line in the water, Moralès thought, but first he would have to eat something. His hopes were not high when he opened the fridge door. He couldn't remember when he had last gone grocery shopping. Still, he managed to salvage three mushrooms, half a tomato, a scrap of green pepper, two eggs, a hunk of cheese and a tiny onion. Not such a bad start to the morning after all.

With Celia Cruz's voice stuck in his head, he was humming 'Rie Y Llora' as he rustled up breakfast for himself. He wasn't expecting Sébastien to join him; he figured it would be a while before the rookie drove him back here after their salsa on the sand. Just as he was sliding his ranchero omelette onto a plate and pouring himself a coffee, he heard a car pulling into the driveway. Cursing under his breath that he'd not even taken a bite, he stepped outside to thank Joannie Robichaud and see what state his son was in.

'You can count on me, Mr and Mr Moralès!' Away she skipped, with rosy cheeks and messy hair.

'You aren't forgetting your service weapon, are you?'

Giggling like a naughty child, she gambolled back to Sébastien's car, grabbed her things and returned to her own vehicle.

'I've never seen her like that before,' Moralès said.

'I guess she needed the Mexican touch.'

'Since when are you Mexican?'

'Since I've been in the Gaspé.'

'And how long have you been in the Gaspé, exactly?'

Joaquin immediately regretted his words. He hated bombarding his son with questions. The sun was starting to feel warm as Sébastien sauntered sheepishly over to his car, packed to the roof with the ruins of a couple's life together. He yanked the back door open, grabbed a box of pots and pans, and clutched it to his chest as if he were gauging a party costume for size. 'I'm here to do some culinary experimentation,' he said.

Moralès reeled back in surprise.

'Culinary experimentation?'

Sébastien was a chef, but unfortunately his dishes always fell flat on flavour. There was something dependable yet ultimately forgettable about his cooking. It was the kind of food that tickled no one's taste buds, let alone their fancy. Moralès had often wondered whether customers ever remembered dining at the restaurant he worked in. He'd like to think the blandness had something to do with following the restaurant owner's recipes, but after tasting Sébastien's home concoctions, he'd come to the realisation that his son, who calculated spices and counted portions by the gram, cooked like an accountant.

'*Si, señor!* I've talked to my boss and he thinks it's a good idea.'

Moralès didn't know what to say. '*Chiquito…*'

'I want to learn more about the local specialities. You know, lobster, crab…'

'The season's over. The fishermen put all their traps away

weeks ago. The halibut catch is in, and their boats are all pretty much in dry dock.'

Sébastien kicked the car door shut. 'Shrimp, then!'

'There's no shrimp fishing in the Baie-des-Chaleurs.'

'Are you sure? Oh, well. I'm not hung up on crustaceans. There are plenty of fish in the sea, right?'

Moralès opened the front door for his son and his box of pots and pans, and followed him inside the house.

'Aw, you made your good old ranchero omelette for me? I haven't eaten one of these in years. Thanks Dad, you're the best!'

Sébastien dumped the box on the kitchen counter and carried his father's omelette and coffee to the table. The first forkful was in his mouth before he'd even sat down. Moralès bitterly remembered why children have to fly the nest and learn to make their own breakfast. Sighing, he threw two slices of stale bread into the toaster and put another pot of coffee on.

'So, you've started fishing again?' Sébastien asked.

'Yes. I was just heading out there, actually.'

'Where?'

'Down by the water's usually a good place.'

'I mean, do you fish right here?'

When the toast was ready, Joaquin realised he was out of butter. He poured himself another coffee, only to see he was out of milk too. 'Yes. There's a wooden staircase leading down to the shore. There's a trench at the foot of the cliff, on the right. The fishermen put their traps there in the summer. I went diving down there once. There's no end of lobster, crab and fish.'

'What do you fish for?'

Moralès was just sitting down at the table, but his son had already wolfed the whole plate down, like a teenager having a growth spurt.

'Anything that'll bite. It's not so much fishing as underwater trial and error.'

Sébastien looked around the room. 'Nice place you have here, anyway.'

It was the first time he'd set foot inside the house his father had moved into three months earlier. What it lacked in size, it made up for with charm. The open-plan living and dining room had big bay windows and a patio door leading out onto a deck overlooking the sea. Only one painting adorned the walls, a piece Moralès had owned forever that went well with the colours of the Mexican flag hanging over the stairs. All the furniture was new, and by the window was a powerful telescope turned to the horizon.

Sébastien collapsed on the sofa. Sitting down at the table, Moralès pushed his son's dirty dishes aside and ate in silence. Sébastien didn't say a word either. Joaquin could sense his son wasn't comfortable mentioning the real reason for his visit. He waited until he'd finished his toast before testing the waters.

'How long are you planning on staying?'

No answer.

'Because there's no bed in the spare room yet.'

Silence. Moving closer, Moralès saw that his son had fallen asleep, sitting on the sofa with his chin buried in his chest. He went to fetch a pillow and blanket, and helped him to lie down. Then, he downed the rest of his coffee in one gulp, grabbed his coat, wallet and keys and went into town to buy a bed. Not that he wanted to spoil his son with luxuries. He just didn't want him crashing on his sofa, spreading his things all over the place and getting between him and his telescope. No matter how temporary a thing it was.

By the time Joaquin eventually made it down to the water's edge, the day was nearly over. He had gone to the furniture store in Bonaventure, only to discover it was closed on Sundays. He ended up driving all the way to Grande-Rivière and ordering a bed for delivery the next day. He stopped for groceries on the way home. Finding his son still snoring away on the sofa, he put the groceries away, navigating around the box of pots and pans, and grabbed his fishing rod before heading down the cliff.

Setting foot on the shore at last, Moralès sighed as flashes of that morning came back to him. Sébastien's inebriated grin, Joannie's unbridled locks. He untangled the line, made sure the silvery spoon was firmly attached, and cast the lure over the water in a long, smooth arc.

Ten hours on the road to get here, and he'd driven into a lie. Did he regret what he'd done? Suffice it to say that Sébastien Moralès wasn't exactly on top form when he opened his eyes at the end of that Gaspesian afternoon with a pounding headache, dry mouth and a blanket tangled around his legs.

Hauling himself upright on the sofa, he picked up his phone. He was sure the ringtone had brought him back to life, but the handset was on silent. A series of texts and missed-call notifications filled the screen. Maude had obviously been trying to get hold of him, but he wasn't going to reply. Not right now, anyway.

He'd been mad at his partner since Thursday night. Since the huge argument they had about infidelity. For every couple, some topics of conversation are like cracks in a home's foundation. When you're caught up in the enthusiastic confidence of youth, you buy a fixer-upper, thinking a few drops of spring snowmelt seeping into the concrete basement won't make the place any less solid. As the years go by, the cracks widen, but laziness or routine means you don't notice the smell of the rising damp creeping up the side of the stairs. Then, one stormy night, you hear an ominous sound down below and are dumbstruck to see the wall has caved in.

In the middle of the night, amidst the nauseating words and misunderstandings, Maude had decided to go to her sister's for a few days to give herself and Sébastien some time to breathe and reflect on their future. She had grabbed a few handfuls of clothes and slammed the door on her way out, leaving him in a hell of a state. Maude's confession had not been the worst thing, rather it was the dagger she'd then thrown at him – 'we're both responsible for what happened' – that had cut his mind to shreds until morning came. How dare she blame him for her own infidelities?

Sébastien didn't go into work the next day, and, as if he hadn't been through the wringer enough already, his mother called to chat about where her career was going next. Since she hit the menopause, she had been swept up in her dream of becoming a great artist. He'd only been listening with half an ear, and Sarah had caught him at it.

'Are you listening to me, Sébastien?'

'Sorry Mum, I didn't catch the last few words.'

'I'd appreciate it if you gave me a hand with my move.'

'To the Gaspé?'

Silence at the other end of the line. 'No. I just told you: I've bought a condo here in Longueuil, right by my studio space. I'm moving in tomorrow.'

'You're not going out to join Dad, then?'

'No.'

'But you're the one who wanted to move to the Gaspé. You're the one who persuaded him to get a transfer out there.'

'Yes, but I've changed my mind.'

'Let me guess: your "agent" Jean-Paul has a hand in this,' he said with a sneer. The one time he had seen his mother with the guy, she was fawning all over him like a teenager with the school heartthrob. It had made him want to puke.

'Well, my artistic career has taken off unexpectedly lately, and…'

'Does Dad know?'

Another silence descended on the conversation, a longer one this time. Then his mother said, 'Your father's a grown man, Sébastien. He's not a victim of my choices. He's just as responsible as I am for the situation…'

With that, Sébastien hung up on his mother. Seething with anger, he grabbed his things and loaded the car to the roof. He didn't bother leaving a note for Maude before he hit the road for the Gaspé. He was furious, but also confused. But who was he angry with? Maude? Obviously. His mother? Maybe. Himself? He wouldn't have been able to see why. His father?

The question struck a chord in his mind. Who else could be to blame for his family's failures besides his father? Just over thirty years ago, Joaquin Moralès had said goodbye to Mexico because he'd got a young Canadian tourist pregnant. The proud, young Mexican police officer left his country behind for a life as a good, malleable suburban husband just outside Montreal. Had he not essentially abandoned his homeland, turned his back on his family and cast his culture aside – all for Sarah, his wife? The more Sébastien thought about it, the clearer he could see his father, silent and obedient at his mother's feet. Subservient. And because no woman respects a man who acts like a doormat, now his mother was waltzing off with her art agent. How did they not see that coming? Maybe she'd been cheating on his father for years. Who knew? She'd even managed to get him out from under her feet by roping him into moving to the Gaspé.

Sébastien had jumped to these conclusions as he drove away from his home, and the resentment had come flooding in. Because children tend to mimic their parents, he told himself, he had made the same mistake as his father, bowing to his partner's whims. And he was now suffering the humiliation of her cheating.

He had to face the fact that the failure of his own relationship was rooted in the example of behaviour his father had set him. And so, all fired up, he had made a beeline for the highway, de-termined not just to take a break from Maude, but also to confront his progenitor and free himself from the filial subser-vience that was ruining his life.

As the miles went by between Montreal and Quebec City, he had pictured the entrance he was going to make. Between Quebec City and Rimouski, he had hashed out his argument. Between Rimouski and Amqui, he had fine-tuned the words he was going to use to take his stand. The further he had driven, the clearer his thoughts and the sharper his tongue had become. But driving into Carleton, he had realised he was hungry. He only had an hour left to drive, but he couldn't show up at his dad's place with an empty stomach. That would have been em-barrassing, for a chef.

So, he had pulled over at a bistro for a bite to eat. It doesn't take much for hunger to turn to thirst. Especially in a seaside town on a Saturday night. He had soon slipped into the drink and when the Latin American rhythms had filled his ears, for the first time in forever he'd washed up on the dance floor. Caught up in a whirlwind of his own making, he had twirled one girl after another by the hand. And when they had whispered in his ear, 'Ooh, Moralès, that's Mexican, isn't it?' he had figured, why the hell not? And rolled his tongue around an accent only his father's family had owned. As the night had advanced, the drink had quenched his moral thirst and cooled his temper such that he found himself seeking refuge from his claustrophobic relationship in the arms of his doting father.

Joaquin hadn't asked any questions that morning, but Sébastien – too exhausted to get into a father-and-son heart-to-heart – had felt an unspoken pressure to justify his surprise visit. Of course, he could have just said something vague and pressed pause on the confrontation he had come here for. To buy himself some time, he could have told a harmless fib and said he'd got the week off unexpectedly and decided to surprise his father. But he had felt an obligation to come up with something more tangible. A project.

That was why, when he saw the pots and pans jammed against the rear window of his car, he had opened the door, grabbed the box and spun this yarn: 'I'm here to do some culinary experimentation!'

His father had shaken his head, and at that point Sébastien, like a child caught telling tall tales, should have kept his mouth shut. But leaving it at that, he figured, would only have proved that he was lying. He needed to add weight to his words, so had laid it on thicker: 'I want to learn more about the local specialities. You know, lobster, crab…'

He'd been drowning in lies for years. And what did he do when he was sinking like a stone? Make up more untruths. The strange thing was, the more he lied, the easier it was to convince himself he was telling the truth. He knew he was digging himself a hole, but somehow he found it comforting. To pull the cover of a project over his pain, the way others might hang a fancy tapestry to hide a crack in a wall. It was like last night: the more he danced, the more he felt like dancing.

Sébastien folded the blanket, stood up from the sofa and went over to the patio door. It was hard for him to admit, but he'd had the wind knocked out of his sails. That morning, he hadn't been able to break the news to his father that his mother had bought herself a condo in Longueuil and wouldn't be coming out to join him in the Gaspesian dream they had shared. Sébastien would have felt embarrassed, spouting about his father's blind subservience to his wife while eating his food. And now, waking up to the sight of the sea with a vaguely clear head, he didn't feel like dredging up the reasons why he'd left Maude. Come to think of it, maybe it was better that way: he should catch his breath and reconnect with his father before standing up to him.

The sea was shimmering in the sun. Down at the foot of the cliff, to the west, Sébastien could see his father setting up to fish. He checked his line, then cast it over the water. The lure made a little ripple as it broke the surface. The line started to reel out. It looked like he'd got a bite. On the first cast? That'd be a stroke of luck. Sébastien watched his father give the line some slack, walk a few steps to the left and try to reel the line in. Ah, no. The hook must have caught on something. He gave it some more slack, walked a few steps to the right, and tried to reel the line in again. Still stuck. That was strange, Sébastien thought, because his father had said it was deep around there.

Maybe a deer had fallen off the cliff, or something. In sync, father and son both turned towards the rock face and squinted. This was going to be painful. They looked back towards the trench, wondering what the hook could have snagged on.

Of course, Joaquin could just cut the line. He wasn't worried about losing a cheap lure. But there shouldn't have been anything down there to get snagged. Sébastien watched from inside as his father shrugged his shoulders and made up his mind. Joaquin leaned his rod up against the red rocks and took off his shoes and socks.

Then a phone rang. It startled Sébastien. Wait, wasn't that the same ring that had woken him? He looked around for the device and found it sitting on the kitchen counter. 'Private number', said the caller ID. Sébastien hurried back to the patio door, opened it and called down to Joaquin, but he was too busy taking off his shirt and trousers and readying himself to wade into the chilly water to hear.

Sébastien answered the call. 'Wait a sec, my dad's just gone for a dip. I'll go fetch him.'

He grabbed a towel from the bathroom before picking up the phone again and dashing down the steps that clung to the side of the cliff.

He set the phone and towel down on a rock, picked up the fishing rod and let the line go. And waited. At last something moved, and his father surfaced and swam quickly back to shore. 'The hook got caught on a tree trunk,' he said.

Sébastien smiled and began to reel the line in now that it was free. 'Is it cold?'

'Freezing.' Joaquin emerged shivering from the water and reached for the towel.

'Here, there's someone on the phone for you.'

Moralès raised the phone to his ear while his son busied himself with the rod, tackle box and pile of discarded clothes. 'Hello?'

'Detective Moralès?'

Joaquin Moralès glanced at his son, who was already climbing back up to the house. 'Speaking.'

'Lieutenant Forest here.'

He tried to towel himself dry with one hand.

'Oh good, I was going to give you a call. I'd like to take a few days off.'

He'd been due to take three weeks' holiday since the day he

moved into this place on the shore of the Baie-des-Chaleurs, but his new boss had always found a reason to snatch the time away. She'd thrown a homicide at him as he'd pulled into the driveway of his new home for the first time. After that, there had been a string of thefts inland and a grave-robbing to take care of.

Moralès was a patient man, though. He hadn't brought it up again, because he'd been planning to take the time off when his wife came out to join him. However, with the unexpected arrival of Sébastien and his pots and pans, he thought it would be a good idea to take a few days to be with his son.

'Detective Moralès, I've told you already, the Gaspé is no place to take a holiday.'

'Well, it's just that my son's visiting and … er…'

Moralès wasn't sure how to put it exactly. A mental-health memo had gone around at work recently, and he remembered reading that helping a relative in psychological distress was a valid reason for taking immediate family leave. But none of those words flowed as easily from the lips of a father and detective as they did from the pages of a pop psychology magazine.

'My son needs … er…'

How could he ask for this? Moralès senior and junior hated explaining themselves to their bosses as much as they did father-son conversations.

'I'd appreciate it if you could finish your sentence today, Moralès.'

'I have to help him with his culinary experiments.'

The words sounded all wrong coming from him, like a trumpet in the middle of a piano solo. He could feel himself blushing like an idiot. His boss cleared her throat before replying with the measured control of someone doing her damnedest to quell a wave of sarcasm.

'Moralès, how should I put this? You have to help me with a "detecting experiment" over Forillon Park way.'

He felt ridiculous, but that wasn't a reason to kow-tow to his boss's demands. 'That's not my patch.'

'Homicide detectives are few and far between in this neck of the woods, Moralès, and the SQ detachment in Gaspé needs help with a misper that came to light last night.'

'You're mixing up a disappearance with a homicide, lieutenant.'

Suddenly, Moralès realised he was shivering. He started back towards the house. Meanwhile, his boss was pretending she hadn't heard him.

'We share what resources we have around here, detective. Loaning your talent to our colleagues will buy precious time before they send a team from Montreal to take over. If they even bother.'

'I'm already busy investigating the grave-robbing case…'

'I've put Constable Robichaud on that.'

Moralès stepped inside the house. He couldn't help but wonder whether the young rookie had told their boss precisely how Sébastien had arrived on the peninsula that morning.

'Listen, my son's here and I'd really like to…'

'I hear what you're saying. But whatever you're cooking up, you're doing it out there on the point in Gaspé, all right?'

There was no way he could tell the truth and say it wasn't about cooking. He couldn't say he thought his son needed help when he was right there, behind his pile of pots and pans, riffling through the kitchen cupboards.

'To be honest, I thought about you specifically for this case,' she purred.

Now his son was opening the fridge.

'And why's that, Lieutenant Forest?'

'Because it's a woman who's missing.'

Suddenly his son was the least of his concerns; a chill of fear surged through him.

'A woman?'

'Yes.'

'At sea?'

'Yes.'

Marlène Forest was revelling in the silence. She was clearly taking advantage of his weakness. Joaquin glanced at the telescope he used to scan the horizon every day, hoping he'd see Catherine, the woman who tied his heart in knots, sailing home. He was hesitant to ask the question. His heart was pounding so hard it hurt.

'What kind of boat?'

'A lobster trawler.'

Moralès exhaled slowly, leaned against the door frame, closed his eyes. Standing in the fridge doorway, Sébastien froze.

'Dad? Are you all right?'

Marlène Forest's voice snapped back to her usual scathing tone. 'The women of the sea leave no one indifferent, Moralès. Not you, and not any Gaspesian worth his salt. If your heart's where it should be, you'll drop those pots and pans and hightail it to Gaspé!'

His boss was right, but Moralès couldn't bring himself to actually say yes to her. She'd figured out just how fragile Catherine had made him, and was now playing a heartless mind game with him.

Sébastien closed the fridge door and walked over to his father with a frown. 'You sure you're all right?'

Joaquin looked at the son he loved, who was right before his eyes, music, pots and pans, flaws and all. He drew himself tall.

'I'm not a missing-persons detective, Lieutenant Forest. Call me back when it becomes a homicide.'

He hung up, gave Sébastien a forger's wink and set about towelling the remaining seawater from his skin.

Joaquin Moralès jogged to the cemetery, slowed to a walk and turned left. His anger had mellowed to indecision. He approached the old house without a sound, and sneaked past the pickup truck in the driveway to the stepladder, which was conveniently placed beside the woodpile, beneath an unlocked window. Creeping up the ladder to the window ledge, he peeped into the room. The first thing he saw was a bag of marijuana on a bedside table. The second, the hands of a man rolling himself a joint.

Cyrille Bernard was sitting up in bed. He cast an eye towards the window. 'Heee… This pot is therapeutic, officer.'

Moralès opened the window and ducked into the old man's bedroom. 'You're still alive, then?'

'Not dead yet, at any rate.' Cyrille licked and stuck his rolling paper while Moralès pulled the window shut.

Cyrille lived with his sister, and now the cancer was so advanced, she staunchly refused to allow him any visitors. Since the summer, the old fisherman's friends had therefore taken to clambering up the woodpile beneath the window to pay him a visit. But just last week, Moralès had sent nearly half the pile tumbling to the ground. Unfortunately for him, the wood had been covered with a sheet of metal to stop the rain seeping in, and it had made a hell of a racket. As he fell arse over elbow into the tumbling logs, the Bernard sister, a hefty French-Canadian battleaxe, had stormed out of the house brandishing a rolling pin.

Moralès was unlikely to forget the sight that had assailed his eyes when he blinked them open, lying there in the remnants of the woodpile. Backlit by the afternoon sun, a foreboding shadow with an oddly shaped head, and wielding a blunt instrument, stood menacingly over him. Before he could even get to his feet, she had hissed like a snake, 'Now you pick all that up, and make it snappy!'

Caught off guard, he had fallen over himself to apologise and set about restacking the wood in record time as the shadow watched over his shoulder, or so he had thought. Unbeknownst to him, Cyrille's sister had in fact gone to fetch a little stepladder from inside the house. 'Put that under the window, will you? I can't stand hearing you lot huff and puff your way up that woodpile.' Moralès had turned to thank her, but she had already turned her back and walked away. He had just caught a glimpse as she disappeared around the corner of the porch in her dressing gown, her hair in curlers. Moralès had grumbled to himself, licking his wounds as well his pride. Since then, he'd been tiptoeing in as light as can be, but couldn't quite shake the feeling she was watching him.

The old fisherman lit the joint and closed his eyes as he inhaled.

Joaquin sat down beside the bed. 'These days, the sea is losing its sparkle. The sun's rising ever later, as if it's weary of climbing over the mountaintops. It's not in any hurry to get to work. And it's turning in for the night earlier and earlier. Must be tired of lighting up the sky for so long.'

Cyrille Bernard was no more than a shadow beneath the bed covers now. His breathing was more laboured and whistling than ever. He sounded like a man drowning, fighting for air.

'The wind's not letting up much. Especially not in the daytime. It's been howling across the bay. At high tide, the crests of the waves are peaking tall and white, sharp as Jack Frost's teeth. There's no cold snap in sight yet, but it's a sign that winter's on its way.'

'Heee … you're getting better at that, for someone from the big city! Maybe there's more Mexico left in you than you think.'

Moralès shrugged his shoulders, embarrassed by the compliment.

'Soon it'll be a full moon.'

'Heee … you know what people say here? They say the moon is a liar, and you know what it reflects in the sea? Heee … fool's silver.'

Cyrille was in palliative care now. He had long since finished fishing, but his boat was still in the water. There would be no wintering it this year. Cyrille had a plan to die at sea, at one with the waves, before the season's icy veil smothered them both. He had told Joaquin. He had warned him that the autumn tides would soon be rising.

Moralès knew it was only a matter of time. For nearly a week now Cyrille had been bedridden, so he'd promised to come by and tell him all about the sea. The gulls diving into the frigid depths, splashing up spouts like shards of ice that pierce the lazy rays of the sun. The swell snorting its way through the morning frost on the sand. The wakes of boats sailing home becoming fewer and further between. The tiny nameless beaches deserted by even the most lingering of holidaymakers. The gloom descending gradually as the day gives minutes away to the night. The silence blanketing the shore.

'My eldest showed up here this morning. Drunk, with his car full of pots and pans.'

Cyrille arched an eyebrow through the smoke. 'Heee … sounds to me like his girlfriend's washed up on the rocks.'

Moralès nodded. 'Last year at Christmas, she told the whole family she wanted a baby. My Sébastien went all red.'

'Heee … red as in embarrassed?

'No.'

Moralès had always thought his son should be more assertive. So many times he had seen Maude speak for Sébastien, open the wine, announce the big milestones in their life together and tease him, while he smiled mutely, like one of those men who let their other half dictate the feminist course of their lives. But that time he had reacted differently.

'Red as in angry.'

It had struck Moralès that this was the first time he'd seen any signs of anger in his son in front of his partner.

Cyrille flicked the ash from his joint. 'Heee … he doesn't want kids, then?'

Outside, the blue of the sky was growing fainter already.

'I don't know.'

'Heee … you didn't ask him?'

Staring out at the cemetery, Moralès didn't answer.

'It'll be too late to talk about it when you're resting there in peace. Heee…'

'What am I supposed to say?'

'Heee … you're the detective. You must be able to string one or two intelligent questions together.'

'I'm sure he doesn't need me to tell him how to go about loving a woman.' Moralès stood and leaned on the corner of a dresser, thinking about how his son had unravelled Joannie Robichaud's hair that morning on the beach.

'So what's he doing now, then?'

'When I left, he was trying to make himself a coffee.'

Moralès shifted slightly and watched as Cyrille puffed away at what was left of his joint.

'I had a call from Marlène earlier. She's sending me over Forillon Park way to work on a case.'

'When are you leaving?'

'I'm not done with the cemetery case in Saint-Siméon yet.'

Moralès wasn't going to say so, but he wanted to be by Cyrille Bernard's side until the end.

'Deaths aren't exactly ten a penny in the Gaspé, you know. Heee … Make the most of 'em while you can if you want to stay here and still be a detective.'

'This isn't a death, it's a disappearance.'

Joaquin went to look out of the window. The Caplan cemetery was settling down to rest in the evening mist. Yesterday was the equinox. Autumn had descended in the night without a sound. Now the sun was waiting for the snow to come.

'Heee … who's gone and disappeared?'

The detective hesitated for a moment.

'Moralès?'

'A woman.'

Cyrille stubbed out his joint. The dying man's breaths whistled across the room as if clawing at the walls. 'Heee … why are you still here, then?'

Moralès turned towards the bed.

'They don't need me quite yet.'

'You'll never teach that boy of yours how to love a woman if you keep letting them slip through your fingers.'

Moralès took it on the chin. 'I'll see…'

'Joaquin Moralès. Heee…'

'If Marlène Forest calls back…'

'Then you're going. Heee … and no one's getting on their knees to beg you.'

Moralès swallowed. Was this why he'd left the big city behind? Why he'd taken a step closer to retirement? To live hours away from his wife, muse about a woman who had sailed away, see Sébastien wash up drunk and in disarray, and leave his only friend around here to die alone?

'I have my son to…'

'That girl, she's someone's daughter too, you know! Heee…'

'Cyrille, I…'

The dying man pulled himself up higher on his pillow and drilled his deep-blue eyes into his friend's face. 'Stop that, will you? Heee … I'm sick, not blind! I don't need you to tell me stories about the sea, Joaquin. Heee … and I don't need you telling me not to die, either.'

Moralès jogged faster on the way home. Running away from the darkness that had triumphed over the light, he thought. His legs were heavy and he was short of breath when he got to the end of the gravel track and turned onto the path hugging the shore. Light spilled from the windows of the bistro up the hill, which looked unusually busy. He went out of his way to take a look. Thirty metres away, he could hear the Mexican music blasting through the speakers.

There must have been twenty cars parked out front. Through the windows, he saw the tables had been pushed to the sides of the room. Sébastien Moralès was dancing a fiery salsa with a woman whose every curve was quivering with joy. At least a dozen more folks were trying to keep pace. Renaud Boissonneau had cast off his waiter's apron to gyrate his hips out of time to the music and twirl the seamstress from next door like a rag doll. Joannie Robichaud was there too, hair down and hips lightened of her usual load, dancing with an older man Moralès didn't recognise.

In one corner a group of women merrily practised their steps, counting the beat as they swayed their hips forward and back, laughing and patting each other on the arm, back or shoulder as they fell out of time, winking at their husbands, who were looking on eagerly with a beer or glass of wine from the long table they had made when they pushed everything aside for the women to work on their moves. They must have been hoping the dancing would continue later at home, in the living room, up to the bedroom, between the sheets.

When the young rookie Robichaud saw Moralès standing in the lamplight outside, she bounded over to the window and beckoned him to come inside and join them.

Joaquin thought about it for a second. Something inside made him feel like dancing, but he couldn't bring himself to. He thought about his wife, Sarah, the woman he had chosen thirty years ago. Back then, she had looked a lot like this young woman did tonight, hair as free as the wind. He thought about Sébastien, who had just noticed his father and was also motioning to him through the glass. Joaquin had no idea why his son had come out here to see him, but he loved him no matter what the answer was. Then he thought about this fish-erwoman who had gone missing, and the silence she must be sinking into as the hours went by. About his heart being where it should be.

Cyrille was right. That woman was someone's daughter.

With a friendly wave he acknowledged Joannie and Sébastien, who grimaced in mock disappointment before returning to the dance floor. Detective Moralès then turned away, stepped out of the halo of lamplight and jogged home along the shore.

Monday 24th September

Leeroy Roberts insisted his sons keep scanning the sea, again and again, with the radar and searchlights. They were aboard the *Ange-Irène*, his eldest's shrimp trawler. Bruce and Jimmy, and Guy Babin were out on deck with spotting scopes, but Leeroy stayed inside the wheelhouse to watch the radar and automatic pilot. Even with the naked eye, he could see a long way when the moon was that full.

Leeroy ducked into the galley and emerged with a thermos of coffee, packet of cupcakes and four mugs. He set these down on the ledge inside the front window, then he opened the door and called the men over. They filed inside from the cold night air to rub their hands, pour themselves a coffee and wolf down a sugary snack or two. Bruce peered at the computer screen to check the chart and the heading they were on.

His younger brother was still grumbling. 'We're way off course! I told you, we're not going to find anything here. We should be looking further north.'

Jimmy had been going on like that for an hour or more. Bruce kept his mouth shut. This was his boat and he knew best how to navigate these waters. He had weighed all the possibilities and persuaded his father to head south, the way the tide was going, then follow the Labrador Current. Leeroy trusted his eldest son's wisdom.

But the youngest wouldn't give up. 'Stop messing around with your fancy calculations, will you?'

Leeroy knew what Jimmy was like. Since he sold his fishing licence, he'd been strutting around like a peacock with the Babin brothers, but folks knew it was all bluff and bluster. Nobody dared to bring it up back on the wharf, but Leeroy wasn't deaf. He knew people were gossiping behind his back.

He just kept his mouth shut to avoid any aggro. When he and Bruce went out looking for Angel, Jimmy and Guy Babin invited themselves aboard. It would have been hard to refuse the help, but they weren't exactly lightening the atmosphere.

'It's been drifting more than twenty-four hours, that trawler of hers, so who knows where it's got to?'

Babin nearly choked on his coffee. Leeroy and Bruce whirled to face Jimmy.

'What did you just say?'

Jimmy didn't react.

'How exactly do you know Angel's boat's "been drifting more than twenty-four hours"?' Bruce pressed. 'Cyr said he was at the wharf at ten in the morning yesterday and the boat wasn't there. By my calculation, we don't know it's been gone any more than fifteen hours, do we?'

Seeing he wasn't going to get an answer out of his brother, Bruce turned to Guy Babin instead. 'Where were you boys last night, then?'

Babin clenched his fists. 'Why, are you accusing me of something?'

Leeroy raised a hand. 'That's enough!'

Bruce nodded. He knew what had been going on. Jimmy and Babin knew that he knew.

'Listen, we're not going to go stabbing each other in the back, all right? Not over something like this.'

Bruce turned to his father. Did he know the guys were using Angel's boat? Probably.

Leeroy looked his son in the eye. 'Whatever happens, none of us point a finger at the other, you hear me?'

Bruce took a bite of his cupcake to avoid having to say anything. His brother was looking at their father with an air of suspicion. He wouldn't be surprised if their old man was hiding something. It wouldn't be the first time.

'That applies to you too, Guy. And that brother of yours.'

He nodded. Guy and Jean-Paul Babin weren't from the most reputable of families in Haldimand, but Leeroy had hired them young, and that had made them loyal. Today they were far from rich, but they had learned to work hard. And that was something they owed more to Leeroy than their own father.

'For what it's worth, Mr Roberts, I reckon Clément Cyr must have a hand in it. Him or his uncle.'

Leeroy was sure he'd done right hiring the Babins, but Bruce had never liked them. Finishing his mouthful, he raised an eyebrow.

'Say that all you like to the cops, Ti-Guy, but Clément Cyr was at the auberge all night. He's got an alibi set in stone. That's more than you lot can say.'

'Nobody's dragging the Roberts name through the mud, is that clear?'

'Yes, Dad.'

The men finished their coffee break in silence.

'Now get back out there and keep looking.'

Jimmy couldn't help himself from muttering under his breath. 'We're not going to find anything, I tell you. I wouldn't put it past Angel to do a runner and sink her bloody boat just to get our backs up.'

His words fell on deaf ears, but the others were tempted to think her younger brother might be right.

The night passed under a moon that hung high in the sky even as dawn drew near. As the men rubbed the fatigue from their eyes, the light of day gradually filtered into their darkness-filled pupils.

Suddenly – wait, what was that? Over there. It looked like there was a reflection on the water. Something shiny. Something promising. Bruce was the one who pointed it out.

Leeroy came out on deck and took the scope from his son.

'Huh! How did you know to look over there, eh?' Jimmy's words were full of undertones and spite.

Leeroy looked at his eldest son to gauge his reaction. Bruce didn't say a word as he marched into the wheelhouse and turned the wheel to starboard to steer the *Ange-Irène* onto the right heading. Leeroy lifted the scope to his eye and scoured the horizon. At first he couldn't see anything, but then the scope caught a faint glimmer of light. Leeroy's heart began to race. Because he had a feeling. That reflection was his daughter's boat. He was sure of it.

Joaquin tossed and turned in bed for a while before he went down to the living room. He leaned over the telescope, cast an eye over a night that would soon make way for the dawn, and drew himself tall.

The Gaspé Peninsula was an unforgiving kind of place.

He thought about Sarah and their plan to move here together. Things hadn't exactly gone the way he'd hoped. Moralès had driven out to Caplan at the beginning of the summer to get their new place ready while his wife finalised the sale of their house in Longueuil. She was supposed to have followed a week later with all their belongings. But something had gone awry. Saltwater had somehow seeped in and seized up the plan. Sarah had driven out here unannounced at the end of the summer, when Moralès was out of town. He'd been called to investigate a case out in the back of beyond – near Saint-

Elzéar, where there was no phone signal. He and two other officers had spent a few nights out there in a hunting cabin that had suffered a spate of break-ins. Thanks to their surveillance, the police had made a number of arrests.

The first Moralès had learned of Sarah's flying visit was on his return, when he saw the scathing note she'd left on the kitchen table. Someone had told Sarah he'd had a romantic encounter out here, it seemed. But who? That was a mystery. Still, she had left without waiting for him to return. Since then, she'd been ignoring him, creating a bubble of silence around herself and what was left of their relationship, which now seemed destined to drift onto the proverbial rocks. Did that make him feel sad? He wasn't sure. After thirty years of living together, it would take strength for any couple to keep the flames of passion burning.

He went back upstairs, undressed and sat upright in bed. He looked through the window at the moon splintering on the swell. He thought about Catherine and where she had gone. What had she set out in search of? Fool's silver?

Moralès glanced at the clock on the bedside table. Five in the morning. Sébastien had been out all night, but he wasn't worried. Joannie must have given him a breathalyser and made him sleep on a bench at the bistro. Moralès had left his phone beside the alarm clock, hoping Lieutenant Forest would call back. As reluctant as he was to be dragged away, he hated the idea of being excluded from investigating this disappearance.

He wondered how old the woman on the lobster boat might be. *The woman on the lobster boat.* In the city, that was the kind of name the detectives would use to talk about the victim. Moralès realised he would have been incapable of calling Marie Garant, the victim of the last homicide he investigated, 'the woman on the sailboat'. Out here, the dead were allowed to keep their real names. Come to think of it, what was the missing woman's name? He resisted the urge to call Marlène Forest.

Moralès found life in the Gaspé challenging not only because of its slow pace, but also because he found the demand to embrace intimacy here excruciating. Here you had to know everything about everybody to stand a chance of solving a case. In the city, everything was rougher, more raw. People killed violently – for drugs and money. Murderers took the lives of strangers. Spitting with vengeance, they executed their victims coldly. Here, death was inflicted so gently it hurt. And prison was more therapy than punishment. It was a gentleness that pained Moralès. This investigation was a case in point. It had held him captive all night, and it was yet to begin.

The phone remained silent. Moralès didn't really feel like thinking about his son and their uncomfortable conversations, the pots and pans in a box on the kitchen counter, the round-about ways the two of them found to avoid talking to one another. She'll call back, he told himself. That very moment, his phone rang. Private number. He picked up immediately. He knew it was Marlène Forest. And he knew he'd be getting in his car and driving along the coast.

She didn't bother saying hello. 'They've found the lobster trawler.'

Moralès stood and pulled on a pair of jeans. 'Where?'

'It should have been at the wharf in Grande-Grave, on the south side of Forillon Park, but it was drifting offshore. Out in the gulf.'

'And the woman?'

Marlène Forest drew a deep breath.

'Lieutenant Forest? Where's the woman?'

No reply.

Moralès pulled on the rest of his clothes. 'She wasn't on board?'

'No.'

He ran down the stairs.

'Constable Lefebvre is expecting you at the station in Gaspé. He'll be glad of your help.'

Moralès grabbed his jacket, wallet, car keys and a duffel bag full of clothes he'd packed the night before, and stepped out into the pre-dawn light. 'One more question, lieutenant.'

'Yes?'

'What's the woman's name?'

'Roberts.'

Her voice was shaking, as if she were personally suffering from this disappearance, but Moralès didn't notice.

'Her name is Angel Roberts.'

He hung up, got into his car and set off towards the east along Highway 132. To his right, the liar of a moon paved a path of broken silver on the autumn sea.

Killers make up all kinds of things. Detective Moralès had figured that out long ago. Jane Doe stabbed her husband to death because she was sure he had a string of mistresses, a gang of teenagers massacred an elderly couple they imagined must be sleeping on a mattress stuffed with banknotes, a cult leader brainwashed his disciples into following him into a deadly inferno, convinced of the purifying powers of the flames. Criminals latched on to the things they imagined so firmly, they refused to believe reality could prove them wrong. In their twisted minds, these scenarios played out with cinematographic precision. Naturally, the killers cast themselves in the leading

role. Meanwhile, the victims played bit parts. They were dehu-
manised, reduced to nameless extras on a movie set, roped in
just to fill the shot. What's more, the killers convince themselves
they're acting in the name of justice. Jane Doe had to preserve
her husband's dignity, the teenagers really needed the money,
and the cult leader was trying to make the world better for all
of us. They're so sure their fiction is fact, they'd rather kill than
admit when real life contradicts them.

Over the years, Moralès had come to see that criminals
weren't the only ones who made things up. According to police
psychologists, it wasn't unusual for people to craft their own
inner narratives to try and make sense of their daily struggle.
Many even started to think and act like the character they had
chosen to embody. But far from turning everyday people into
potential killers, this kind of inward storytelling could often be
their saving grace, making them want to keep on living.
However, Moralès had observed that some people tended to
exaggerate the importance of their character in whatever story
was unfolding, which made them particularly insufferable. The
experience that awaited him at the Gaspé police station would
unfortunately add weight to his theory.

After a three-hour drive, sustained only by a lukewarm
muffin and a bitter convenience-store coffee, Moralès pulled
up in front of the nondescript building nestled at the foot of
a cliff across from the mouth of Gaspé Bay. The aroma of kelp
at low tide drifted into his nostrils as he got out of the car, but
he barely noticed. Casting an eye at his silent phone, he strode
inside.

Behind the bulletproof window, a woman as cheery as an
undertaker's assistant sat in the receptionist's chair.

'Good morning. I have an appointment with Constable
Lefebvre,' Moralès announced.

This failed to elicit even a raised eyebrow. Moralès took in his surroundings. On one wall of the tiny entrance hall was a bulletin board full of helpline numbers for drug addiction and violence, mental-health leaflets and business cards for lawyers promising to talk people out of trouble. On the other was an armoured and clearly locked door. Obviously, visitors had to talk their way into this behemoth of a building. *Take two*, thought Moralès, taking the badge from his belt, holding it to the window and declaring his identity.

'Detective Sergeant Joaquin Moralès from the Bonaventure detachment.'

Still the receptionist kept tapping away at her keyboard.

'I'm here to lend Constable Lefebvre a hand. Would you let him know I'm here, please?'

She didn't bother to look up at either the badge or the man standing in front of her. With a huff, she punched a number and curtly announced the visitor's presence through clenched teeth, eyes still glued to her screen. 'Detective Moral-less from Bonaventure is asking for you.' Her voice grated the microphone of her headset like a nail file. After a moment's silence, she spoke again. 'Opening the door is not in my job description.' She ended the call and resumed her frantic tapping at the keyboard.

Moralès was lost for words. He stood there watching her for a moment, wondering if she thought she was working at a federal penitentiary. The armoured door opened to reveal a man with sandy hair who looked to be a little younger than him, sporting a retro eighties shirt, cowboy boots and a pencil moustache over a broad smile.

The man nodded good morning to Moralès before turning to the receptionist. 'I haven't seen you on form like this for a while, Thérèse. It's going to be a beautiful day, sweetheart.'

She gave no indication she'd heard a word he said. The man

ushered Moralès into a holding room where people sat waiting on plastic chairs in front of a small office with glass walls.

'Phew, she's really something, eh?' He extended a hand to Moralès. 'Érik Lefebvre. Sexy as hell, isn't she?'

Moralès frowned. 'Who?'

Lefebvre nodded towards the front desk. 'Thérèse Roch! Quite the catch for men like you and me, right?'

'I'm married.'

Lefebvre smoothed his thin moustache with glee. 'Right, well, she certainly floats my boat!'

The two men went through another doorway into an incident room with six desks, two of which were vacant, complete with the usual computers and file folders. On one side of the room, beside the toilets, stood a closed door with a sign that read 'Archives'. On the other, a row of open doors offered glimpses of police officers at work. Lefebvre led Moralès to the back of the room, down a corridor that split the building in two. 'Let me show you to our office.'

'*Our* office?'

'Every cop who gets seconded here hopes they'll get to work out of a conference room with a sea view, but we don't have anything like that. They're renovating the station at the moment, so we didn't really know where to put you. And because it's moose season, all the builders have gone off to their hunting camps for a week or two. Same goes for our captain. He's a good guy, but don't try and get hold of him when the hunting starts. There's no phone service in his neck of the woods. You've probably noticed there are lots of dead zones out here in the Gaspé. That kind of thing tends to bother the city folk, but I think it's good to get away from it all sometimes. Don't you think?'

Moralès wasn't sure where he stood in that regard.

'Don't you worry, though. I'll take care of all the liaising with the higher-ups. We made that a rule to keep detectives on loan out here from getting swamped. This is our office.'

Moralès followed Lefebvre through a wide-open door – and froze. The room was piled high with precarious towers of random objects, papers, photos, document holders and rocks. They looked like little inukshuks but were constructed with much less intention than the kitsch stone-cairn ornaments. Half-open drawers were bursting with files that hadn't been put back properly. A shredder was overflowing with strips of multi-coloured paper. Memos were stapled or taped to the walls here and there, and a row of hooks was heaving under the weight of jackets and windbreakers for every season.

'Sorry it's a bit untidy. Between investigations I've been going over unsolved cases and trying to cross-reference them. I should have been an archivist, you know. I don't have the talent of a field officer, but I do all right with paperwork. The laptop is yours to borrow. Just don't forget to give it back when you go home. I cleared some space for you last night when your boss called to say you were coming.'

Moralès arched an eyebrow. 'Last night?'

Obviously, Marlène Forest had been sure she'd rope him into this investigation. For as long as he'd been on the Gaspé Peninsula, he'd had the sense he was being taken for a ride. Was he really that much of a pushover? It made him feel ridiculous, somehow.

'I mean, it wasn't ideal…' Lefebvre began.

In the far-right corner, by a window half bricked-up with rocks, was a little table that had clearly been swept free of junk. It looked like a school desk. Lefebvre hadn't bothered to clear the yellowed papers from the bulletin board on the wall above it. A boxy chair stood behind the desk.

'…to be tidying up at night.'

As he spoke, Lefebvre was trying to forge a path to the desk. And failing.

'But I did my best to set aside a corner for you.'

Piles of case files stood on either side of the school desk, boxing the chair in. The only way to get to it was to climb over the desk itself.

Lefebvre gave up trying to wade his way through to the desk and took stock of the situation. 'Maybe I can rearrange a few things.' He grabbed a pile of case files and turned, trying to find an alternative work surface. Something in one of the files caught his eye. Intrigued, he opened the file and leafed through a few pages as surprise spread across his face. He dumped the pile on the desk he had set aside for Moralès with the open file in plain sight on top and grabbed a rock from the window to weight it down. Then, turning to Moralès as if he were surprised to see him there, he changed tack completely. 'Come on, let's see where Simone's at with her research.'

They left the room and crossed the corridor to a small meeting room, where a woman stood with her back to the door, making notes on a map pinned to a bulletin board. The fabric of her blouse draped in a perfect triangle from her shoulder blades to the middle of her waist. Her hair was pinned up loosely in a bun, held in place by a spindly piece of driftwood, but it wasn't her hairstyle that had caught Moralès's eye. She'd tilted her head forward a touch, revealing the slightest tease of bone through the skin at the nape of her neck. What was that vertebra called again? C3 or C4, a number that conveyed nothing of the gracefulness of this mound elongating the epidermis like a delicate knot in the stem of a cherry that would disappear as soon as the woman looked up. A mirage of a dimple flirted with the strands at her hairline.

'Simone?'

She turned to look at them. Late forties, dirty blonde hair, pendant dangling from a silver chain in a plunging forest-green neckline. Sleeves rolled up, she was the picture of physical fitness and wearied efficiency.

'Let me introduce you to Detective Moralès. He's with the Sûreté du Québec too, at the Bonaventure detachment.'

Simone Lord looked him up and down. 'Usually they send us a guy from Montreal.'

Her eyes were an almost translucent green, the faint lines in the corners like elegant little arabesques.

'Actually, I used to be part of the personal crime team in Montreal. I've just moved to—'

'The woman was reported missing yesterday afternoon. Why weren't you here earlier?'

Moralès opened his mouth, but found nothing to say. His phone started to ring. He muttered a vague excuse, rummaged in his pocket and checked the number on the screen. It wasn't one he recognised. He turned the ringer off and Lefebvre resumed the introductions under the wry regard of his colleague.

'This is Simone Lord. She's been a fisheries officer for … how long?'

'The last ten years or so. I was with the coast guard before that. Search and rescue. Every time we have to work with the police, I'm the one they send.'

She said it with an air of disdain, or contempt, presumably directed at the police, or those who sent her. Or both. Then, silence. The two Gaspesians watched the newcomer, and waited.

Moralès spoke up. 'Who's in charge of the search efforts?'

'At sea? That's Simone.'

'No, on land. If the boat was empty, that means Angel

Roberts is officially a missing person. Who's in charge of the investigation?'

The locals shared a puzzled look before Simone Lord turned on the sarcasm.

'I'm not sure I caught that. Are you a real detective, or are you here to deliver a pizza? Because I'm pretty sure no one here ordered a pizza. Hey, Lefebvre, did you order a pizza?'

'No, but maybe later…'

Moralès frowned. His boss hadn't said anything about him leading the team. Constable Lefebvre didn't finish his sentence. He went into the corner of the room, bent over a portable heater that had just rattled to life making a hell of a noise, yanked the plug out of the wall and started to tinker with it.

Meanwhile, Simone Lord kept going. 'When it's a man who goes missing, the SQ scrambles its finest team of specialists from Montreal, but when it's a woman…' She cast a disapproving eye up and down Moralès. 'When it's a woman we're looking for, they send us the loser in early retirement who takes seventeen hours to drive two hundred kilometres. Oh, it's all right if you don't want anything to do with this investigation. No problem at all. Just go ask Thérèse Roch for a pair of slippers and make yourself comfortable in the waiting room. We'll call someone else. And in the meantime, we'll pretend this disappearance is a big deal, shall we?'

She turned and glared at Lefebvre. 'What's up with you? Are you an appliance repair man now?'

Lefebvre pushed the heater aside. 'We were given the order to wait for you, detective.'

Inside, Moralès was cursing the crumbs of information Marlène Forest kept throwing to him, and the corners she backed him into. She'd told him he was going to lend a hand, not run the bloody investigation. He had to admit the fisheries officer was right, though. He should have come the night before. Why had he been so resistant to the idea? Was it because of Sébastien and Cyrille? Because he didn't want to be away from either of them, as the reality of losing Sarah slowly sank in? Regardless, Lord had struck a nerve. He did feel old. And ridiculous.

He cut to the chase. 'Where was Angel Roberts last seen?'

Lefebvre riffled through a pile of papers, found his notes, and answered without looking at them. 'Her husband drove her home on Saturday night, around half past eleven. They'd been at a party in the village of Rivière-au-Renard. After that, he went back to the party, and that was the last he saw of her. He found her car the next morning by the wharf where she docks her lobster trawler.'

Lord chimed in with the rest of the story. 'The boat wasn't there. The men in the Roberts family went out to look for her. They took the eldest brother's shrimp trawler. They found the boat, but they didn't find Angel.'

The fisheries officer moved over to the marine chart pinned to the bulletin board and tilted her head forward a touch. In spite of himself, Moralès was watching for the mirage to reappear at the nape of her neck, but saw nothing. With the tip of her pencil, she pointed to a spot that was circled on the chart. 'The lobster trawler's home port is Grande-Grave, on the other side of the village of Cap-aux-Os, in Forillon Park.'

Moralès stepped closer to the chart. 'Does that mean fishing is allowed in the national park?'

'Yes, but it's strictly regulated. The boat was found here, near Percé, off the shore of Bonaventure Island. About eighteen nautical miles, let's say thirty-five kilometres, away from her home port.' She pointed to another spot circled on the chart, with geographic coordinates scribbled alongside. This was much further south, where the gulf opened into the ocean.

'How did it get there?'

'You tell me. You're the detective.'

Moralès turned to look at the fisheries officer. He wanted to tell her he wasn't indifferent to this woman's disappearance. He wanted to clarify why he had hesitated to come, tell her his son needed him, explain to her that his only friend in the Gaspé was dying, and at least try to establish a healthy working relationship. But Moralès had never enjoyed those kinds of conversations.

'If someone had untied the trawler from the dock, would the current have carried it out to sea?'

'No, it would have been pushed ashore. Grande-Grave is in a little cove. You'd have to navigate the boat out of the cove just to get out into Gaspé Bay, and that's not the open sea.'

'What if the engine had broken down somewhere in the bay? Would the current have carried the boat towards the shore or swept it out to sea? Was the tide coming in or going out that night?'

Lord muttered a half-hearted reply, as if she were discouraged to hear him asking all the right questions. 'Depends what time you're talking about. High tide was around midnight on Saturday. The first couple of hours after that, there was a northeast wind blowing stronger than the current, which was pretty much standing still. If the engine had been turned off, the boat would have drifted ashore on the south side of the bay sometime between midnight and three in the morning. To make sure it didn't find its way back to shore, someone would have had to take it much further out, almost to the other side of Forillon Park. Past the point. After two in the morning, the tidal flow would have increased. If it was out in Gaspé Bay any time after that, then yes, the boat would have been carried out to sea.'

'Was the engine running when they found the trawler? Do you know if the boat had been having engine trouble? Did Angel Roberts make a distress call? Could she have launched a lifeboat?'

Moralès had called the woman by her name. Simone Lord would almost have rather given Angel a nickname instead, something that would create more distance, the way cops often did to allow themselves to pass judgement.

'No. She didn't make a distress call, and the lifeboat was still on board when they found the trawler. I don't know about the engine.' She seemed reluctant to admit it.

Moralès turned his attention away from her and back to the chart on the wall. If Angel Roberts didn't launch her lifeboat, that meant she must have gone overboard. He looked at the vast expanse of the Gulf of St Lawrence. The water out there was frigid. Four degrees Celsius at most. If she had fallen in, she was a dead woman. Simone Lord reached out and pointed to one of the places she had circled on the chart, then the other.

'We've been combing the area between these two circles, along this line from Gaspé Bay to Bonaventure Island.'

Lefebvre sidled over, placing the heater discreetly beside his notes, and tried to peer at the chart over Moralès's shoulder.

'What if Angel didn't go aboard?' Moralès asked.

Moralès turned to find his new colleague standing uncomfortably close. Lefebvre backed away without having managed to get a proper look at the chart.

'Did you initiate any search efforts on the shore, Constable Lefebvre?'

'We don't tend to look on dry land for people who've gone out to sea. Plus, she's only just been officially reported missing.'

Moralès's phone started to vibrate. Simone Lord rolled her eyes as he checked the caller ID. It was the same number as before.

'I'm going to need your help, Constable Lefebvre,' Moralès said.

Lefebvre was rummaging through the papers on the table in nervous haste.

'Just stop it, will you!' Simone Lord laid into him. 'Do you really have to turn everything upside down?' She pulled a pile of documents out of Lefebvre's reach while he, momentarily taken aback to see so many tidy papers had escaped his sticky fingers, returned to the task of leafing through his own pile in search of a blank page to write on. Lord passed him a pen.

'Do we have a photo?' Moralès asked.

'Right, well, I thought you could ask the husband for one,' Lefebvre replied.

'As soon as we have a photo, I want you to show it around at the train station, bus terminal and taxi rank, OK? Ask if anyone has seen her. If so, was she leaving town, and where was she going? Have you thought to do a sweep of the area where her car was found?'

'Well, since it looked like she'd gone out to sea…'

'Do it. We're looking for a missing woman, but we're also looking for clues. You're going to need a warrant to get a record of her recent bank transactions. Has she withdrawn any large amounts of money? Has she opened a different account? Have her debit and credit cards been used?'

Moralès turned to Simone Lord. 'When is the boat getting here?'

She glanced at her watch. 'Not for another hour. The guys are on their way to the wharf at Rivière-au-Renard. I'm going there to interview them to find out how—'

'I'll be the one conducting the interview, Ms Lord.'

She pouted as Lefebvre fell over himself to point out how efficient the Gaspé detachment could be when they tried. 'The forensic technicians are already down at the wharf.'

Lord cracked half a smile. 'I bet they're sitting in their van eating doughnuts.'

Lefebvre took the wisecrack as an attack on the entire police force. 'Hey, those guys are professionals!' he protested.

Moralès cut him off. 'Do we have time to pay the husband a visit?'

'He doesn't live far away. I'll give you the address.'

'Do you have a mobile phone, Constable Lefebvre?'

'Yes.'

'Then you're coming with me.'

'I'm really better at my desk.'

'I'll drive, and you can do your research on the way. I want you to sit in on the interview.'

Moralès wasn't taking no for an answer, and Lefebvre was a good sport. 'I'll get my jacket,' the constable said, and left the room.

Simone Lord was now tidying her files. Moralès decided to try to smooth the waters. 'Do you think she's still alive?' he asked.

She drew a deep breath. 'If she's out at sea with no way to send a distress signal, the chances of finding her are slim. Negligible at best. Probably nonexistent. Even if she's found something to cling on to, the area we have to search is immense, and…'

Moralès's phone started to vibrate again. He checked the screen. Again, the same number. Simone Lord didn't bother finishing her sentence. She picked up her files. 'Just keep an eye on your pacemaker, all right? I'll see you on the wharf.'

As she brushed past Joaquin on her way out, he couldn't help but notice how nice she smelled. She had an earthy, garden-like scent about her, mixed with the hint of a sea breeze. When she'd gone, he took a deep breath and answered the phone.

'Have you found her?'

The husband of Angel Roberts stood imposingly broad and tall in the doorway. He was a beefcake of a man with legs like tree trunks and slabs for hands. But a note in his gravelly voice suggested he was treading a narrow tightrope of hope. Érik Lefebvre retreated a step and shook his head in resignation. He hated working in the field.

'Not yet.'

The house on the north side of Highway 132 in the village of Cap-aux-Os had its back turned to the life in the town of Gaspé, enjoying instead a sweeping view of the bay and its south shore, all the way from the point at Sandy Beach to Haldimand Beach, where a handful of out-of-towners would be waiting for Thanksgiving to come and go before boarding up the windows of their holiday cottages and abandoning the place until the spring.

Clément Cyr was leaning all his weight against the door frame, burying his giant, powerless head in his chest. Moralès took a mental picture of the man and filed it away with all the others. This collection of snapshots, which he had committed to memory and never talked about, was like an old family photo album – negatives he hung on to despite the passing of time, fragments of stories associated with the smells, sounds and attitudes of humanity in tears.

The time he knocked at the door in the middle of the night to break the news of a teenager's accidental death to parents who had been fast asleep without a care in the world just minutes earlier. The time he picked up the pieces of a snowmobiler who had wrapped himself around a tree while his wife was waiting for him to get back to their cabin in the woods. The time he retrieved the body of a young girl who had caught her hair in the filter of the family's new swimming pool. The time he entered the room where one Christmas, a father dressed in a red Santa suit had committed suicide while his wife went to wake the children so they could open their presents.

These bombshells were so devastating, the officers who dropped them found themselves absorbing the shock waves and dodging the shrapnel. To deal with the pain, some cracked distasteful jokes; others made cheerful banter. But none of them were fools. They knew they would carry the weight of it all home with them, down to the strangest of details. The blood spatters on a necklace, the colour of the scarf caught between skin and metal, the label on a shirt torn to shreds. Scraps of tragedy stitching a patchwork of painful recollections in their minds.

Compared to that, handing out traffic tickets, catching car thieves or investigating a settling of scores between biker gangs was a walk in the park. Not to mention the shoplifting, disputes between neighbours, and fender-benders the patrol officers had to sort out. Rising through the ranks meant dealing with more drama. And pain.

'I'm Detective Sergeant Moralès and this is Constable Lefebvre. We're looking for your wife. If you don't mind, we'd like to come in. We have some questions to ask you that might help us find her.'

If it weren't for the slumped shoulders, unwashed hair and face ravaged by anguish, Clément Cyr would have been a striking figure. Dragging his feet like a condemned man, he led the way into the kitchen and gestured for Moralès to join him at the kitchen table.

Érik Lefebvre followed at his own pace with his hands behind his back. He stopped in front of the refrigerator to look at the snapshots of friends, grocery lists and sweet nothings held up by magnets. On the wall to the right of Moralès, framed photographs of the young couple suggested a life full of shared travel and adventure – cycling, skiing, hiking, camping and all. Angel Roberts and her husband were the picture of two sporty, energetic thirty-somethings in love.

Clément Cyr was lost without her. Struggling to gather his thoughts, he was staring at the other side of the room. And then, he saw her. Right there. Angel. Just like he'd seen her appear when he opened the door to the detectives. When she saw them coming, she'd hurried into the kitchen to put a pot of coffee on, prepare the milk and brown sugar, bring out the nice cups and her mother's best spoons. She turned around and swept her hair behind her ears, folding her arms as she leaned her hip against the kitchen counter and smiled at her husband.

Moralès followed Clément Cyr's faraway gaze as the man desperately tried to stop his wedding photos from turning to sepia. He decided to leave him another minute before breaking the spell, while Lefebvre made his way around the living room, taking everything in as if this were a memorisation exercise.

'I'd like you to tell me what you did on Saturday,' Moralès began.

Jolted back to reality, Cyr realised the coffee pot was empty and dirty. 'It's our tenth wedding anniversary the day after tomorrow. Every year we celebrate in style. Angel puts her wedding dress on, I have to dress up smart, and we go to either my family or hers for dinner. Because it fell on a weeknight this year, we arranged with my father-in-law to have dinner at his place on Saturday. We didn't stay late, but there was a party in the village for the end of the fishing season, so we went there afterwards.'

'Around what time?'

He hesitated. 'About ten o'clock, I'd say. It's never a late night with Angel's old man.'

'Where was the party?'

'At Corine's.'

Moralès turned to Lefebvre, who, without looking up from the rock collection he was studying, said: 'It's an auberge in Rivière-au-Renard. Every year, in the autumn, Corine puts on a party for the fishing folk. After that, she closes for the off season.'

Angel poured the coffee, passed the milk around and put the little spoons on the table.

'So, you both went to Corine's.'

'To the auberge, yes. But we didn't stay long.'

'Why?'

'Angel wasn't well. All night she'd been complaining she felt queasy. She said she was tired and her head was spinning.'

'Has she been tired a lot lately?'

Angel pulled out the chair nearest her husband's and sat. She held her cup to her face and breathed in the steaming morning aroma. Cyr glanced over to Érik Lefebvre as he wandered off down the hallway.

'Fishing's not an easy job. It's only natural to be worn out by the end of the season. Don't go spreading that around, will you? Angel likes to play the strong woman. She doesn't want people thinking she has moments of weakness.'

Moralès nodded, as if making a promise. 'So, you went to Corine's auberge, but Angel wasn't feeling well.'

'That's right. She had one drink, then she asked me to drive her home.'

'What time was that?'

'Before midnight.'

'And you brought her back here?'

'Yes.'

'Did you drive through the park?' Lefebvre interjected bluntly as he came back into the kitchen.

'When do you mean?'

'When you brought Angel home.'

Clément Cyr shook his head. 'No. Angel was feeling sick, and that road has a lot of twists and turns. Plus, my wife doesn't like us driving that way at night. She's always worried we'll hit a bear or a moose. We took La Radoune instead. I took it slow. Even stopped the car once or twice because she thought she was going to throw up. She didn't, though.'

Moralès turned to Lefebvre to fill him in.

'La Radoune is what the locals call Highway 197. It's a longer route, but at night it's safer than the coast road.'

'And when you got back here, what did you do?' Moralès continued.

'Well, I turned around and went back to the bar. It was the big end-of-season party. That's when all the skippers pick up the tab for their crew.'

'Around what time?'

He hesitated, toying with his watch as if it would give him the answer.

'Well, I did get changed, because I was still in my fancy wedding clothes. Then I drove back. The guys were still there.'

'And what time was that?'

'One o'clock, maybe quarter past.'

'And when did you come home again?'

'I'd had a bit to drink, so I spent the night at the auberge and came home Sunday morning. Around ten.'

This was getting uncomfortable for Clément Cyr, but he carried on. 'Angel wasn't here. I knew that as soon as I got here, because her car wasn't in the driveway. When I came into the kitchen, I found this on the table.'

He held up a scrap of paper with a few words of feminine handwriting on it: *Gone out for a bit, see you later.* Two x's – two kisses – concluded the message.

'Is it all right if we hold on to this note?'

Clément Cyr nodded. Moralès handed it to Lefebvre, who seemed only too happy to fish a plastic evidence bag out of his pocket.

'Anyway, I went down to her slip at the wharf to see if she was there,' Cyr continued. 'Her car was there, but the *Close Call II* wasn't. That's the name of her lobster trawler. Angel's never sunk a boat, and there never was a *Close Call I*; she just thought that name would show some bravado and reflect her sense of humour. She says the sea is too macho a place for its own good, but she makes the best of it. She's a fearless woman, my wife. A fighter.'

Cyr lowered his eyes, as if doing so could hold back the wave building in his throat.

'Were you worried to see her boat was gone?'

Cyr drew a deep breath before he answered. 'Angel loves the sea. Not just working out there, but being out there. She likes to take her boat out to get some peace and quiet, see the whales, gaze at the horizon, that sort of thing. It's not a big boat, so it's good on fuel and she can tie it up by herself. My wife is a real seafarer, detective. When she takes her boat out, it's not a cause for concern.'

'But still, you were worried about her.'

'Yes. Because I tried calling her phone and marine radio, and she didn't answer.'

'And when was that?'

'Between ten in the morning and noon.'

'So, around half past midnight was the last time you spoke to her?'

Clément Cyr's eyes wandered across the kitchen table, noticing the absence of coffee cups, milk, sugar and spoons. Were she here, she'd have been shooting daggers at him, because he hadn't told the whole truth. He was too ashamed to speak up. That was the story of his life. He had always wanted to live up to his father and his wife, but now he had lost everything. Everything but the guilt and the shame. Now that was all he had left.

'That's right. I checked her car, down by the wharf, and found her handbag there with her phone inside. Then I called Jean-Paul Babin. He's Angel's deckhand. He phoned his brother Ti-Guy, and Angel's brother Jimmy. They put their heads together, and Jean-Paul called me back not long after. He said the Roberts guys were taking the *Ange-Irène* out to look for her. That boat's a big trawler, so I figured they must be going offshore. I asked Laurent Lepage if he'd take me out to comb the coastline. He hasn't taken his lobster boat out of the water for the winter yet. So we went out and looked around my wife's fishing grounds. Around three that afternoon, Lepage said I should report Angel missing. That was when I called the police. After that, I came ashore. I didn't dare go out to sea again.' His last words were barely audible, as if the water had risen around them.

'Why not?'

'I was scared.'

Lefebvre didn't catch on.

'Scared of what?'

'That we wouldn't find her.'

Lefebvre's phone started to vibrate. Moralès and Cyr turned to him with question marks in their eyes. Lefebvre checked the screen and shook his head. No news. He left the room to take the call.

Moralès kept the tone gentle. 'Is your wife happy? Has she been feeling all right?'

Cyr bowed his head to the table, as if trying not to see her spirit appearing all over the room. 'You're asking if she might have taken her own life. I don't know. Maybe. Often when people kill themselves, their family and friends act all shocked, as if no one had ever dreamed it could happen. I don't think Angel's unhappy, but now you bring it up, I don't really know.'

Moralès thought it better not to mention the possibility that she might have wanted to leave her husband. Perhaps for another man. He decided to try a different tack. 'Did you find her purse too?'

'It's in her handbag.'

Clément Cyr stood, went into the hallway and returned with a fairly large shoulder bag, which he placed on the kitchen table. He unzipped the bag, pulled out a red leather purse and held it out for Moralès to look through. Embarrassed by the openness of the gesture, Moralès refused to take it.

'I'll leave that to you, all right? You know how particular women can be. Could you just tell me whether her driver's licence and bank cards are still in there?'

Cyr nodded and opened his wife's purse, extracting the said cards and putting them on the table.

'Is there anything missing?'

'I don't think so. There's even some cash in here.'

There was an air of dejection in his eyes as he held the purse in his hands, as if the object confirmed that Angel was gone. 'She won't be happy if she knows I've opened her handbag.'

'Maybe you should put the cards back where you found them.'

Moralès stood while Angel's husband covered his tracks. This house was laden with shadows, and he needed a breath of fresh air. As if on cue, he saw Lefebvre hang up and give him a wave from the kitchen doorway. The boats must be close to shore now, he figured.

'I have to ask you for a photo of your wife, Mr Cyr.'

Angel's husband went to the wall of happy memories in frames. 'I took this one myself,' he said, taking one off its hook, removing the back and teasing the photo out by the bottom corner, as if worried he might drop it.

'We were camping up north in Sept-Îles. She was chopping the vegetables for dinner.'

Stray locks cascaded gently around the image of Angel's face, blown around by the unbridled freedom of a relaxing getaway, or maybe just by the wind. Her eyes were brown. She was laughing. Neither her hands nor the vegetables were visible. Just the edge of the forest in the background.

The man gazed at his wife again before handing the photo to Moralès.

'We've got people out there looking, and we're stepping up the efforts too. Did you know your father-in-law has found the boat?'

'Yes.'

'We're going to have it examined.'

Cyr shrugged his shoulders. 'It's not the boat I care about.'

Érik Lefebvre coughed discreetly in the hallway. It was time for them to go. Moralès had said he wanted to get to the wharf before the boats docked, to make sure no one contaminated a potential crime scene. He was also keen to meet Angel's father and brothers before they had a chance to speak to other fishermen and embellish their stories.

'Who's your wife's best friend?'

'Annie Arsenault. She lives in the blue house next door,' he replied, pointing to it.

'Could you describe what clothes Angel was wearing when you last saw her?' Moralès asked.

'I told you, her wedding dress.'

'She must have changed before she went out, then.'

Clément Cyr shook his head. 'No. I checked. There's nothing else missing from her wardrobe.'

Lefebvre opened the front door. Clément waved a futile hand from the kitchen. He let his wife walk the officers out and shut the door behind them.

Sébastien Moralès felt like he was in a nightmare when he woke to the sound of his ringing phone echoing around the room. Which room, though? Blinking his eyes into focus, he saw he was lying on a sofa in a corridor. Above him loomed a giant figure of Christ wearing a crown of thorns, nailed to a white crucifix.

The phone stopped ringing. 'Hello! Renaud Boissonneau here, honorary dean of the high school and businessman with business aplenty. Let me tell you, if you're calling about dance classes, you're going to have to wait your turn, they're not half popular.'

It was all coming back to him now. Last night he'd crashed on a sofa in the back of the bistro.

'What? He's a chef in Montreal? Well, he didn't exactly shout about that last night!'

Sébastien realised he must have left his phone hooked up to the stereo in the bistro last night. That's why the ringer was so loud.

'This is the bistro in Caplan, Quebec, Canada. We've got the sole on special for lunch today.'

Sébastien tried to stand but had to sit down right away. His head was spinning. He could just about remember climbing the stairs.

'Yes, miss. But Mr Sébastien Moralès is sleeping at the moment.'

Sébastien pricked his ears. How many times had his phone rung?

'While you're on the phone, you might as well make a reservation.'

He folded the blanket he had used.

'Well if you're in Montreal, then let me tell you, you'll have a hard time getting here in time for lunch.'

What? Renaud Boissonneau had answered his phone? Sébastien sprang to his feet and ran downstairs to find himself face to face with the salt-and-pepper moustache of the server from last night, who had seen him coming and was in a hurry to wrap up the conversation.

'Well, miss, it's just rude to call a bistro at this time in the morning and not make a reservation.'

Renaud ended the call, but kept the phone in his hand.

'You're a chef and you didn't tell me?'

Sébastien approached the counter, but he didn't know what to say. But Renaud still had a bone to pick with him.

'Because, let me tell you, I've always wanted to be a chef myself. I was even made cook's helper last summer. But I had my heart broken, so I went back to waiting tables.'

'Renaud, who were you talking to when I came downstairs?'

'What? Who was I talking to? I'm afraid that's classified information.'

The rows of stools that had been pushed aside last night

formed a barrier that kept Sébastien from getting too close to Renaud, who was standing behind the counter as guarded as a soldier in a trench.

'Were you just talking to my partner?'

Renaud's cheeks flushed. Not in embarrassment. In anger. He slammed his fist onto the counter. 'Let me tell you one thing, you and that father of yours are both the same. You come gallivanting here to court the women of the Gaspé while your own sweethearts are sitting at home in the big city waiting for you.'

Sébastien felt the words like a slap in the face and retreated a step.

'What are you insinuating about my father?'

'Don't try and get me to spill the beans,' Renaud snorted. 'Whatever romance there was between your father and the lovely Catherine is their business, and theirs alone. I didn't breathe anything of it to your mother when she came here, but don't you worry, she'll make whatever decisions she has to. She's not a woman to let the wool be pulled over her eyes, you can tell that straight away.'

Sébastien was wide awake now. 'Listen, Renaud…'

'The men in your family, you're nothing but liars.'

The phone rang again, making Renaud nearly jump out of his skin. He answered in a split second. 'Hello! Renaud Boissonneau here, honorary dean of the high school and businessman with…'

Renaud's words and behaviour left Sébastien dumbstruck for a moment.

'Inspector Moralès, your son is a chef, and you didn't tell me.'

A second later, he added, 'Yes, he's here, but he's not available.'

'Hey, what do you mean, not available?' Sébastien protested, moving the stools aside. He leaned over the counter to grab his phone, but Renaud stepped back.

'No, no, nothing's happening.'

'Renaud, give me my phone!'

Sébastien put one foot on a stool and jumped over the counter. Seeing him coming, Renaud Boissonneau deftly stepped aside. 'I'll give him the message. Have a nice day, inspector!' Then he hung up, put the phone on the counter and motioned for Sébastien to leave the premises with a dismissive wave of his hand.

'You have to go to your father's place. He's having a mattress delivered. And you have to go buy sheets and pillows in Bonaventure, too. He'll pay you back, he says.'

Discouraged, Sébastien pocketed his phone and grabbed his coat from the rack. On his way out he heard Renaud calling after him, 'Mr Sébastien! When are you coming back to dance for us again?'

When they left Cap-aux-Os, Moralès and Lefebvre looped around the bay to the station in Gaspé to pick up a second car before they headed north to meet the boat in Rivière-au-Renard. As they drove through the national park, the sky clouded over but stopped short of turning grey. There wasn't much to see along the way. Only the odd house emerged haphazardly from a dense forest of black spruce, where every tree seemed to be twisting its spiked head to get away from the wind or attack those surrounding it. At last, the horizon opened up as the road drew nearer to the coast.

Lefebvre turned onto Rue de L'Église, forked onto Rue du Banc and brought his unmarked car to a halt in the pot-holed wasteland of a car park behind the coast-guard building. Moralès followed. The air felt cool, bordering on cold, when he opened the door and got out of the car, giving his back a stretch and lifting his head like a cormorant spreading its wings after a snooze. The village of Rivière-au-Renard had gathered its houses in a proud semicircle facing the sea. Standing stoically on the hill behind the wharf, they seemed to watch over the water the way a lighthouse guards the shore.

Lefebvre and Moralès walked through the parking area to a service road for the wharf where all the small trawlers were moored. The place was all but deserted. Lefebvre led Moralès to the forensics van, where two tight-lipped technicians were waiting. Moralès remembered having crossed paths with them a couple of times in recent investigations. He had to admit Simone Lord was right: one of the technicians emerged from the van and promptly threw an empty doughnut box in the nearest rubbish bin.

Lefebvre barely said a word of introduction. 'This is the guy who's in charge,' he said, pointing at Moralès.

Moralès nodded. Now it was official. He was leading the in-vestigation. And no one had forced his hand. That had sunk in earlier, as he held the photograph of Angel Roberts in his hand. He had known, in that moment, he had to do right by this proud fisherwoman who'd gone missing in her wedding dress.

'Hmm,' said one of the technicians.

'OK,' said the other.

Moralès wondered who had sent the forensics team here, because he hadn't taken the initiative himself. Surely not Lefebvre, who was trudging around this patch of wasteland with his eyes glued to the ground like he was studying the geology of the place.

'Who told you to come?'

They shrugged.

'Orders always come from high up,' said one technician.

'Hmm,' said the other.

'You do know we're investigating a disappearance, not a homicide?'

One of them reached into the van for a sheet of paper, read the address on it, and nodded towards the wharf. 'Well, this is where we're supposed to be.'

Moralès turned to take in their surroundings. The wharf stretched to the east and ended in a loading basin where a huge gantry crane loomed overhead like a giant metal spider. Dozens of trawlers were strewn around at the back of the basin, resting in their winter storage cradles. Parked here and there between the vessels in dry dock were pickup trucks that must have belonged to the owners, mechanics, welders, and whoever else had business being there.

Beyond the basin Moralès could see stacks of fishing bins amidst an armada of seafood-processing plants and semi-trailers. Beyond those another, larger, wharf extended out from the shore, perpendicular to the wharf they were standing on now. It looked like it was built in the shelter of the breakwater that protected the port from storms. That was where all the big midshore shrimp trawlers docked, Lefebvre had said.

The place had none of the charm of a marina. It was clearly an industrial area filled with heavy machinery for extracting fish from the sea. To the north, the St Lawrence River estuary was whipping white foam atop the black waves. The other shore was too far away to see.

Lefebvre pointed to the boats approaching from the east. As they forged closer to shore, fishermen emerged from the boats in dry dock and began to file down to the wharf. Cars carrying fishermen's wives and onlookers arrived too. People were coming out in droves, not so much to see the boats motor in, but to show solidarity among seafarers. They were all wearing windbreakers, gathering in a silence broken only by whispers. Fingers pointed here and there. A man in his early fifties was explaining that they'd found the lobster trawler on the other side of Bonaventure Island. He'd heard it on his VHF. The others remarked how far away that was, that at least this cloud had a silver lining, though the insurance would have paid out anyway. Not that any settlement could ever replace a woman like Angel, though.

Simone Lord was leaning casually against a sporty-looking pickup truck emblazoned with the Fisheries and Oceans Canada logo, exchanging vaguely polite nods of greeting with fishermen at a distance. Her arms were folded. Her face gave nothing away.

The moment she looked at him, Moralès felt his phone vibrate in his pocket. He glanced at the screen and ignored the call when he saw Sébastien's name. Now was not the time.

'That's them,' said Lefebvre, slipping a few rocks into his pockets as he sidled up to Moralès.

A bright-yellow trawler bearing a red lobster and the name *Close Call II* charged around the windswept and wave-lashed breakwater into the marina basin and docked almost too swiftly alongside the trawler wharf, in front of the coast-guard vessel.

Moralès gestured for Lefebvre to follow him as he made his way through the crowd to the boat to meet the two men in their early thirties tying it up. One of them jumped down onto the wharf. Moralès stepped forward, introduced himself and flashed his badge. The fishermen gave him a chilly nod as well as their names: Jimmy Roberts and Guy Babin. Babin was quick to turn his back on the officers and clamber back aboard.

'Not so fast,' Moralès intervened. 'I have to ask you to turn the engine off and disembark. My forensics team have work to do on board.'

Jimmy Roberts tipped his chin defiantly and dug his hands into his pockets. 'And why's that?'

'Because this boat is potentially a crime scene.'

The onlookers were silent, hanging on every word, taking in every detail of the interaction like reporters keen for a scoop.

'Who says a crime has been committed?'

'Your sister's disappearance is being treated as suspicious. Now turn the engine off and leave the boat.'

Jimmy Roberts and Guy Babin dragged their heels.

'I'm not so sure. How long's this for?' Jimmy Roberts protested.

'As long as it takes!' barked a female voice of authority behind Moralès.

Simone Lord stepped out from the crowd in a windbreaker bearing an official Fisheries and Oceans logo. A semicircle of curious bystanders formed around them. Roberts and Babin grimaced.

'What did you not understand? We need the boat. Fishing season's done, anyway.'

Babin was a short, stocky man, built like an ox with a thick neck and bear paws for hands. He had been staring at Moralès with fierce contempt since the men started talking. Joaquin let Simone Lord play her hand and kept his own in his pockets, resolving to take her down a peg when he had the chance.

Jimmy Roberts was reluctant to obey the fisheries officer's orders. 'Yeah, but we have to get the boat out of the water for the winter before it gets too cold.'

Lord glared at him. 'You'll have all the time in the world to mess around with it later, Jimmy boy. Now turn off the engine and leave that boat, or I'll keep it off the water for the first two weeks of the season next year. You might be in line to inherit, you never know. Where do you think you'll put those traps once all the good spots are taken?'

Jimmy Roberts was still dallying, but it was just for show. This round was over, and it was clear that Simone had played the winning hand. Roberts grudgingly complied and stepped onto the wharf. Babin leaned overboard and spat into the water between him and Moralès.

Jimmy nodded to Babin. 'Come on, Ti-Guy.'

Babin followed his lead.

'My colleague here will make a note of your contact details, and the forensics team will take your prints,' Moralès explained.

Waiting in the wings, Lefebvre opened his notebook while the forensics guys pulled on their overalls and set about doing their job. Simone Lord beckoned to Moralès. 'We'll take my truck over to the *Ange-Irène.*'

The onlookers began to disperse as she led Moralès to her vehicle. Lefebvre had already finished with the fishermen, so Moralès gestured for him to come too. If Angel Roberts' father and other brother were as unwelcoming as this one, he preferred to have backup.

Lefebvre jumped into the back seat of the truck. 'Wow, Simone, you didn't beat around the bush! Don't you think you came on a bit strong?'

'Those guys swagger around like they rule the waves. They had it coming.'

Moralès was listening, but looking out of the window. He wasn't saying a word. For now. Simone's little tirade had ruffled the men's feathers and put him in a tricky situation as the in-vestigating officer. Now it would be harder for him to get any information out of them. He could certainly appreciate the fisheries officer's influence, but it would get them nowhere if she couldn't be a team player. She took her role too seriously and that bothered him. But he was hesitant to lay down the law with her. Now was not the time.

Simone turned left at the La Marinière fish market, towards the main wharf. The waves were pounding against the rocks of the breakwater, sending spray across the road. There were onlookers here too, though they had the sense to be keeping warm and dry inside their vehicles. Only two men were out braving the elements, standing by the edge of the wharf where the shrimp trawler would be docking.

The huge boat with a navy-blue hull motored into the port and turned head to wind, flaunting the hefty white structure of her double deck, complete with solid metal doors and stabiliser cylinders, steel-cabled web of pulleys and winches, grey out-riggers carrying green midwater trawl nets, and orange buoys bearing her name in salt-worn black letters: *Ange-Irène*.

Now the vessel was advancing almost gracefully towards the wharf, pitching to her port side in the wind and swell, then rolling back to starboard under her own weight. A man in his late thirties wearing green deck boots, dressed in orange overalls and jacket with a black woolly hat pulled tightly over his ears waited patiently for the shrimp trawler to nestle against the wharf. Then he threw the mooring lines, one by one, to the men onshore, who hooked them over the bollards on the wharf without a word.

As soon as Moralès ventured out of the truck, the wind caught him and forced him back a step. The door slammed shut behind him. The waves were hitting the breakwater harder than he'd thought, drenching the wharf with blasts of spray. Before he saw it coming, one of the breakers gave him a faceful of saltwater. Cursing, he shook himself off and found shelter from any further onslaughts behind a shipping container.

Simone Lord and Érik Lefebvre, who had seen fit to grab a Fisheries and Oceans weatherproof jacket each from the truck, soon joined him. The wind ballooned its way under their clothes, making them look like they were about to take flight.

The man who had thrown the mooring lines looked at them and called hello to Simone.

'This is Detective Sergeant Moralès, the officer in charge of the investigation,' she replied.

The man turned to Moralès. 'Bruce Roberts. I'm Angel's brother. My dad's in the wheelhouse.'

'Can we talk?' Moralès had to shout to make himself heard in the wind.

'Come with me.'

Moralès let Simone Lord go first – to be polite of course, but also to watch how she climbed aboard. She sprang nimbly across the gap between the wharf and the boat and made way for the two police officers to follow. She said something to Bruce Roberts that only the fisherman could hear. Moralès figured she was explaining who Lefebvre was. The fisherman nodded and opened the door to the wheelhouse.

On the wharf, onlookers and their vehicles were backing up and making their way back to the village. Leeroy Roberts had seen them all from the windows of the wheelhouse. That was enough to show who was standing by him.

Moralès hadn't been aboard a vessel like this before. The wheelhouse was bigger and more comfortable than he had thought it would be. A deep, grey, leather bench stretched along the entire port side below the windows. Charts, papers and pens were strewn across a black console unit edged with wood trim, which ran the length of the front windows to the plush captain's swivel chair on the starboard side. Six screens displayed marine charts, the position of the nets and images of the aft deck and engine room. A dozen or so VHF transceivers were attached to the ceiling. There was no traditional ship's wheel, rather an array of joysticks, levers, keyboards, compasses, depth gauges, inclinometers and sounders – all the gadgets you'd expect aboard an ocean-going vessel. Behind the cockpit stood a rack of orange safety jackets. To the rear, by the window overlooking the deck, was another console, formed of more screens and joysticks. In the middle of the space, encased on three sides by a low wall made of wood, was a staircase, descending into the belly of the beast.

Lefebvre whistled in appreciation. A man in his late sixties was standing, quite still, by the stairs, behind the captain's chair. It was Angel Roberts' father. His lips were pressed tightly together, either in anger or because he was trying not to cry. Without moving a muscle, he watched Simone Lord approach.

The fishermen here knew that she'd never hesitated to put her own life on the line to save theirs when she was working with the coast guard. They'd come to accept she could be stubborn and difficult, but they'd wished she wasn't a woman. It would have been easier for them to look up to a man. Later, though, when she became a fisheries officer, they weren't shy about bad-mouthing her to her face.

'Hi, Leeroy.'

They shook hands warmly. He looked at her gratefully. He could never hold anything against her. When his wooden boat caught fire fifteen or so years ago, he, his son and his crew would have perished in the fog if she and her colleagues hadn't come to their rescue. Lord had moved to Fisheries and Oceans after that – she and her watchful eye. Leeroy wasn't known to be a generous man, but he would remember and show gratitude when he had to.

'We're going to find your daughter.'

'Thank you, Simone.'

She made the introductions. Leeroy Roberts eyed Moralès intently from behind his grey-framed glasses. His daughter's fate was in this man's hands. His name wasn't from around here, and his face was too tanned for the season.

'Where are you from, then?'

'Caplan. I work at the Bonaventure detachment.'

That was good enough for Leeroy. You didn't have to be born here to be a Gaspesian. You just needed to have your heart in the right place.

Moralès felt like an imposter. Angel Roberts was missing and her father was standing here in front of him – with an air of distrust, yes, but also a shred of hope. He wanted to give this man his daughter back, but he doubted that was possible. He hoped this was just a case of a woman who needed a breath of fresh air. It did happen. Husbands and wives sometimes decided to get away from each other without telling anyone. And it wasn't always because they were having an affair. Often they just wanted or needed to be alone for a while, to pull themselves together or gather their thoughts. Moralès thought it was completely unreasonable for anyone to worry their friends and family sick just so they could 'gather their thoughts', but what could he do about it? He thought about Sébastien and his 'culinary experiments' and shook his head. He'd have a word with his son later. He'd talk to Marlène Forest about his holiday time later. And he'd call his wife later too.

'Talk about a sweet setup,' Lefebvre enthused. 'I can't believe all the gear you've got. I can see why these boats cost so much.' He seemed to have completely forgotten why he was on board.

Simone Lord was scandalised. She glared at him, but his insensitive words seemed to have fallen on deaf ears. Neither Angel's father, nor her brother, who had followed them into the wheelhouse and closed the door behind him, paid any attention.

Moralès knew he was going to have to act fast if he didn't want either of his colleagues to wreck his investigation. 'When did you learn your daughter was missing?'

Leeroy remained standing in spite of his fatigue. They were

talking about his daughter's possible death and he wasn't the kind of man to sit down when fate came knocking. He rested a hand on the low wall around the stairwell and turned to face the detective. 'Yesterday morning, Ti-Guy Babin called my boy Jimmy to tell him Angel's boat wasn't at Grande-Grave no more.'

Simone Lord interrupted. 'And around what time did you set out?'

Leeroy looked at her suspiciously and chose to ignore her. He turned back to Moralès to finish his answer. He was an old-school kind of guy and would only talk to the boss. 'It was his brother, Jean-Paul, who called him. He's one of Angel's deckhands. He must have gone down to the wharf and seen the boat wasn't there.'

'And around what time—?'

Moralès cut in – he wasn't going to let Lord continue. 'Who's the other deckhand?'

'Jacques Forest – Angel's uncle on her mum's side.'

Lord was seething, but dropped her question. Érik Lefebvre wandered to the starboard side and sat down in the captain's chair, turning it from side to side with an annoying squeak. Bruce Roberts leaned back against the door and stared at a stain on the floor.

'Was Angel the sole owner of the trawler?'

Leeroy nodded, turned to the portside window and looked out across the water at his daughter's boat, where the crime-scene technicians were busy doing their job. 'Her home port's on the south side of Forillon Park, but we brought her back here because I live right there.' He pointed to a house by the water's edge. 'I wanted to feel like she was close to me. At least for today.'

Moralès was thinking. Clément Cyr had said he was the one

who had raised the alarm with Jean-Paul Babin, but Leeroy didn't seem to know that. Or was pretending he didn't. He decided to ask a different question to check whether the omission was intentional.

'As I understand it, yesterday your daughter's deckhand Jean-Paul Babin went down to the wharf to go fishing, but—'

'No, no, no,' Simone Lord interrupted. 'The fishing season's over.'

Moralès turned to face her squarely, but addressed his other colleague. 'Constable Lefebvre, would you go and inspect the inside of the boat, please?'

Lefebvre sprang to his feet, keen as can be. 'Right away?'

The Roberts men hadn't reacted to the unexpected intrusion, so the detective nodded. 'Now would be a good time.'

Lefebvre scurried over to the stairwell.

'Officer Lord here will join you, since she's the expert.'

The fisheries officer took an indignant step backward.

'Come on, Simone. I need you down here. I've never been aboard a trawler before, so…' Lefebvre's voice trailed away as he descended into the shrimp trawler's bowels. Simone Lord scowled at Moralès as she reluctantly followed suit.

Leeroy nodded to the stairs. 'They're your best field agents, are they?'

The man was bitter. That was understandable. His daughter was missing and they'd sent the B-team to investigate. Moralès had nothing to say to that. So he waited, letting Angel's father pick up the thread of his story where he felt he could.

Leeroy Roberts was ready to carry on. 'I think my dear son-in-law, Clément Cyr, had a bit of a late night on Saturday,' Leeroy said, with more than a hint of sarcasm. 'He spent the night at the auberge, and his wife wasn't home when he came back the next morning. He must've gone down to the wharf and thought it was strange the boat wasn't there, then called Jean-Paul Babin to see if he knew where Angel was. He must've known Jimmy would get wind of it. And us too.'

'Why wouldn't he have called you directly?'

Leeroy pursed his lips in contempt. 'Just because we're Gaspesians, it doesn't make us friends. And just because he married my daughter, it doesn't mean we like each other.'

'Does your daughter often go out to sea alone?'

'Yes, and it's something she enjoys.'

'So what was it that worried you?'

'It was Jimmy who had me worried. We don't call each other often. Then the phone rings out of the blue and he tells me his sister's gone off with the boat. That was a strange thing for him to be phoning me about. I mean, she's a fisherwoman, so there's nothing unusual about her taking her boat out. So anyway, I tried Angel's mobile. No answer. Then I asked my Bruce to call her on the marine radio.'

'She didn't answer,' the older of the Roberts brothers said flatly, still leaning against the door. This man had the kind of lean, tough strength that only came from working outdoors. His arms were covered with boats and mermaids tattooed in shades of black and blue. He wasn't a talkative man, but that didn't make him distant. He was the kind of skipper who wouldn't hesitate to go out on deck in a raging storm.

Angel's father picked up the conversation. Slowly. 'Do you have children, detective?'

Moralès nodded. 'Two grown-up sons.'

That seemed to buoy Leeroy's confidence. 'You know how they are. They're not kids anymore, but you still worry about them all the time. And these bloody phones! We're so used to people picking up right away, when they don't answer, we don't know what to think. So anyway, I was umming and ah-ing for a bit, then I thought I should get Bruce to call Clément back and ask him how long it had been since he'd heard from Angel. And when that son-in-law of mine told me he hadn't heard a word from her since the night before, and that she still had her wedding dress on…' Suddenly, the words were hard to find. 'That gave me the shivers. Like in the films, when they set things up so you know something bad's going to happen. So I said to Bruce, "Let's go out and have a look." And off we went.'

'What time was that?'

'We hadn't eaten, so probably about four o'clock.'

'Who was on board when you went out?'

'Bruce and me. We came down to the wharf, and when we got here we saw Jimmy as well. He twisted my arm to let him and Ti-Guy Babin come aboard too. Angel's his sister. I couldn't exactly say no. He said if we found the boat, we'd need help bringing it back, and that convinced me.'

Simone Lord and Érik Lefebvre raced back up the stairs.

'It's the first time I've seen a boat anything like this. I can't believe all the berths you've got down there. They must be practical.'

No one turned to look at Lefebvre, so he felt awkward. He shuffled over to the long grey bench, sat down and casually crossed his legs, showing a flash of his cowboy boots.

'Listen, I don't know where you're at, but I need to know how these guys went about finding the boat,' Simone cut in rudely.

'We're getting there,' Moralès said softly.

Leeroy carried on telling his story. He was looking at her, that fisheries woman, because she knew the sea, but the detective from Caplan was the one he was talking to, because he had children of his own.

'We went to the end of Forillon Point and looked all around

the mouth of Gaspé Bay, but we couldn't see anything. So we started calculating.'

Simone Lord's eyes widened. 'Calculating what?'

It was the son who answered. 'The wind and the tide in the last twelve hours.'

'And that led you to the boat?'

Bruce Roberts shook his head firmly. 'Nope. You know as well as I do, twelve hours is far too long a time for anyone to calculate exactly where a boat will have drifted.'

A suspicious smile crept across Simone's lips. 'So what did you calculate?'

Bruce Roberts chose to keep his mouth shut. He didn't like the fisheries officer's sarcasm. Instead Leeroy turned to Moralès and gestured to his eldest son.

'My Bruce knows his navigation. He's better at it than I am. He said we should head south to follow the Labrador Current. If we went in the right direction, but faster than a boat would drift, we might find it, he reckoned. That made sense to me. So we went out that way and kept our eyes peeled the best we could.'

He hesitated before saying more. He knew what they'd done sounded fishy. Even he thought Bruce seemed a bit too confident about where they should be looking, but he'd defend his son if he had to.

'By a stroke of luck, this morning Jimmy saw something reflecting the sun on the horizon. "That's it," I said. So we went for a look-see, and that was it.'

Leeroy Roberts seemed to drift away. He let his gaze wander to the stairs, as if his daughter might be down there.

'When you got there, what did you see?' asked Moralès.

The old fisherman looked up and frowned, not grasping what the detective meant. 'Well, the boat, of course.'

He had felt a sharp pain in his chest when they pulled up alongside it.

'What kind of condition was it in?'

This time, it was Bruce who answered. 'It was in good shape. We didn't go aboard, us two. Jimmy took charge of everything. The engine was off, but there was fuel in the tank. When he turned it on, we saw the boat was all right.'

He was going to say something else but stopped himself and clenched his jaw.

Moralès pressed him. 'Is that all?'

Bruce Roberts shrugged.

Simone chimed in. 'What did your brother say, exactly?'

'Jimmy said, "Well, it's a nice surprise all the same."'

Leeroy looked at Moralès, wondering if he knew what it was like to have children who said stupid things sometimes. Children who, even as adults, said things that could break your heart. Children you might even be a little ashamed of sometimes. Moralès met the man's gaze and nodded. Maybe it was human nature to pass the worst of our indiscretions on to our children.

'Did you notice anything else?'

Bruce Roberts drew a breath. 'The deck was open.'

Moralès didn't understand, but had the feeling this might be something important. Bruce noticed the question mark hanging in the air.

'Come look at the other lobster trawlers,' he explained, walking over to the portside window and pointing to the only two still in the water this late in the year. They were moored near the processing plant. Moralès joined him at the window.

'See how the deck is closed at the stern? In Nova Scotia, where the conditions are harsh and the boats go fishing for lobster way offshore, the shipyards started building boats with open transoms. The fishermen string their lobster pots together by the dozen. Each one of those they call a line of traps. Then when they pull up a line, they bring it over the side of the boat. They empty the traps, bait them and stack them up on the deck so when they go back out again, they just have to pitch the first one overboard and all the others will slide right off the stern, one at a time.' Bruce Roberts was still looking out at the water as he spoke. 'My sister doesn't like to strain her crew, so she wanted to make it easy for them to send the traps out the back, like the guys in Nova Scotia do. But because her boat isn't too big and she likes taking her friends out for a spin, she didn't want to have a transom that was open all the time. So she put a tailgate in the back instead, like a pickup truck. She opens it when her deckhands are dropping the lines of traps. And when she takes the boat out for pleasure, she keeps the transom closed to make sure no one falls overboard.'

Moralès picked out the *Close Call II* and studied it a little more closely, and saw for himself that the stern looked a lot like the back of a pickup truck. 'And what was so unusual about that tailgate when you found the boat?'

Bruce Roberts moved away from the window before he answered. 'It was open. The season's over, and my sister was getting ready to put the boat on its cradle for the winter. She was going to keep it in the water a few more days to cruise around for pleasure first. That's what she liked to do.'

'And you think she would have kept the tailgate closed?'

'I don't *think* she would, I'm sure she would.'

Simone Lord came back for another try with Leeroy. 'Did you notice anything else?'

'No. We found the boat, we approached it.' That was all he said. He would have liked to go aboard, but he couldn't bring himself to.

Bruce Roberts picked up the thread. 'Jimmy and Ti-Guy Babin went aboard. And they didn't find anything.'

A spark of inspiration furrowed Lefebvre's brow. 'They didn't find anything? What do you mean? Were they looking for something?'

The old fisherman glared at the hapless constable with a huff of exasperation. 'My daughter. They were looking for my daughter.'

'Ah. Of course. Sorry, I'm not good with this kind of thing.'

Leeroy Roberts looked exhausted.

'We notified the coast guard. Ti-Guy and Jimmy started up the *Close Call II* and we brought both the boats back to shore,' Bruce said.

Moralès gestured to his colleagues. That was enough for today. 'Try to get some rest, Leeroy. We're going to keep looking.'

Simone Lord stood up. Bruce Roberts stepped aside and opened the door to let them out. The men shook hands in silence.

On the way out, Moralès heard Lefebvre trying to be reassuring. 'We're doing everything we can to find her.'

As Simone drove them back around the quayside to the *Close Call II*, Lefebvre gave Moralès the address of Corine's auberge, where he had booked a room for him, and promised he would drop by that evening. When the truck pulled up to the wharf, he made his way to his own unmarked car, keen to drive back to the police station in Gaspé.

The onlookers must have grown tired of waiting in the cold wind for information and gossip that failed to materialise, because the wharf was now empty. The lobster trawler had now been sealed off with yellow crime-scene tape. Simone Lord strode purposefully towards the forensic technicians as they were taking off their gloves. Moralès felt his phone vibrate in his pocket again, but he didn't bother to look at the screen. He didn't want to let the fisheries officer take the lead in this investigation.

'Did you find anything?' he asked the technicians.

'Nothing in the wheelhouse or at the bow. We lifted some prints, but they were probably from the guys earlier. Those two clowns touched everything, by the looks of it.'

No surprise there, Moralès thought.

'Nothing in the bilge or around the engine compartment.'

Moralès looked across at the area of the deck behind the wheelhouse. 'It seems the tailgate was open when the men found the boat.'

'Evidently.'

'Why do you say that?'

The forensic technicians put their gloves back on, walked to the stern, one to either side, and opened the tailgate. The younger of the two then explained what they had found, but without making eye contact with the detective or the fisheries officer. 'She must have been sitting there.'

'Hmm,' said his colleague.

Moralès frowned and walked over for a closer look. 'Where, exactly?'

'With one hand behind her back.'

'What do you mean, one hand behind her back?'

The young forensic technician looked down his nose at Moralès, as if he'd interrupted a groundbreaking lecture about the survival of the human race. He was hesitant to bother gracing Moralès's question with an answer but, after a silent debate with himself, decided he probably should. 'She was slumped on the deck with her back against the wheelhouse, right there, with her right hand behind her back, palm facing down.'

'Hmm,' the other guy confirmed.

'There are clear prints of a female's fingertips here. But the rest of the print is weird. It's like the hand had flipped itself over somehow.'

'Hmm. Flipped.'

The young guy turned away from Moralès and twisted his arm behind his back, palm facing out.

'Like this.'

He let his hand fall, but kept his back to Moralès.

'Then, it's as if she was pulled downwards.'

'Hmm. Towards the sea.'

'Sorry?'

The young guy whirled around and glared at Moralès. 'It's hard to explain when you keep getting interrupted.'

The other guy nodded.

The detective ignored the comment. 'Are you saying someone dragged her towards the stern?'

'Towards the water.'

'Is there anything else that would confirm this theory?'

'Hmm. Something white and frilly.'

'Caught on the hold-hatch bolt, there.'

'Here?' Moralès pointed to the hold hatches.

'Hmm. Hair, as well.'

'In both bolt heads. The angle suggests she slid towards the stern, not the other way.'

'Hmm.'

'And we found more in the tailgate hinge.'

'As if she'd been dragged towards the sea and the hair had got caught there along the way?'

'Hmm.'

'Any evidence there was some kind of struggle?'

'None.'

'Hmm.'

'She was attached.'

'Attached? To what?'

'To the line that was spliced to the anchor chain. But the anchor itself is still in its well, up front.'

'What was at the end of the chain?'

Both forensics technicians shrugged in unison, as if they were practising a synchronised-swimming routine. 'We don't know.' Then the younger one turned to his colleague. 'Can you summarise?'

'Hmm. Let me summarise. So the woman was lying there, slumped against the wheelhouse, dressed in her white frilly whatnot with one hand behind her back. She was attached to a line, and that line was attached to an anchor chain, both of which had first been taken out of the anchor well up front. We don't know what was on the end of the chain. The tailgate was open. The woman was dragged off the boat in a reclined position. There are fibres from the line and marks where the chain slid over the tailgate. The tailgate itself was closed later, presumably when the two deckhands came aboard.'

The young guy raised an admiring eyebrow to his colleague, who nodded in return, as if to say 'that's the way you deliver a brief summary of the chain of events at a crime scene'.

Moralès interrupted their silent exchange. 'So she came aboard without putting up a fight, laid down on the deck in her frilly dress, put one hand behind her back and let herself get dragged overboard without blinking an eye?'

'She must have been unconscious,' Simone said.

'Or already dead,' Moralès countered.

'The murderer must have dived into the water after he tied her up to the chain.'

'Or jumped onto another boat,' the young forensic technician suggested.

'Did you notice any marks on the side of the hull?'

'Hmm.'

'There are some traces of red paint.' The technician pointed to a part of the hull near the stern on the starboard side.

'Anything else?'

'We're going to analyse the paint to see what kind of vessel it might have come from. We're also going to pay her deckhands a visit and examine the woman's house. Take some hair samples and fingerprints. Not just hers, the people close to her too. We're going to need permissions for that.'

'Constable Lefebvre is back at the station. He'll arrange all that for you. Let him know when you've got the results of your analysis.'

The forensics technicians nodded. Moralès turned to Simone Lord, but she was already halfway back to her truck. He watched her walk away. In spite of her temperament, he couldn't help but think about that intriguing little vertebra at the nape of her neck. Moralès skirted around the coast-guard building and walked back to his car. Then he drove away from the wharf.

Before he went into the auberge, Joaquin paused to look out at the sea. And breathe. Angel Roberts must be out there, he thought. Somewhere in that breezy expanse of blue. In her wedding dress, sinking into the seaweed and silt. If the search turned up nothing, she would slip away into stillness, leaving him on shore to get to the bottom of the turbulent mystery of her death.

According to Cyrille Bernard, there was no better place to die than the sea. Especially for someone like him, who had spent his whole life loving and fishing its depths. That was how he wanted to die, Cyrille said. The sea would turn his body to sediment and coral. And that coral would be fashioned into magnificent, illicit jewellery, almost like something a bride wears on her wedding day.

The wind was easing with the setting sun, as if it were feeling the fatigue of a hard day's work lashing the sea, whipping the whitecaps, keeping the waves alive. Moralès could feel the sea spray's salty residue lingering in his hair and on his skin. He was damp and sticky, and not just where his wet trouser bottoms were clinging to his ankles.

In the city, everything he had seen was clearly defined. The contours of the buildings, the files on the desk in front of him. There, he'd had to make the facts fit together, shuffle them around until he found the right order and the pieces of the puzzle started to resemble a picture of the truth. What it had been, or what it would be. Here, things seemed to take on another dimension. Another rhythm. Things emerged as specks on the horizon, imprinted themselves like transparencies on the seascape, and were filed in order by the precise, calculated movements of the tides. Rarely was there any sense in rushing. Bruce Roberts had proved that earlier, by calculating the flow of the current and orienting the search in its direction.

Joaquin shook his head. The sea had been seeping into his veins since the day he arrived on the Gaspé Peninsula. Cold and harsh, but also spectacular in all its northern beauty. Joaquin fished his phone from his pocket. Two missed calls from his son. Sébastien could wait. He called Cyrille's sister's number. No answer. He walked towards the auberge, where he'd parked his car on the street outside about half an hour earlier. Before long, he was walking through the door.

If anyone had asked him how he had imagined Corine, when Clément Cyr had told him about the auberge, he'd probably have said she was a woman of a certain age – a world-weary tavern owner who smoked, had a hacking cough and gave sailors what for when they puked in her bar. But in truth, Moralès hadn't given her a thought.

Her slippers were what first caught his eye. Not that he had a fetish for slippers or anything. He just happened to be looking down just as she breezed towards the reception desk and turned to greet him. And there they were. Leather slippers, open in the back like clogs. And in those slippers, her sprightly young feet. Moralès didn't have a thing for women's feet either. But sometimes, something strange just happened. Something incomprehensible. That concave curve between the end of the heel and the beginning of the ankle, those mere centimetres of perfection, showing between the rolled-up leg of a pair of faded jeans and the top of a mule slipper, were sometimes enough to get a man's blood pumping and make his heart skip a beat.

Corine smiled and offered her hand. 'Moralès, that's Mexican, isn't it? Can I call you by your first name? Do you pronounce it Hwa-keen or Zho-a-keen?'

Inside, the auberge was divided in two. To the right of the entrance was an informal dining area, with red leather bench seats and wooden chairs. The kitchen door was at the back of this room. To the left was the pub side of the auberge, with its square tables and dozens of bottles of spirits racked up behind the bar. Both rooms had floor-to-ceiling windows on the far wall offering a spectacular view of the water.

Corine had officially closed her doors the previous day. 'Business is slow this time of year. Not much point staying open,' she said, beckoning him to take a seat at the bar and pouring them each a glass of white wine.

Moralès didn't even think to decline her offer. He was going with the flow, in keeping with the rhythm of the afternoon. Corine joined Moralès at the bar, leaving a stool's distance between them. He resisted the foolish urge to sneak a downward peek, but as she sat, he could imagine the slipper dangling from her toes, the curve of her heel tightening.

'So…' She smiled and nodded, as if she were a teacher encouraging a child to speak.

'I hear you had a party here on Saturday?' Moralès felt ridiculous asking the question. So he tried to relax and let the interview flow like a conversation, taking small sips of his wine as he listened.

'Yes, I saw Angel. She was with Clément. She's been married ten years, and she puts her wedding dress on for every anniversary. If you want my opinion, it's more a pretty white dress than a bridal gown tarted up with lace and frills. No one blinks an eye anymore. Clément was all dressed up as well, but not in his wedding suit. It doesn't fit him anymore. But I imagine that's not what you came here to find out.'

She took a sip of wine and thought hard. It looked like she was trying to remember an important detail. When did women start having this kind of effect on him? Was it when he met Catherine?

'They had a drink, but they didn't stay long. Angel was tired. She said she was asleep on her feet. It's true, she was pale. I was so busy, I didn't really have the chance to worry about her, though.'

Was it when he stopped hearing from Sarah?

She took another sip without breaking the rhythm of her story. 'Clément went to drive her home, maybe around midnight, and he came back an hour later, I'd say. He wasn't away for long. Then he was here until about nine the next morning. He slept in room two.'

'Who came to the party?'

'It wasn't a private party, but not far off. Only fishermen. No tourists. Between you and me, tourists like fishermen when they're down on the wharf. They think they're exotic, with all their talk of quotas, longlines, zones and groundfish, but the shine wears off after half an hour. The rest of the time, the tourists keep to themselves and chat about their favourite camping spots and spout on about seeing whales in Percé.'

She extended a mocking pinkie as she raised her glass to her lips. 'They just want their perfect holiday photo – eating their lobster dinner and drinking their glass of French wine in front of a warm red sunset.' She gave him a knowing wink. Joaquin lowered his gaze and took a quick sip of his wine. 'Propping up the bar with fifty-odd fishermen isn't quite their thing.'

'Would you write me a list of the people who were here that night?'

'The fishermen?'

'Yes. And their guests, wives…'

'Gladly. But the only guests were the deckhands. This kind of thing is like an office party. The wives stay home.'

Corine finished her wine and carried her empty glass to the sink behind the bar. 'Will you be wanting to stay here?'

Moralès nodded. 'I live in Caplan. Constable Lefebvre at the Gaspé detachment told me you could put me up while I'm here for the investigation.'

'Come on, I'll show you around.'

Moralès obediently fell into step. He couldn't stop his eyes wandering to those heels in their slippers, flip-flopping up and down as she led him across the dining room.

'Feel free to bring your own food in and make yourself at home in the kitchen.' Corine showed him the cooker and opened a fridge. 'There's enough in here already to throw three or four halibut fillets in a pan with some vegetables. Oh, and look, some lobster as well! You're welcome to all that, if you're hungry. I'm having dinner at my mum's tonight.'

Moralès was already salivating. He'd barely eaten a thing all day.

'Want to pick a room?' She led the way through a door behind the reception desk to a narrow staircase.

The detective followed her upstairs.

'This is my apartment,' Corine said.

Moralès averted his eyes, discomfited by his hostess's openness. She turned left and went along a corridor and down three steps. The maze of rooms, corridors and levels seemed to defy both logic and fire-safety regulations.

'I know it's a bizarre layout. This used to be a corner shop and the former owner had a whole cottage moved from somewhere else and placed alongside it. And two extensions were built after that. They were designed by a crazy old English woman who wanted all the rooms to have a sea view – all except the servants' quarters. But the place still has a certain charm, don't you think?'

'Yes, it's all very charming.'

Corine opened a door with the number 9 painted on it. 'How about this room? It's got two windows and a nice big bathtub, see. You can pick another one if you'd rather. Rooms nine to fifteen are all clean.'

'This one's perfect.'

'The quickest way down to the bar is via the emergency exit here.' She turned on her heels, descended a spiral staircase, turned right at the bottom, passed the toilets and somehow emerged in reception, between the bar and dining room.

Simone Lord was there waiting for them. She said hello to Corine and made her way over to the bar. Moralès followed.

Again, he found his eyes wandering to the intriguing protrusion at the nape of her neck as she bent over to pour herself a glass of water.

Corine picked up a pen and scribbled something on a piece of paper. 'Here's the code for the front door. The room keys are hanging on the wall behind the reception desk, if you want to lock your room. But don't worry, it's just you and me, and I'm not the nosy type. I'm sure you'll be all right. How's it going, Simone? I'm off to my mum's. I'll leave you two to work in peace.'

While she'd been talking, Corine had grabbed her jacket, put it on and made her way to the entrance. She was just heading out of the door when Érik Lefebvre arrived and held it open for her. 'Thanks a lot, Corine. Just keep track of everything and send the bill to the detachment, will you?'

'Yes, of course, it's not the first time. Have a good night.'

Moralès took a seat at the bar. The wall of windows at the end of the room looked north over the estuary, where the river met the sea and the pale late-afternoon light slipped into the water. Cyrille Bernard must have told him a hundred times that the Gaspé was an ageing land, with its mature soil and wrinkled pebbles. That wasn't the way Joaquin Moralès saw it, though. Since his son had set Celia Cruz playing on a loop in his mind, these Gaspesian shores had been sparkling with Joannie's unbridled locks, Simone's intriguing neck and Corine's alluring heels.

He discreetly thumbed the band on his wedding finger. All these years, and the ring hadn't lost its shine. But the inscription engraved in the metal had worn away a little, weathered by their marital storms, perhaps, or smoothed by the rising tide of monotony.

The first week after his wife had come to Caplan and turned right back around again, he had tried dozens of times to call her. The second week, he had spaced the calls out; perhaps she thought she'd lost the upper hand with her husband and, ironically, might get it back by renewing some contact with him. Nothing. Next, he had written to say he was leaving her time to think and giving her the leisure to reply when she was ready. He hadn't heard a word from her.

The sea turned a pastel shade of blue as the wind dropped a few more knots. Lefebvre found his way behind the bar while Simone Lord perched herself on the stool Corine had vacated earlier.

Simone filled them in. 'The coast guard is trying to cover as broad an area as possible between the shore – the wharf at Grande-Grave, to be precise – and the place where the Roberts guys found the boat. They've put three quarters of their resources into the search, but let's not get our hopes up too much. If she went overboard, Angel Roberts has probably been dead for a while. When a fisherman – or woman – decides to take their own life at sea, they usually go someplace where they know the tide won't wash a body ashore.'

Lefebvre eyed the bottle of wine Corine had left on the bar, the two empty glasses by the sink, then his watch.

'We're still on duty,' Moralès said.

Where did they go, the women we loved? Why did they surround themselves in silence?

Lefebvre leaned on the bar. 'Do you think it's suicide, then?'

Simone Lord took a sip of water before she replied. 'That's probably the conclusion you'll have to draw if they don't find the body.'

Moralès had nothing to add. If his wife came out to join him now, today, would that make him happy?

'The local wildlife conservation officers have joined in the search efforts too. There's an emergency plan in case someone gets lost in the forest. They've set that in motion. Apparently they've called in all their employees and each of them has scrambled a team of citizen volunteers who know the park inside out. There aren't that many of them, but they're efficient. They'll be out looking until sundown. Then they'll start again in the morning. They're starting out at Grande-Grave and combing the woods nearby. The officer I spoke to told me they'd have more people helping tomorrow.'

How come he couldn't remember things like that about Sarah's body?

'It's a waste of time. Forensics said Angel Roberts went overboard,' Moralès replied.

'Right, well, everyone knows we're looking for clues, not just a victim,' Lefebvre said. 'I checked all the things you asked me to. No one at the train station, bus terminal or taxi rank had seen her. I'm still waiting for the court order so I can check her bank account.'

He missed his wife's company. Or was it just female company he missed? Joaquin had to admit, he could have asked for holiday time and gone to see her. That was another way to look at it. But he had stayed here.

'Detective Sergeant Moralès,' Simone piped up, 'would Your Highness deign to join this conversation, or is that too much to ask? Do tell us if we're bothering you, and we'll go inspect the cellar.'

Without batting an eye, Moralès turned his attention to Lefebvre. 'As soon as you have the warrant, cast the net far and wide on Angel Roberts. We need to know the state of her finances, and what she's insured for. I want to know who stands to inherit. It's probably her husband, but you should still ask the notary to do a will search. We also need an asset statement for the husband and any other beneficiaries. A victim always has a value, and that might be monetary or symbolic. If we can figure out what Angel Roberts was worth, so to speak, that could put us on the trail of a potential killer.'

Now he turned to Simone Lord and plunged, without expecting to, into the depths of her green eyes. 'Is there much competition in the fishing sector?'

'Fishers tend to make a decent living, but maybe someone wanted to take over her licence and her fishing zone.'

'Check that. Could someone have harboured a grudge against her for being a woman in the fishing industry?'

'Everyone hates women who do men's jobs. Wives worry, and their husbands become misogynists.'

She cast him a scathing smile, but Moralès refused to acknowledge it. His gaze lingered for a moment on the delicate arcs at the corners of her lips before he turned away.

'Did forensics take any prints in Angel's car, Constable Lefebvre?'

'No, but I'll ask them to.'

'Are there any known sexual predators in the area?'

'I'll check the movements of those we keep on our radar.'

Lefebvre nodded enthusiastically. At last, here was some action that would keep him at his desk. Right on cue, Moralès's phone rang.

'Are you running an escort service, detective?' Simone asked.

He pretended not to hear and dug the handset out of his pocket, checked the screen and put the phone on the bar. Lefebvre peered at it inquisitively.

'It's my son. I'll call him back later.'

Simone Lord pouted, but Érik Lefebvre's curiosity was piqued. 'You have a son? How old is he?'

'Two sons, actually. Sébastien's thirty. He lives in Montreal, but he's passing through.'

'Passing through? You can't pass through the Gaspé. It's a peninsula. You have to go out of your way to come here. Is he on holiday?'

'I don't know. He only arrived yesterday and I came here at the crack of dawn. I haven't had a chance to talk to him yet.'

'Is he on his own? Tell him to come here and keep you company. There's plenty of room.'

'What, so it'll be Moralès the father, the son and the holy spirit?' the detective scoffed. 'Don't you think that's a bit much, Lefebvre?'

'Listen, Leeroy Roberts has just lost his daughter. He must be wishing he could still talk to her. Tell that son of yours to come and join you. Corine will be happy to have him stay.' With that, Érik Lefebvre left the bar and went over towards the dining room.

Simone Lord turned to Moralès purposefully, as if she'd been waiting to get him alone so she could speak her mind. 'This isn't the first fishing accident we've seen, you know. In Nova Scotia, they report at least one a year. But we don't see deaths like this very often. It doesn't look like an accident to me. And believe me, men despise women with balls.'

What was she insinuating? He knew very well that women often had to have a thicker skin than their male counterparts to claim their place and defend it.

'I've been working around these wharves for nearly twenty-five years. I know all these men. It's hard for a woman to earn their respect.'

Not wanting to add fuel to the fire, Moralès kept his mouth shut and his eyes on the sea as it settled beneath the colourful blanket of the sunset.

'Sergeant Moralès, don't you ever send me down into a ship's hold again. Is that clear?'

The detective turned around slowly. 'Officer Lord, I saw you in action on the wharf. Granted, you're good at your job. But you seem to have forgotten that this is a police investigation. Let me suggest you refrain from flexing your muscles in my presence. In fact, that's an order, because I'm the one leading this investigation. Your role is to coordinate the search efforts at sea. And it's your duty to follow my instructions.'

It felt wrong to be putting her in her place. Moralès tried to tell himself she'd asked for it, and that it was best for the investigation that everyone knew the roles they were expected to play, but still, he felt terrible. He turned away. Shades of mauve and lilac danced across the water.

Simone took it on the chin. 'What are you actually leading right now, Moralès? Truth is, your investigation depends on my team. If we don't find Angel, you'll have been here for nothing. And if we do find her…'

The sea was slowly vanishing. Simone stood, unintentionally moving closer to Joaquin in the process. In spite of himself, he savoured the scent of an autumn garden that floated on the air around her.

'Lefebvre has a point. Phone that son of yours while you can, and go play tourist for a while.' She took her jacket from the back of her stool. 'Because I'm going to do my damnedest to make sure we find her.'

She leaned in and whispered the last words into his ear. Moralès took them to heart. He knew precision weapons were often fitted with silencers.

'And when we do,' she continued, 'the real detectives from Montreal will show up to take your place, and you'll go back to your cosy early retirement in Bonaventure.'

She turned and went towards the door. Moralès swivelled his stool around and just caught a glimpse of the vertebra teasing the skin at the nape of her neck as she pulled her jacket on. With that, Simone Lord opened the door and stepped out into the fading evening light.

Lefebvre emerged from the kitchen. 'Right, well, Simone's gone and it's the end of our day, so why don't we polish off that bottle of white that's sitting on the bar, Moralès? I thought you might fancy a lobster club sandwich.'

Moralès smiled and went to fetch the bottle of wine and two fresh glasses. Lefebvre brought out all the fixings, ready to serve dinner on a table at the far end of the dining room.

'She's sexy all right, but stubborn as a mule.' Lefebvre whistled.

'I thought you only had eyes for the receptionist at the station.'

Lefebvre put the cutlery on the table. 'No, that was for you, not me. I've seen the way you look at her. And since your marriage is in trouble, Joaquin … You don't mind if I call you Joaquin when it's just the two of us, do you?'

Moralès put the glasses down and poured the wine. 'Who said my marriage was in trouble?'

'You were playing with your wedding ring earlier. You've been at the Bonaventure detachment for three months now and you said your son's on his own in Caplan, so that means your wife stayed behind. It's not hard to figure out why your wedding ring's burning.'

'You should be a detective, Érik Lefebvre…'

'Anyway, about Simone: I feel your pain. I've always fallen for women who are a real handful too.'

They sat down to eat.

'My father loved an unattainable woman. My mother had the sea breeze in her soul. My father was a pharmacist in town, and we lived down by Haldimand Beach. Often, my mother would wander off along the shore and lose herself out there.'

They slathered a few slices of bread with butter, mayonnaise and sliced tomatoes, added bacon, lobster and more bread on top to close their sandwiches, then sliced them in half.

'My father would always go and look for her. He'd find her in a world of her own, and bring her back home. He took care of her. He adored her. She wasn't crazy; she was just a free spirit. Eventually I realised I'd been trying to do the same thing as my father. Trying to tie down a woman who wouldn't be tethered.' Lefebvre downed a mouthful of wine.

'And now you've fallen for Thérèse Roch.'

'The thought of her fuels my passion for the unattainable, but I'm not getting my hopes up. What would I do if she actually said yes? I'm not sure I'd want to make life complicated by bickering over who got to sleep on which side of the bed or choose the colour of the curtains, and put myself on the hook for alimony down the line. But don't worry, I'm a red-blooded Gaspesian, so I'm not wasting any time. I take advantage of tourist season.'

'Which means?'

Lefebvre smoothed his pencil moustache with a suave touch. 'I have summer flings with tourists who get stars in their eyes at the sight of my police badge.'

'What?'

'Well, I spend my whole year hunting down burglars, fraudsters and murderers, so when the tide of women in bikinis flows into town, I keep my eyes open. Plenty of women want to take home saucy souvenirs from their summer holiday, you know. You'd be surprised. In a way, I suppose you can say I'm doing a service … And catering to some needs more than others.'

Joaquin burst out laughing.

'It keeps me on my toes, and it's a great way to test my police gear. All the women ask me a bunch of gruesome questions and want me to slap the cuffs on them.'

Proud of his little speech, Lefebvre finished his sandwich while Moralès poured what was left of the bottle into their glasses.

'So is that son of yours unlucky in love as well?'

'I think so. He's in a long-term relationship, but he's dancing with other women.'

'Sounds like he's going the right way about making it all go wrong.' Lefebvre drifted off into thought for a moment. 'I don't know if you've noticed, but when you're in love, you only have eyes for one woman. You're blind to all the others. You don't notice their little movements, the way they laugh, even their dresses blowing in the wind. The only woman who treads that red carpet is your own. It's like she's bottled all the beauty in the world. When you go twirling a bunch of girls across the dance floor, that pops the cork and lets the beauty flow away.' Lefebvre stood up. 'And when that happens, your marriage is over.'

Moralès didn't move. He was taking his time to finish the wine and let what Lefebvre had said sink in. Maybe that's what had happened when Catherine breezed through his life. She had shaken the bottle and popped the cork. And now all the beauty he had once seen in Sarah was floating away.

'Right, well, I'm going back to my desk,' Lefebvre announced. 'Mind if I leave you to do the washing-up?'

Tuesday 25th September

'Good morning, Joaquin! Sleep well?' His name was a song on Corine's lips. 'I've drawn up the list of people at the party you asked me for yesterday.'

She placed a sheet of paper on his breakfast table. Moralès picked it up and leaned in for a closer look, trying to hide the fact that he had stolen a glance at her heels, covered in thin socks inside her slippers. He had woken early and gone for a run in Forillon Park. Back at the auberge, he had showered, eaten a hearty breakfast and taken his papers downstairs to set up a makeshift office in the dining room. He scanned the list of names.

'They're organised by boat,' Corine explained.

'Do you have a minute?'

Corine smiled and sat down beside him.

'You told me Clément Cyr slept here, the night Angel Roberts went missing at sea.'

'Yes. In room two.'

'Did he sleep alone?'

She blushed, reluctant to answer. 'That's a delicate question.'

'Delicate for whom? For you?'

'It's just that I run an auberge in a small village. If I start gossiping about what goes on in these rooms, I'll lose half my business.'

Moralès promised to keep her answers to himself and repeated the question. 'Did he sleep alone?'

'I think so, yes.'

Something seemed off. What – or who – was she trying to protect? Her auberge, or Clément Cyr? Or someone else?

'Corine, are you aware of any amorous or sexual relationship between Clément Cyr and a person other than his wife? Any encounter that might have happened here, or somewhere else?'

'To my knowledge, he's a faithful man.'

Moralès knew that was all he was going to get for now. He scanned the paper she'd given him, quickly found the names he was looking for and pointed to them. 'I see Bruce Roberts and his father were here the night Angel went missing.'

Corine nodded.

'Did they stay late?'

'Leeroy only stopped in to say hello. Bruce stayed until about half past one, two o'clock.'

'And Jimmy?'

'He wasn't here. He doesn't have a boat anymore. He doesn't mingle much with the others. Not since he lost his fishing licence.'

'Lost? How do you mean? In a card game?'

Corine stared at the list, as if she regretted giving him a document that would prompt her to reveal her customers' misdeeds. She looked away, and was saved from her awkwardness by a car pulling into the driveway. She sprang to her feet and made for the door.

'You'll have to excuse me, my friend is here. We're going out to help with the search and…'

The rest of her sentence was lost in the wind. Moralès watched Corine walk up to the driver, who was now standing beside the car. She kissed the woman on both cheeks and drew her into a long monologue. The woman nodded to show she'd understood. Moralès turned his attention back to the list of names, and a moment later the two women breezed into the dining room.

'Detective Moralès, this is Kimo. She lives next door.'

The young woman shook his hand firmly. Moralès's phone rang. He remembered there had been a message waiting when he got back from his run, but had forgotten to listen to it. He didn't answer. Kimo was wearing leggings and a fitted workout jacket that did nothing to hide the lean strength of her body. Tiny pearls studded her earlobes. Her eyes looked a little red. Her short, boyish hair was damp.

'Looks like you've been for a swim.'

'Yes, in the bay.'

'I went for a dip myself on Sunday, in Caplan. The water was freezing.'

'The water stays warmer for longer in the bay than anywhere else on the coast, and I've got a good wetsuit.'

'Kimo won the silver medal in the Gaspé triathlon last year,' Corine said.

'That was two years ago.'

'Same difference. She teaches yoga classes in town.'

'Are you ready?' Kimo was clearly keen to get going.

The two women said goodbye to Moralès and drove off. He checked the list Corine had given him. Kimo's name wasn't on there.

Sébastien Moralès poured himself a coffee and called his father's number. He had got out of the wrong side of the bed again. The previous day, he had done as he was asked and received the mattress delivery, then gone to buy pillows and sheets to make up the guest bed. After a nap, he had made dinner for two, in vain. Sébastien had tried several times to reach his father, also in vain.

As a boy, he had always thought his father's sudden absences were mysterious and somehow heroic. He used to tell anyone who would listen that he wanted to be a police officer too. A detective. Because it was in his blood. That dream had evaporated in his teens – perhaps around the age of fourteen, when Detective Moralès discovered his son's first joint and gave him a guided tour of the local prison to scare the living daylights out of him.

Today, Sébastien wondered what the real reason for those hasty departures might have been. He was puzzled by Renaud Boissonneau's allegations. Was his father really an unfaithful husband? If he was, Sébastien wouldn't be able to blame paternal mimicry for letting Maude walk all over him. He refused to believe it.

'*Holà, chiquito.* How are you doing?'

Sometimes it could be awkward to give an honest answer. 'Not bad. You? Where are you?' Not to mention that he'd feel like a complete idiot hunkering down in that new guest bed in Caplan, waiting for his father to come home so he could deliver his little speech about pride, if Joaquin was hard at work between a frisky Gaspesian *chiquita*'s thighs.

'I'm at the police station in Gaspé,' Joaquin replied.

'On your own?'

Joaquin responded with a puzzled silence before he answered the question. 'Pretty much. I've just pulled up out front in my car. Did you sleep all right? I tried to call you back last night, but you didn't pick up. I didn't leave a message. Your voicemail was full.'

That was true. After she'd heard from Renaud Boissonneau that Sébastien was on the Gaspé Peninsula, Maude had bombarded him with phone calls and text messages. At first he'd tried to ignore her, but she'd been so insistent he had turned his phone off.

'I went to bed early. Are you going to be there long?'

'I don't know, but why don't you come and join me?'

Sébastien let that sink in for a moment. He was still thinking he might turn around and go back to Montreal, even if his life there was crumbling to pieces. The previous morning, he had called his boss to arrange two weeks of holiday. His boss had always prided himself on treating his employees like gold, or so he said. But Sébastien's request had been met with a frosty silence.

'My father's sick. He's all alone in the Gaspé, so I'm at his bedside.' A nervous Sébastien had blurted out this curious choice of untruth with all the ease of a teenager called to the headmaster's office.

'Right. And my grandma's on her death bed. If you're not here by noon, Moralès, you're fired.'

His boss had promptly hung up and Sébastien's cheeks had flushed with shame. He didn't really care that he'd been shown the door. The decent restaurants in the city were always looking for chefs, and this one wasn't the greatest place to work. But why had he lied?

'I'll give it some thought,' he told his father. 'If I leave Caplan now, Renaud Boissonneau might send out a search party. He's desperate for another dance class.'

'Forget about that and come here, OK? I'm staying at Corine's … er … Auberge Le Noroît in Rivière-au-Renard.'

'It won't be easy to leave this comfy new mattress behind, you know.'

Joaquin Moralès cleared his throat. '*Chiquito* … I have a favour to ask you.'

Sébastien couldn't remember his father ever asking him anything so bashfully. 'All right, what is it?'

'I'd like you to go to my telescope, look out at the sea, and write down what you see.'

'The boats?'

'Everything.'

'OK.'

'Then, I want you to go and … er … see someone.'

'OK…'

'Go down to the café by the wharf. Leave your car there and walk up the dirt track that goes under the railway bridge.'

Moralès junior realised he was holding his breath. Was his father sending him to see his mistress?

'At the end, you'll see the cemetery on the right and a house on the left. Under a window, beside a woodpile, there's a short stepladder. Climb that and duck inside the window.'

'Listen, Dad, I'm not sure I…'

Joaquin pretended not to hear. He carried on as smoothly as a gynaecologist slips on a pair of gloves.

'You'll find yourself in Cyrille Bernard's bedroom.'

'Cyrille? That's a man's name?' Now Sébastien didn't know what to think.

Joaquin thought it was a strange thing for his son to say. 'Yes. A fisherman. A friend who's sick. Why do you ask?'

'No reason. Wait a sec, let me jot that down.'

Sébastien went to find something to write with.

'Tell him the name of the woman whose disappearance I'm investigating is Angel Roberts, and she went missing from a lobster trawler around Rivière-au-Renard. Got that?'

'Yep.' Sébastien found it a bit ridiculous for his father to be sending him to see a fisherman as part of his investigation.

'He might know her, so be diplomatic. Then, tell him what you saw on the sea this morning. Or the other way around. Yes, tell him about the sea first. Understand? Do that first.'

Sébastien agreed.

'Tell him everything. Even the stuff you don't think is important.'

'Got it.'

'He's a sick man.'

'I understand. You get back to your investigation. I'll go see this friend of yours.'

'Thanks, *chiquito*.'

'Talk to you soon.'

When he'd driven around the waterfront, Moralès had been surprised to see that the *Close Call II* had disappeared. He had stopped at the wharf to ask people there if they'd noticed anything, but no one had even seen the lobster trawler leaving the port, let alone who had made off with it. At the coast-guard office, three men sitting comfortably in front of a big flat-screen TV lackadaisically replied they weren't paid to keep watch over the waterfront.

When Moralès walked into the station in Gaspé and approached the bulletproof glass at the front desk, the receptionist's fingers were flying across her computer keyboard at a dizzying pace.

'Good morning, Ms Roch. I'm here to see Constable Lefebvre again.'

The recalcitrant receptionist gave no indication that she'd heard or seen him. Moralès knocked gently on the glass and spoke a bit louder, this time saying 'please'.

Thérèse Roch quickly tapped a code into the phone.

'Officer Moral-less to see you.'

She hung up without waiting for an answer. With a manner like that, she should be working airport security, Moralès thought. A second later, Érik Lefebvre opened the door and blew the receptionist a kiss, which she dismissed with a shrug.

How she saw him do it was a mystery, because she didn't look up.

'Simone and I are reassessing the search area. Want to join us?'

Moralès followed Lefebvre into the depths of the building. 'No. I trust you to do your job. And I don't know the area. You're better off with Officer Lord. The boat has disappeared, though.'

Lefebvre stopped and frowned. 'Angel's boat?'

'Yes. It's not at the wharf in Rivière-au-Renard anymore.'

Lefebvre led the way to his office.

Moralès paused when they passed the meeting room, where Simone Lord and two other people were scrutinising a map of the Gulf of St Lawrence. 'Officer Lord, I need you for a second.'

She looked up disapprovingly, but fell into step.

The three of them went into Lefebvre's office, which was somehow filled with even more stuff than the day before. Even the little school desk he had cleared was now buried under piles of who-knows-what that seemed to be growing by themselves.

Moralès turned to Simone Lord. 'The *Close Call II* isn't at the wharf anymore. Besides the deckhands, who else would have a key to the boat?'

'Angel's brother who brought it back yesterday. Jimmy Roberts. He probably kept the key. And the husband.'

Lefebvre rubbed his chin, grabbed one of several half-empty mugs of coffee, took a sip, winced, pushed it away and picked another one instead. 'Why would they take off with the boat? Should we assume they've stolen it?'

Simone Lord shook her head. 'No. The guys must have taken it back to its home port to get it ready for winter. Didn't you seal it off?'

'No. I thought the tape the forensics team put up would be enough to stop anyone going aboard, let alone take it to sea.'

Simone Lord smirked condescendingly. 'Do you really think a scrap of yellow tape is going to intimidate a fisherman?'

Moralès had worked in the big city on cases far more dangerous than this, so he wasn't going to let a fisheries officer lecture him about intimidation. 'How are the search parties on land doing?' he asked, turning to Lefebvre.

'They've managed to cover the whole of the south sector since yesterday.' He pointed to a heavily annotated map of Forillon Park on his desk. 'They've been down the coast from Grande-Grave to L'Anse-Aux-Amérindiens cove and up to the campground at Petit-Gaspé. In between, it's steep and hilly, so they can't get everywhere, but they're making good progress. The park rangers put out a call for help to people with season passes, because they know the trails. They're doing a good job. This morning they've split up into teams. There's one covering the area south towards Land's End, another that's set off across the headland to Cap-Bon-Ami, and a third that's gone up towards Petit-Gaspé and Angel's house. People in Cap-aux-Os are searching their village too.'

Simone Lord touched a finger to the map. 'Our Zodiacs are trawling the coast, and the park rangers and SQ officers have boats out there too. The search and rescue aircraft—'

Suddenly, a shrill voice rang out above all the others from the main office area. Simone turned in surprise, tiptoed towards the door and glanced out into the corridor.

Lefebvre took Moralès by the arm. 'Quick, come with me.'

Leaving Simone to her own devices – she had turned her back on them, anyway – the constable crouched and ran with his head low to the far end of the corridor. Moralès followed suit. His reflexes kicking in, the detective flattened himself against the wall and dropped a hand to his holster.

Lefebvre waved at him to stop. 'Whoa, don't get carried away!'

'What's happening?'

'Oh, it's only Dotrice paying us a visit.'

'Who the heck is Dotrice?'

Lefebvre motioned for Moralès to stay quiet and pulled him to the shelter of an emergency exit around the corner. 'She's a woman who lives in Cap-des-Rosiers.'

'What's she doing here?'

'She sees things.'

'What kind of things?'

Lefebvre kept peeking into the corridor. 'Every time we're working a big case, she shows up and tells us she's seen something.'

'And has she usually seen something?'

'Of course, she's a clairvoyant.'

Moralès burst out laughing. Major investigations did tend to draw a medium or two out of the woodwork. 'How does she get into the station?'

'Ah, Thérèse is such a free spirit. Don't ask me how she runs the front desk.'

Moralès followed Lefebvre out through the emergency exit. 'Where does Angel moor the *Close Call II*, then?' he asked.

'Simone said she had a mooring at the wharf in Grande-Grave. That's down the south end of Forillon. Look…' Lefebvre wedged a rock in the door frame, tiptoed around to the east side of the building and pointed across to the north shore of Gaspé Bay. 'Over there. Want to see it for yourself?'

'Yes.'

'Take the bridge, keep going on Highway 132, and keep right at the T-junction. The wharf is about six or seven kilometres further on. It's inside the national park. There's a barrier on the road, but it'll be open today. Anyway, the park rangers will let you through if you tell them you're investigating Angel's disappearance. Grande-Grave is a historic site. You'll drive down from the road into the parking area. There's a wharf there, but the boats moor up at the wooden dock just behind.

'OK.'

'I'll go back inside to create a diversion. See you later!'

The box of pots and pans was still sitting shamefully on a corner of the kitchen counter. It occurred to Sébastien that cooking vessels weren't the only things he'd been piling one on top of the other. He'd been doing the same with his tall tales. On his third sip of coffee, he walked over to the telescope in the bay window. What was he supposed to be looking for, exactly? And how was he going to explain it to the old fisherman?

He thought the Baie-des-Chaleurs was pretty, but not as spectacular as the St Lawrence. Here, he could see the coast of New Brunswick across the water, where the Acadian Peninsula began to narrow the entrance to the bay. But the St Lawrence around Rimouski seemed to open up and stretch on forever, like an ocean. He had never been all the way to the end of the Gaspé Peninsula. He had no idea what beauty awaited him there.

Sébastien looked out across the bay and saw a flock of Arctic terns circling a patch of turbulent water. There must be a shoal of fish down there, he thought. The birds were dancing in the sky, sending flashes of light with every flap of their grey-tinged wings before tucking them tight and diving like darts into the sea, smashing the surface and sending up spectacular splashes as they plunged for a split second then resurfaced with a shake of their feathers. Their catches weighing them down, they struggled to take flight again before soaring away to the south.

Sébastien's phone vibrated. Her again. Maude. He kept the device in his hand until it stopped buzzing.

He was looking at the sea, but what was he supposed to observe? He tried to take it all in. A westerly breeze rippled the surface into a rumpled silk sheet that soon ironed itself out. He peered into the telescope again. Suddenly the sun came out and the sea was dazzling, a carpet of shimmering gold coins stretching all the way to the horizon. Sébastien squinted and took two steps back. The view was making him dizzy. He closed his eyes for a moment. The sun disappeared behind a dark cloud. The wind began to pick up, and the swell started to roll. Soon the fog drifted in to settle over the water, and the window was a mirror reflecting his ghostly image: left hand holding the coffee mug, right hand gripping the phone like a buoy that was slowly taking on water and sinking, dragging him down with it.

Sébastien turned away and put some music on. He cranked up the volume to flush himself out of this mess, hoping the rhythm of Orishas would drown the sound of his own voice in his mind. But the Cuban hip-hop did more than that and he soon felt his knees softening up and his hips swaying side to side. He tried to tell himself he wasn't running away.

Sébastien finished his coffee. He was hungry now. Of course, he could mess around with his pots and pans, but since his father wasn't here, he figured the culinary experiments could wait. Forcing yourself to play the game when there was no one to watch was a bit like putting on a cheery clown costume right before bedtime. He decided to go to the bistro in the village for an early lunch. After that, he'd walk down to the fisherman's house. Doing his father a favour made him feel like less of an idiot. Less ashamed. He pulled his jacket on and was just about to head out, but stopped short of opening the door. What was he going to tell Cyrille Bernard? The phone buzzed in his hand

again. He glanced at the screen. It was Maude, again. He buried
the phone in his pocket, went back into the living room, peered
into the telescope again and swept the dense layer of fog on the
horizon. Two container ships. That was it.

Moralès drove into the parking area behind the wharf. Down
the far end, a couple of kayak-rental and diving-school shacks
stood nestled at the foot of a tree-lined cliff. To the southeast, a
wooden wharf and dock reached out into the little cove of
Grande-Grave, which opened up into Gaspé Bay. As he got out
of the car, Moralès noticed a pickup truck parked facing the sea
by the dock, at which he saw the *Close Call II* was moored. He
was striding towards it when his phone rang. A quick glance at
the screen told him someone at the police station in Gaspé was
calling. Now wasn't the time to take a phone call. A man was
carrying things off the lobster trawler and onto the wharf.
Moralès could see an oilskin jacket, a blanket, a backpack and
a cool box.

There was no need for him to hurry, because the man had
seen him and was waiting with an outstretched hand.

'Jacques Forest, I'm one of Angel's deckhands. You must be
Detective Moralès.'

'Yes. Was it you who moved the boat here from Rivière-au-
Renard?'

'No. Jean-Paul Babin called me about half past nine and told
me to collect my things. Season's over, anyway.' His voice
cracked as the last few words came out. He looked away. 'Jean-
Paul Babin's the other deckhand on the boat.'

'Yes. But he's not your boss.'

'No, Angel is.'

'Did he tell you who brought the boat here?'

'No, but it was probably Jimmy. He's Angel's kid brother. He used to fish for scallops in the Baie-des-Chaleurs, you know. But he sold his boat three, four years ago. The Babin brothers were his deckhands. I reckon if Jimmy needs help now, they're the ones he'll take on. But like I said, the season's over anyway. No point leaving my things on board, is there?'

'How long have you been working for Angel?'

The deckhand turned to look out at the bay. The sky was ugly and a sadness hung in the air.

'Since the beginning.'

His eyes were filled with the kind of pain you could see, and it spilled out across his face as if he were feeling the loss of his skipper physically. Moralès recalled this was Angel's maternal uncle. The man's gaze was lost in the foul weather.

'I used to work marine search and rescue when I was young, you know,' he said. 'Down in the States, with a crazy-ass crew. We used to go out to sea in raging thunderstorms to save pleasure boaters who'd got themselves out of their depth.' A string of gulls battling against the wind caught his eye. 'I thrived on the adrenaline when I was that age, I suppose. Then one day, I came home. I heard young Angel was buying herself a boat, so I offered my services. She said yes. That was, what, ten years ago?'

Moralès's phone rang again. He apologised and checked the screen. It was the station in Gaspé again. The phone went back in his pocket.

'You were at the party on Saturday night.' It was a statement, not a question. The detective fished Corine's list out of his pocket and showed it to the deckhand.

'Yes. I was there until about midnight.'

'Does this look like a complete list of who was there that night?'

Jacques Forest pulled his reading glasses from his shirt pocket, scanned the list and frowned as he ran through the names, trying to remember.

'It's hard to say, just like that, but yes, that was pretty much it.'

'Are there any people who should have been at the party but didn't go?'

'Obviously. Only about half the fishermen in the area ended up coming. Not everyone likes to stay out late, you know. Then there are some who would have been away hunting, and others who'd had a falling-out with their skipper at the end of the season.'

'Do you know anyone who might have had a run-in with Angel Roberts?'

'No, not with Angel. Plenty resent her, mind you. She's a woman in a man's world, so no one's going to do her any favours. You know the way we are, us blokes. We love women, all right, but we'd rather they didn't stick their noses in our business. At the same time, I think everyone respects her. And we're all reeling from the shock of her … disappearance.'

The phone rang again. Moralès checked and saw the same number as before. He excused himself and stepped away to take the call.

'Hi, it's Lefebvre. Turns out there is a sex offender who was released last month. We're trying to track him down. Do you think I should let the park rangers know so they can inform the search-party volunteers?'

'No, find the guy first. There's no point spreading panic.'

'OK. Did you find the boat at Grande-Grave?'

'Yes. But I'm busy right now…'

'Oh, and it's none of my business, but I wanted you to know: Simone's beside herself.'

'Officer Lord? Why?'

'It wasn't my place to ask. You're the boss, you deal with it.'

'OK. But I'm busy at the wharf. Tell her to stay calm, I'm going to—'

'She did try to call you, but you didn't answer, so she asked me where you were. I said you were at Grande-Grave. She should be there any minute.'

'Lefebvre! You could have—'

'No, Moralès. I couldn't.' He hung up.

Jacques Forest walked up to the detective. 'If you have a minute, I'd like you to come aboard with me.'

On the road through the park a vehicle was fast approaching in a cloud of dust.

'Some things have gone missing…'

The Fisheries and Oceans Canada truck thundered down the hill to the Grande-Grave parking area and came to a screeching halt.

Jacques Forest stopped mid-sentence. 'That's the fisheries watcher. She's always sniffing around our boats. I'll give you my details and we'll meet up later, all right?'

'Don't worry, I'm the one she's here to keep an eye on.'

Forest gaped in surprise, feeling sorry for the detective, as the door of the truck flew open and Simone Lord stormed towards Moralès, sporting her official Fisheries and Oceans windbreaker.

'If you wouldn't mind waiting, this won't take long,' Moralès said.

Jacques Forest waved to Simone from a distance. Then he hurried off to fetch his bag, cool box, blanket and jacket from the wharf and loaded them into his truck.

🦞

If there had been more dining establishments to choose from in Caplan, Sébastien Moralès would probably have gone somewhere else for lunch. Maybe not, though. Behind the bar, Renaud Boissonneau was polishing wine glasses with a dish towel as if his life depended on it. He raised an eye towards his only customer, who had his head buried in the menu.

'Let me tell you, I'm going to recommend the sole. Because there's plenty left and the chef wants me to shift it.' He dropped his cloth and hung the glass on the rack.

'OK. I'll have the sole, then.'

Renaud Boissonneau scurried into the kitchen to place the order and returned waving a bottle enticingly. 'Unless you're allergic, I've got a lovely local wine here…'

'A local wine?'

'Well, it was local when they made it in France. There's half a bottle left. It goes off quick, you know.'

'I'll have a glass.'

Renaud Boissonneau plucked a gleaming polished glass from the rack, placed it on the bar in front of Sébastien Moralès and poured him a white wine. 'I'll leave the bottle here, in case you feel like another.'

'That's very kind of you.'

Renaud nodded and dutifully returned to polishing his wine glasses. 'So, are you here to give us a dance class?'

'Not today.'

'Show us a recipe, perhaps?'

'Nope.'

'So you're just here as a customer?'

'Unfortunately.'

'Ah, never mind.'

Sébastien took a sip of wine. He wanted to ask Renaud Boissonneau to elaborate on what he had insinuated about his father and that woman, Catherine, but he didn't know how to go about it.

Renaud, who was clearly preoccupied, leaned across the bar and passed Sébastien a pen and paper. 'Can I have your phone number, in case I ever have any culinary questions?'

Sébastien Moralès gave it to him without thinking of the potential consequences.

A bell dinged in the kitchen. Renaud collected the plate from the serving hatch and placed it in front of his customer, who picked up a fork and dug in to the sole. Renaud was watching him like a hawk.

'Very tasty,' Sébastien said after the first mouthful. Seeing he was satisfied, Renaud slipped Sébastien's number into his shirt pocket and returned to his wine-glass polishing.

'So you came to see your father, but he's not feeding you, then? Because, let me tell you, you wouldn't be here if he was making your lunch.'

'He's working in Gaspé.'

Renaud Boissonneau opened his eyes wide. 'There's been a murder in Gaspé?'

'I don't know,' Sébastien replied between two bites.

'I imagine you'll be going up the coast to join him, then. You must be a bit of a detective too, I bet. That sort of thing runs in the family, doesn't it?'

'No, it doesn't run in the family.'

Renaud seemed puzzled. He was now blowing on the glass to fog it up between two rubs of his dishcloth. It looked like his head was spinning a little, but still he kept polishing. 'Well, it's not a job for making friends, is it? Here, have another glass of wine. Your father always has two. I'll bring you the dessert of the day as well.'

Renaud refilled his glass, scurried off to the kitchen and returned with a slice of upside-down fudge cake.

Sébastien looked at the cake and the wine hesitantly. The picture Renaud was painting of his father didn't match the man Sébastien had always envisioned.

'Let me tell you, the road to Gaspé will take you through Percé. Aren't you the lucky one? Tourists come from all over the world to see the rock! Perhaps you've already been?'

Percé Rock was precisely the kind of place Sébastien Moralès couldn't give a damn about. He'd seen too much of it already on other people's photos, postcards and Quebec tourist brochures.

'No.' Sébastien picked up a spoon and tasted the dessert.

'Never? Well, it's one place you have to see before you die! Go on, what are you waiting for?' Renaud finished polishing his last glass and hung it from its stem on the rack.

'Have you seen it?'

Renaud froze. He seemed surprised by the question. 'No, never! But it's not the same for me. It can wait. I'm not ready to pop my clogs.'

Sébastien's phone started to vibrate in his pocket. He took it out, glanced at it and stuffed it back into his jacket.

Renaud Boissonneau followed the movement with his eyes. 'Seems to me the Gaspé's the best place for folks not to answer their phones…' He pointed to Sébastien's jacket pocket, looking worried. 'You will answer if I call, won't you?'

'Depends…'

'On what?' Renaud opened the dishwasher and wafted away the cloud of escaping steam with his towel.

'Renaud, you led me to believe yesterday that my father had, er, encountered certain women…'

The server held up his hand to stop him. 'Ah, I can't answer questions about private matters. I'm a restaurant server, so let me tell you, I'm bound by professional secrecy.' And then he leaned across the bar with the air of a secret agent. 'All I can say is your father's good at getting himself into trouble with women…'

'Detective Moralès. I imagine you're proud of yourself. Looks like you've found the lobster boat you were looking for.'

'Thank you for your assistance, Officer Lord. I'm sure I couldn't have done it without you.'

'I was wrong about you, Moralès. You're not a lazy detective from the city easing his way into early retirement; you're a sexist boar. You're so full of yourself. Just another bastard who steals his female colleagues' thunder and runs away, out the back door, like a naughty schoolboy.'

Moralès couldn't believe his ears. 'Run away? What are you talking about?'

Jacques Forest got into his truck and slammed the door. For a second, Moralès was worried the fisherman was going to drive away.

'You breezed into the station, consulted with me for help finding the boat and then ran away in the middle of the bloody conversation.'

'I didn't consult with you…' As the words started to come out, Moralès realised it would be better to keep his mouth shut. The fisherman turned the stereo on in his truck and looked away so he wouldn't have to witness the scene.

'Am I dreaming? Is the lonesome cowboy telling me I can't see what's right in front of my nose? Was I hallucinating when I saw you waltz in and ask where the boat had got to? Did I imagine telling you it would probably be moored here? And what about you doing a disappearing act while I was filling you in about the search parties? Did I just make that up?'

Moralès could feel his blood starting to boil. This was ridiculous. She was the one who stormed in here throwing her weight around and now he was supposed to apologise?

'It's not going to work between you and me, Officer Lord.'

'I couldn't agree more. This is definitely not working. Because you don't seem to give a damn about team—'

Moralès cut her off and took a sterner tone. 'You've just barged in and interrupted a detective interviewing a potential witness because you don't think I praised you enough? Well congratulations, Officer Lord. I'll be sending a report to your superior to commend your valuable work in pointing out the home port of a lobster trawler. How about that?' He turned his back and started towards the fisherman's truck.

'You're sidelining me because I'm a woman,' she spat as he walked away.

Moralès stopped and turned to look at her, but kept his distance. 'No, Officer Lord. I'm not sidelining you. I'm putting you in your place because you're not doing your job. What are you doing here? You tracked me down and raced here to give me a dressing down. But it's Angel Roberts you're supposed to be looking for at the moment, not me. Why aren't you out there doing everything you possibly can to find her? Is it … because she's a woman?' he mocked.

Shaken by his scathing retaliation, Simone Lord wavered, took a step to the side, turned on her heels and strode purposefully back to her truck. Climbing behind the wheel, she slammed the door and skidded away in a cloud of dust.

Now the fisheries officer had gone, Moralès was lost for words. Why had he taken such a hard line with her? Was it because she'd flashed her badge to the fishermen the day before? Because she had told him off like a child? True, he had left the police station through the back door after asking her advice, but she wasn't the reason for his hasty departure. It would have been easy enough to explain that and even apologise. Why hadn't he done so?

'Don't you worry, she'll come back. She's a fisheries officer. You can never get rid of that lot.' Jacques Forest had emerged from the safety of his truck. 'I can't decide if the sexiest thing about her is her body, her eagle eye or that pig-headed character of hers. What do you reckon?'

Moralès acknowledged the observation with a half-smile.

'Can't hold it against her, mind you. I used to work with women in search and rescue. They'd never think twice about putting their own life on the line to help men in trouble. But those men would rather it hadn't been women who saved their lives. It would've been easier for them to look up to other men, you see. It must have been hard enough for Simone with the coast guard, but then she became a fisheries officer. Angel's always nice to her, but I bet she must get a lot of flak from the men.'

Moralès felt uncomfortable and changed the subject. 'You said some things had gone missing from the boat?'

'Come with me.'

It was the second time in his life that Moralès had boarded a lobster trawler. The first was not long ago at the wharf in Caplan, when Cyrille finished his season and put a picnic table on the deck of his boat to take his friends out for a beer on the water when the seas were calm. The *Close Call II* was built differently. In the bow there was an inside area with a kitchenette, two berths and a small bathroom with a shower. Moralès could certainly see why Angel would want to take her boat out for a jaunt in the summer.

'We never slept on board, but Angel wanted us to leave sleeping bags just in case. I've always thought there wasn't much point, because Angel's always kept nice warm bedding in the cupboard.' Jacques Forest opened a small closet and showed the detective the empty shelves. 'It was all here last week when I helped Angel carry some empty water bottles ashore.'

'Was there a lot of bedding?'

'I don't know. Four or five sheets, maybe. And some old blankets of her mother's, I think. Rag blankets, we used to call them. Throws, or quilts, I suppose you'd say nowadays. Old-fashioned things, in any case. I think she'd use them to stay warm when she went out to sea to look at the stars. Anyway, all that was there, with those water bottles and oilskins.'

Moralès could see half a case of bottled water and three water-proof jackets.

The fisherman pointed to the bottom of the closet. 'Her old trap isn't there either.'

Moralès leaned closer. 'What old trap?'

'We fish with plastic or mesh lobster pots these days. But in the old days they were made of wood, and we called them traps. We had a quota of a hundred and twenty traps. Angel always kept one extra on board. I don't know why. We used to tease her about it, because even when we needed it, she would never use it. She would always buy another one or fix one that was broken. So anyway, her spare trap never got used. Like the family silver. Four years ago, she replaced all the old traps with mesh pots. They're bigger and lighter and catch more lobsters. I asked her what I should do with the old wooden trap, and she said, "Leave it there, it's our lucky charm!" She was joking, but the trap stayed where it was.'

'What did the trap look like?'

'Like a lobster fishing trap. Rectangular, about so big, made of strips of wood. Angel painted it red, I don't know why. It still worked. It had a funnel made of netting and a parlour to stop the lobsters from getting out, and the cement block was still attached.'

'The cement block?'

'Right. To keep the cage on the seabed, you have to weight it down with a hundred-pound cement block. That's why lobster fishing's so hard. It's not just the traps full of lobsters you have to lug around, but the great lumps of cement too. They're damned heavy.'

'What else is missing?'

'That's all, as far as I can see. The old trap and the bed linen.'

As they were disembarking, Jacques Forest veered off course and went up to the bow, as if he had just thought of something. Before Moralès could say or do anything, the fisherman bent down and opened the anchor well.

He gritted his teeth, held his breath and then said, 'The anchor chain and line are gone as well.'

The man's eyes filled with tears and his nostrils flared wide as he drew a deep breath. He was trying to hold himself together as a scene played out in his mind like something in a horror movie: Angel trussed up in those blankets with the anchor chain and line, and the lobster trap dragging her to the bottom of the sea. He closed the anchor well.

Moralès's phone rang again. It was the station in Gaspé. 'I'm sorry,' he said, both for stepping away to talk and for what the fisherman must be feeling. He figured it would be wise to answer to avoid getting Simone's back up even more.

'Any news from Corine? Are you at the auberge?' It was Lefebvre.

'No, I'm at the wharf with Jacques…'

'You're going to think I'm worried for nothing, but that sex offender I told you about was at the prison in New Carlisle and he was released three weeks ago. We're trying to track him down right now, because he's got the profile of a potential repeat offender, but we don't know where he is.'

Moralès moved towards the wheelhouse. 'What's the connection with Corine?'

'Well, I asked the park ranger to check where all the volunteers were, and he couldn't reach Corine or Kimo.'

'And you've tried their mobiles?'

'Yes. And the land line at the auberge. No answer. It might just be poor phone reception, but…'

'I'm done here. I'm heading back to the auberge now.'

'I never consult clairvoyants, Moralès, but this morning, Dotrice said there was a naked monster on the loose, so…'

'I hear you. I'm on my way.'

Moralès ended the call and jumped out onto the wharf. The deckhand followed and locked the boat behind them.

'Who else has a key to this boat?' Moralès asked.

'Angel, and Jean-Paul Babin. She had one cut for each of us in case we have to repair anything when she's not around. Maybe Clément has one as well.'

They started up towards the parking area, walking side by side.

'Is the boat always kept locked?'

'Yes. Angel's had stuff stolen before. The fishers' association put up a sign beside the kayak shack to say there's a camera, but it's only to scare people away. They've never installed one.'

'I'd like you to keep this key with you until the investigation's over. I'll call you if we need to go aboard again.'

'All right. It's not like I'm in a hurry to give it back to anyone,' the deckhand replied.

Moralès said goodbye and drove away. He soon found himself at the main T-junction in the park. Instead of hugging the shore of Gaspé Bay and taking the road the locals called La Radoune to get back to the auberge, he turned right to stay on Highway

132 the whole way. According to the satnav, the driving time was about the same. But as the road wound its way up into the mountains, Moralès had to keep his speed down. He could see what Clément Cyr meant the previous day about this road being dangerous after dark. There were signs everywhere warning drivers about wild animals, and it must be darker than a bear's pupils out here at night, he thought.

Moralès didn't believe in fortune tellers, but he couldn't help but wonder. Could they be dealing with a sex crime? Paradoxically, trying to nab a psychopath who kept targeting one woman after another was the kind of case that both sickened him the most and made him feel the most alive. Maybe it was the sense of urgency, the need to act fast, and the number of victims that could grow by the day, or the hour.

His pulse quickened. He tried to picture the scene. Clément Cyr drove his wife home, not realising they were being followed by a psychopath who had been watching the couple and suspected the husband might well be kissing his wife goodnight and going back to the pub for the rest of the night. The guy waited for Clément to drive away, then rang the doorbell, so Angel would think her husband had forgotten his keys. Or maybe he just walked right in, because plenty of folks in the Gaspé didn't lock their doors. Maybe he grabbed Angel and made her go down to the wharf. But how? Did he blackmail her? Did he say her husband had been in an accident? Was he the one who had driven her car?

Moralès had to slow down as the curves in the road grew tighter, but his mind kept racing faster with the scenario he was inventing.

The psychopath raped and killed the young woman in the park, then carried her body aboard, programmed a route into the GPS and pushed her boat away from the dock.

He should have gone the other way, taken La Radoune instead of the coast road.

Scratch that: the engine wasn't running. So the psychopath must have taken her out on the boat. Then maybe he swam back to shore. No. If that were the case, the body would have gone overboard nearer to shore and washed up somewhere for the search parties to find.

Moralès was beating himself up. He should have insisted Lefebvre leave the station and go to the auberge. But in his mind he could hear his colleague protesting 'I'm not a field officer'. Lefebvre be damned! It seemed to Moralès that all the people he'd worked with since he arrived on the Gaspé Peninsula had their own bizarre quirks. Joannie Robichaud, who never took her baton off her belt; Érik Lefebvre, who refused to leave his office; and Simone Lord who … Who what? Who insisted on sticking her nose in. Who kept overstepping her mark. Who was hot-headed and … wanted only to be respected. Moralès felt ashamed of himself. Just focus on the road, he told himself.

Then he had an idea. He would call Lefebvre and tell him to meet him at the auberge. That should light a fire under him. Moralès slowed down, picked up his phone, dialled the number, glanced at the screen – no signal – looked up, saw the curve in the road, braked, yanked the wheel, stayed on the road by some miracle, swore … and accelerated.

He picked up the longest knife, wiped the blade meticulously and set it aside. Then he reached for the steaming-hot cutlery holder, pulled it out and dropped it on the bar with a bang.

Sébastien observed Renaud in silence. He could feel his phone vibrating in his pocket again. The stream of texts, calls and emails from Maude was both erratic and unrelenting. Questions, accusations, sweet nothings, fits of rage.

He asked for the bill. Renaud went to the till, rang up his customer's meal, printed the bill and handed it over. Whistling, he cleared the empty plate and full glass, and put the clean cutlery away. Sébastien paid and donned his jacket.

'You have a nice time in Gaspé now, let me tell you.'

Sébastien said goodbye to Renaud and went outside, He walked down to the water, then along past the chalets on the shore to the café by the wharf. He saw the dirt track his father had described and started along it at a stiff pace, tormented by Maude's messages and Renaud's insinuations. He felt like listening to some music, but realised he'd left his earbuds on the kitchen counter. He took a deep breath to calm his nerves, only to realise he'd quickened his pace since he turned under the railway bridge and was breaking into a run, driven by the unvoiced anger that was boiling deep inside. He couldn't go on like this. He needed to get away. To lose his bearings. To drink, dance and run, become breathless, sweat it all out, get all these questions off his chest. His feet felt heavy from the wine at lunch, but he didn't care. His father had once told him that running helped you to not lose your footing. His father. The wind was biting through Sébastien's clothes and whistling its way into his too-long hair.

A familiar vibration in his pocket demanded his attention, but he focused on running – the pounding of his feet on the ground, the firmness of his calves, the bend in his knees. His father, unfaithful? Sébastien regretted not being able to listen to his music. He picked up the pace. You grow up certain that the values you've learned are good and strong. But what if that isn't the case? Could you build a life on a foundation of lies? He tried to focus on his running – the tensing of his thighs, the movement of his hips, the tightening of his abdominals. His pulsing torso, pearling sweat and burning lungs. He should have put his earbuds in his jacket pocket.

The cemetery gradually came into view. Sébastien ran faster. He'd had enough of the questions running through his mind. He ran past the cemetery, old house and woodpile. How many hours, how many kilometres did a man have to run to overcome his inner turmoil? He kept going and turned onto a trail in the woods. His legs were hurting. His life was a mess. He was out of breath. This wasn't the solution. He looped around and retraced his steps, slowed his pace and walked through the cemetery to cool down and catch his breath, so he wouldn't be going into the fisherman's bedroom dripping with sweat. Sébastien looked at the window above the woodpile. Two container ships. That was it. He took a deep breath in. Then he put one foot on the stepladder.

Kimo's car was parked in front of the auberge. She and Corine had put some music on and were making something to eat when Joaquin walked in, still unnerved by their potential abduction. They said hello and gave him friendly but distant smiles. Moralès went straight up to his room to call Lefebvre.

'Yes, I managed to reach Corine about fifteen minutes ago,' his colleague explained. 'Turns out they were just in the car. They forgot to report that they'd finished combing their area and were going home. Oh, and I tracked down that sex offender too. He's living with his brother in Rimouski now. He found a job there as a security guard and he was working the night shift on Saturday. Nothing to worry about, in the end.'

Moralès wasn't sure if he felt relieved or exasperated. Lefebvre had made him hurry for nothing.

'Never believe a clairvoyant, that's what I say. Seriously, a "naked monster"? What a load of codswallop.'

'Did you get the warrants, Lefebvre?'

'Yes, they just came in. It's Wednesday tomorrow. We'll see if there's been any activity in her accounts in the last three days, then we'll go from there. I'll check what insurance she had and get the notary to do a will search.'

'Any word from Simone Lord?'

Lefebvre whistled between his teeth. 'She often gets a bee in her bonnet, but I've rarely seen her this hot under the collar. I don't know what you did to get her knickers in a twist, but this afternoon we've been daring each other to see who can last the longest with her in the meeting room.'

'And?'

'Thérèse Roch's the clear winner. I'm not surprised. She's untouchable.'

'What about the searches?'

'I don't think the weather today's helping. Don't worry, though. If Simone finds something, we'll know about it, all right.'

Sébastien scaled the little stepladder and thrust the sash window open. Cyrille Bernard slowly turned to look at him. What was he doing here? He jumped down into the room. It smelled of marijuana. Beneath the sheets he could see the thin silhouette of a man who was struggling to breathe.

'Mr Bernard? My father, Joaquin Moralès, asked me to come.'

He moved closer to the man's bed. All he could hear was a whistling 'heee…' sound – the laboured in-breath of a dying man. Sébastien felt awkward. The man scrutinised him through his pale-blue eyes.

'He said I should tell you what I saw through the telescope.'

Beside the bed was a wooden chair, clearly placed there for visitors. Sébastien was too restless to sit down, so he stayed standing. He shifted his weight from one leg to the other, like a teenager who couldn't make up his mind. The old man sat up a little.

'Heee… Tell me, then. What did you see, son?'

Sébastien was ill at ease in this antechamber of death. 'Not much. Two container ships.'

Cyrille Bernard gave him a cynical look. 'Is that all?'

'They looked like they were heading towards New Brunswick.'

'Heee…'

'That's all I saw.'

The old fisherman shook his head in disbelief. 'Heee … young people today. You're still of an age to be counting your rights and your wrongs.' Then he closed his eyes.

Sébastien felt his anger boiling over. 'There was nothing else to see, all right!' he protested.

Cyrille didn't even bother opening an eye. 'Well, you're not going to see anything if you watch the sea like an accountant, are you? Heee…'

The insult was like a slap on the cheek. Why did everyone have to lecture him about the way he saw things? What was he supposed to say? Was he supposed to make something up?

Sébastien sat and inched the chair closer to the bed. He leaned in and spoke to the man in a voice he hoped was soft enough to contain his anger. It wasn't.

'OK, then. I saw a patch of water that was teeming with life. The birds were diving beneath the surface and emerging with fish in their beaks. And I saw three whales as well.'

There weren't any whales in that area, and Cyrille knew it.

The old fisherman cracked his eyelids open and cast him a sideways glance. 'Heee … what are you going on about, son?'

Sébastien shrugged. 'I don't know what to say, so I'm making things up to make you happy.'

'Heee … Why not just tell me what you saw?'

'Because nothing I've seen lately is exactly uplifting.'

Cyrille turned to look at the angry young man. 'Heee … How so?'

'Last week, my mother bought a condo in Longueuil behind my father's back. Yesterday, my boss, who thinks he's oh-so understanding, told me I was out of a job if I wasn't there by noon. And the server in the bistro insinuated my father had an affair with a woman called Cath—'

'Heee … Your girlfriend's pregnant and she didn't tell you?'

Sébastien showed almost no surprise at these words. He just nodded and carried on, like a spinning top caught up in its own momentum.

'Do you know what all that is, Mr Bernard? It's just a whole lot of thrashing on the surface with no fish – or whales – in the water. And I'm the one circling hungry overhead and diving into the sea for a meal that isn't there. It's the lure that's been hooking my whole life for years. That's what I saw in the telescope this morning.'

Cyrille closed his exhausted eyes. 'Heee … That's a lot of things to see on your first time.'

Sébastien pushed the chair back and stood up. 'You're just like everyone else, telling me I'm seeing things all wrong. It's like my life's constantly slipping between my fingers.'

'Heee … If you didn't want to open your eyes to the sea that's right in front of you … heee … staring you in the face, why bother coming to tell me about it?'

'Because my dad asked me to.'

Cyrille opened his eyes again and looked Sébastien up and down. 'How old are you?'

'Thirty.'

'Thirty years old and you're foaming at the mouth over two bloody ships? Heee … Thirty years old and you're still doing everything your father says? Heee … Thirty years old and you don't know the difference between a rogue wave and a shoal of fish?'

Sébastien was lost for words.

'Heee … If you came here just to keep your father happy, you'd have told me about those two ships and gone on your way. Heee … Don't let an old man like me, on his death bed, keep a young man like you.'

All of a sudden, something clicked for Sébastien. He felt like he wasn't going around in circles anymore. Like a spinning top that ran into something in its path, he teetered and swayed his way back to sit in stillness in the chair at Cyrille Bernard's bedside. And apologised.

The old fisherman shrugged. Lying at death's door, he wasn't about to start chalking up faults now.

'Sometimes it's like I don't know who I am anymore.'

'Heee … You sound like your father. You dream of the wide blue yonder, but you never take your eyes off the shore.'

Sébastien took a deep breath and edged a touch closer to the old fisherman, who was still studying him with his ocean eyes.

'You'll have to tell me what you want me to look out for.'

'Heee … Stop asking other people what you should see. Just open your eyes and look.'

'I can come back again tomorrow…'

'Son, it's been a long time since I needed anyone to tell me stories about the sea. Heee … Everything I need to know is in here.' He pointed an experienced finger to his heart. 'Heee … Some fishermen say when you're on a boat, you rise up above the waves. But, you listen to me, son: it's the sea that rises in you. It's just like everything else. We always think fear, jealousy, resentment and lies are things that come from other people. Heee … But they're lurking inside all of us. Like a winter tide.'

Sébastien had run out of things to say. Then he remembered her. 'My dad wants you to know he's in Rivière-au-Renard investigating the disappearance of a woman. Angel Roberts.'

Cyrille had been resting his eyes, but he blinked them open. 'The young lass with the lobster boat?'

'Yes.' Sébastien held his breath, as if holding back a tear.

'There are families that have hated each other for so long, it welds them together. Heee … Your father's caught a hell of a pot of crabs there.'

Sébastien stood and moved towards the window.

'The suffering we put ourselves through is worse than all the rest. Heee … It takes a whole lot of horizon to calm your own troubles.' Cyrille shifted position in the bed, slowly succumbing to his fatigue. 'Do you know what the word "Gaspé" means? Heee…'

Sébastien turned to him and shook his head. 'No.'

'It means "the end of the world". Go out there and see your father. Heee … Listen to an old fisherman who's on his last legs. Heee … Keep looking at the sea and I promise, one day, you'll see it.'

Moralès had been going round in circles. Where could he go to write his report for the day? He didn't feel comfortable going down to the dining room again, for fear of disturbing Corine and Kimo, and sitting alone in the empty bar was a depressing prospect, especially as he was getting hungry. He grabbed his things and decided to go into downtown Gaspé. Lefebvre had recommended a pub called the Brise-Bise.

Arriving at the pub, he sat at the bar in what looked like a quiet corner. The barman came over, a heavyset type who probably knew all the regulars by name and looked like he could be a ship's captain: forearms inked with sailor tattoos, a single earring, close-cropped black hair and beard, hours of gym time in his biceps.

'Today's special is chicken chasseur, with a pear tart for dessert. I'd suggest a pint of Pit Caribou amber ale to go with it. I can bring you the menu if you like.'

'No, that will be perfect,' Moralès replied.

It was an easy-going kind of place. A gentle blues soundtrack filled the air while a football match played on one of the TV screens. Moralès felt happy. He glanced at his phone. An email had just come in from a former colleague and friend in Montreal, a Detective Sergeant Doiron. He replied to the message, then opened his file, grabbed a blank sheet of paper and started writing his report.

'Is it you who's investigating the disappearance of the fisher-woman?' the barman asked, stealing a glance at the file as he put the pint on the bar.

Moralès took a sip of the beer. 'Do you know her?'

'No, but her husband comes here often.' He reached a hand over the bar. 'My name's Louis.'

A bell dinged in the kitchen, and the barman went away. Moralès made a note about discovering that the lobster trawler had been moved, probably by Jimmy Roberts and the Babin brothers; he'd have to clear that up. The beer was good. He made a start on the report of his conversation with Jacques Forest. The serving staff were buzzing like bees around the kitchen, flying up and down the stairs between the two floors of the pub, smiling and cracking jokes with customers. Moralès chose not to put the tumultuous episode with Simone Lord on the record. His chicken chasseur arrived.

'Do you think it's a revenge thing among fishermen?' the barman asked.

Moralès leaned back in his bar stool. 'What makes you say that?'

'Well, fishermen might seem friendly enough when you see them on shore, but out on the water they can be different beasts.'

'Have you ever worked as a fisherman?'

'No, but I hear them talk.'

'And what else have you heard?'

Louis gave him a half-smile, shook his head and returned to his duties, leaving Moralès to tuck into his chicken. The file stayed closed while he was eating.

He'd demolished the chicken and the pear tart before big Louis opened his trap again. Moralès had asked for the bill and was standing between the pillar at the end of the bar and the closed kitchen door when the barman, peering down at the screen on the till, spoke up.

'The guys don't like seeing you sniffing around the *Close Call II*.'

'Which guys? The Roberts brothers?'

Louis shrugged. 'I'm not one for getting myself into hot water, but you're in fishing territory here. Don't go making too many waves with your investigation.'

'Would anyone in particular have a vested interest in that boat?'

The barman handed Moralès his receipt. 'Be careful. That's all I'm saying. When all's said and done, we're no different here than anywhere else. We like our peace and quiet.'

Wednesday 26th September

Sébastien's phone rang, and again he ignored it. He loaded the stuff into his car. Some for him, the rest for his father. He was trying to take his time and go with the flow, but he couldn't. His movements were stiff and choppy. He had woken early and gone for a run, kept going until his muscles ached. And he had run past Cyrille Bernard's window without stopping. What would they have said to each other? He had followed a trail for a long time, then retraced his steps in the half-light of a milky dawn, a haze that seemed more opaque where the sky met the sea.

The previous evening, he and Joaquin had exchanged silence over the phone. You couldn't really call it a conversation. His father had reminded Sébastien he was waiting for him in a village near the town of Gaspé. He had given him the address of the auberge, adding that they would be the only guests staying there. Sébastien had been sitting outside. The drizzle had stopped and the sky was filled with high clouds torn into strips, letting the stars shine through. After a pause on the line, Sébastien had said he would come.

His mind was made up. He was going to settle the score with his father. That was why he had come here, after all. He locked up the house, got behind the wheel and drove onto Highway 132, heading east. He couldn't see the sea that morning. A tenacious mist had settled over the bay during the night, turning the red cliffs pale and the horizon opaque and colourless. These days, the bitterness was so thick it felt like he was walking around in a cloud. No wonder he couldn't see clearly.

Sébastien drove through the village of Saint-Siméon, then the town of Bonaventure. The sea was still hiding in the fog. He had seen plenty of colourful adverts for the Gaspé Peninsula. In summer, the daisies, lupins and other meadow flowers must really brighten up the landscape, he thought. Today, everything was monochrome. Little Anglican churches popped up here and there with a ghostly, abandoned air about them. The hodge-podge of buildings, closed shop fronts and faded or broken billboards along the road made the drive feel a bit creepy. Sébastien saw a few big trucks coming the other way, carrying gigantic wind-generator blades that flexed when the wheels ran over a pothole, of which there were many. The road surface was in such poor condition, it looked like a mosaic of ruined asphalt.

The decay in some of the villages was an assault on the eyes. There seemed to be no light at the end of this tunnel of overcast sky. Sébastien had put some music on, but his heart wasn't in it. He couldn't remember what he had to say to his father. He tried to rehearse by voicing the blame out loud. That didn't help.

Sébastien drove through the village of Sainte-Thérèse-de-Gaspé. The wind was starting to pick up. He pulled into the first rest stop he saw on the approach to Percé. A number of wide, straight wooden staircases invited him to visit a bijou beach edged with red cliffs. The mist seemed to be rising a little, and there was a hint of late summer floating on the mild autumn air. The waves rolled low and heavy onto a shore lined with pink pebbles and beige sand. The sea was throwing itself at Sébastien's feet. This must be September's way of smiling on the Gaspé, he thought. He got back in the car and kept driving.

He must have laid eyes on it dozens of times in travel guides. He'd seen so many photos, he'd ended up dismissing it as a cheesy tourist trap. But in spite of himself, as the town of Percé drew nearer, Sébastien was surprised to be crossing his fingers that the lingering fog would lift enough for him to make out the iconic Percé Rock as he drove by.

The wind was blowing harder now. As the mist drifted away from the shore, the sea became an ocean and the sun came out to paint the water blue. Cresting the summit of the well-known and aptly named Côte de la Surprise, he saw it as the horizon opened up. The Percé Rock. It was pink. Or rather, green and pink.

Sébastien drove into a town that tourism had only recently deserted, hypnotised by the rock, which looked like it was leaning back on its elbows in the shallows. He decided to find somewhere to park. He turned onto the Rue du Quai and pulled up by the museum. As he got out of the car, his eye was drawn to Bonaventure Island, sitting offshore like a giant beached whale. His ear picked up the clinking sound of the waves rolling pink and green pebbles on the shore. He got back into the car.

On the other side of Percé, the road climbed, hugging the headland. Sébastien kept going. Coin-du-Banc, Bridgeville, Barachois. Pointe-Saint-Pierre, Saint-Georges-de-Malbaie, Prével, Bois-Brûlé, L'Anse-à-Brillant, Douglastown.

As he drove into the town of Gaspé, his phone rang. It was a local number.

'Hello?'

'Hi, my name's Corine. Are you Joaquin Moralès's son?'

'Yes.'

'There's a ground search in the park to look for the woman who's gone missing, and I want to go and help. So there won't be anyone here when you arrive. Do you mind if I give you the code for the door and leave you to make yourself at home? Just go upstairs and choose any room you like.'

'Where's the search happening?'

'Do you want to help?'

'Where is it?'

'I've arranged to meet a friend and we're going up to the lookout at Cap-Bon-Ami, but she's not free for another hour. I thought I'd go down to the water at Grande-Grave before I head out there. Are you nearby? Would you like to join us?'

Sébastien smiled. Why not? It would do him good to get a breath of fresh air with Corine and her friend, and surely he could find somewhere in this town to buy a pair of hiking boots. It couldn't hurt to put off confronting his father for a few more hours, could it?

'Hello, Ms Roch! Could you open the door for me, please?'

She didn't bat an eye.

'Constable Lefebvre is expecting me.'

The receptionist passed Moralès a folded piece of paper. It was addressed by hand to 'Detective Moralless'. He glanced at Thérèse Roch. She was still tapping away at her computer keyboard, oblivious to his presence. Intrigued, he unfolded the paper. The words he saw were in small, forward-slanting hand-writing and followed by a local telephone number.

Detective Moralless,
I have some confidential information to share with you. I SAW
some extraordinary things the night Angel Roberts disappeared.
Call me.
   Dotrice Percy

'Thank you, Ms Roch. Now, would you kindly…'

The outside door flew open to reveal Simone Lord.

'Hi Thérèse! Having a good day?'

The receptionist glanced at her, nodded and pressed the button to buzz her in. The fisheries officer breezed right past Moralès as if he wasn't there, but he seized his chance and slipped through the door behind her. Simone Lord held herself tall as she walked. She was wearing an autumn wool sweater with a round neckline.

She didn't say a word or throw him even the slightest look of contempt. He followed her into the small meeting room. Lefebvre wasn't there. She turned around to leave, and Moralès walked right into her. He caught her full in the chest and the damage was done. He couldn't help but breathe in the earthy, breezy scent of her. She shoved him away and he dutifully stepped aside. She hurried down the corridor to Lefebvre's office and he followed her.

The door was open. Lefebvre gestured to them. 'I've got some answers for you, Moralès.'

Proud of himself, Lefebvre slapped a palm on the desk and inadvertently knocked two sheets of paper onto the floor. 'Oops!' He bent down, picked up his papers, resurfaced, dropped one of the sheets into the recycling bin, retrieved it, looked at it intently and put it on top of a pile to his left. 'Where was I?'

Moralès was wondering where he could stand so he could close the door behind them. Every time he came in here, the office seemed to get smaller. As files and random objects accumulated, it began to look more and more like a lair.

Simone found a solution. 'I can see how you thrive in this environment, Lefebvre, but I'd rather we do this in the meeting room. My update won't take long.'

Lefebvre looked up in surprise. 'Is that right?' He frowned and threw Moralès a questioning look. 'I suppose if that's what you'd rather…'

As the two men sat down in the other room, Simone Lord stood tall and clasped her hands behind her back to report on the search efforts in the last few hours. 'Our people have combed the area between Gaspé Bay and Bonaventure Island several times, to no avail. The fog has hampered our efforts severely. The skies are clearing, but time is ticking. The Zodiacs haven't found anything along the coast. We're specifically looking for any white objects that might be part of a wedding dress. We're not leaving anything to chance.'

She spoke in a monotone with a professional detachment, looking only at Lefebvre. Uncomfortable being the sole object of her attention, he didn't know what to do with his eyes. His attention flitted between the fisheries officer, the marine chart pinned to the bulletin board and the detective.

'We're planning to keep this pace going on the search for two more days,' Simone continued. 'The chances of finding Angel Roberts alive are getting slimmer by the hour.' She fell quiet.

Lefebvre tried to pick up where she left off, taking pains to sit up straight and adopt an official tone, as if Simone Lord had imposed a decorum he was obliged to follow. 'With respect to—'

'Ahem,' Simone interrupted. 'The other aspects of this investigation do not concern my area of expertise, so I'm going to leave you now and return to my duties.' Without further ado, she left the room.

A bewildered Lefebvre stared at Moralès. 'I think you two are going to have to kiss and make up after your little tiff if we're all going to work together, don't you?'

Moralès wasn't sure if he felt pride or shame. He did feel a bit sheepish for having taken her down a peg, but did he really have to apologise?

'So, where are you at?' he asked the constable.

Lefebvre sighed. 'With respect to the will…' He rummaged through his papers, failed to find the information he wanted, gave up and looked at Moralès. 'There isn't one. There's nothing at all. The notary said everything goes to her husband. She hasn't used any of her bank cards since last Thursday evening; she spent enough for two bottles of wine at the government liquor store. Her finances are in very good shape. Almost too good. You have to wonder how she managed to pay off her lobster trawler so quickly.'

'Does she have any debt?'

'No.'

'And her husband?'

'Not much. Clément Cyr was twenty years old when his father died. He inherited his old man's fishing licence. He's making a comfortable living, but he bought a new shrimp trawler three years ago.'

Moralès mulled that over for a moment.

Lefebvre took advantage of the time to rummage through his papers again. 'Do you have a will? I've never thought about it myself, but the notary said I should look into it, since I don't have kids.' He pulled a paper out of the pile. 'See, he wrote his rate down for me. Do you think it costs the same everywhere or do people shop around?'

Sébastien parked in front of the general store. Corine was waiting for him.

'We've got time for a walk on the beach before Kimo gets here. She's teaching a yoga class. She should be here in half an hour. Have you been to the Gaspé before?'

'Never.'

The sun shattered the sea into a crazed mirror of blinding fragments.

'In 1970, the government expropriated land from three thousand people on this part of the peninsula to create the national park, did you know that?'

Sébastien shook his head. Corine skipped towards a shuttered general store with an old-fashioned sign out front that read W^M HYMAN & SONS. The ancient clapboard building had been tarted up with a lick of fresh paint.

'For two centuries, the Gaspesians were treated like slaves by the Robins, who came from the island of Jersey, and the Hymans, who were from Russia. Exploiters, they were. Instead of paying the fishermen, they gave them vouchers to exchange for goods. This used to be their general store. The building might look historic, but it hasn't been closed that long.'

Corine led Sébastien onto a gravel path as she continued her story. It wasn't long before they arrived at a lookout overhanging the cliff, surrounded by bushes. Little islands of spruce were dotted here and there, the trees huddling together to resist the relentless onslaught of the wind. The bushes were blushing with autumn colour.

'In the summer, you can see the fishing buoys all along here,' Corine said.

Down below, Sébastien saw an inaccessible pebble beach, invaded by mocking gulls. The shadowy forms of rocks beneath the surface were all that tainted the crystal-clear water. The seabed was a blue so clear it looked almost green. The cliff with its layers of limestone traced a daring arc out over the water. Where the waves had toiled to shape the shore, spruces sprouted from the concave curve of the stone, taking root against all odds – clinging to the cliff like thrill-seeking mountaineers.

Between this copse of black spruce that veiled the easternmost point of Forillon Park, and Haldimand Beach on the south shore of Gaspé Bay, the ocean drew the eye and swallowed it whole. Sébastien took a few steps to the side of the lookout to try and see above the spruce tops.

'Don't go over there! There's poison ivy, you'll be itching all week.'

'Is there a trail that goes to the end of Forillon Park? Can you walk all the way out on the headland?'

'Yes, the path to Land's End will take you to Cap-Gaspé. But today, we're going up to the lookout at Cap-Bon-Ami. It's at the top of the mountain. The view will take your breath away. You won't regret coming.'

Corine glanced at her watch. 'We'd better get going. Kimo will be here any minute. If you're keen to see the sea we'll take the walking path back to the wharf.' She flashed him a smile full of energy and set off along a path that snaked along the clifftop.

Sébastien envied her. He envied her joy and lightness. That was all he wanted. To be happy. She gambolled along ahead, daring him to keep up with her. Caught up in her own momentum, she sprinted away and was out of sight by the first corner in the path. For a brief moment he could hear the crunching of her shoes on the gravel and the swishing of the long grass against her legs, and then the silence returned, broken only by the pounding of the shorebreak against the rock face below.

Sébastien was happy to let her take the lead. He was taking his time. The squawking of the gulls, the cooing of the chickadees and the tumbling of the waves were all he could hear as he inched closer to the edge of the cliff, which glistened in the sea spray.

Suddenly, he felt rather than heard his phone buzzing in his small daypack. He hesitated. Should he take the pack off, open it and read the text message? No, Corine would be waiting for him. He continued along the path, past an old fish-curing hut, onto the walkway beside the old general store. Down in a dip mid-way between the store and the wharf, he noticed a tiny isolated cove, where the sea was sweeping a narrow shore lined with round, polished pebbles. He went to take a look.

The sound of the waves wasn't the same as in Percé. Here, the pebbles tinkled a more scintillating ballad, the chinking of a pearl necklace released by a languid hand onto a bed of rumpled blue velvet. Bustards and their young were enjoying the gentle rolling of the swell before their migration. The stones under his soles clinked together as if he were walking on gold coins. He reflected on the irony of that image. If what Corine had said was true, these were poor man's pebbles on a beach for exploited fishermen.

Sébastien thought about the poverty and subservience that must have been passed down through the generations. He had to talk to his father. Make a decision. Go back to the city.

The sea was making some order of the pebbles. As Sébastien walked back up to the path, they fell silent once more. But he could still hear the beating of the waves against the cliff as he made his way to the wharf. The path skirted a thicket and an animal kind of smell, an earthy, salty scent, wafted into his nostrils. His new boots felt solid on the ground. The parking area by the wharf was deserted as he approached. To his right, Sébastien saw an area with some picnic tables. He went over to see.

'Corine?'

He shivered. She wasn't there. She must be on the wharf, he thought. His phone vibrated again. At last, he drew near and saw that the wharf was empty. He had a look around the shacks he found behind the wharf, and a boat that was moored alongside. The sea was dazzling. He moved towards the floating dock down below. And he saw her. At least he thought he did. He wasn't certain it was her. Worried, he quickened his step. Yes, that was her. Sitting cross-legged on the pontoon beside a boat with the name *Close Call II* painted on the side.

'Corine?' he called again.

She didn't answer. He moved closer.

'Has something happened?'

She pulled herself together and shook her head. 'No. I'm sorry.'

She dried her eyes and got up. 'This is Angel's boat. The woman who's missing. She's the reason we're going on the search.'

Behind them, a car drove down the slope into the parking area.

'That's Kimo. Come on, I'll introduce you.'

He turned into the driveway of the blue house. Annie Arsenault's home was both simple and appealing, surrounded by trees on all sides except the south, which offered a partial sea view.

As he parked his car, Moralès noticed, on a gentle slope at the rear of the house, a big vegetable garden, which extended onto Angel Roberts' property. Foil plates hanging from strings attached to long sticks planted in the ground were dancing in the westerly breeze, scaring the birds away. Around the perimeter was a trellis fence to keep the hungry deer and hares out. The yellowed leaves of climbing beans covered the west side of the fence. Leaning against the north side was a disorderly bundle of stakes that must have been tied together after the tomato plants had withered and been pulled up. Just in front, wilted flowers drooped their brown corollas towards the ground. Through the trellis, the bright orange splotches of pumpkins, gentle green spheres of autumn cabbage and ochre-red background of turned soil painted a pointillist work or art befitting of the season. Beyond the garden was a wooden compost bin and a small shed with tools hanging on the side.

Annie Arsenault opened the door before Moralès had time to knock. She stepped outside and guessed what he was looking at, without having to turn to see.

'Angel and I planted that garden together. Just last week, we turned some of the soil.'

She was an attractive woman with thin lips and green eyes. Her face was flushed from crying. Moralès had called that lunchtime to arrange to see her.

She smiled, and Moralès saw the whole woman appear before his eyes. The lines on her face had been shaping themselves forever around this graceful smile he guessed came naturally, usually, but not so much today. Her short, tangled hair bounced in a tousle of curls around a colourful headband. She was wearing a pretty yellow top under a navy jacket.

'We were at school together. She decided to go into fishing, and I became a teacher. I teach maths at the college in Gaspé. People sometimes say we grow apart from our friends as we get older. But Angel and I, we bought houses next door to each other, we planted a shared garden and we do all our canning together. In the winter, when I finish late, she watches my boys, and in the summer I've been known to give her a hand on the boat. Time has made us sisters.'

She paused and took a deep breath to keep the tears at bay.

Moralès stayed quiet. He had stopped consoling people a long time ago. What would he say to her, anyway? That he would find Angel Roberts? That he would bring her friend home alive? That the two of them would get to sow their pepper seeds again in the greenhouse in March, plant their tomatoes in May and harvest their carrots in July?

'Let's sit outside, shall we?' she suggested. 'It's a nice day.'

She had made some herbal tea and put a box of tissues on the patio table. Moralès sat while she poured the tea. It smelled of fir, hawthorn and wintergreen.

'My husband's gone out there with our three boys. To help with the search. I'm…'

Tears streamed down her cheeks, following channels carved by the last few days. She pulled two tissues out of the box.

'I'm sorry.' She dried her eyes. 'I just can't bring myself to go.' But there were more tears eating away at her from the inside. 'I'm too scared of finding Angel, wearing her wedding dress.'

Moralès could understand. She was afraid she would find her friend beaten, raped, tortured. She was afraid of the fear she would read on the face of her confidante, her bloodied dress dragged through the mud; she was scared she would have to live with those images burned into her retinas and would never again be able to crouch in the garden and do the things they both loved.

He waited until she was back in her depth. 'You've known each other a long time.'

It wasn't a question, but she nodded. 'Our mothers used to work together. They were nurses at the hospital in Gaspé. Cancer took hers a decade ago. Angel's mum was the daughter of a prominent local doctor, who had spent some time in politics too. The family was very active in the community.'

'Was her father's family from around here as well?'

Annie Arsenault pulled a face. 'Yes. Angel's grandfather on her father's side worked at the Hyman general store in Grande-Grave, which belonged to a company that exploited fishermen. He wasn't well-liked because he played at being rich. Even when the store closed down, he pretended he was a cut above. But when he died, he left his children nothing but debts. Debts and shame.' She cocked her head. 'It's sad when you think about it. My own father used to tell me how, when he was young, Angel's father wanted to be a fisherman, but no one would take him on because his father had been so arrogant to the locals. He ended up having to go to New Brunswick to find work. One day, he came back. He met Angel's mother and they got married. She was the one who paid for his first boat. But grudges run deep. Even with a fancy boat, he had trouble finding deckhands because people from around here refused to work with him. There are families that pass their squabbles from one generation to the next.'

'Was he the one who bankrolled his children's boats?'

'I don't know.' Annie Arsenault bit the inside of her cheek pensively and took a sip of herbal tea.

'What about Angel's?'

She put her cup down and leaned back in her chair. From the corner of her eye, she could see a bit of the garden plot. The corner where they'd had to dig down and bury a wire fence because the raccoons had tunnelled superhighways under the trellis to sneak in and munch on their precious heads of lettuce.

'I doubt it. Angel was fifteen years old when she set her heart on this career. The men said she could never do it. Even her own father. He never wanted to take her on board. Leeroy can be quite the chauvinist. Like any other fisherman, I suppose. It wasn't cod or shrimp she was interested in anyway, but lobster. She dreamed of cruising up and down the coast.'

She smiled softly as she spoke about her friend, as if remembering her would suspend time and delay the moment she would have to admit that Angel was gone.

'She went to study in Rimouski, at the Maritime Institute. I don't remember the details, because I was doing my degree in Quebec City then. What I do know is that Angel got her boat just after her mother died.'

Lefebvre had said that Angel's boat was paid off. Probably thanks to an inheritance, Moralès thought.

'When Jean Morrissette retired, she bought his boat. She was twenty-two years old. He wrote into the sales contract that he would lend a hand if need be, but that never happened. To be fair, his wife was sick; they ended up moving to Quebec City to be closer to good healthcare. In the dead of winter. So Angel was on her own when spring came around.'

Moralès sipped his tea. He wasn't a fan of the woody taste, but he didn't let it show.

'Most fishers learn the ropes working on other people's boats, but no one wanted to take her on. And no one wanted to work for her either. Angel was "just a woman", you see?'

'Did the fishermen try to sabotage her operation?'

'It did happen, yes.'

'How?'

'The lobster traps are connected to a cable. There's a dozen on each line. That line is weighted with lead so it won't catch the engines of any small boats that pass by on the surface. The whole setup sits on the seabed, and at each end of the line is a buoy that floats on the surface. To pull up the traps, the fishers come along and pull on the buoy, and haul the line in with a winch. Are you with me?'

He nodded.

'The first year someone went around cutting Angel's lines. She'd get to her zone and find her buoys had gone. The first few times it happened, she had to bring in divers to retrieve her lines and traps. After that she kitted herself out so she could dive herself. She never talked about it. Not to anyone. She coped.'

Moralès turned towards the garden while Annie Arsenault caught her breath. He admired this courageous Angel, who toiled the land and the sea.

'Then it just stopped. We never found out why, but I've always suspected her uncle Jacques went and had a word with another fisherman.'

'Jacques Forest?'

'Yes. He used to do ocean search and rescue in the States. He came back when Angel's mother passed. Maybe she called and asked him to watch over her daughter. I don't know. Anyway, he went on board with her. He's always been her most reliable worker, but he'd never fished before either, can you imagine?'

'Who else worked with her?'

Annie sipped her tea and clenched her jaw as if she'd nibbled a bitter endive. 'She's had plenty of deckhands over the years. Unreliable young lads who gave up when the going got rough, Indigenous guys from the reserve who only stayed a year, and other youngsters who didn't have a place on their fathers' boats. When her brother sold his scallop trawler, she took on one of his deckhands, Jean-Paul Babin.'

'Her brother doesn't fish with her?'

'No.' She said it coldly.

'Do she and her brothers get on well?'

Annie poured a fresh stream of tea into her cup and didn't mention the fact that Moralès had barely touched his. It wasn't the detective's favourite thing to drink, but she didn't seem to notice.

'For a long time Bruce worked up north on the big tankers. It wasn't long ago that he bought his father's licence. Five years, maybe. He didn't make a big song and dance about it though.'

'And Jimmy? Did they have a falling-out?'

She hesitated a moment. 'I don't think the Robertses have ever been an easy family to like. It's like they inherited a flaw from the grandfather. They get hung up on money and fight among themselves – and with others too. I don't know the full story. I lost track of all their spats when I was away at uni in Quebec City. I do know the Robertses weren't a happy family at Angel's wedding, though.'

'Why not?'

'Leeroy's never got on with Clément's dad. The Robertses were irked because they thought, if Angel died, Clément would get to take over her fishing operation. You get the picture? Anyway, they looked into it and found out that if Angel didn't have children, her dad and brothers would be the ones to inherit. I mean, who even thinks to find out about that sort of thing? No one!'

'And what did she think about all that?'

'Every year on their anniversary, she put her wedding dress on and invited herself and Clément over to her dad's for dinner.'

'She was rubbing their noses in it.'

'No. I think she just wanted to show them she was happy and in love, and remind them that that was more important than money.'

He had always preferred shadowed eyelids, perky eyelashes, shiny lips and hairstyles created with an expert feminine touch that you could undo with the stroke of the hand, to naked faces. For him, until now, the pinnacle of femininity had risen half from a woman's natural beauty and half from the art of making herself beautiful, the meticulous skill of nuancing jewellery, mascara and hair clips.

Sébastien put one foot in front of the other in a continuous and conscious effort to conquer the mountain. Kimo wore nothing but tiny gold studs in her ears. Her face was free of makeup, tanned by the sun and flushed with emotion. There was an air of sadness and honesty about her that gave her a certain *je ne sais quoi*. She had taken it upon herself to race up the trail, sweating out a pent-up energy that was soon dripping down her skin. Sébastien wasn't about to criticise her decompressing technique.

Kimo had only said a brief hello before the three of them set off walking towards Cap-Bon-Ami. 'What are you doing out here in the Gaspé?' she asked Sébastien now.

'I'm working on some culinary experiments, with local products.'

She shrugged her shoulders like she didn't believe him.

Corine intervened. 'Ooh, I'll have to take you beer tasting!'

Kimo shook her head. 'Corine has a thing for craft brewers.'

'It's better than having a thing for fishermen!'

Corine regretted the taunt immediately and apologised. 'It came out all by itself, Kimo…'

Her friend quickened her step and swallowed her pain.

'Sometimes, I should just keep my mouth shut,' Corine whispered in Sébastien's ear, mortified.

She moved aside to let him pass. At first Sébastien felt uncomfortable as he followed Kimo up the first part of the steep climb. Then after a while he found himself appreciating the view of the young woman ahead of him. Her muscles, her calves, her thighs, especially her buttocks, and her lower back. When they got to the first lookout platform, he sneaked a glimpse at her bare neck and the beads of sweat pearling on her skin.

An awkward silence hung in the air between the two friends. Out of the blue, Kimo turned to Sébastien and took him to task. 'So, as far as men go, would you say you're the loyal type?'

He was taken aback. The question was abrupt, but rhetorical. Yes, he was the faithful type, but she was beautiful and standing right in front of him. He needed to take a deep breath. This was a question best left unanswered.

'Because I've got bad karma when it comes to romance. I always end up being manipulated. Are you the kind of man who thinks he's decent?'

Definitely best not to answer that one. Kimo was a strapping young woman and the cliff below was mighty steep.

Sébastien chose to subtly change the subject, a technique that had often come in handy. 'When things aren't going well, I dance. Do you know how to dance the salsa? There's not a lot of room up here on the lookout, but we can dance a few steps.'

Kimo gave him a death stare, turned her back and bolted off up the path.

Sébastien turned to Corine. 'Well, that's the quickest I've ever scared a woman away.'

Corine burst out laughing and kept on climbing. 'Come on, Moralès, you're such a slowcoach.'

Sébastien followed, not daring to pass Corine or try to catch up with Kimo. They stopped at a second lookout platform. The view was impressive. He couldn't see the mountaintop, but the horizon stretched all around and gave them a little room to breathe.

'Is that your phone vibrating?' Kimo scowled.

He blushed. He didn't think there was any service here, but as they'd climbed higher the phone must have picked up a signal from a high tower.

'If you didn't want to answer it, you should have left it in your car.' Kimo turned and made her way back to the path.

Corine awkwardly tried to apologise for her friend. 'She's had a bad experience…' She opened her palms in a gesture of power-lessness and hurried in pursuit.

Sébastien leaned against the railing and reached into his backpack for his phone. That was the twelfth time she'd called that day. He thought about everything his life had been until just last week, and it felt like a punch in the stomach. He looked at the path ahead. Why hurry? He wanted to give himself the chance to see his life from a different angle, didn't he? So why shy away from that? He felt attracted to this girl, Kimo, perhaps because he sensed in her a turmoil not unlike his own. He could get close to her – not to cheat on Maude, just to feel under-stood. By mutual consent. Without any ulterior motives, just to console one another. He realised he wasn't being truthful with himself. He wanted to get close to her to escape his life, to end things with Maude. He buried the phone in his pack, hauled it onto his back again and kept on climbing. He'd do something about all that later. Not now.

By the time he made it to the top of the mountain, the girls had been waiting for a while. They were sitting on a wooden bench at the lookout, snacking on some fruit and nuts, when he arrived. Sébastien gazed out to the horizon. Anticosti Island to the north, Percé the other way. The ocean was all around. Sébastien took his backpack off and put it down on the bench.

Corine stood up and moved towards him. 'Well, if you're offering, I'm up for that salsa class.'

Sébastien Moralès bowed, took the young woman by the hand and pulled her into his arms. She laughed as he showed her a few steps before leading her into some fancy footwork and twirling her around on the cramped platform. She soon felt dizzy from the altitude and all the spinning, and had to sit down.

That was Sébastien's cue to approach Kimo and offer his left hand. She stared at him with an air of defiance, then placed her right hand in his palm. She stood rigid and defensive, consenting in spite of herself, pushing through her reluctance to avoid looking like a poor sport. Keeping her right hand in his left, he took her other hand and placed it on his right shoulder, and moved a little closer.

Treading gently into the moist, woody aroma of her space, he led her a step to the side, and another step back. She followed his lead, albeit with a certain reticence and fragility. He was dancing in slow motion, because he could sense the tension and pain in the young woman's body. For a brief moment concentrating on Kimo and the way he was leading her forward and back made him forget his own. He decided to try a twirl. As she turned, he caught a glimpse of the sea stretching all the way to the horizon and felt the fresh air swallow him up. Abruptly, Kimo froze, not quite facing him, held only by the hand of her suitor, which was hanging over her head like a string. She let go, and for a second Sébastien thought she was going to burst into tears. Instead, she pulled away. This dance was over.

'We saved you a snack. I hope you enjoy it,' Kimo said. Then she slipped her backpack on, turned her back and set off down the path.

'Would you say Clément is the loyal type? Was he faithful to Angel?' Moralès asked.

Annie Arsenault turned her gaze to the vegetable garden. She was playing for time; that was never a good sign.

'Something strange happened this summer. There was this girl, Kimo. That's a nickname. Kim Morin is her name. I think she's from Cloridorme. I'm not sure, but there are a lot of

Morins that way, up the coast. She moved to Rivière-au-Renard a few years ago. She teaches yoga classes in town.'

She paused, waiting for a nudge from Moralès that didn't come.

'Something happened between Clément and her.' She looked at him as if to say *you wanted to know, so I'm going to tell you everything.* 'I think I'd heard she'd been seeing Bruce, but I'm not sure. Anyway, she'd been spending a lot of time down at the big trawler wharf. Angel's never liked women who hang around on the wharves. It's not the most subtle way to woo a fisherman. One night we were all together. Angel made some silly jokes about yoga, but it was obvious she was having a dig at Kimo. Clément was there. He didn't say a word, but apparently he showed Kimo around his boat the next day.'

The way she talked about the visit made it sound like an act of high treason. She poured the rest of the herbal tea into her cup.

'Men talk, you know. My husband says it's just gossip and that Kimo seems nice enough. He must think I'm jealous because she's what, twenty-three? And pretty.'

Moralès smiled. Annie Arsenault was a charming woman who had nothing to envy the other – not her physique, nor her smile.

'But he's wrong. I'm not jealous. I admire strong women. When Kimo first came here and opened her yoga studio, I thought that was fantastic. She was always out training for her triathlons, running in the park, cycling on Highway 132, swimming in Gaspé Bay. I was impressed. But when a woman starts lingering on a commercial wharf like the one in Rivière-au-Renard and invites herself aboard a married man's boat, I have a hard time thinking she's not scheming.'

She sipped her tea and composed herself.

'I don't know many people more in love than Clément and Angel. I really don't think Clément would have cheated on Angel.'

'And Angel? Has she ever had a lover?'

Annie Arsenault looked at Moralès in surprise. 'No. I'd know if she had.'

'Did you hear any noises coming from your neighbour's house on Saturday night?'

'What kind of noises?'

'Vehicles coming or going, for example.'

'Clément and Angel both fish, so they're often out at all hours. We got used to hearing them come and go a long time ago.'

'Do you think she could have run away?'

'No.'

'Could she have … taken her own life?'

'That wouldn't be her style.'

'What would be her style?'

Annie Arsenault turned towards the sea and gave a gentle, sad smile.

'Her style, Detective Moralès, is to stay alive.'

Joaquin stopped for groceries on the way back. Maybe Corine would join him for dinner. Join *them*. He was going to introduce her to his son. His phone vibrated as he pulled up at the auberge. A message from his friend Doiron. He sent a quick reply. He hated thinking about relationship issues during an investigation. Afterwards, he'd see. After all this.

He got out of the car and looked out to sea before he went inside. The sky was navy blue. The swell was running high. The crests were whipping hard. That's what he would say to Cyrille if he were in Caplan. He gazed out over the water. *Where are you, Angel?* The horizon was narrow when the waves were steep.

He grabbed his case file and made his way to the entrance. His son's car was parked there. It was getting late and Sébastien must be tired of waiting, he thought.

A woman's laugh. That was the first thing Joaquin Moralès heard when he stepped inside. A bright, carefree laugh. A touch on the shrill side, the way it goes when a woman is enticing or being enticed. Frivolous, playful, unbridled. A laugh that lingers, fizzles in the breath, then quickly comes back for more.

Moralès walked towards the dining room. There she was, sitting on one of the red bench seats. She first emerged to him in profile, head tilted back slightly, unpretentiously. In jeans and a long-sleeved top. Hair held back by a colourful bandana. Beer bottles on the table. And Sébastien, sitting across from her.

His son stood when he saw him walk in. 'Hey Dad! Long day? I picked up some beers at L'Anse-à-Beaufils. Do you know the brewpub there?'

Moralès grumbled to himself. It made him uncomfortable to see his son apparently courting a woman other than his partner. All of a sudden, he felt irritated by Sébastien's presence – and his music, which he insisted on taking everywhere he went. He wouldn't say no to a beer, though.

'I've bought all the fixings to make a seafood pizza. I was waiting for you to get here. Sit down and relax. I've got this.'

Moralès felt like a fool for grumbling. Ridiculous.

Corine got up as well. 'Good evening, Joaquin. How are you doing?'

His name sounded almost glacial in the young woman's mouth. He returned the greeting.

She turned to Sébastien. 'Want to try the amber ale?'

'I'd love to.'

She didn't smile at him the same way she smiled at Sébastien. It made him feel old. He watched Sébastien pick up the dough he must have prepared earlier, and press it down. Moralès took off his jacket and sat down at a table with his papers to make a note of the new information he'd gathered. Corine came back and opened the beers.

'Here you go, Dad.' Sébastien came over with two glasses of amber ale and put one on the table in front of his father. The two youngsters went off into a quiet corner and tried to whisper so they wouldn't disturb him.

Moralès turned his attention to the *Close Call II* and drew up a timeline of events. He dug out the paper he had used to take down the deckhands' details, added that Jacques Forest was Angel's maternal uncle, and wrote a few lines about the others Annie Arsenault had told him about. He picked up a fresh sheet of paper. Like it or not, he could hear Sébastien and Corine chatting, laughing, saying everything and nothing. She said she'd better go have a shower before dinner. Nah, you're all right, he replied. She stood and took three steps, said he shouldn't hold it against Kimo, for the dance. She's a sweet girl who's had her heart broken, that's all. I'm not sure the shower can wait, he joked. She laughed.

Moralès pushed his chair away from the table and went over to check on the pizza dough.

'Are we bothering you, Dad?'

'No, of course not. I just wanted to see how the dough was doing.'

'Corine was just wondering if she should go freshen up before dinner.'

The auberge owner cringed. 'Don't say that to your dad, it's embarrassing.'

Moralès punched the dough down to get the air out, covered it again, then returned to his seat.

'Dad, you haven't even tasted your beer!'

It was true, Joaquin had forgotten all about it. Now he took a sip. 'It's nice.'

Now he had to put his notes in some kind of order. Who could have taken the bed linen and the wooden lobster trap? He had made Jacques Forest swear not to mention that to anyone. On the blank page, he wrote Annie Arsenault's name and the date of their meeting. He added that she and Angel had gone to school together, planted a shared garden and built a fence around it, and that Annie made her own herbal tea. That she'd be harvesting the rest of their produce alone. What else? Moralès took another sip of his beer. Weather's supposed to be nice tomorrow, he heard Corine say. We should hike up to the lookout on Mont Saint-Alban. Have you ever been? No, Sébastien explained, this was his first time on the Gaspé Peninsula. Good job he'd bought some hiking boots. We can invite Kimo if you like, she offered. Joaquin was trying his best to concentrate.

'Right, I'm off to have a quick shower now,' Corine said, and left the dining room.

Sébastien came over and sat beside his father. 'Making progress?'

'Slowly.'

'We're bothering you, aren't we?'

'No, I just don't have an office at the police station.' He took another sip of beer. 'This is really tasty, actually.'

'So we are bothering you.'

Joaquin looked his son in the eye. What was going on with Maude? He didn't dare ask.

Sébastien recoiled at the question he saw in his father's gaze.

Not now. He wasn't ready. He needed time and distance. Alcohol, perhaps, and music.

Both father and son were weighing each other up. Joaquin didn't feel like having to explain himself either.

'I think the dough's ready,' Joaquin said. 'I'll put the pizza together.'

They stood.

'You grate the cheese, I'll take care of the rest.'

Joaquin tossed and stretched the dough while Sébastien took out the seafood and washed it. Without realising it, his father was muscling him out of the kitchen.

Sébastien decided to leave him to it. He was taking the cutlery to lay the table when Corine came down the stairs with a spring in her step, humming to herself.

'Oh, there she is. Doesn't she smell nice?'

She burst into the kind of laugh that wells up like a wave, peaks and washes up gently on the beach. Moralès put the pizza in the oven.

'Corine, you wouldn't have a conference or meeting room here by any chance, would you?'

'Why?'

'Because my dad needs somewhere to work.'

Corine turned to Moralès. 'Oh, I hadn't thought about that. They don't have any space for you at the police station, do they?'

'Not really.'

'There is a spot right at the other end of the building. It's a holiday apartment I rent out in the summer. It's empty now. It's above the bar; can you see where I mean? There's a sign on the door that says *Le Chalet*. The key's in the lock. You can set yourself up in there. No one will bother you. There's a kitchenette with a table, a mini fridge and a coffee maker. There are

two adjoining bedrooms, so you can each have one if you want
to bunk down together.'

'Oh, that sounds perfect. Thank you.'

Moralès felt awkward sharing the table with the youngsters,
so he ate quickly and went upstairs to move his things.

Half an hour later, against all odds, Sébastien came upstairs
with his own luggage and put it in the second bedroom. Moralès
had thought his son would have rather stayed longer with
Corine and chosen another room to have more privacy. He put
his pen down and tidied his papers.

Seeing he was winding down, Sébastien reached into his bag
and pulled out two cold beers.

'You didn't tell me the Gaspé was craft-beer paradise!'

He reached into the bag again for his Bluetooth speaker and
put his music on. Then he opened the bottles and took two
glasses from the kitchen cupboard.

'What's this music?' Joaquin asked.

'Control Machete. Do you like it?'

Joaquin Moralès looked at his son. His eldest was here, now,
with him. And that was a good thing.

Thursday 27th September

It had been a late night for both of them. Sébastien had taken it upon himself to show his father the dance moves for Control Machete, but Joaquin had shaken his head: his son's movements were too jerky, even for Mexican hip-hop. Dancing was all about seduction; that was no secret. Even birds knew that.

'You have to let your body sway more gently, *chiquito*. You're taking the music into your ears, but you have to let it fill you up. Your movements are coming from your arms and your feet, but you have to let them come from your belly, from the centre of your body, and let them roll out. Wait. Let me show you.'

That was how, at fifty-two years old, Joaquin Moralès ended up dancing with his son in the middle of the night in the kitchenette of a seaside holiday apartment. He still didn't know what Sébastien was running away from or had come here to find. But who was he to judge? Joaquin was wading his way through muddy waters of his own. What was he trying to escape? And where were his desires coming from?

They had turned the music up loud. Corine's room was a distance away and the auberge was otherwise empty. They had drained the beers and every last drop of their strength. They had turned out the light and spent a long while contemplating the already-waning moon as it illuminated the estuary and sprinkled the water with silver sequins. The moon was a liar, that's what Cyrille had said. It gave Moralès the shivers to think that the same moon might be shining on Angel Roberts' white dress.

Father and son had then gone to bed at last, happy to be

together, out here on this peninsula, as far as the road would take them.

In the morning, Sébastien had joined his father for his morning run. When Joaquin had said he was getting up early to go back and explore a trail in Forillon Park with his running shoes on, his son had jumped at the chance to tag along.

Now Sébastien went over to the coffee maker and poured himself a refill. It had been a week since he made up his mind to confront his father and get things off his chest, but he still hadn't done anything about it. It was hard to find the right time. The day before, when he was on the road, he had resolved to get it out of the way as soon as he arrived. He had even made an effort to remember his arguments, but these had soon been dissolved by the fog, the scenery, the walk in the woods and the sweat that had soaked Kimo's top where it clung to her hips.

Now might be the right time, he thought.

'Dad?'

Joaquin looked up from his papers. He had been working since breakfast.

'I … er … Can I have a word?'

Joaquin put his pen down and pushed the case file aside. He had never been very good at father-son chats, but he would try his best. Because Sébastien was his son and he loved him.

'Of course. Sit down.'

Sébastien would almost have rather he had said no. In fact, if his father had got angry, it would have buoyed his spirits. The moment he sat down, he regretted it. Standing would have given him more presence. Sitting across from his father made him feel like a child again. How could he explain that he'd spent his whole life being submissive?

'It's about … er … Maude. But not just about Maude. Er … About her and—'

He was interrupted by the vibration of the phone on the table. Joaquin glanced at the screen. The call was from the Gaspé police station.

'That can wait,' Joaquin said.

Sébastien had seen his father's eye wandering.

'No, no. You should answer. It must be important.'

'Are you sure?'

'Of course, Dad.'

The detective took the call.

'Officer Lord here.' She sounded serious. 'We've found Angel Roberts.'

Without a word, Moralès looked at his son, who had heard the voice on the other end of the line. In an instant, a gallery of images illustrating the love between a father and his son, something they never talked about, flashed through their minds. Childhood hugs, cheers of encouragement in team sports, episodes of teenage rebellion, outbursts they never thought themselves capable of, moody silences filled with loathing – but also painful apologies and infinite forgiveness, because loving your child, loving your father, was something stronger than yourself. All these emotions that made a family and were woven into the intimate filial fabric welled up between this father and son because a woman was dead. Because she was someone's daughter and someone else's wife. Because she had left people grieving and her story would forever sink into memory.

'Where?'

'Apparently she's anchored somewhere off Gaspé Bay.'

'Anchored?'

'Looks like her body's attached to something underwater.'

Moralès knew what anchored meant, but there had been no sarcasm in Lord's voice, so he said nothing.

'We're going out there to get her. We'll be waiting for you on the coast-guard boat in Rivière-au-Renard.'

'I'm on my way.'

Sébastien got into the passenger seat without asking any details. They said nothing on the road, and nothing more when they arrived at the wharf. He followed his father aboard the coast-guard launch. Moralès simply nodded to Simone Lord and didn't explain why his son would be joining them.

'They spotted her from the coast-guard plane. They've given us her position. We'll be there in two hours.'

They went into the wheelhouse while Sébastien stayed out on the aft deck, watching the seamen cast off the mooring lines.

'That's the spot,' Simone said, leaning over a large paper marine chart and pointing to an area off the tip of the peninsula, just outside the mouth of Gaspé Bay.

The boat left the wharf.

Simone Lord moved her finger on the chart. 'Angel's dock is here. She probably followed this trajectory for about eight nautical miles before going into the water here. Her boat was carried away on the currents and found here.' She moved her finger much further south. 'We were looking in the right general area, but we didn't think she'd be that far offshore. The sea was calm this morning. Perhaps that made it easier for the guys on the plane to spot her. Unless the body only went into the water recently. Or maybe it was there all the time and only just resurfaced. We'll retrieve her and bring her ashore at the Sandy Beach wharf in town. Constable Lefebvre said the hearse would be waiting there.'

Moralès was silent, saddened by the sombre reason for this

outing. He looked out at Sébastien, being buffeted by the wind and the rolling of the boat. Stray locks of hair were whipping around his face. He hadn't said a word. He had just gone along with his father as if it were any other day, even though it had been months since they spent any time together. Joaquin had never told his son how this kind of death haunted him. Sébastien turned, saw his father and raised an inquisitive eyebrow. Joaquin gave him a sad smile. There was so much to say, but he preferred to respect the silence and let the time go by.

Sébastien stayed outside in spite of the cold. He had felt relieved when his father's phone rang earlier. The boat was sailing down the coast off Forillon Park. The big, loud birds – northern gannets and gulls – were slowly circling overhead, while the razorbills and seals kept their distance. The boat rounded the headland and veered to the south. After twenty-five minutes heading offshore, they slowed down and started to sail in increasingly concentric circles.

Officer Lord went out on deck in a diving suit, accompanied by another diver. She pointed to the place with a tip of her chin. 'There she is.'

The captain veered to one side and slowed the boat as much as possible.

Suddenly, Moralès saw her. And froze.

'*En la madre…*'

Sébastien was surprised to hear his father speaking Spanish. He leaned over the side to see. The woman was floating in midwater, a metre and a half below the surface, with her arms wide open and palms turned to the sky as if waiting to take flight. Her face was cupped by a halo of hair that swayed in the swell like Medusa's mane. Against the transparent darkness of the water, her white dress fanned out around her, concealing her legs and feet. She looked like an angel rising from the watery depths.

Moralès turned his gaze to Simone Lord. She swallowed, clearly shaken by the strange apparition as well, then gave a sigh and turned to the captain.

'We're going to dive from here.'

Not that the captain cared. He and his two crew members thought the whole thing was ridiculous. They'd made that clear on the way here. They had a rescue basket. That's what they'd told the detective. Just cut the line, hook the body, pull it into the basket, and bring it ashore like that. Just think how gross it'll be, they had added. All crab-eaten and stinky. They'd even cracked jokes along the lines of 'remember that time when…'. Officer Lord had told them to shut up. She was diving, no matter what.

'We're going down with cameras to take photos and see how she's anchored. Then we'll decide how we bring her home.'

The men had rolled their eyes; Moralès had frowned at them. There was no way he was going to let those coast-guard comedians make lame jokes at Angel's expense. He'd had to put his foot down – 'Is that really any skin off your noses?' – to shut them up. No, no, of course not, they'd replied. Anyway, it was their investigation. They could figure it out themselves. Simone Lord hadn't thanked Moralès for standing up for her, or at least leaning the same way. She had simply gone to put her diving suit on. Earlier, she had taken the initiative to call a diver she knew. A guy who took photos for the police sometimes.

She and the other diver adjusted their suits, masks, air tanks and gloves. Then they tipped themselves overboard, about three metres away from Angel Roberts.

Moralès went out onto the deck. One of the crewmen leaned out towards the divers and passed them the end of a steel cable with a hook, then winched it out to give them some slack. He and Moralès watched the divers descend beneath the surface, circle the body and take some pictures before turning a light on and plunging to darker depths. Soon the detective lost sight of them and could only follow the fading beam of light so far. He waited. His son stood a few steps away, not moving a muscle. The crewman felt two tugs on the cable. He turned on the winch to reel it in.

Suddenly, something in the water caught Moralès's attention. The bride had moved. She was floating closer to the surface. The divers had freed the rope and whatever was tethering Angel Roberts to the seabed. The other crewman lowered a cradle into the water beside the hull. The second diver lined the body up over it and gave the signal to winch it up. Slowly, the cradle rose. When Angel's body reached the surface, Simone Lord motioned for the crewman to stop the winch. They stabilised the body against the hull. The dead woman's tangle of hair was wrapped around her face like a net.

The second diver resurfaced. Something was attached to the rope. A red box. No, it wasn't a box. It was a trap, painted red. An old, wooden lobster-fishing trap. It had been filled with things to make it heavier. A block of cement and a pile of wet blankets. When they brought it up, a flood of water came pouring out. The crewman waited until most of it had drained away before swinging the trap on board. There was a chain attached to it. He set the winch going again to haul up the chain, which was connected to an anchor line. Meanwhile, Simone Lord clambered up the ladder, followed by the other diver. Moralès watched patiently. The cradle swung over the deck and Angel Roberts was finally on board.

Simone Lord approached the detective and spoke without looking at him – helping her colleague take off his diving gear as she did so.

'The trap was snagged on a bunch of half-sunken logs that

were slowly drifting offshore. If the seas had been any rougher, the logs would have carried her further out and we'd never have spotted her.'

She stopped, rattled that her superior officer had turned his back on her. Then she saw it was because he was moving closer to the body, crouching beside the cage-like structure they had lowered the cradle into when they carried Angel Roberts to the surface.

Moralès had heard what Simone said, but had nothing to reply.

'Well, she's all yours now,' she mumbled, shrugging her shoulders and leaving the deck.

Sébastien had observed the whole procedure. Now he watched Joaquin lean over the mesh that separated him from the dead woman. He thought about everything his father must have bottled up over the years as he investigated. He wondered if he was anything like a detective in a crime novel – haunted by the evil in the world. The crimes, the screams, the cruelty of the killers, the blank stares of the victims, the gallows humour of the other cops. It struck him that his father must have seen so much and tried, not to repair, but to understand and cast light on the things others had done that ultimately solved nothing. He thought about everything the man never talked about. His father was a vault of silence that never opened more than a narrow crack.

But now here he was, talking to *her*. Standing beside the cage, leaning over the bride inside. He was wearing gloves, but he couldn't touch her. She was too far away through the mesh. So he did what he could. He looked at her. And said something to her. Her name, Sébastien deduced. He was calling her by her name.

Angel Roberts.

She wasn't much older than his sons. Moralès looked up and saw Sébastien watching him. He waved and asked if he was all right. Yes, Sébastien replied. That was a lie. Moralès knew his son was lying. Out of pride, or just so his father could get on with his work. And his son knew that his father knew it. They were united by a kind of loyalty in spite of everything, a silent pact they kept renewing.

The captain was heading for a wharf somewhere down the end of Gaspé Bay. Where exactly, Moralès didn't know. The captain had slowed the boat with a shrug, seeing how insistent the detective was to linger on the port side, leaning over the corpse. He'd heard the guy's name earlier. Moralès. Another Mexican who'd come over here to take a local's job, he figured. A Latino who was doing some weird Day of the Dead stuff with the body of a girl from the Gaspé. Maybe the guy was a necrophile. In any case, he wouldn't have hired the guy. Not him, and not that Simone woman either. When she'd been with the coast guard, she'd done nothing but get a bee in her bonnet. Plenty were happy she'd gone off to play at being the fishing police. Wouldn't be surprised if she ended up the same way as that fisherwoman. The sea was no place for a woman. No. Not for a Mexican, either.

Moralès was still leaning over her. This was all the time he was going to get with Angel. As soon as they went ashore, she would be in the hands of the medical examiner, autopsy technicians and undertakers. They would examine her, cut her and reduce her to ashes. And she would elude him once more. Under the water, she had looked like she was flying. Now, her dress clung to her skin like long, slimy fronds of seaweed. Under the water, she could have turned to coral. Someday, her bones might have made some pretty jewellery. But she had decided to float to the surface. Why? Joaquin Moralès was profoundly shaken.

She was still dressed like a bride. Tiny hoops sparkled in her earlobes. Well, he could see one, at least. She still had her wedding band on her left ring finger. She wore no other adornments. No necklace, not even a simple chain at her neck. The fabric of her white clothing was torn. Moralès hoped the scrap the forensics technicians had found on board the lobster trawler would match one of the layers of material the garment was made from. There was a bluish tinge to her body. Her feet were bare. The sea fleas had made short work of her eyes.

The autopsy would tell him the rest of the story. What she had eaten, what she had drunk, the time of her death. Moralès wished he could hold up a hand and make her a promise. *Angel, daughter of Leeroy Roberts and wife of Clément Cyr, I will find who did this to you.*

But he couldn't. How many promises were impossible to keep?

Now the boat was approaching the wharf, Moralès stood up. No one had touched the lobster trap or its contents. Forensics would take care of that. The crewmen were getting ready to dock.

It was mayhem on the Sandy Beach wharf. The local SQ officers had closed the barrier to block access to unauthorised vehicles, but they didn't seem to have done much to stem the flood of reporters and other onlookers. It was going to be a challenge for them to dock.

Moralès walked to the stern, where Simone Lord was standing. 'Corine's rented me an apartment with a kitchenette on the west side of the auberge. That's where I'm going to work.'

She was facing the wharf, holding her diving gear, paying him next to no attention.

'I'm calling a meeting in ninety minutes' time.'

She shrugged. Moralès knew he could order her to be there. She knew that too. Neither of them said anything else.

She watched the crew carry out their docking manoeuvres. As soon as she could, she jumped down onto the wharf and went on her way.

Moralès looked around for Lefebvre. He was nowhere to be seen, but he had sent the two monosyllabic forensic technicians. They were there, and ready to get to work. They came aboard and picked up the wooden trap, examined the chain and rope, took pictures, cut the rope attaching the chain to Angel Roberts' legs, and loaded it all into their van. Then they returned to Angel's side, accompanied by two undertakers.

'Looks like you're needed over there, detective,' said one of the forensic technicians.

'Hmm,' said the other.

Moralès looked at them. They nodded towards the wharf.

Clément Cyr had not only vaulted a metal fence intended to keep onlookers back, but also ducked under the yellow tape the police had stretched between the wharf and the undertakers' hearse. Moralès watched as the officers on the wharf struggled to intercept the giant of a man. Too distraught to be mindful of his own strength, he could easily floor them if they didn't watch out. He was clearly in shock.

Moralès hopped over the side of the boat, back onto dry land. He turned for a second and saw his son disembark, taking in the whole scene. Now he wished he had spared Sébastien this experience. He wished he could spare him every painful experience in life. Not just the surface physical pain – scraped knees, scratched hands, bruised legs, sprained joints, sunburn and flu – but also the deeper, emotional pain of broken hearts, sleepless nights, work worries, personal qualms and the infernal tragedies of daily life. Some people said suffering turned boys into men. Moralès had always thought that was a load of rubbish. He looked at Clément Cyr. Suffering was no good to him.

The undertakers zipped what remained of Angel into a body bag. It wasn't the first time they'd collected a body from this vessel. Balancing it expertly, they slid the bag towards them and onto a small stretcher. Because the tide was out, the boat was sitting low in the water and no one on the wharf could see them at work. But when they carried the stretcher onto the wharf, Clément saw them and screamed that he wanted to see his wife and they had no right to stop him. The police officers securing the area were struggling to restrain him, but when he saw Moralès, the man called his name and calmed down, as if he were sure the detective would understand.

Detective Sergeant Joaquin Morales walked unhurriedly towards Clément Cyr. He was mostly trying to buy some time and give the undertakers the chance to load the stretcher into the hearse, which they had reversed as close as possible to the gangway.

'I want to see her.'

Moralès wanted to say yes. It was hard to deny a man something like that.

'What if it was your wife, Moralès?'

He wanted to give the man a word of advice, tell him to keep calm and not to be rough with people, not to touch the body, not to…

'Come with me,' he found himself saying.

The undertakers were just sliding the stretcher into the hearse. They stopped what they were doing when they saw Cyr with the detective. Moralès was surprised to see these were the same undertakers he had met some time ago in Caplan: the Langevin brothers. One of them was an insufferable chatterbox. He had to avoid talking to him at all costs. He turned to the other undertaker instead.

'Would it be possible to open the bag?' he asked.

From the other side of the stretcher, the chatterbox said, 'We can't do that, it's against the rules. There's too much risk bacteria will spread. Our code of ethics forbids us from—'

His brother, a thin, upright man, stepped towards Clément Cyr. The fisherman was much taller than him, but the undertaker looked at him the way a parent pacifies a needy child.

The chatterbox turned to his brother. 'You know full well it's not hygienic. You said it yourself…'

The quiet undertaker brought a finger to his lips to shush his brother. Now he spoke to Clément Cyr. 'Usually I tell people it's important to see their loved ones after they die, because it helps them to grieve.'

The giant's face cracked with pain. He understood what Langevin was about to say.

'But it won't help you.'

Thick tears rolled down Clément Cyr's face.

'I can do it. Open the bag and show her to you. But I'd advise against it. I can also take her back to my laboratory, make her a bit more presentable and give you a call.'

'When?'

'After the autopsy.'

'That's too long.'

The undertaker nodded. He knew that would be the answer. 'I'll tell you what you're going to see, all right?'

The husband acquiesced in silence.

'She doesn't have eyes or lips anymore.'

Clément Cyr looked down at the ground, either conjuring a mental image or trying not to.

'Her body is bloated from the water, and her skin is blue.'

He hung his head as if he might throw up.

'She's still in her wedding dress.'

Clément Cyr drew himself upright and lifted his gaze to the stretcher. He wanted to see her.

'I'm going to show you just her hair, all right?' the undertaker said.

The giant nodded.

Langevin opened the bag, just a little. The zip opened to reveal nothing but a tangle of wet hair, and Moralès understood that the undertaker had planned ahead for this. That was all Clément Cyr needed to see before he crumpled to his knees in tears. Tremors of grief rocked his body as he knelt there in a daze, mumbling his love for his wife.

Someone from social services came over and crouched beside him, had a gentle word in his ear and pointed to a waiting ambulance. Clément nodded and got to his feet like a disoriented puppet, allowing himself to be ushered into the vehicle and driven away.

Two men stood observing the scene from a distance. Leeroy Roberts and his son Bruce. Now the undertakers closed the bag, slid the stretcher into the hearse and drove Angel Roberts to the morgue.

The dead leave everything behind them. Especially the living. Angel's death was a tremor, and a shock wave of suffering was now spreading onshore. Her husband was beside himself, her brother looked like he'd been punched in the face and her father was hanging his head. The sun was beating down on the wharf mercilessly, almost too viciously.

Moralès watched the father and son weave their way through the crowd of onlookers, get into their pickup truck and leave the wharf. He looked over at his own son and saw that Sébastien was clenching his jaw. Moralès went to stand by his side. 'Maybe you shouldn't have come.'

'It's all right.'

The detective's mobile rang. It was Lefebvre.

'Now you're investigating a suspicious death, Detective Sergeant Moralès.'

'It's time for you to poke your nose out of your office, Constable Lefebvre. Come pick me up at the Sandy Beach wharf, and bring the whole case file with you … in duplicate.'

Sébastien was mentally going around in circles. He had no desire to go down to the kitchen and see Corine, answer her questions and make small talk.

He picked up his phone. In the hurry that morning, he had forgotten to take it with him. A stack of text messages and missed calls greeted him. Maude. He was suffocating. Seeing the dead woman's husband that morning, Sébastien had pondered the meaning of love. He threw the phone onto the bed, grabbed his windbreaker and left the room. He nodded to his father and Lefebvre, who were getting down to work in the kitchenette, then went downstairs and out the door to let the fresh air wash over him.

He walked east for a while, then turned on to the Rue du Quai. He wanted space to breathe, to let everything spinning around his head to percolate through his mind, but he couldn't even put words to what he was feeling. All he could think of was his father leaning over the dead woman and uttering those three words, *en la madre*.

He walked down the side of the coast-guard building and made his way to the water. There were five boats moored in the port: the coast-guard launch, which the crewmen were busy cleaning; three small trawlers; and a shrimp trawler at the big wharf around the corner. He kept on walking in that direction.

When he and his brother were younger, their mother had a habit of saying, whenever their father came up with a crazy idea, that it was the Mexican blood boiling over in his mind. They used to laugh about it. But did their father used to laugh too? Sébastien couldn't remember.

To his right, dozens of boats – a few massive shrimp trawlers, but mostly fixed gears, lobster trawlers and sailboats – were lined up on a patch of wasteland, resting in their winter cradles. Most of the fishing boats had a pickup truck parked beside them, a sign that men were at work.

Was there a chance he could be wrong about his father? What if he wasn't the cowardly, submissive man he had come here to confront?

He walked past the boat ramp and fish market, and continued along the paved road towards the big wharf. To the north was a low, wide cement wall, on the other side of which an army of concrete tetrapods formed a solid breakwater to deflect the energy of the waves. Vehicles were parked here and there along the big wharf.

A dozen souls were standing on the wall casting their lines into the water. Sébastien kept churning his and his father's stories over in his mind. All the things they'd said and all the things they hadn't were tumbling together in one big nauseating knot of deceit.

People nodded to him in greeting and resumed their fishing in silence. The lines caught the sun as their bait arced through the air, their lures breaking the surface with some of the few tepid sounds there were to be heard in the late afternoon.

The fishermen reeled in their hooks with an unhurried rhythmic cadence, slowing, delivering their coups de grâce, doing it all again. But the fish weren't biting. Time enveloped the fishermen's movements in its mechanical cycle, suspending them in its eternal waiting room. Sébastien stood and watched.

Lefebvre was impressed. Moralès had turned the kitchenette of his holiday apartment into an active incident room. Laid out in meticulous order across the large table were all the documents typical of a criminal investigation: timelines for the day and night prior to the disappearance, and the search efforts; names of people, grouped by family and boat crew, with the names of the boats as well; descriptions of places and the distances between various points on land and at sea. A map of the Gaspé Peninsula, complete with handwritten notes, was taped to the wall. A list of questions was poking out from under another page.

Lefebvre gave his superior officer a look of admiration. This was how a real detective did things. The constable tidied some papers to make room at the table for himself and Simone Lord, who was yet to arrive. Moralès reached into the fridge for three cans of ginger ale, then sat down. Lefebvre hadn't seen him take any notes at all, and had started to think the detective was disorganised and, quite frankly, a bit of an amateur. Now he stood corrected. This was where it was all happening. He took a seat at the corner of the table.

Moralès passed him a large notepad and pen. Lefebvre was thrilled; he had left his in the office. He opened the pad to a blank page.

'I want us to run through the list of people Angel saw last Saturday,' Moralès began.

He wasn't waiting for Simone Lord. He wasn't sure if she was even going to be there. He had to admit, he had admired her work that morning. When he had seen how the captain of the coast-guard launch treated her, he had realised what a bunch of macho men she must have had to work with, and figured that might explain her vehement determination. Then, she had bravely thrown herself overboard. Moralès had tried to imagine what she must have felt: the chill of the water against her diving suit, the contrast between the white of the dress and the darkness of the water, the suffocating sense of being confined by the diving gear, the waves and the proximity of the body of a young woman who could almost be her daughter. He didn't know if Simone had children. He knew nothing about her. Cyrille Bernard had given him grief before for being obsessed with death and not taking enough interest in life.

'Four days before their tenth wedding anniversary, Angel Roberts and Clément Cyr went to dinner at her father, Leeroy Roberts' place,' Lefebvre summarised.

The door opened discreetly. Simone Lord came in and sat at the other side of the table, opposite Moralès. The detective felt strangely relieved by her arrival, as if he had been holding his breath while waiting for her. She pulled a clipboard out of her bag, flipped to a blank page and picked up a pen. Lefebvre said hello to her and turned to Moralès.

'Just before that, they stopped in to see Clément's mother for an apéritif.'

Moralès frowned. 'I didn't know that.'

Simone Lord gave a sarcastic little laugh. Moralès tensed. He understood very well what that laugh meant: he didn't know anything about Angel Roberts. Come to think of it, what *had* he learned about her? That she liked to go camping with her husband, that she tended a vegetable garden with her best friend, that she worked with her uncle at dawn? Not very much. What Simone Lord didn't know, was that Moralès was most interested in the way other people saw Angel Roberts. Who might have imagined a scenario that led the fisherwoman to her death, and why?

Lefebvre opened his can of ginger ale. 'They went there at the end of the afternoon,' he continued. 'Clément's mother's name is Gaétane Cloutier. She lives around Penouille – not far from Cap-aux-Os, with her partner, Fernand Cyr.'

'I assume that's Clément's father?'

Simone shook her head. She couldn't believe the detective's ignorance. 'No. Fernand is his uncle. Clément's father died fourteen years ago and Gaétane Cloutier got together with the guy's brother after that. Fernand Cyr.'

Lefebvre got up and went to rummage around in the kitchen cupboard.

'How did he die?'

The constable returned with three glasses, but neglected to pass them to his colleagues. He seemed happy just to line them up beside his own can as Simone answered Moralès's question.

'Fishing accident. His boat capsized not far from L'Anse-au-Griffon. He drowned.'

'His name?'

'Firmin Cyr.'

Lefebvre burst out laughing. 'Firmin. Firmin and Fernand … Well, their parents had a sense of humour!'

Moralès tore a page out of his pad and made a note of this rough family history. Taking it upon himself to imitate the detective, Lefebvre tore a page from his own pad. Then he hesitated, decided he'd rather make a photocopy of Moralès's notes, and folded that page and pushed it aside.

'Does Clément Cyr have any brothers and sisters?' Moralès asked.

'Not that I know of,' Lefebvre replied.

'So, the couple went for a drink at Clément's mother's and stepfather's place at the end of the afternoon,' Moralès summarised. 'Then he and Angel went to Leeroy Roberts' place for dinner.'

'The two families don't get on well,' Lefebvre said.

'I've gathered that. Do you know why?'

'Old quarrels.'

'Can you be more specific?'

Officer Lord was compulsively doodling, the tip of her blue pen never leaving the page.

'Simone?'

His voice snagged on something. Moralès cleared his throat while she raised an eyebrow in his direction.

'Officer Lord, are you aware of any particular disagreement between these two families?'

Her concentration on her doodling didn't waver. 'You do know I'm just a fisheries officer…'

'Precisely. Would the disagreement have something to do with fishing?'

'When the cod moratorium happened, there were plenty of disputes over fishing grounds. That was a good fifteen years ago.'

Moralès wanted to ask her about the moratorium, but he wasn't going to indulge her. He could do without the attitude, and would do his own research. He carried on. 'Around six in the evening, they arrived at Leeroy Roberts' place for dinner. Bruce, the eldest son, who owns the shrimp trawler, was there. So was Jimmy, the youngest. He used to have a scallop trawler, but he sold it. Now he works at the processing plant in Rivière-au-Renard. Why did he sell it? Debts?'

Simone Lord shook her head. She tore off the page she'd been making notes on. Her peculiar handwriting looked like scattered islands of drawings. 'Lobster fishing wasn't going well in the area. Scientists explained to the lobster fishers that the lobsters were scarce because of the scallop trawlers dragging the seabed. Marine deforestation, that's what they were doing. Destroying the lobsters' ecosystem. So, the owners of the lobster trawlers joined forces to buy and tear up the scallop trawlers' licences. Since then, the lobster fishing has bounced back.'

'So, Jimmy Roberts basically sold his fishing licence to his sister?'

Simone started to fold her page as she spoke. 'Not just to his sister, to the group of lobster fishers she was a part of.'

'Did the scallop boat owners get bitter about it?'

'Not to my knowledge. They were paid well.'

Lefebvre tore another sheet off his pad and made notes here, there and everywhere, in an order all his own.

'And the couple ended up here, at the bar downstairs, at the end of the evening. I have the list of people who were here that night. I'll send it to you. Then, around eleven-thirty, Clément Cyr drove his wife home. He was back at the bar by around one. When he went home, around ten the next morning, his wife's car wasn't in the driveway. We all know how the rest of the day unfolded.'

Simone Lord kept turning and folding her sheet of paper. That was her way of being present without being subservient.

'There are three possible windows of death,' Moralès continued. 'Between eleven-thirty at night and one in the morning, when Clément Cyr was with his wife before he returned to the auberge. Between one and ten in the morning, when Angel Roberts was either alone or with her killer or killers. Or after ten in the morning, if the discovery of the boat was staged and Angel Roberts was dumped in the water in the last three days. Did the searches turn up any clues?'

Lefebvre finished his drink and stood up. He was getting

itchy feet. 'Nothing. But the autopsy report should help us to narrow down the day and time of death.'

'In the meantime, what are the possibilities?'

'Right, well, we can rule out the accident theory,' Lefebvre said.

'Yes, we can rule out an accident.'

'Let's be honest, it looks like suicide.' Lefebvre returned with a packet of nuts he had found on the counter.

'Let's explore that idea. Angel Roberts goes to her boat, sets out from the dock, motors fifteen kilometres or so, then turns the engine off. She fills a trap with blankets, drags it to the stern, ties herself to the trap and throws it overboard, and lets herself get dragged down to the depths.'

Lefebvre was chewing a mouthful of nuts. Simone agreed that could be a possibility. 'The knot was in front of her, so she could have tied herself up.'

'But forensics said she had an arm behind her back. Do you really think she tied herself up then twisted an arm behind her back?'

Simone Lord stopped doodling for a second.

Lefebvre sat down again. 'Maybe she had to scratch her back,' he suggested.

Moralès glanced at the constable's flotsam of notes and shook his head. 'That doesn't make sense. Why would she do that? So, in the middle of the night, she goes to her boat, casts off her moorings and says to herself, "Well, I've been married ten years, fishing season's over, so I might as well kill myself"? Seriously? Why go to the trouble of tying herself to a lobster trap? She was a long way from shore. All she had to do was throw herself overboard. That would have meant certain death.'

'Because she didn't want her body to wash up on the shore?'

'She could have just tied herself to the anchor. And she kept her wedding dress on. Why?'

'I suppose it might be a ritual or something.'

'An esoteric trip, really?'

Lefebvre wandered over to a shelf filled with board games in the corner of the room. 'Women can be like that, sometimes.'

Simone Lord threw daggers at him, but chose not to say anything.

Moralès continued floating the possibilities. 'She sets out to sea, contemplates the moon shining on the water…'

'Well, I suppose she might have had a bit too much to drink.'

'And she decides to "marry the sea"? Do you think that's plausible?'

'How should I know?'

'A wedding ritual with the sea on the night of the equinox? Is that something you've ever heard of?'

'No, but that doesn't mean it's not a thing.'

Moralès looked at Simone Lord, who was still silent, focused on her page. He had a vague sense that her silence, perhaps even her whole attitude since the beginning, might be hiding something.

'I don't know a thing about the women of the sea. Throw me a lifeline, Officer Lord.'

'Now you want me to help you?' She didn't turn away from her page.

'How many female fishing boat skippers are there out there? Maybe two or three in the whole of the Gaspé? Why do they do what they do? Why devote their lives to such a tough job?'

She shrugged, this time without any contempt. What could she say? She didn't even know the answer herself.

'Maybe they're obsessed with the sea?' Érik Lefebvre dropped a Monopoly box on the table beside the jetsam of his empty nut packet, three unused glasses, empty pop can, notepad, pen and torn-off sheets of paper.

Moralès raised an eyebrow. 'I'd like you to look into any groups with, er, interesting beliefs we should be aware of in the local area.'

'OK.'

'Go have a chat with Dotrice.'

'You're the one she wants to see, though.'

'You take care of it.'

Moralès stood and went over to the map he had pinned to the wall. Meanwhile, Lefebvre couldn't wait to get his curious hands on a decorative inukshuk that was sitting on a high shelf.

'Is there a reason why she might have chosen that spot? Is it a significant place for fishing?'

Simone Lord replied half-heartedly. 'Not to my knowledge.'

'For her?'

'It was completely by chance that we found her. The trap had snagged on a raft of dead tree trunks that was half floating in midwater. The chain was long, but it was probably just meant to weigh her down. It would have been easier just to use the anchor, though,' Simone explained.

'Why might Angel Roberts have wanted to take her own life? Let's take a closer look. Was she in therapy? Any reasons why she might be depressed? Any abuse or addiction? Is there any history of suicide in her family?'

Moralès turned to Érik Lefebvre, who was now turning the inukshuk over in his hands; the stones were glued together. 'Call her doctor tomorrow. Don't take no for an answer.'

'OK.'

They both returned to their seats at the table. Simone was still folding and refolding her paper.

Lefebvre still couldn't take his eyes off the inukshuk. 'Can you believe that, Moralès? You're supposed to balance the stones on top of each other, not stick them together!'

An awkward silence fell around the table. It was hard enough to get answers from the living, so it was better not to ask too much of the dead.

Moralès picked up where he had left off. 'What if she was murdered? She goes down to the wharf. How? In her own car?'

'Maybe she had arranged to meet someone.'

'At one in the morning?'

'A lover, or at least someone she knew.'

Could Angel have pretended she wasn't feeling well so she could go and meet her murderer?

'So, she and a mystery person go aboard the lobster trawler. Why?'

'I don't know. But still, they go aboard and head out to sea.'

'What next? She just lets someone tie her legs to a lobster trap and slide her overboard?'

'Maybe she was drugged.'

'Who would have drugged her? Her mother-in-law over drinks? Her family over dinner? Someone at the bar? Her husband?' Moralès hated that vile moment when loved ones became suspects.

'We'll get the blood test results tomorrow or the day after,' Lefebvre said.

'So, when she gets to the wharf, she goes aboard with her killer,' Moralès continued to speculate. 'They set out to sea and after a while, she passes out because she's been drugged. The killer ties her legs to a makeshift anchor, pitches her overboard and lets the boat drift. But how does he get back to shore?'

'It must be two or three in the morning at that point,' Lefebvre added. 'The boat is fifteen kilometres offshore and the water is only about four degrees Celsius. There's no way he could have swum back to shore. Maybe he brought a dinghy. Or a kayak. Or some kind of inflatable. That would have been strange, though. She would definitely have smelled a rat.'

'Or a second boat picked him up.'

Simone cracked a wry smile.

'Do you have something to add, Officer Lord?'

'You're just clutching at straws! You don't have anything concrete to go on.'

Moralès leaned back in his chair and looked her square in the face. 'Every suspicious death is the end of a story, Officer Lord. My job is to find the beginning. There are only so many possible reasons. Someone gets all wound up about something, whether it's revenge, money, love, gang business or wounded pride, and ends up so convinced they're right that they'll kill to have the last word.'

Exasperated, Simone Lord put her pen away and closed her clipboard.

Lefebvre sighed and placed the inukshuk on his notepad like a paperweight. 'Well, I'm on board with the suicide theory.'

Simone had made a hasty exit, and Lefebvre had gone off to make photocopies of the meeting notes. Now his hands and the chairs around the table were empty, Moralès saw the door to the holiday apartment opening.

Sébastien tiptoed in sheepishly. Looking at his son, Joaquin was moved. The whole day came flooding back to him, especially the striking vision of Sébastien standing watching him, pretending everything was all right as Joaquin leaned over the dead woman in her bridal gown.

He had never known how to talk to his boys, and now, here in this seaside holiday apartment kitchenette, he regretted that.

Too busy reconstructing other people's stories, he had always lacked the words to tell his own. No, not his – *theirs*. Sébastien had driven for more than twelve hours to come and see him. It had been four days since his son arrived, and Joaquin still didn't know what had motivated the trip. Cyrille was right, he had to talk to him before it was too late. Joaquin cleared his throat. He started to say something, then lowered his eyes.

Where Lefebvre had been sitting, an empty pop can still stood, along with a notepad, a scattering of papers, three untouched glasses, a game of Monopoly and, in the middle of it all, a glued-together inukshuk. *Is everything all right?* he wanted to ask. *What's going on with Maude?* All the questions were on the tip of his tongue. *Did she break your heart? Is it your job? What's troubling you?* In the spot Simone Lord had vacated, he saw an origami creation that looked like a seabird, adorned with graceful drawings in blue ballpoint pen. What did she know that she wasn't saying?

Moralès looked up. 'Are you hungry?' he ended up asking.

His son nodded. 'Yes, I'm starving.'

Father and son walked into the Brise-Bise and sat at the bar with their backs to the southwest-facing window, in front of the tap handles showcasing the local brews. Neither of them had said a word on the drive over here. They had listened to music instead. The barman came over. It was the same guy, with short hair and a long beard, as the other night. Louis. Behind him, the dishwasher was loitering impatiently, waiting for the next bin of dirty dishes.

'We'll have two amber ales.' Joaquin decided for them both. If they had nothing to drink, they wouldn't be able to eat.

Louis served their beers, handed them each a menu, and went to lean his hips against the bar a few steps away, beside the dishwasher. The Moralèses could hear the gist of their conversation.

Seems like they've found the missing woman. You know Clément, the tall guy who trawls for shrimp? He's here a lot when there's a live band playing. Yeah, I know the guy you mean. Turns out it was his wife. Oh, I didn't know he was married.

Sébastien waved the barman over. As he approached, he pulled his notepad and pen slowly from his apron pocket. 'Is your investigation going well?' he asked, playing the journalist.

A waitress came down the stairs from the mezzanine with a bin of dirty dishes, which the dishwasher promptly whisked away to the kitchen.

'We'll have the catch of the day,' Joaquin replied.

If he was disappointed not to glean anything about the investigation from them, big Louis didn't let it show.

'Could you put the TV on?' Sébastien asked.

'For sure, but I'll have to mute it.' He grabbed the remote and a football match sparked to life on the screen.

Joaquin raised an eye to the match and his glass to his lips, took a sip, then lowered his beer. 'That's the unfortunate thing about normality: it's just the ordinary spiced up with suffering.'

That was all he said, but it left him almost out of breath. At least he'd said something. When the incomprehensible squeezed you by the throat, you had to latch on to small talk about the weather, the sports scores, the ups and downs of fuel prices, your weekly chores and the daily grind to keep your head above water. His son nodded, and Joaquin felt a fleeting sense of relief.

The barman slid their plates of fish across the bar. A loud group came into the pub. Louis picked up a handful of menus and hurried over to greet them. The Moralès men ate their dinner, watched the match without seeing any of it, and then pushed their plates away. The barman cleared their places. Joaquin ordered another beer for his son and a coffee for himself. He still had work to do when they got back.

Suddenly, with his eyes glued to the screen, Sébastien dropped a question as naturally as a comment about the football match.

'Do you miss Mum?'

Moralès struggled to catch his breath. Did he miss his wife? He kept seeing the tangled mat of hair that had brought Angel's enamoured giant of a husband to his knees. He recalled Lefebvre's comment about beauty: when it seemed to have flowed away somewhere, the well of love must be running dry. Try as he might, he couldn't shake the images that had tempted him these last few days: the cascading of unbridled locks, the curve of a heel, a face shaped around a smile, the intriguing hint of vertebrae beneath the skin.

The barman put their drinks in front of them.

That morning, when he had seen Angel Roberts floating in the water, her arms wide open to the sky, her hair and her dress billowing around her, DS Joaquin Moralès had felt his heart pounding in his chest. He had stayed there for a while, kneeling over her, wondering why his heart was beating that way. Cyrille Bernard had told him many times that he was the kind of man who'd easily get carried out to sea – the kind who wanted to hold in his palm the infinite possibility of the world. Sitting in the bay window of his living room, Moralès had often wondered what the old fisherman meant. Tonight, staring at a soundless screen, it finally dawned on him what Cyrille had been trying to say.

What are you supposed to say to your thirty-year-old son? He hesitated. A moment too long. He took a deep breath, only to discover he had lost his voice. Again. Time to take a sip of coffee, he thought.

'I went down to the wharf in Rivière-au-Renard today.'

It almost made him jump to hear Sébastien speaking again.

'There were some people fishing. I stayed and watched them for a long time. All afternoon. I think I might take that up. Fishing, I mean.'

Louis brought the bill over. Joaquin placed his hand over it and finished his coffee.

'Fishing, that's a good idea.'

The two men stood. Joaquin wished he could wrap his arms around his son, reassure him, help him to make sense of the turmoil he could detect in his grown child's mind. He wished he could answer Sébastien's questions and talk to him about men casting off moorings, dispersing beauty at sea and holding the endless ever-after in their hands, but all he could bring himself to do was pick up the bill, pull out his credit card and pay for the meal.

Friday 28th September

Moralès had gone to bed late again. He had tried, in vain, to reach Cyrille Bernard. Then he had written up his report of the day on the kitchenette table and tidied away the random things Lefebvre had put there earlier. He had hesitated to do anything with the origami creation Simone Lord had left behind, and had held it in his hand for a long while as Sébastien contemplated the blurry horizon of a sea cast in the weak light from a moon caught in the clouds.

Now, as his son still slumbered, the detective decided to pay a visit to Jimmy Roberts. He drove down to the water and parked by the seafood-processing plant, where the end of the big wharf met the winter mooring yard.

A number of men were busy putting the *Ange-Irène* into dry dock. One of them was driving a huge winch on wheels that looked like a giant spider; he manoeuvred it over the rectangular loading basin that opened into the port.

Moralès got out of the car and walked over, staying close to the side of the processing plant so he'd be out of the wind. Two curious onlookers stood on the wharf commenting on the manoeuvre.

'They're going to slide those straps underneath to hoist 'er up.'

'Aye, but they'll have to be careful not to overload the lift like they did in the spring.'

They waved to Moralès.

'Is that Bruce Roberts' shrimp trawler?' the detective asked.

They nodded.

'Everyone here used to fish for cod, but since the moratorium, they've had to go after shrimp instead.'

'What moratorium?'

The men looked at Moralès as if he was from another planet.

'You must've come a long way to be asking questions like that.'

'Aye, that's proof no one in the city takes any interest in that sort of thing. They all want to eat fresh fish and juicy shrimp, but none of them'll stand up for the fishermen.'

The *Ange-Irène* motored slowly towards the loading basin. The onlookers didn't bother answering Moralès's question. Two men were holding a strap in place, ready to slide it under the bow before doing the same at the stern once the engine was turned off.

'You the one investigating the death of Leeroy's girl, then?'

Moralès said yes.

'What happened?'

The detective gave them a taste of their own gruff silence. Let them read into that whatever they would.

'Aye, well, she's not the first to kill herself around here.'

'Remember Jean Bournival?'

'Aye, but that wasn't the same.'

'What are you on about? Course it was!'

The man turned to Moralès. 'Bournival, he climbed up on top of his boat, right here in the marina, and he yelled to God to send him some fish. Gave him proper grief, he did. And what do you think happened? He got struck by lightning. Right under all our noses.'

'Aye, well like I said, that wasn't suicide, was it?'

'What do you call it, then? It wasn't even stormy out.'

'Course there was a storm brewing. It was cloudy and windy,

it just hadn't started to rain yet. That's why he went up on top of his boat, remember. The wind was ripping his antenna off.'

'Still, shouldn't have summoned the man upstairs, should he?'

'He was only messing around.'

'That's not something you joke about.'

'Well, we know that now.'

Suddenly, the door at the back of the processing plant opened and a sea of employees flooded out. Moralès saw Jimmy Roberts and Guy Babin. As soon as they saw him, they turned and walked in the opposite direction.

Moralès hurried after them. 'Jimmy Roberts, I'd like to—'

'He doesn't have time. We're only on a fifteen-minute break.' It was Babin who answered.

'I could bring you down to the station for questioning. The whole village would get wind of that. Or we can have a nice informal chat here, just the two of us, shooting the breeze.'

'Now you listen to me, the bloody police—'

Jimmy Roberts raised a hand to stop Babin from saying any more.

'It's all right, Ti-Guy. I'll take care of this.'

Babin glared at Moralès and sloped off reluctantly. The detective fell into step with Angel's younger brother, who pulled out a packet of cigarettes and lit one as they crossed the paved road that led to the wharf.

'What do you want to know?'

'I hear you used to have a scallop trawler. I'd like to know why you sold it.'

Jimmy slowed his pace, raised an eyebrow. He had probably been expecting to be questioned about moving the lobster boat, his relationship with Angel and his comings and goings.

'The lobster fishers banded together to buy all the scallop-fishing permits and tear them up. The biologists told them it was our fault there weren't many lobsters in the Gaspé anymore. They offered us a good deal. So I sold, like everyone else.'

The two men stopped on the other side of the road, where the breakwater for the big wharf embedded itself into terra firma. The huge boulders were there to protect the road from the autumn high tides. Now, the retreating tide had exposed a broad strip of kelp. Mushy waves were licking the muddy foreshore.

'And after that?'

Jimmy Roberts exhaled a breath of cigarette smoke full of contempt. 'What do you mean, *after that*?'

An odour of sulphur and salt wafted towards them on the breeze. A flock of gulls swooped down with a shriek and landed on the muddy rocks, beaks to the wind.

'What did you do with that money?'

Jimmy Roberts took a long drag of his cigarette. 'I paid off my boat.' He breathed a long breath out. 'And I got divorced. Costs a lot of money, a divorce, when you've got young kids.'

The gulls were jerking their heads haphazardly, lifting their beaks to the sky with shrill little snickers and smirks.

'I started work at the fish plant after that. Not as many responsibilities. The pay's all right.'

Jimmy Roberts tried to squeeze one last drag out of his cigarette, only to realise he was already down to the filter. He let the end fall to the ground and crushed it with the toe of his boot.

'Did you and your sister get on well?'

'Yes, why?'

'Because Jean-Paul Babin went to work for her, but you didn't.'

A refrigerated truck rolled by. Offended by the noise, the gulls took off with surly shrieks and whirled around overhead before swooping down again to take their places on the rocks and mounds of kelp.

'My sister Angel asked me if I wanted to work for her two years ago, but I said no. She came with the other lobster fishers to tear up my licence, you know. I have a bad temper and it was her boat, so I didn't exactly want to make her life miserable on board.'

The other employees were starting to file back in to work. Jimmy Roberts started back towards the processing plant. Moralès walked with him. The gulls looked like they were sleeping as the men left the boulders of the breakwater behind them and crossed the road.

'Mr Roberts, are you or your friends, the Babin brothers, going to try and take over your sister's boat and fishing licence?'

Jimmy Roberts barely broke his stride. 'I'm going to be late.' He had seen something in the corner of his eye that was turning left and accelerating towards the processing plant. 'I don't want them to dock an hour off my pay, OK?'

Moralès looked over his shoulder to see what had made Jimmy Roberts so quick to scarper. Jimmy's father's pickup truck was pulling in to park in the winter mooring yard. When the detective turned back, he saw the door to the building closing behind the youngest Roberts son. Moralès walked back towards the loading basin. The two onlookers were still there, watching the dry-docking manoeuvre in progress. 'I still say fishing's too hard a job for a woman. I mean, it's hard enough for a man, so can you imagine?' one said to the other.

As Leeroy Roberts let two big dogs out of the truck, the onlookers sidled over, took their caps off and shook hands with him. They were too far away for Moralès to hear what they were saying, but he understood they must be expressing their condolences.

The dogs ran towards the water and came to a stop near Moralès, who bent down to pet them. Leeroy Roberts bid farewell to the onlookers and walked over to the detective.

'My daughter was allergic. I had to put them outside whenever she came over to the house, even though she always took her allergy pills. The last time, her pills didn't work.'

Like the others, Moralès offered the man his condolences. Leeroy tightened his lips, because there was nothing more to say. None of these expressions of sympathy could bring the man's daughter back. He turned to watch the gantry crane hoisting the *Ange-Irène* out of the water. It was no consolation to see a fine boat like that, but it did give him a sense of pride. Because Bruce was good at his fishing. He knew how to bring in a good haul.

'They're going to bring her in right there, on the slipway. They park the *Ange-Irène* near the water's edge in the winter, because my Bruce's boat's the biggest. She's a bit too heavy for the boat lift, tends to overload it if they're not careful. So they don't want to carry her too far.'

Now that he thought about it, Moralès could hear a warning bleep sounding on the breeze.

'That's why they bring Bruce's out last. If the lift were to break down now, at least everyone else wouldn't still be waiting to put their boats in dry dock while they got it fixed.'

The shrimp trawler was now suspended in midair. Leeroy Roberts wished the detective knew more about big mobile machinery so that he'd appreciate what an impressive piece of kit this was. The travel lift started to carry the big boat forward.

'Do you often go aboard with your son?'

'Never. Two skippers on a boat are never going to get along. And Bruce is better than me. He went to university to study marine biology, and to the Maritime Institute. He knows all the technology, computers, sonars, and electronic whatnot in the trawl nets to measure the catch. You went aboard the other day. You must have seen all the gear. It's all lost on me.'

The travel lift was inching its way forward under the weight of the heavy trawler.

'These days, you have to study to go out fishing. Back in my time, it was the opposite. Fishing was what you did if you wanted to stay out of the classroom. "You're no good at school? Let's sell you a boat nice and cheap and you can teach yourself how to fish." It's no wonder fishermen were poor, they didn't have an education.'

A sporty-looking pickup truck drove up and parked. Two men got out and exchanged a discreet nod with Leeroy. The boat lift continued to inch towards its destination, warning sound and all.

'I've always said the sea's full of treasure; you just have to know how to find it.'

Moralès resisted the urge to ask Leeroy any more questions. He was worried he might put the man on his guard while he was still opening up.

'I learned the ropes as a deckhand in New Brunswick, then I went down to Maine. When I came back up here, I got married and bought my first boat. An old wooden beauty, she was. I chose to fish for cod. It paid well, but it was hard work. Back then, we used to haul up the nets by hand, over the side of the boat.'

The travel lift arrived at its destination. The men from the sporty-looking pickup truck went around to either side of the stern and started to stack big wooden chocks under the hull. Caught in a wave of nostalgia, Angel's father fished a crumpled black-and-white photograph from his wallet and handed it to Moralès. It was a picture of an old boat, on which a young, proud Leeroy stood facing the camera, arms folded across his chest.

'But down in Maine, I'd seen boats that hauled the nets up at the stern, not over the side. It made more sense, but the boat had to be built differently so the nets wouldn't get sucked into the propeller. And guess what, they pulled everything up with a winch! So when I came to buy my own boat, I found one with a winch in the back. It wasn't cheap, but it was worth the money.'

The dogs had now sniffed around all the potholes full of water and came back to sit at their master's feet.

Leeroy took the photograph back from Moralès and looked at it. 'It was a blessing in disguise, though, that boat going up in smoke.'

'Who set fire to it?'

'It was an accident. We were out at sea, me, my boy and my two deckhands. Not far, mind you, but there was a pea soup of a fog that meant we couldn't see a thing. On our way back to shore, we must have hit a rock lurking under the surface and bent the propeller shaft or something. Not that we noticed. We were out on deck sorting the fish. Unbeknownst to us, the engine had started to labour and it ended up catching fire. When we saw and tried to put it out, it was already too late. The whole stern was ablaze. We sent a distress call to the coast guard, launched the life raft and jumped aboard. At first, we wanted to stay close to the fire so it'd be easier for the rescue boat to locate us. With that fog though, it took a while for them to find us. It was dead calm out there, and all you could smell was barbecued fish.'

The two men from the pickup truck moved to the front of the *Ange-Irène* now and started to stack wooden chocks to support the bow.

'It all went south from there. My wooden boat was full of distress flares, you see. You have to buy new ones every year; that's the law. I never used to throw out the old ones, so I had a big box full of them. When the flames caught that box, boy, did we ever know it! The flares started to explode, and they were shooting out all over the place! My deckhands were scared a spark might catch the life raft. It was inflatable and made of rubber, you see, so we'd have sunk. So anyway, one of the guys took the little oar that was in there and started to row with all his strength to get us away from the fishing boat. But it was one of those circular rafts with a roof and just a little door on one side. And all we had was one little oar. What do you think happened? We just turned around in circles like a bloody spinning top!'

Now the chocks were in place, the man manoeuvring the lift started to release the tension on the straps cradling the shrimp trawler.

'The coast guard found us in the end, but my wooden boat sank. I ended up missing the rest of the season. It was hard because the cod-fishing moratorium was brought in around that time. You must have heard about that, I imagine?'

Moralès was reluctant to say no.

'From one day to the next, the government closed the cod fishery. Just like that, it was all over. Because my boat had just gone up in smoke, I had another one built, especially for shrimp, with a winch in the back.'

The warning sound stopped. The men unhooked the straps and let them fall to the ground.

'Some spiteful tongues went around saying I'd set fire to my wooden boat on purpose. It's not true. I'd never have risked my life, and especially not my son's and my deckhands'. But when the stars align like that, there'll always be a few jealous folk who make up untruths.'

These were bitter memories for Leeroy to recall. In his mind, he had always been a cod fisherman.

'When the moratorium came, our hands were forced. There was no arguing with the biologists and the government pen-pushers. Every last cod fisherman had no choice but to switch over to shrimp.'

He told Moralès how, the first time he moored his new boat at the big wharf, the others had come out to spit on it and had called him a shrimp thief. It seemed that Leeroy had earned his success the hard way.

Slowly, the boat lift backed away from the trawler. The men picked up the straps.

'It's easy to badmouth people who've been successful, but I've had to work hard for what I've achieved. Damn hard. And my boy Bruce has too. It's no coincidence he's got himself a fine boat like that.'

The two men hooked a metal stepladder on wheels to their truck and towed it over to the shrimp trawler while the boat lift, freed of its load, zoomed by them on its way to park in its usual spot over the loading basin.

'I ran into your son Jimmy before you got here…'

Leeroy motioned for Moralès to stop. He was expecting to hear that his youngest had slung mud at him. But he wasn't going to stand for his whining. Leeroy had raised all his children to work hard and hold their heads high; he had never had any time for leeches.

'Jimmy never stops complaining. He got a girl pregnant at seventeen. He married her at eighteen and before he was nineteen he wanted his own fishing boat. His mum and me, we told him he was too young, but he wouldn't hear a word of it. You must know, kids won't do anything unless it's their idea. Then afterwards, when it's all gone belly up, they come and blame us for it. Jimmy went through some hard times. He ended up selling his fishing operation. We all have to live with the consequences of our own lives, don't we?'

Leeroy Roberts tipped his chin and crossed his arms over his chest, becoming the proud man in the black-and-white photograph again.

'Was it you who asked your son to bring the *Close Call II* back to the Grande-Grave wharf the other night?'

'Yes. That boat's worth money, you know. We can't leave her just anywhere. We have to get her ready for the winter. Jimmy's taking care of it.' Leeroy shook his head in distaste. 'I told Angel she should choose another way to make a living, that fishing wasn't a woman's job. She wouldn't hear a word of it. Stubborn as a mule, she was. I'd never have thought she'd take her own life. But what do we really know about our kids?'

Leeroy Roberts turned and walked away with a weary step. He opened the back door of his pickup. The dogs bounded in and curled up obediently on the blanket covering the backseat. He closed the door. In the yard, dozens of boats were waiting for some end-of-season TLC. Their sides were streaked with wings of rust. They'd have to be repainted, again, to ward off the insatiable appetite of the salt and the sea in which they immersed themselves, such tiny hulls atop the infinite murky depths.

The fisherman trudged back over to the detective.

'Mr Roberts, last Saturday, your daughter Angel and her husband had dinner at your house. Who made the food?'

'The caterers. Corine took care of it, with the Morin girl.'

The answer came mechanically.

'Are you talking about Kim Morin, who teaches yoga?'

'Yes.'

Leeroy Roberts looked up and for the first time Moralès saw the grief that haunted him.

'I've been feeling like this since yesterday. The same way I did when my wooden boat went down. I'm spinning around in circles with my little oar on the life raft and all the distress flares are trying to shoot out of my body.'

He nodded goodbye to the detective, then sloped off towards the stepladder on wheels that was now docked alongside the shrimp trawler. Resting on her wooden chocks, a steady stream of seawater trickled off the *Ange-Irène* as she settled into dry dock for the winter.

Corine had tied her hair in a topknot and was just about to take stock of her freezers when he came into the kitchen. 'Are you heading out to investigate with your dad again?' she asked. She was holding a notepad, pen and marker.

'No. It's not really my place. I went down to the wharf yesterday and watched people fishing. I think I'd like to give that a go.'

Her eyes widened in surprise. 'Have you never fished?'

'Once or twice, when I was a boy. It looks pretty easy. Hold the rod to one side, cast the line, reel it in. How hard can it be?' Sébastien mimed the action of winding a little handle.

Corine smiled, unimpressed. 'And what lure are you going to use?'

'What lure?'

'What are you going to put at the end of your line?'

He rolled his eyes, as if that went without saying. 'A hook, of course!'

'A hook?'

'A hook and a worm.'

She laughed out loud. 'You don't have a clue!'

'Why do you say that?'

'No one fishes with worms in the sea. What do you think you're going to catch – river trout?'

Truth be told, he hadn't thought he might actually catch a fish. The day before, he had stood and watched the fishers casting their lines and reeling them in, and that choreographed performance alone seemed satisfying enough. Like those Far Eastern disciplines that consisted of endlessly repeating the same movement, integrating it into the body to free the mind. A kind of seaside Tai Chi to untangle his mental knots. The old man, Cyrille, had told him he didn't know how to look at the sea. Maybe that would come if he could just learn to see clearly. Lures and catches seemed incidental, somehow.

'I don't know. I saw my dad fishing the other day in Caplan, but all he caught was a log.'

'Do you have a rod?'

'I'll pick up a cheap one in the village.'

Corine shook her head in desperation. She put her notepad and pens down. 'Follow me. I've got a few I rent out to tourists in the summer.'

The auberge owner led Moralès's son outside to a storage shed by a rocky outcrop at the end of the property. The air smelled of kelp, and there was a chill in the wind. Corine opened the door. Inside was a meticulously organised treasure trove – equipment for the perfect summer holiday: windsurf boards, canoes, buckets and spades for the beach, and fishing rods.

She went straight over to the wall on the right. The rods were standing upright in little wooden compartments, as if they were a precious collection. On a workbench to one side sat two tackle boxes, one large and one small, each filled with hooks, floats, flies, lures of all colours – some articulated, others slimy-looking – each in its own little bag or in a packet with others.

From the large tackle box, Corine pulled a long silvery spoon with a red dot for an eye at one end and a hook with three barbs on the other. 'Here's your lure.'

She slid behind Sébastien towards the rods on the wall. There were a dozen of them, all in a row. She picked a simple-looking one, about two metres long, with a silver-coloured reel, and disengaged the bail to release the line. She pulled out some slack and attached the hook to the swivel at the end of the line. Then, she engaged the bail again, dug one of the barbs of the hook into the cork handle and tightened the line. Now she pulled the rod out of its stand and handed it to Sébastien.

'Why don't you try your hand at mackerel fishing for starters?'

She led him to a little jetty that reached out over the water.

'First, you release the hook,' she instructed.

He did as she said.

'Now, take the rod in your right hand. Let a bit more line out, it's too high. Hold it out to your right. Wait…'

She came to stand facing him, closer than strictly necessary, to show him what she meant. Sébastien was surprised by the physical proximity, but Corine seemed to think nothing of it.

'Slide your right hand higher up the rod and hold the line with your index finger against the handle. Now flip the bail open with your left hand.'

She touched his hand to show him, then stepped away. 'Now, swing it back and let the line go as you throw it forward…'

He did what he was told.

'There you go! Now give the reel half a turn, that'll set the bail back in place.'

He turned the reel.

Corine looked at the line, then at the rookie angler, and smiled. 'Not bad for a beginner. Now try reeling it back in. Not too fast. Find the right rhythm. That's it. Every once in a while, you can give the rod a jiggle to the side, so it'll look like the lure's trying to get away. That's supposed to get the fish excited.'

He looked at her. She was kind of pretty, he thought.

'You can borrow the rod. I'll lend you that small tackle box too, and a pair of pliers to take the hook out of the fish, and a few other bits and bobs. You'll be all right down on the wharves. If you've got any questions, just ask someone. Anyone else who's fishing will give you a hand. Oh, and you'd better put a bucket in your car as well, unless you want your carpets to stink of fish for the next ten years.'

Sébastien reeled the line in and stuck the barb into the cork handle like Corine had shown him. They walked back to the shed. Corine picked a few things out of the big tackle box and tucked them into the smaller box as she handed it to him.

'There you go, now you're all set for your first day of mackerel fishing!'

As Sébastien thanked her, he realised he didn't even know what a mackerel looked like. But that wasn't important. He walked to his car and drove off towards the wharf. As he turned the corner onto the Rue du Quai, he saw his father driving the other way, and waved.

Sébastien parked in the middle of the big wharf, on the same side as the breakwater. There were no other people fishing as far as he could see. It didn't matter. He took the rod out anyway.

On his way into the police station, Moralès was surprised to see the prison guard of a receptionist get up from her desk.

'Ah, good morning, Detective Moral-less. I have a message for you. Ms Dotrice Percy came by asking for you. She's a serious woman. You never know, you might be glad of her help. The night Angel Roberts went missing, Ms Percy says she witnessed an important event. She'd like to meet with you because no one here takes her seriously. Here, I've written her number down in case you've lost it.'

'We'll pay her a visit this afternoon. Thank you, Ms Roch.'

Moralès took the note, somewhat troubled that the receptionist had given him the time of day, although it had hardly been the kind of civil conversation he was hoping for. She buzzed him in without him having to ask.

Moralès walked down the corridor to Lefebvre's office, where the second surprise of the day awaited him. Lefebvre handed him a copy of the case file, photos, coast-guard report and all, without having to resort to an archaeological dig. In return, Moralès passed him the note he had been given by the keeper of the reception desk. 'Dotrice Percy called this morning, it seems.'

'I know, I've just got off the phone with her. She really would rather you went to see her. I think she'd be disappointed not to speak to the detective in charge.'

'That's not possible. I'm busy. Nice try, Lefebvre, but you're my best field officer.'

Lefebvre chose to ignore the comment. 'I stopped by the clinic earlier this morning. I spoke with Angel Roberts' doctor. She was in good health. No known history of depression or therapy, no hidden cancer that might have caused a premature death. No known legal or illegal drug use, either. She wasn't depressive, just overwhelmed by the world. Like you and me.'

'Is that what her doctor said?'

'I read between the lines.'

'Is that all?'

'She had trouble sleeping.'

'Have you had a chance to look into her husband's finances?'

Lefebvre nodded. 'They're pretty healthy. He paid off his shrimp boat with his share of the inheritance from his dad. He wants to buy a factory boat now so he can freeze his shrimp catch on board. Simone says it costs a packet though, and there's not much local expertise with that kind of boat. It's a risky move, but he's got the money.'

'Where is Officer Lord now?'

'At the Fisheries and Oceans office. Are you missing her already?'

Lefebvre's mobile vibrated. He took it out and read the text message. 'The medical examiner expects to have a preliminary autopsy report ready for us by tomorrow morning, about eleven. Meet me here and we'll call together?'

'I'll be here.'

Lefebvre replied to the text and pocketed his phone. He grabbed his jacket and walked with Moralès to the reception area.

'Come and see me at the auberge on your way back to keep me posted, will you?' the detective asked.

'OK.'

They were nearly at reception.

'Do you have a family doctor?' Lefebvre asked.

'No, I don't,' Moralès replied.

'Earlier, when I saw Angel Roberts' doctor, I asked her if she'd have me in for some tests.'

'You can't do that, Lefebvre. You have to put your name on the waiting list, like everyone else.'

'I know. I just thought it couldn't hurt to ask while I was there…'

As they walked through the door, he smoothed his thin moustache and said goodbye to Thérèse Roch.

'It's just a mutual agreement between a doctor and a police

officer. You scratch my back, I'll scratch yours. You never know when one of us might need the other's services. Plus, my mum used to be one of her dad's patients. Can you believe it? There've been three generations of doctors in their family. They must give each other stethoscopes for Christmas.'

'What did she say?'

'Her secretary gave me an appointment. I have to go in for some blood tests. Get my heart and my prostate checked. The job lot. You can tell she's a doctor who takes things seriously.'

Standing on the cement wall atop the Rivière-au-Renard break-water, Sébastien pressed his index finger onto the line, flipped the bail of the spool open and cast. In a golden arc, the spoon flew through the air and plunged into the water some twenty metres away. He gave the spool a turn to re-engage the bail, then set about reeling the line in slowly, jerking it a touch to one side and then the other.

His movements lacked flow. The rod trembled every time he turned the spool, and he was holding the line too high. Everyone he saw yesterday had been holding their line parallel to the water. He repeated the exercise. Two, three, four … soon fifteen times. Gradually he found some balance with the energy of his cast, the rhythm of his reeling and the angle of his line.

The waves were sweeping his lure towards the breakwater near the end, though. He would have to reel it in faster for the last few metres.

Moralès picked up a shrimp sandwich and made his way down to the Grande-Grave wharf. He ate his lunch under the tourist shelter, then walked over to the *Close Call II*, past the wharf where the anglers were teasing the mackerel. Something drew his attention as he stepped onto the dock where the lobster trawler was moored. The detective tried to put his finger on it. Whatever it was, it wasn't obvious. Some objects had moved since he was here with Jacques Forest. Buckets, buoys, maybe. Moralès pulled out his phone and took some photos of the boat. Tomorrow, he would come back and check if the objects were still in the same place. He walked back to his car. A few anglers looked up and followed him surreptitiously from the corners of their eyes.

Clément Cyr and Moralès pulled into the driveway at the same time. The men got out of their vehicles, but the giant didn't invite the detective in. His face was sunken, ravaged by a dark pain he was struggling to contain.

'Do you never call before you show up at people's houses?'

'I saw you coming, so I decided to stop in. I have a few questions to ask you. Do you mind?'

Cyr folded his arms across his broad torso. 'Go ahead.'

'Are you busy? Where did you just come from?'

'The Langevin brothers' funeral home. They've got branches all around the Gaspé Peninsula. They're all right, the two of them, but the eldest talks too much. He used to be a car salesman. Is that all?'

Moralès let a moment of silence go by. This wasn't the first time he hadn't been welcome somewhere.

'Can we go inside and sit down? I won't keep you long.'

'The house is a mess.'

'That's understandable.' He ushered Angel's husband towards the front door, as if he were the one inviting him in.

Clément Cyr sighed, threw his arms by his sides, trudged up the steps and opened the door.

Angel's already there, standing in the shadows.

Moralès followed Clément into the kitchen. The room was in disarray. Dirty dishes piled up, clothes and shoes lingered, papers were strewn here and there. Cyr was blind to it all. He only had eyes for the memory of his wife. It was all he could do just to keep a handle on his pain. He flopped into a chair beside the table. The detective sat down in turn in this haunted kitchen.

'How had your wife been doing, lately?'

'You've already asked me that question. She was tired. That's normal at the end of the season. She was having trouble sleeping. She was taking pills – melatonin, I think. Something she could buy over the counter, anyway.'

'Do you still have the container?'

'I would imagine so.'

He stood and went into the bathroom, on the left at the end of the hall. Moralès heard him open one door, then two, and close them again. Then the drawers. The widower returned empty-handed.

'I couldn't find it.'

'That's all right. Maybe it was empty.'

Clément sat down again.

Angel hasn't moved.

'Did you know the Robertses had taken the lobster boat to Grande-Grave?'

'Well, it needs to come out of the water for the winter. Jimmy will take care of it.'

Moralès was surprised how easily Clément Cyr seemed to have relinquished control of his wife's boat to his brother-in-law, but he did remember what Simone Lord had said about fishermen having their own ways of handling the sea. He changed tacks to throw the fisherman off.

'Did your wife have any food allergies?'

Clément barely blinked an eye. 'No.'

'Were there any other people at dinner on Saturday who had the same symptoms of nausea and dizziness that Angel was complaining of that night?'

He shook his head. 'No, but she was allergic to dogs. She had taken allergy pills, because there are two at my father-in-law's.'

'Was that the first time she'd taken that medication?'

'No, but she did complain during dinner that the pills weren't working. At one point, she took another one. With alcohol.'

'Did she drink a lot?'

'No.'

'Did she drink more than usual last Saturday?'

'I don't remember.'

The man's tone had turned aggressive as he clammed up. Moralès wondered what he was hiding. He decided to ask some less compromising questions before getting down to the nitty-gritty.

'Do you know if your wife had any esoteric beliefs?'

This time, Cyr raised a genuinely questioning eyebrow. That had caught him by surprise.

'Was she into meditation, or any other rituals?'

'I don't think so.'

Moralès took advantage of the fisherman's confusion to cut to the chase.

'Mr Cyr, are you a loyal man?'

Clément's eyes narrowed and his nostrils flared like a bull's.

Thick veins pulsed at his neck. He was clearly making an effort to keep a lid on this sudden welling-up of anger.

'What are you insinuating? That's all I am, bloody loyal! Do you hear me? Ask anyone you want: we Cyrs are honest folk. There's no wonder all the villagers were gobsmacked when they saw me with Roberts' daughter!'

'What's the story with your father-in-law?'

Clément Cyr composed himself. 'There's nothing to tell.'

'You seemed to be suggesting—'

'It's water under the bridge. We've settled our differences.'

Moralès sensed a lull in the man's temper; he had got the better of his anger and was probably regretting the outburst. The detective wanted to knock him off balance again, but knew that would be harder to do. He tried another angle.

'I'd like you to tell me if you know Kim Morin.'

'Yes, she teaches yoga in town.'

'How would you describe your relationship with her?'

Clément Cyr sighed in exasperation. 'She's nice enough, but she's a bit of a pain. She's obsessed with the sea. So she hangs around the wharf and flits around from boat to boat. Once I thought I'd be polite and invite her aboard to show her around. After that, she never stopped coming back, as if we were the best of friends.'

'Is that the case?'

'No. I'm a fisherman. I spend all my time working with men. I don't have any female friends.'

'Have you seen Kimo again in the last few days?'

'I've run into her in town. She says she wants to console me or something like that, but she just gets on my nerves.'

'Why?'

'Because nothing can console me.'

'Mr Cyr, were you faithful to your wife?'

The man swept a hand angrily away from his face, as if trying to get rid of something obstructing his view. 'Look, I can't be guilty of everything!'

Moralès wondered who he was talking to. 'What do you mean?'

Cyr couldn't take any more of Angel's scornful gaze or the shadows floating around this shambles of a home. 'That's enough. Leave me alone, now.'

Angel's exhausted husband looked down at his powerless hands. Nothing made sense, and nothing could change that. Joaquin Moralès understood that the widower was troubled by his wife's death. It would be strange if he wasn't. He resolved to make sure social services kept an eye on him. The detective stood, but his reluctant host remained seated.

'I spent the night alone at the auberge, if that's what you want to know. I like to let my hair down a bit, just like my old man, but I'm an honest person.'

Moralès nodded, turned his back and saw himself out. Before he got into his car, he went over to Clément Cyr's garage and peered through the window. He saw buoys, nets and waterproofs, a diving suit that would be too small for Cyr, snow tyres for the vehicles, a couple of bikes and camping chairs. Nothing resembling a boat. The detective walked around the back. Behind the garage were a number of metal cages for fishing lobster strung together. On the other side, he saw Annie Arsenault, kneeling in the vegetable garden, planting garlic. She looked up, nodded to Moralès in greeting and returned to her bulbs and cloves.

The detective returned to his car. He opened the driver's door and cast a glance towards the house. Through the kitchen window, Cyr was watching him with a hostile eye.

A different ringtone to the one he heard when Maude was calling caught his attention. Sébastien reached into his pocket for the phone and checked the screen. It was a local number. He answered the call.

'Ah! Let me tell you, this is Renaud Boissonneau on the line.'

'Hold on a second, just bear with me.'

Intrigued by the call, Sébastien reeled his line in, hopped down from the wall and propped his rod up against it.

'I'm all ears, Renaud.'

'I suppose you're in Gaspé with your father?'

'Rivière-au-Renard, actually. We're both staying at the Auberge Le Noroît, but I'm on my own at the moment. What can I do for you?'

'Well, let me tell you, I'm calling to see how the investigation's going.'

'Sorry, what investigation?

Sébastien had been so absorbed in his fishing efforts, he realised everything else that was going on had completely slipped his mind.

'The investigation about that young fisherwoman found dead in Gaspé. They're talking about it on the radio all the way over here. Was it your father who fished her body out?'

'The coast guard did, but he was on the boat. Why?'

'And are they saying it was a murder or an accident?'

Sébastien scratched his head. Renaud Boissonneau was only calling him to stick his nose into the investigation.

'I could always wait and read it in the paper, but nothing's better than hearing the news right from the horse's mouth, is it?'

For a moment Sébastien was taken aback by the server's

shamelessness, but then he had an idea. 'Tell me, Mr Boissonneau, is it true that my father has had affairs with women in the Gaspé, or is that just gossip you've made up?'

A surprised, uncomfortable silence trickled down the line. 'Jesus, Mary and Joseph! Let me tell you, I've never told or even dreamed such a wretched tale. No, sir. Your father is as sensitive to women as any Mexican police inspector, I imagine; no more and no less. And that's all perfectly understandable for a hot-blooded man. But don't you worry, he's as faithful as your mother would want.'

A wave of unease welled in Sébastien's throat. He had no idea whether his parents had spoken to each other or whether his father knew Sarah was moving into a condo in Longueuil. He had no desire to even think about it, especially as the fish weren't biting, Maude was whirling around his mind like a nauseating carousel and the sleek, choreographed movements that made the other anglers look so Zen, for him were all discombobulated and made him look like a ridiculous puppet.

'But let me tell you, the last time I saw her, she was really the one fishing for reasons not to come. Men like you and your father, you're perfectly able to dance with other women without taking them to bed.'

Sébastien couldn't deny that.

'And let me tell you just one thing, these investigations break my poor little heart too, you know. So anyway – that fisher-woman, are you telling me it's an accident or a murder?'

'I don't know, Mr Boissonneau.'

'I'm not asking for myself, you know, it's just in case I have any customers who are curious…'

'I don't know. I honestly don't. My dad's doing his detective work, and I'm out fishing.'

A disappointed silence travelled down the line. 'It's all right if you don't want to answer, we won't be any worse enemies than before.' Then Renaud Boissonneau surrendered his weapons and changed the subject. 'So what are you fishing for?'

'I'm trying my hand at mackerel.'

'Ooh, have you caught any? Chef says it's not easy to cook a fish as hefty as that. Have you found a good recipe?'

'Listen, if ever I find one, I'll call you back, all right?'

'Okey dokey. And tell me, before you hang up, is it true people in Percé eat like northern gannets, or is everyone here just pulling my leg?'

At the end of the line, what sounded like a bistro full of customers burst out laughing around Boissonneau. Sébastien ended the call.

'You're the detective's son. I saw you on the wharf yesterday.'

Sébastien looked up. A pickup truck had rolled to a halt behind him. The truck bed was loaded with buoys, lines, waterproofs and fishing rods.

'You're not fishing in the right spot. Your dad's investigation isn't going to wrap up overnight. As early as you can tomorrow morning, come and meet me at the Grande-Grave wharf. That's where they like to bite.'

The truck drove away, and Sébastien watched it disappear behind the fish-processing plant.

Joaquin Moralès parked outside the auberge. Sébastien's car wasn't there. He went inside, dropped his bags of groceries in the kitchen, crossed the dining room and climbed the stairs, glancing at his watch as he walked down the corridor to his apartment. Under one arm he had the file Lefebvre had given him that lunchtime and a notepad from his car that he had used to jot a few things down from his interviews that day – Jimmy Roberts' resentment, his father's nostalgia and Clément Cyr's latent guilt – but he wouldn't have time to write it all up before dinner.

Suddenly, he stopped and held his breath. There was a noise coming from inside the apartment. He put the file on the floor, took his revolver from its holster and double-checked it was loaded. The door was three steps away. Moralès crept forward and pricked his ears. Someone was rummaging around his apartment. He remembered leaving most of the case file on the kitchen table. He reached for the door handle and turned it slowly without a sound. It wasn't locked. He inched the door open. For a second, there was only silence, then Moralès thought he heard the sound of water, a gentle lapping.

He glanced warily around the room. The intruder was leaning over the detective's work table with a look of intense concentration, head covered with a colourful bandana Moralès recognised immediately. He swiftly holstered his weapon, picked up the file again and pushed the door wide open.

The young woman jumped and took three steps back. 'Oh, hello Joaquin. You scared me.' I was just giving your kitchenette a clean. Have you had a good day? Is your investigation going well?'

The bandana was holding her hair back from her face, and sweat was pearling on her throat. She had a bucket of soapy water at her feet and was holding a wet rag in one hand. There was a broom leaning against the wall just inside the doorway.

'Thank you, Corine, but I'd rather you dropped the cleaning routine until the investigation's over.'

She put on an overly formal smile.

'Ah, this is all highly confidential.' Moralès strode into the room and placed the file on the table with authority. As she wasn't showing any signs of moving, he walked back to the door and put the broom out in the corridor. Then he stood back and waited until she finally got the message that he was showing her the door.

'Thank you,' he said curtly as she left the room.

She forced a rigid smile and scurried away. A second later, Moralès cursed himself. He really wasn't acting very courteously or tactfully towards women lately, was he? He stepped out into the corridor and hurried after her.

'Corine?'

She stopped and turned around.

'I think I was a little short with you. I'm sorry.'

She gave a little nod, but said nothing.

'Do you have any dinner plans?'

She hesitated. 'Is it the detective who's asking?'

He shrugged apologetically.

She thought for a moment. 'Shall we meet in the kitchen?'

Moralès agreed. He returned to his apartment and hung up his jacket. It had been a bit over the top for him to draw his weapon and kick into action when it was just Corine doing a bit of cleaning. Of course, you could never be too careful, but still he felt ridiculous to have overreacted. To think he'd been ready to pull the trigger on an auberge owner who was tidying up the mess he and his son had created. From now on, he would keep the case file with him. That would eliminate any concerns.

Moralès went downstairs to the kitchen. He had tried to reach Cyrille, but no one had answered the phone. Corine wasn't there yet. He was taking out the ingredients for his recipe when he saw Érik Lefebvre park in front of the auberge and stroll in through the front door.

'Reporting for duty, boss!'

Moralès smiled. 'Have you eaten, Constable Lefebvre?'

'Is that an invitation?'

'If you like chilli.'

'Not only do I love chilli, but I think I also deserve a beer.'

The constable went to fetch a couple of bottles from the bar.

'I understand Dotrice Percy gave you the run-around?' Moralès said.

Lefebvre opened the bottles and took a long swig of his before collapsing on a chair at the corner of the service counter. 'Some people live in parallel worlds, Moralès. You'll never believe it.'

'Hurry up and tell me what she said. Corine and Sébastien will be here soon.'

'It's a sin to spare you the details of the decor in her meditation room. You really missed something there. Anyway, remember what you asked me to look into? It turns out lunar cults are a thing. Apparently the moon worshippers get quite excited on equinox nights. There are cults in the Middle East, cults in China, cults in…'

'Gaspé? Was there a cult thing here last Saturday?'

Lefebvre was disappointed; he didn't appreciate being rushed. 'Dotrice spent the night meditating at L'Anse-aux-Amérindiens cove, out on the whale-watching point.'

Moralès cast him a sideways glance. 'Is that all?'

'Yes and no. She said the moon had revealed some things to her – woo woo! – but she would only talk to the detective in charge.'

'You did tell her I was too busy?'

Sébastien's car pulled into the parking area.

'I laid it on as thick as I could, but she wasn't hearing any of it. As it was, she made me wait for an hour on the doorstep before she finally opened up, then as soon as I got a foot in the door she threw me out and cast a spell on me.'

'Did she have anything to tell you besides her tale of the naked monster?'

Sébastien walked into the dining room. Just as he was saying hello, Corine came downstairs.

Lefebvre mumbled a hasty reply. 'I'm afraid I can't answer that question right now, even if you are the detective in charge, because there are civilians present. Oh, hi Corine! Can you put these two beers on my tab?'

Corine had changed into a pretty autumn dress. Sébastien turned to look at her. 'Did you finish your stocktaking?'

'Yes...' She neglected to mention that she'd done some cleaning as well. 'Your hands are empty. Fish weren't biting, then?'

'No. Not even a nibble. Tomorrow morning, I'm going down to the Grande-Grave wharf, in the park. That's where they're biting, I hear.'

'Good plan,' Lefebvre chimed in. 'Hey, am I the only one who's hungry?'

Moralès smiled. 'I'm working on it. You'll have time for another beer.'

Saturday 29th September

'Good morning, Moralès. This is your favourite constable calling. Clément Cyr's down at the station. He says he has to speak to you, and he's not taking no for an answer.'

Joaquin looked at his watch. Barely eight o'clock. He and his son had just got back from their run.

'Where are you, Érik?'

'On my way into work.'

'Set him up in an interview room when you get there. I'm on my way. Make sure you record—'

'Relax, this isn't my first rodeo, cowboy.'

Twenty-five minutes later, Moralès gained entry to the police station with unusual ease. Thérèse Roch wasn't working the front desk that Saturday. A young, cheery receptionist was sitting in her place. She buzzed him in without batting an eye. A female officer he had crossed paths with a few times that week came to greet him and walked him to the interview room. There the detective found Clément Cyr, sitting on a chair that was too small for him, rubbing a nervous right hand against his thigh.

He stood and took a step towards Moralès. 'I'm sorry, I know it's Saturday, but I have to speak to you. It's important.'

Moralès greeted the man, closed the door behind him and the two of them sat down. Érik Lefebvre was already sitting behind the two-way mirror. Not that Cyr was paying attention, but Moralès read him his rights and stated his name and rank for the benefit of the recording. He had spent the night drifting between his bedroom and the kitchenette. Between his guilt and his wife's resentment.

'I'm listening,' Moralès began.

Clément Cyr was staring at the table. He didn't know where to start. The words seeped out one by one. 'I feel guilty. I can't live with myself anymore.'

His voice faded to a whisper.

'I killed my wife.'

The detective frowned. Clément Cyr had only been away for about an hour and a half that night. Moralès couldn't see how the man could have killed his wife, taken her out to sea aboard the *Close Call II* and dumped her overboard, let alone getting off the boat, swimming for kilometres, going home to change and getting back to the auberge in such a short time. And why would he have left the boat drifting? If the man had wanted to get rid of his wife, surely he would have just thrown her overboard and taken the boat back to the wharf.

'Can you tell me how it happened?' the detective asked.

Clément Cyr's eyes were crazed with fatigue. He could barely focus. His hands were clammy and trembling.

'Let's run through things in order, shall we? Tell me what happened when the two of you got home.'

The fisherman nodded, still staring at the table, but seeing right through it.

The road, La Radoune, slowly comes into focus in the twin beams of the headlights. White and yellow lines mark the way, ditches lie on either side for those who stray.

'Angel said she was feeling dizzy.'

Her hair is a little tousled, and she looks pale in that pretty white dress of hers that still fits after all these years.

'When we got home, she drank a glass of water. She was sitting in the kitchen. She was feeling queasy too. I just thought she'd had too much wine. I waited a while, not long, then I said I wanted to go back into the village.'

She looks at him with more than a shadow of doubt. Seriously? It's our tenth wedding anniversary, I'm not feeling well and you've got somewhere better to be?

'It was the end of my season too, and I wanted to let my hair down with the others. Plus, it's the done thing for the skippers to buy the rounds for their crew. I didn't want to look cheap.'

Angel stands and totters to the bathroom in her pretty dress with a heavy head and eyes filled with disappointment. He tries to follow her, but she shuts the door and locks herself in with her hurt feelings. He's talking to her, trying to argue his case.

'When you're an adult and you're feeling sick, you throw up and go to bed and ride it out. I told her she was grown-up enough to look after herself. There's never anyone there to hold my hand when I throw up.'

There's no answer on the other side of the door. He can hear some sounds, though. She's opening the medicine cabinet, popping the lid off a bottle, maybe an antinausea pill. He figures that will help her to sleep. She fills a glass with water. He keeps talking, but she refuses to break her silence.

'But Angel got in a huff.'

Eventually, she emerges from the bathroom and breezes right past him, doing her best to make him feel pathetic, him and his stubborn determination to go back for a drink with the boys. It works. He feels ashamed, but he's entitled to go back to the bar if he damn well wants to. Except he'd rather he had his wife's blessing. He wishes she would just say 'It's all right, go have fun. I'm going straight to sleep anyway'. Because she loves him and she wants him to be happy, that's what she always tells him. Because they do love each other, don't they?

'So I got changed, because I wasn't going to spend a night on the tiles with the boys in my fancy suit, was I?'

But she doesn't. She doesn't say it's all right. She doesn't say I love you, I'm going to sleep and have a fun night, sweetheart. She's sulking. And that rubs him the wrong way. He feels hurt and humiliated. He tears off his suit angrily. He tells her it's over. That's the last time he's going to dress up in that fake wedding suit and play this stupid masquerade every bloody anniversary. Do any of their friends do that? No, they don't.

'But we had a fight. Every couple has rows, don't they? I'm sure you've had plenty.'

As well as feeling nauseous, she's angry because he's showered her with hurtful words. So she replies with a sharp tongue, and the vein pulses at her temple like it always does when she loses her temper. But he's not going to be a pushover. She always gets the last word, and he's not going to let her steamroll him again. Because that's always the way it goes, isn't it? No it isn't, she protests. Everything's fair and equal in their relationship. That's not true, he hurls. He tells her she's being petty. Selfish. A spoilt child.

'Then I left.'

He's taking out his anger on the road, yanking the wheel, putting his foot down too hard. He's a free man. He loves Angel, but she has no right to control him. He can't say he's spent the last ten years of his life obeying her, that wouldn't be true, but they certainly do what she wants more often than not. He's sure of it. She makes a lot of their decisions. Usually that's all fine by Clément, but not all the time.

'I went back to the auberge.'

Clément Cyr couldn't hide the shame in his eyes as he looked across to Moralès again. 'Listen, detective, I'm not proud of what I did. But I hate being talked to like a naughty child and told I'm not allowed to go out.'

'What happened?'

'When I got back to the auberge, I hit the bottle. Hard.'

Moralès frowned in puzzlement.

'And I turned my phone off. I didn't want her ruining the rest of the night by calling me all the time. I just thought, if I didn't pick up, she'd be angry, but at least she'd sleep on it and we'd smooth things over the next day. She knows how religious I am about paying for my crew's rounds. Not every skipper still does it religiously, but my old man always did and I've kept the tradition going. I'm a man of my word when it comes to that sort of thing.'

He rubbed his clammy hands together.

'I got myself hammered and I slept it off at the auberge. But now I can't stop thinking that my wife wasn't well and I left her. I should never have done that to her, you understand? While I was out getting bladdered with my crew, Angel, she was…'

The giant of a man let his words sink into silence.

Moralès understood. Clément Cyr had been playing the scenes from that night over and over again in his suffering, grieving mind. One never-ending loop of the events he had experienced and the parallel events he imagined had unfolded in his absence. The fisherman was drinking and laughing with his workmates, reminiscing about the season they'd had and getting so drunk he could barely walk and had to be helped to bed in the auberge, in the nearest room, of course, since he was such a heavyweight. He had passed out fully clothed, sleeping off the drink while the few still standing at the bar joked about him. Meanwhile, Angel, his wife, was unwell. She was wearing her wedding dress, because she'd just celebrated ten years of marriage with the man she loved, but he'd left her to hold her own hair back over the toilet bowl. She was exhausted from the season that just ended, confused, perhaps depressed. She felt bitter and alone. So she decided she'd had enough. Of fishing, of her husband, of the ridiculous choice he'd made that night. She felt humiliated because the others at the bar would obviously have seen that her husband would rather abandon her, the woman skipper they all poked fun at behind her back, for them.

The young woman who had built her whole life on pride and forced her family to accept the choices she had made, who had taught herself, with the help of only a clueless uncle and a couple of unreliable deckhands, to fish for lobster, to dive to retrieve her sabotaged traps and to sell her catches; she who had stubbornly pursued this tough profession to live life immersed in the beauty of a sunrise over the sea, had suddenly had enough. Without even changing her clothes – because she didn't care anymore, because she loved that dress or because she wanted to make her husband feel guilty – she staggered out of the house and into her car and drove down to the wharf. There, she clambered aboard her trusty lobster trawler, started the engine, cast off her moorings and motored out to sea, where she decided to put an end to it all, her relationship and her life, in the middle of the night of the equinox. She'd just let the boat drift in the ocean she called home. Because it was her boat and hers alone, and she'd rather leave it adrift in the gulf than have it commandeered by a man.

Moralès looked at Clément Cyr. Usually, it was the parents of missing children who made confessions like this. They were haunted by their pain, by the shock of the grief, and when they realised they were powerless to save their offspring from their fate, they convinced themselves they were to blame. I thought he was at his friend's house. I got home five minutes late. I let her walk home from school alone. So many ordinary sentences and turns of phrase that belonged in every family's everyday life when conjugated in the present tense. But in the past tense, in a detective's office, these words spoke of personal trials, unforgivable mistakes and consciences wrecked for nothing.

The fisherman sitting in front of Moralès was almost begging to be found guilty. But how could any man know his wife has gone missing before it's been discovered? Moralès cast a glance at the two-way mirror. He suspected Lefebvre would be drawing the same conclusion he was.

'As soon as I woke up, I tried to call her, but her phone was off. She didn't answer the landline at home either. I thought she was still mad at me, because I'd turned my own phone off the night before, you see? I got home around ten the next morning. That was when I found her note. She'd put two kisses at the end, so I thought she'd calmed down. I thought everything was all right. But it was a farewell note and I didn't even understand.'

His gaze drifted around the room, as if he were recreating her in every corner, and recreating the spaces she used to fill.

She's there, standing at the kitchen counter, leaning over a drawer that's ajar, sitting in the armchair by the window. She's everywhere. She's chopping vegetables, drinking a beer, laughing out loud.

The more Angel filled the room with her presence, her voice, her jokes, the smaller the room became, and Moralès understood that. The void of this woman he had never met was taking up all the space.

'Angel's dead because of me.'

Moralès shook his head. 'No.'

But he didn't say anything else. He'd let social services do their job.

'If it weren't for my new doctor, I think I'd take up smoking.' Constable Érik Lefebvre was visibly shaken. He collapsed into the chair behind his desk. 'I hate that.'

Moralès pushed a box out of the way, closed the door, moved

two thick files to one side and freed an old armchair for himself.
'You hate what?'

'Working on the front lines!'

Moralès smiled in spite of himself. 'Have you ever had to
draw your weapon, Lefebvre?'

'My weapon?' He looked left, then right, to make sure the
walls hadn't sprouted ears. Then he leaned towards Moralès se-
cretively. 'It's not loaded.'

'Are you serious?'

'I'm a bad shot.'

'That's not a reason.'

'Yes, it is. If I fire an unloaded weapon, there's no way I can
shoot an innocent person. Anyway I figure my weapon can have
a persuasive power or a destructive power. I like to rely on the
power of persuasion.' He leaned back in his chair.

'I think it's time to call the medical examiner for the autopsy
results,' Moralès said.

Lefebvre looked at his watch. 'You're right!'

He put his desk phone on speaker and dialled a number. A
monotonous doctor engaged Lefebvre in conversation before
filling him and Moralès in on Angel Roberts' autopsy results.

'The external examination tells us lots of things. There are no
marks of violence, other than some slight bruising at the nape
of the neck. Nothing that would have caused unconsciousness
or a fall. No dirt or flesh under the nails either.'

'That doesn't tell us much,' Moralès replied.

'If you say so. The official cause of death is drowning. The
lungs are full of saltwater.'

'Would you be able to estimate the time of death?'

'Yes.'

'And what time would that be?'

'Hard to say.'

'But you said it was possible.'

'Do you know what time she had dinner?'

Moralès reflected for a moment before he answered. 'Between six and seven.'

'She died about ten hours later.'

'Around four-thirty in the morning?'

'If you say so.'

'Do you have the blood-test results?'

'Not yet.'

'When will they be ready?'

The medical examiner marked a pause. 'It's Sunday tomorrow. I'll ask if the lab can get the results to you this afternoon. I imagine I can email them to you?'

'If you say so,' Lefebvre smirked. He hung up and whistled between his teeth. 'Four-thirty in the morning. That means there's going to be a whole bunch of people with no alibi.'

Moralès stared at him blankly. 'What time did the party at Corine's wind down?'

Lefebvre shrugged. 'Late, I imagine. We're meeting the forensics guys at one. Time for lunch?'

Sebastien drove into the parking area at Grande-Grave. He had been awake half the night. He still hadn't talked to his father, but he wasn't avoiding it – or so he told himself. He just needed some time. Plus, he found fishing very calming. It was helping to give him the distance he needed before he broached that kind of topic. He got out of the car. Another angler's truck was abandoned in the far corner, between a kayak rental shack that was closed for the season and the trees at the foot of the bluff.

The horizon drew its gloomy curtains as the sky turned to

rain. The angler who'd told him yesterday that Grande-Grave was the place to fish was standing alone at the end of the wharf, with a bucket at his feet and a rod and line in his hand. He was dressed head to toe in green waterproofs. The man cast his line in one swift, assertive movement.

The boat belonging to the woman in the wedding dress was still moored at the dock. Sébastien shivered. He thought about Maude and tried to snap himself out of the nauseating melancholy that still smothered him. It was Saturday, and he was hoping to find somewhere to go dancing that night. He wondered if he should invite Kimo. He reached for his phone and texted Corine.

Suddenly, Sébastien saw the angler's line tighten. He had a bite! Sébastien was rooted to the spot. He was torn between getting his own equipment and going over to help the angler reel the fish in. Too late. The angler had reeled the line in quickly, and the fish was hooked good and proper, but all its writhing had attracted the seals. As soon as the fish was above the surface, one of the hungry mammals leaped out of the water, swallowed the fish whole, snapping the line in the process, and plunged beneath the sea again with a satisfied splash.

Mesmerised by this marine ballet, Sébastien Moralès quickly grabbed his rod and bucket and hurried towards the solitary angler.

Moralès and Lefebvre made their way down a staircase at the rear of the building and found themselves in the forensic-science laboratory. The place was small but well equipped, and impeccably clean. The two forensic technicians Moralès had spoken with when the men in the Roberts family brought the *Close Call*

11 back to shore were standing at a stainless-steel table, examining the severed rope that had been attached to Angel Roberts' legs, the anchor chain, the bright-red lobster trap and the blankets inside.

Lefebvre was happy to let Moralès take the lead. Given the choice, he would have stayed in his office.

'Where do we start?' the detective asked.

'Hmm. The rope,' said one of the technicians.

'Tied at the front, quite tight, around the calves, with what you'd call a bowline.'

'A bowline?'

'A common sailor's knot.'

The younger of the technicians pulled out a rolling chair, sat and slipped a length of rope, similar to the one on the steel table, behind his legs.

'Could she have tied it herself?'

'Hmm.' The technician stretched his legs out, pulled on both ends of the rope and tied the said knot with dexterity and ease.

'Good job,' said Lefebvre as the other technician gratified his colleague with a proud smile.

Moralès peered at the knot. 'Do you have to be a sailor to be able to do that?'

'Or a climber. One thing's for sure, you'd have to know that knot well to be able to tie it under pressure – in other words, if it's pitch-dark, you're on a boat in the rolling swell and you're about to kill a woman.'

'Hmm.'

'Especially as it's not a slipknot.'

'Which means?'

'It won't slip.'

'Hmm.'

Moralès didn't understand.

'It won't tighten when it's pulled. With a knot like that, someone who didn't know what they were doing might easily make the eye too big, and then the rope could have easily pulled right off whatever it was tied around – in this case, the victim's legs.'

'OK. So we should assume a certain familiarity with that knot.'

'Hmm.'

'Could she have tied it herself?'

The young technician nodded. 'I'm sure she did. There's a direction to this knot. The victim was sitting on the deck of the lobster trawler, on the port side, leaning against the wheelhouse. Logically, a killer would have been crouching in front of her. In which case the knot would have been tied in the other direction.'

The technician passed the rope to Moralès. He saw what the man meant. The knot looked like it had been tied the same way as the one on the table. Either Angel had tied the knot in the rope herself before putting her hand behind her back, or someone deliberately tied the knot that way to make it look like she'd killed herself. The detective turned back to the table. The technician stood and followed.

'Right, now the anchor chain. Nothing to flag there. It was probably already attached to the anchor line with this swivel. The line and chain were taken from the anchor well. The lobster trap had never been used before that night. The paint on the trap is the same as we found on the hull. The ropes of the funnel inside the trap were cut with a knife to make space for the three blankets. All three are old *catalogne* blankets. You know, the traditional kind woven from rags.'

'Hmm,' the older technician said.

'We wondered why the victim would have used the lobster trap instead of the anchor,' the younger technician continued.

'Perhaps the anchor was too heavy,' Moralès suggested.

'We thought about that, but the trap was weighted with a cement block and it's more cumbersome.'

'Hmm. I think the trap has a sentimental value.'

The younger technician turned to his colleague to acknowledge his contribution.

'Perhaps. Now, as well as the chain, there was a frayed length of thin cord attached to the top of the lobster trap. The other day, we found the other end of that cord on the lobster trawler. Attached at the stern.' He pointed to both lengths of thin cord on the table. 'It snapped under stretching force.'

'What do you mean?'

The two forensic technicians exchanged a knowing look.

'We think the trap was suspended from the stern of the boat, over the water, with this cord. It stayed there until the seawater soaked into the blankets. When they got wet, the material became heavier…'

'And the cord snapped,' Moralès deduced.

'Hmm.'

'We'll have to go back to the boat to test that theory. We need to know the height of the gunwale to see how it compares to the length of the cord.'

'We can go there now,' Moralès said.

'OK. And regarding the dress, we didn't find any signs of tearing, other than the scrap at the back that snagged on the bolt heads.'

As the technician spoke, he and his colleague had gathered their equipment and were eager to get going. 'Are you ready?'

Lefebvre looked at his watch. 'Listen, Moralès, I'm going to leave you to it. I'll take care of the lab report and see you at dinner time, all right?'

Moralès took a photo of the trap and blankets with his

phone. Then he called Jacques Forest to see about borrowing his key to the lobster boat, and followed the forensics technicians out the door.

Moralès was surprised to see his son's car was the only one parked by the Grande-Grave wharf. Then he noticed a familiar pickup truck beside the kayak rental shack. The rain had stopped, but the sky was far from inviting. The detective parked his own car and got out. He made his way over to the figures on the wharf, who were watching the seals cavorting in the water.

'When they're thrashing around like that, it's usually a shoal of mackerel,' the other angler told Sébastien.

Suddenly, one line pulled tight, then the other. The anglers swiftly reeled them in.

'Look at that, son, what did I tell you? There's a shoal of mackerel down there! You'll see, they're a solid and skittish kind of fish, they'll tug at your line. I'll have to take you out for a canoe in the bay. When you paddle through a shoal like that, the fish bash themselves up against the fibreglass, it's quite something.'

Son. That's what he had said. As he approached, Moralès found himself envying the man who was sharing this moment with his son. Fishing like this looked fantastic. The mackerel had silvery blue stripes, and the unexpected appearance of the sun on this greyest of days made them dazzling, even below the water's surface. They looked like shards of shimmering glass as they flirted with the lines. Joaquin reflected that the men were pulling glimmers of light, not just fish, out of the sea.

'Hi, Dad! Are you coming fishing?'

Jacques Forest greeted him in turn.

'I can't. I've got the forensic technicians in tow. We're going aboard the *Close Call II*.'

Forest nodded as Sébastien tried to unhook his first mackerel with a pair of pliers. With such an abundance of food, the seals had let him get away with one.

Moralès walked up to Forest and turned his phone towards him. The deckhand, encumbered by the line he was holding in one hand and the key to the boat in the other, set his rod down.

'Is that the lobster pot and the blankets that were on board?' Moralès asked.

Forest peered at the screen to see the photo the detective wanted to show him. 'Yes.'

Before Angel's uncle could string together a question, there was a sharp tug on his line. He quickly bent down to pick up the rod and busied himself with the fish he had hooked. Moralès went over to the forensics technicians, who were now waiting for him on the dock. He touched his phone screen to life again to scroll through the photos he had taken the previous day.

The younger of the two technicians beat him to it. 'We can confirm, without a shadow of a doubt, that the boat has been used since we examined it the other day.'

'Hmm,' his colleague concurred.

'We know the victim's brother brought it back here from Rivière-au-Renard with one of his friends…' Moralès explained.

'I mean it's been used for fishing.'

Moralès compared what he saw of the boat now to the photos on his screen. Perhaps the forensic technician was right.

'How can you be so sure at first glance?'

'Everything had been washed down with fresh water, probably because the fishing season was over. Now there are traces of salt all over the place.'

'Hmm. Fibres, too.'

'Elastic bands as well; the kind they use for lobster claws.'

'Hmm. Better check the hours on the engine log.'

Moralès looked at them both in turn. 'Can you check for prints and then clean everything when you're done?' He handed them the key and waited while they got to work.

The forensic technicians set off in separate directions without a word. The younger one went towards the stern, while his colleague took the key and opened the wheelhouse door.

On the main wharf, it looked like the fishing was going well. Sébastien was having a whale of a time. Moralès wished he had the Saturday off too, in spite of the drizzle.

'I've already lifted some prints in the wheelhouse,' the older of the technicians said, motioning for Moralès to come inside. 'We'll run them when we get back to the lab and let you know if we find a match.'

Moralès ducked inside and sat on the captain's swivel seat. What did Angel think about when she sat there? The wheel, levers, buttons, compass, duo of screens and trio of VHF radios: none of it revealed anything about her. The screen on the left was bolted to a shelf; the computer keyboard and mouse had been pushed to the back of another shelf below.

The technician came over, holding a spool of thin cord. 'This is the stuff the lobster trap was attached to.'

He led Moralès outside to join his younger colleague, who was taking measurements at the stern. 'The victim was sitting over there, on the deck, with her back against the wheelhouse,' he said, standing and pointing to the bow. 'There was a length of line tied around her legs. That was attached to the anchor chain, which was piled here, on the open tailgate. You can see where it was sitting, from all the scuff marks.'

'Hmm.'

'The other end of the anchor chain was attached to the lobster trap, which was stuffed with blankets and a concrete block. The trap itself was suspended over the water from this metal rod here at the stern, by the same kind of cord my colleague just found in the wheelhouse.'

He crouched and pointed to the rod that held the tailgate latch when it was closed.

'Hmm.'

'So, how long did it take for the waves to soak the blankets in the trap? We'd say ten, fifteen minutes, maybe longer. Depends how big a swell was running. The cord holding the trap above the water wasn't very strong, so it snapped under the weight of the wet blankets. The trap plunged into the water, dragging the anchor chain overboard, then the line, and then the victim, who was slumped over there. Suspending the trap with a cord that would take a while to break would have given her enough time to go sit over there and tie herself up.'

The forensic technicians exchanged a look of satisfaction and gave each other a high five, like two baseball players celebrating a home run.

'Why?' Moralès asked.

The technicians were putting away their equipment.

'Existential questions are not within our jurisdiction, detective.'

'Hmm.'

They left Moralès to lock up the boat and sauntered back to their van.

'How about we stop for doughnuts on the way back?'

'Mm-hmm.'

They got into their van and drove away.

Moralès looked at his watch and paused for a moment. He wanted to hang on to the key, but he didn't feel like giving

Jacques Forest an explanation. He waved to his son and Forest from a distance, and hurried back to his car as if he had an urgent matter to attend to, an excuse to forget he still had the key. He jumped into the driver's seat and drove away in a cloud of dust.

Annie Arsenault looked up from the window as Moralès approached. She smiled. Again. In spite of herself, perhaps, if she was as used to weathering heavy storms and staying afloat as he suspected. She had cried a lot, but didn't seem as fragile as she had the last time.

She came out onto the porch, closed the door behind her and apologised. 'My husband and sons are in the house. Maybe we can sit outside on the deck.'

Moralès remained standing on the steps and leaned against the handrail. 'I only have one question.'

'I'm listening.'

'Who's using the *Close Call II* to go poaching?'

The smile froze on her lips.

'Her uncle Jacques?'

She shook her head. 'No. At least, I don't think so.'

'Jimmy? With the Babin brothers?'

She sighed. 'Those guys are a piece of work.'

'Did they threaten her?'

Annie Arsenault took a deep breath and filled herself with all the strength and pride her friendship with the woman had bequeathed her – a woman who had not lacked courage.

'No. But Angel knew they were poaching with her boat.'

Moralès frowned. 'Did she see them do it?'

'Yes. She spied on them once or twice.'

'She turned a blind eye?'

Annie sighed. If there was one thing all fishers knew, it was that poaching came at a heavy price. Not only did they risk losing their licence, but also all the equipment that had been used for the poaching: the traps, the boat, even the vehicle used to carry it all down to the wharf.

'She did at first. But she didn't say anything, because her brother hadn't had an easy life. But just recently she asked him to pull up his traps.'

'When?' Moralès pressed.

'About ten days ago.'

'Why?'

'Someone threatened to report her.'

'Who?'

She pinched her lips and turned away.

'How do they do it?'

'They take the boat out in the middle of the night. They have a very narrow window to work with: two to three hours after high tide, when the current's running the fastest and they're sure no other fishing boats will be out on the water. Their buoys don't even break the surface, not even at low tide. They keep track of them by GPS.'

'Where do they go?'

She bit the inside of her cheeks. She wished she hadn't opened her mouth. 'Listen, this kind of thing is complicated.'

'Why didn't you tell me this the other day?'

She shrugged. 'I've got a husband and kids…'

She didn't say any more, but Moralès got the message. She was afraid they would end up in the middle of the bay themselves.

'All right. Thank you. Don't worry. This will stay between you and me.'

'I know nothing will happen to us, but…'
She was brave, but she wasn't naive.

Lefebvre was already there, sitting in the dining room of the auberge with his nose in a file, when Moralès walked in the door. A dessert plate and a potato masher sat on the table in front of him. He looked up briefly and turned his gaze back to the page.

'Turns out Angel Roberts had alcohol and sedatives in her stomach. A whole boatload. But death was caused by drowning. I've photocopied the autopsy report for you.'

Moralès sat down and opened the file Lefebvre had copied for him, while the constable, powerless to resist his urges, stood and went over to the counter to stare at a sugar bowl that had caught his attention.

'Shall we get to work, Constable Lefebvre?'

'That's all I ever do, Detective Sergeant Moralès.'

He brought the sugar bowl back to the table and put it down beside the file, a pen Moralès hadn't seen, the plate and the potato masher. Then he sat down again. 'Let's remind ourselves of the series of events. There's the drink at Angel's in-laws', followed by dinner at her dad's place and the soirée at the auberge. Angel isn't feeling well because she's drunk too much, and her husband drives her home. There, the couple has an argument and Clément Cyr goes back to the bar. Meanwhile, Angel gets into her car, goes down to the Grande-Grave wharf, hops aboard her boat, casts off her mooring lines and leaves the dock. When she's a fair way offshore, she takes some sedatives, ties a rope around her legs and attaches it to a lobster trap filled with blankets and a block of concrete that she then suspends over the water with a length of cord just strong enough to give her time to pass out before it snaps so she won't panic when she gets dragged overboard to her death.'

'What makes you think that's how it happened?'

'There were no signs of violence, and she left a note for her husband before she went, so he wouldn't worry.'

Moralès cast Lefebvre a questioning glance.

'I suppose the note was ambiguous,' the constable admitted.

'Suicide notes are rarely literary masterpieces,' Moralès replied.

Lefebvre stood and went over to the counter by the till. 'Shall we close the case, then?'

Moralès shook his head. 'Not yet.'

The constable leaned forward and then drew himself upright again. He returned to the table with the reservations book and added it to his little collection, beside the sugar bowl, his copy of the report, the dessert plate and the potato masher.

'Why not?'

Moralès remained tight-lipped. If he told Lefebvre about the poaching, he would be falling over himself to relay that information to Simone Lord. It was more than likely that she knew what was going on, although why she was hiding the information from him, the detective wasn't sure. In any case, he wanted to ask her himself, so he could catch her by surprise and gauge her reaction.

'I still have one or two leads to follow up. Any word from Simone?'

Lefebvre shrugged as he leafed through the reservations book. 'She's busy with an investigation, so I'm told.'

'Isn't she supposed to be working on *this* investigation?'

'What do you want me to say? Women aren't always at our beck and call, Moralès. It's the same for me. Thérèse Roch doesn't work every day, you know. Do I chase her home at night? No, I don't.' He kept flipping through the pages. 'I wouldn't dare. Did you know she lives with Dotrice Percy?'

'The woman who said she saw a naked monster?'

'Yes. I figured that out the other day when I went to see the seer. Don't you think it's strange to say I went to see the seer? Isn't she supposed to be the one who sees me?' Is that like a *mise en abyme*, you know, one of those images within an image?'

He thought for a moment.

'If she had seen my future in a crystal ball, I'd have been able to say I saw the seer who saw me. Anyway, turns out they're housemates. That explains why Dotrice always manages to sneak into the station, but don't get me wrong, I'm not the one who's going to blow the whistle on my sweet Teresita.'

'I need to see Simone urgently. Find her,' was all Moralès said.

Lefebvre closed the book and gave Moralès a knowing wink. 'Ah, I knew she'd got that Mexican blood of yours pumping.'

'Officer Lord?'

Lefebvre stood and put his jacket on. 'Who else do you think I'm talking about? I know you find her outrageously sexy, Moralès. I've seen the way you look at her.'

And with that, he walked out the door of the auberge.

Sébastien returned around mid-evening. Soaked to the skin, but smiling.

'I've got fish. Are you hungry?'

His father was still sitting in the dining room and had almost finished writing his report for the day. Sébastien took the fish out of the newspaper he had wrapped it in as he made his way to the kitchen.

'I think I'll try my hand at striped bass tomorrow. Jacques told me about a place he knows…' He might as well have been talking to himself.

Why would that happy young woman have taken her own life? Moralès just couldn't wrap his head around it. He wanted to be sure the poachers had nothing to do with it before he closed the case, before he called his boss and told her he was on his way back to Caplan.

Sébastien busied himself in the kitchen, boiling pasta, sautéing vegetables and flouring the mackerel, going on about spoons, bait and tides as his father pored over his report on the other side of the serving hatch.

Moralès cleared the table as his son brought out two plates and sat down.

Sébastien continued his enthusiastic monologue throughout dinner. 'Dad, you wouldn't believe it, seals basically have their own built-in fishing lures on their bellies, like an army general's rack of medals!'

The fish was a bit overdone. Joaquin didn't mention it.

Sébastien reached into his jacket and turned his phone on. It started vibrating like mad to deliver the backlog of text messages that had piled up. Moralès saw his son's face harden as he glanced quickly at the screen and put the device back in his pocket.

He wasn't particularly paranoid, and he wanted to trust her, but when Simone Lord took the Babin brothers and Jimmy Roberts down a peg on the wharf that first day, it had been obvious to Moralès that she knew them. Could she be covering up their poaching, or at least turning a blind eye? Moralès had a hard time believing it, but it wasn't impossible that they were blackmailing her. Maybe they had some kind of hold over her. Alternatively, she might not have a clue what had been going on. That would almost be worse, Moralès said to himself.

Sébastien ate quickly, then announced he was heading upstairs for a shower before going into town. 'Well, Gaspé's not exactly Montreal, but Corine's invited me to a thing tonight at the Brise-Bise. I have to get going. OK if I leave you to do the washing-up?'

Once Sébastien had driven away, Moralès got into his own car. He wanted to go and see what was happening at the Grande-Grave wharf after dark. If Angel Roberts' boat wasn't there, he would be making a call to Fisheries and Oceans Canada. He wasn't going to be doing anything too daring. He'd had his fair share of adrenaline rushes and broken ribs in his younger days as an undercover officer. As he grew older, the idea of getting beaten up somehow seemed less appealing.

He had a flask of hot soup and his case file beside him on the passenger seat. You never knew how long a stakeout might be. He could easily park at the side of the road and walk down to the wharf and back a few times throughout the night. He'd have something to read while he was warming up in the car, and it would keep Corine from poking her nose into his papers. Corine. He had crossed paths with her that morning. Rounding the curves in the road, his mind drifted to the young woman, and to Sébastien. He still hadn't had the chance to talk to his son. The time would come. Soon.

He passed the sign welcoming visitors to the national park, arrived at the toll booth and cursed: since the end of the tourist season there had been no camping allowed in the park and the barrier up ahead was closed after nine at night. There was no way to drive any further.

Moralès was reluctant to go back to the auberge. The police

had been milling around the lobster trawler for the last three days, so the poachers must be getting antsy. He didn't know how many traps they still had in the water, but they must be keen to pull them up. Maybe they had already collected them all. If they hadn't, there couldn't be many left out there. He should have tried harder to reach Simone Lord and alert the fisheries officials. It was eleven-thirty already. No one would want to help him on a risky stakeout at this time of night and at such short notice. Not to mention he hadn't opened a file about the poaching or requested permission to mobilise other officers.

He turned around and drove away from the toll booths, but just before he left the park, he noticed a dirt track on the left, between the road and the sea. He turned onto the track and saw that it led to a special pump-out station for emptying the waste from motorhomes. He parked at the end of the track in a little clearing in the trees and got out of the car to see if he could find somewhere to keep watch near the toll booths. Instead, he found the entrance to a walking trail. He took a few steps forward, then a few more. The ground was soggy and slippery from the rain. It was a dark night, but his eyes soon got used to the half-light. The trail led to a string of rustic plots for tents overlooking the sea. Moralès walked to the edge of the cliff.

About six hundred metres to the east, he could see the silhouette of a boat floating still in the shadows. He felt a rush of adrenaline, but soon saw that the boat wasn't the same shape as Angel Roberts' lobster trawler. Perhaps it was just a couple trying to enjoy a romantic night on the water at the fringe of Forillon National Park.

He walked back to the tent plots. Rustic camping areas like this were intended for people who liked the peace and quiet that came with having to leave their vehicles at the trailhead and hike in with all their gear, and it wasn't uncommon for several different clusters of tent plots to be connected by scenic trails that also led to the main points of interest for visitors. Maybe there was a path that hugged the water's edge and would take him nearer to that boat, ideally all the way to the Grande-Grave wharf. He reached for his phone, turned on the torch function and soon found a trail that seemed to lead the right way. Then he walked ahead, into the darkness.

They made it there eventually. He didn't really know why there had been such a delay. If he'd known it was going to take their trio that long to mobilise, he would have stayed with his father a while longer to ask how the investigation was going.

Corine and Kimo had had dinner together and he had gone to pick them up around ten. He didn't really know why the two of them hadn't joined him and his father to eat. Kimo lived right beside the auberge, a bit further back from the road, towards the shore. Maybe they had secrets to share with no one other than themselves. That was possible, Sébastien supposed.

He parked the car and the women got out. Corine gave him an almost consoling look. Kimo seemed so intent on giving the world the cold shoulder that Corine was worried her friend would put a damper on their evening. Kimo certainly seemed to like making things complicated. Especially her love life, Sébastien thought.

He wondered how she found the head space to do yoga. He watched her walking ahead and felt the urge to touch her. If only he could get her to dance with him. What the hell, he thought, and did a pirouette on the side of the street, took a bow and looked Kimo straight in the eye before they went into the pub. '*Vamos a bailar!* Come on, let's dance!'

It was the echo of a woman's voice, Joaquin Moralès was almost sure of it. He couldn't see the boat very well though, especially since it had no lights on and the night was as dark as a bear's cave. He had followed the trail until he was about level with the vessel, then forged his own path towards the cliff edge. Luckily the vegetation wasn't too dense. Still, his clothes were soaked through and his shoes were muddy. He was starting to feel the cold as well, but wasn't too concerned. Since he could barely see anything, he listened.

He could hear a few low voices, but one stood out above them all – a woman's. It was the intonation. It reminded him of Simone Lord when she was giving orders. He tried to see if it was a Fisheries and Oceans Canada vessel, but still he could only see a vague silhouette. What was that boat doing there at this time of night?

If Simone Lord had been planning a nocturnal mission to catch the poachers red-handed, she would have mentioned it to him, wouldn't she? This was his investigation, after all. He stopped, realising she would say exactly the same thing: 'This is my investigation, Moralès!' Unless she was in on it with the poachers. No. Moralès refused to believe that was possible. He heard the voice echoing again. It was only a murmur, but even the slightest sound carried over the water. He closed his eyes, listened, and then it dawned on him. It wasn't a voice. It was the muffled cry of a night bird. Moralès felt ridiculous. Old and ridiculous.

He tramped his way back to the path, troubled by how easily that woman could work her way into his mind. Was there any truth to what Lefebvre had said? Could there really be a spark between him and Simone Lord? He was haunted by that little bump beneath the skin at the nape of her neck. And oh, the scent of her. The aroma of damp earth, salt and a soupçon of woodiness.

Moralès found himself back on the path. It was barely any further to the wharf at Grande-Grave than it was to his car. It would be silly to turn around now, with the *Close Call II* just a few hundred metres away. Anyway, if he retraced his steps, staking out the area from his car would be pointless. The poachers couldn't come or go that way because the barrier was locked. The only way to shed light on what they were doing was to press on towards the wharf.

Sébastien had left his phone in his jacket pocket. He wanted to keep his hands free and feel unencumbered. The music was hitting the spot. He felt like a rum would go down nicely too, and made his way to the bar. That morning he had gone for a run with his father on a trail in Forillon Park. Then he had gone to meet a fisherman who'd helped him land his first mackerel and made seals leap out of the water. Later he had eaten dinner with his father and had a beer with the girls. Now he was going to dance.

He ordered a shot of rum. And thought about Maude for a second when he saw a bottle of gin behind the bar. He always used to drink gin with her. It was strange how living with someone had changed the way he defined himself. He realised he had done the same thing as his father.

The barman slid the glass of rum in front of him. Sébastien knocked it back in one. 'Another one.'

The barman nodded.

Could he really just leave her this way? After all these years, all those promises and plans, all those photos of her still on his phone?

The barman put a second glass of rum on the bar. Sébastien paid for his drinks. He knocked the second one back as swiftly as the first. Yes. He could. The alcohol burned his throat deliciously. He felt like he could roar. He span gracefully on his heel and swaggered over to the dance floor.

Now, where was Kimo?

Joaquin walked down the slope towards the wharf. Not a soul in sight. He crossed the deserted parking area, sneaked behind the diving school and crept his way along the bottom of the bluff to the back of the kayak rental shack. From there, he had a clear view of the wharf and the *Close Call II*. He shivered, even though he was dressed warmly. The path wasn't very long, but it was so wet and muddy he'd had to wade through the bushes to avoid the biggest puddles, so his trousers were soaked. He paced up and down behind the ramshackle building and checked the time. It was a quarter to two.

His phone battery was nearly dead. He should have told Lefebvre where he was going. He could have been better prepared. What was the plan now? What would he do if the poachers showed up? He would have to try to use the radio on the boat, or maybe even get hold of one of the poachers' phones, to call for backup. And what if they didn't come? He would have to walk back to his car. This time he would take the gravel road. It was a longer way around, but it would be easier going.

Still, he should let someone know where he was before his phone battery died. He could always call Sébastien. Why hadn't he thought of that earlier? He touched the screen to life and called his son's number. It was ringing. Still ringing. Then Moralès remembered his son was going out in town. The call went to voicemail. Sébastien hated checking his messages, especially these days. And Joaquin hated leaving them at the best of times. Beep.

'*Holà, chiquito!* I'm on a stakeout tonight in…'

Suddenly, the roar of an engine came down the road.

'…the park and…'

All-terrain vehicles. At least two of them. Moralès should have thought of that. Lots of Gaspesians used ATVs for hunting. The poachers must have made their way around the barrier somewhere. A dying melody told him his phone had given up the ghost. Moralès pocketed the device.

The ATVs came down the slope, their headlights scanning the area like search lamps. Moralès reached for the weapon in his holster and crouched as low as he could behind the kayak shack. He took in his surroundings. As soon as the poachers left the wharf, the detective could hop onto one of their ATVs and go to fetch backup. He smiled to himself. It wouldn't be that hard to collar them, after all.

That was when he saw the tyre tracks, an approaching beam of light illuminating the ground at his feet. How had he not noticed them before? There were several deep ruts leading from the parking area, which suggested more than one vehicle had recently driven behind the shack, reversed and gone back the way it had come, presumably on more than one occasion. The tracks ended right where he crouched. Evidently this hiding place was not as safe as he had thought.

He puffed out his chest. That was where the music came in. Not through the ears, but the lungs and the belly. He raised his arms above his head and let the dancing begin. The movements of the others on the dance floor didn't bother him in the slightest; he was oblivious to them. Dancing was his domain. It was the fire that pulsed through his veins, swaying his hips and haunches, legs and thighs, warming everything it touched with its glow. He bowed his head and clapped his hands in the air, channelling his inner rock star and tango king. With a laugh and a smile, Corine approached and gyrated around him. Men who liked to dance were few and far between. He took the young woman by the hand and the hip and pulled her towards him, then twirled her back into the crowd. Cool, untouchable Kimo was the one he wanted. Because dancing was a release for pain, and she must be a volcano just waiting to erupt beneath all those layers of stuck tectonic plates.

He caught her unawares, as she had her eyes on the band and her back to the dance floor. He walked up slowly, until she could feel the heat of his body behind her. He knew she could feel it, because he could see the goose bumps tickling the skin at the nape of her neck. She knew it was him, because he had provoked her the other day, because she was cold and distant, and he was a hot-blooded young man who would take it upon himself to try and remedy that.

He placed a firm hand on her hip, dug his thumb in just enough so she would yield a little, while he reached his other arm around her shoulders to hold her close. There was nothing vulgar or aggressive about his approach. He pressed a knee against the back of one of hers. She wasn't watching the band anymore. Her stillness was an almost desperate struggle. He bowed his head. She could feel the warmth of his breath against her neck, her earlobe.

'Let yourself go,' he whispered.

Suddenly, she yielded. As if a giant pair of scissors had snipped the strings holding her puppet of a body to a wooden crosspiece, she succumbed to his embrace. And Sébastien Moralès held her tight.

The ATVs were coming around the foot of the bluff now, just behind the diving school. Moralès seized his chance to slip around the corner of the kayak shack and stay out of sight. Now there was nothing between him and the lobster boat to hide behind. If the men parked where the tracks suggested they usually did, he would have to sneak along the facade of the building and turn the other corner before they caught up, like kids chasing each other around the sides of the house when they played cowboys and Indians.

The ATVs slowed down and came to a stop behind the shack. The men jumped down from their vehicles. Moralès could hear their voices bouncing off the water. He flattened himself against the wall and scuttled to the other end. When the men came around to the water side of the shack, he would slip around to the back side behind them. He certainly wasn't cold anymore. He could feel the sweat beading on his neck. On tenterhooks at the corner of the wall, he was watching, waiting.

Jimmy Roberts made a move towards the wharf, followed by another man, Jean-Paul Babin. Moralès seized his chance to dash to safety behind the shack, at the foot of the bluff. He breathed a sigh of relief, then poked his head out to see them going aboard. But the two fishermen had stopped halfway to the wharf. Moralès froze. They were looking right in his direction. He took a swift step backwards and instantly regretted it: he had just backed into the solid, unyielding chest of the third man.

Ti-Guy Babin grinned in the darkness. He had always wanted to teach a cop to mind his own business.

The music was choosing the rhythm. Sébastien guided Kimo slowly, rolling her like a wave against his body, gently breathing movement back into her. Now he slid his hand down to hers and turned her to face him, his other hand sliding from her waist, and drawing it to his.

He held her in a firm but gentle embrace. 'Dance with me, Kimo, feel the beat of the music in your heart. Remember, we're nothing but dust floating on the wind. Move your arms in mine, let's twirl under the stars.' But was it her he was trying to convince, or himself?

Sébastien Moralès leaned his face closer to hers. He lowered his eyes to look at her.

But Kim Morin stiffened and pulled away. 'I'm going home.'

She left him on the dance floor. The gig was over, anyway. The audience was clapping as Sébastien made his way to the exit.

Sunday 30th September

Moralès could feel the pain before he even opened his eyes. It hurt just to breathe. His whole upper body ached, especially his ribs. He blinked his eyes open.

'Good morning!' said a nurse in blue scrubs, giving him a gentle smile.

Foggy recollections started to drift back to him. The one blow harder than all the others that had sent him reeling into the side of the building and crumpling to the ground. The yelling and the reasoning: 'Are you nuts? He's a cop! I'm calling an ambulance!' 'It won't be able to get into the park.' 'The paramedics have the code to the barrier.' The blaming and the panic: 'You idiot, as if we weren't in enough trouble already!' 'What do we do?' The sound of the ambulance's sirens approaching – 'We have to get out of here!' – then the men roaring off on their ATVs, and the others who picked him up and took him away.

'Are you feeling better?' the nurse asked. 'The doctor's on her way.'

'What time is it?'

'Nearly eight o'clock. The doctor gave you a sedative earlier. Your wife is here. She wanted to be with you when you woke up, but I think she's gone to powder her nose.'

His wife? Moralès struggled to sit up. Had Sarah come all the way here? He tried to calculate how many hours had passed, but it hurt just to think about it. Still, he realised Sarah couldn't have driven here in such a short time. She must have flown.

The nurse took his pulse. 'I'll leave you to rest for a moment,' she said.

He closed his eyes. He had walked right into Ti-Guy Babin. That much he remembered. He moved a little. That wasn't too bad. Pain was something you got used to. He felt like he had a migraine. Everything was fuzzy. Had Sarah somehow found out that he had asked his ex-colleague to tail her. Who would have told her? Surely not Doiron himself. He was the colleague Moralès had always trusted the most, back in Montreal. His friend. He should invite him out here fishing sometime. He must have hit his head. Nothing was clear. How did he get here? He opened his eyes again. The nurse finished writing her notes on his chart and was just about to walk out the door. He could ask her to stay, but he didn't feel like asking a stranger all these questions. She left the room. He heard her run into someone in the corridor.

'Go ahead, he's just woken up.'

Moralès forced a smile. He would rather discuss his marriage issues elsewhere, and above all, in different circumstances. The door swished open and a woman stepped in. But it wasn't Sarah.

'Ah, we meet at last!'

He blinked, disoriented. A tall redhead with short, tight curls was standing at the end of the bed, peering at him. He felt a surge of panic and tried to sit up straight.

'Don't worry. I don't mean you any harm! But you must listen to me, detective. I've tried no end of times to get in touch with you. I've been to the police station, I've left my details at the front desk, but you haven't made time to see me or pick up the phone.'

Moralès sighed with discouragement and pain and flopped back onto his pillow.

'My name is Dotrice Percy, Detective Moral-less. I hope you don't mind me passing myself off as your wife, because I have some important revelations for you.'

She pulled a big hospital armchair closer to the bed and perched herself on the edge of the seat to make sure the detective could see her clearly. She was wearing a loose dress with the loudest of patterns. Moralès closed his eyes. Was this a nightmare, or were the drugs giving him hallucinations? Either way, it was an acutely unpleasant experience.

'I see things, Mr Moral-less.'

He thought about Lefebvre's idiotic utterance – 'I saw the seer who saw me' – and consoled himself with the thought that the painkillers would take the edge off the insufferable interlude he knew was coming.

'I know you can hear me. You're a sceptic; I can sense it. Your eyes are closed, but you can hear me. That's the way most people live. My eyes are wide open. The eyes in my body, and the eyes of my mind. That's how I see things other people don't. With the eyes of the soul.'

There were worse things than getting beaten up by Ti-Guy Babin, Moralès thought.

'Like every true seer, I adhere strictly to certain rituals, such as those devoted to the passing of the seasons. These are special moments, when one can make contact with the forces of the ascendant and transcendent universes. I know these realities escape you, but when the equinox comes, the air is charged with a raw vibration that must not be wasted. Especially in a time of lunar growth. The stars, Mr Moral-less, speak to us in a language all their own, through waves that sound, to the uninitiated, like whispers.'

She took a deep breath. Audibly, as if she were trying to suck the dust from every corner of the room. 'It's not easy for me to be in this place. It reeks of cancer and sick energy. This hospital is hurling silent screams. Within these walls, it's a world of suffering that's crying out to us.'

Moralès opened his eyes and stared at her without a word. If he ruffled her feathers, she would surely tell him he had the rancid energy of the lungs of a subhuman smoker. Or some other sort of nonsense. He hoped that a glare of hardened steel would be enough to make her spit out whatever she had to say. She took another deep breath and raised her arms to the sky like two halves of a circle and brought them down again, interlacing her fingers at her navel in a gesture of receiving.

'The night of the equinox, I was there.'

'When do you mean? Where?'

'The night when Angel Roberts went missing, I was meditating on the land of our red ancestors. Like a good sister-daughter of the moon, I was practising an ancient meditative custom where the all-powerful breath of the whales meets the earth. And that's where the vision came to me. The monster.'

'The monster?'

'A naked monster, with a translucent appendage and a shrivelled phallus.'

'*En la puta madre!*'

Before this investigation had started, Moralès couldn't remember the last time he'd uttered that old curse; and this time it was a more vulgar version than the one that had crossed his lips when they retrieved Angel Roberts' body. It was the one he used to hear from the toothless mouth of his maternal grandfather, who had been a fisherman. Now it surged forth of its own volition, and he was sure the clairvoyant would claim it was her – making things resurface from the depths of time.

Dotrice advanced towards him with her hands at her navel, joined and open at the same time, as if she were a baker carrying an armful of bread. 'The monster came right towards us.'

Joaquin raised his arms to push her away. The clairvoyant was so caught up in reliving her moment of enlightenment, she didn't seem to notice.

'The humans. The seers.'

'Dotrice, get out of my room.'

'He crossed right through the meditative circle and disappeared into the heather.'

Moralès rummaged beneath his bed sheets and eventually found and pressed the call button to alert the nurses' station. Dotrice stood and lowered her arms, then opened them wide and welcoming in front of her. She looked like Jesus with the children, Moralès thought.

'Our mothers, and our mothers' mothers, and their mothers before them read the signs and placed trembling fragments on the surface of the depths. They warned us that the sea is a liar, and all men are traitors!'

She walked towards Moralès like a zombie, then stopped and pointed both index fingers at him.

'Hypocrites,' she said in a throaty whisper.

The door to the room opened abruptly. Sébastien walked in, followed by the nurse, but that didn't deter Dotrice, who continued as if in a trance.

'I implore you to ask me, Moral-less, what celestial truth is holding my mind captive.'

'Ah, don't be swayed by father's Mexican charm,' Sébastien purred, taking control of the situation. He grabbed the clairvoyant by the hand, snatched up her bag – and her bloody crystal ball, Moralès thought – and set about ushering her out of the room.

The nurse kicked into action, her recent training on victims of family violence still fresh in her mind. Powerless to prevent Sébastien strong-arming Dotrice from her parallel universe into a hospital corridor, she turned her wrath on Moralès with an icy stare. 'What makes you think you can treat your wife like that?'

'Listen, she's not my—'

'If I have to strap you down to your bed, I will…'

'Be my guest, sweetheart!' Constable Lefebvre rushed into the room; he had obviously heard what the nurse was saying.

The nurse turned to see the new arrival and her face flushed bright red. She fled the room in a fluster, bumping into Sébastien on her way out, and slammed the door behind her.

Lefebvre looked at Moralès. 'You see, that's why I don't like working on the front line.'

'Hi, Lefebvre.'

'Hi Moralès, father and son.'

'I went down to the Grande-Grave wharf last night. I wanted to see who was taking the *Close Call II* out at night,' Moralès began.

'I know. We got a call at the station to tell us one of our own was wounded in action. So we sent two patrol cars out to the park, and guess what? They stopped two quads driven by Jimmy Roberts and the Babin brothers. Ti-Guy Babin span them a yarn about going out to the wharf to see who was poaching with Angel's boat, and spotting some suspicious character in the shadows. They thought the guy was dangerous, he said, so they wanted to take him down.'

Moralès couldn't believe his ears.

Lefebvre shrugged. 'You're an idiot for going out there alone.'

'Listen, Érik—'

'Good morning.' The door swished open to reveal an attractive woman in a white coat with a stethoscope around her neck. She had a slim, athletic build, narrow blue eyes and frizzy blonde hair tied back in a high ponytail – and a smile that brought a breath of fresh air into the room.

'Dr Turcot. Remember me? I'm Constable Lefebvre, your new patient. You saw me just last week. This is my colleague, Detective Sergeant Joaquin Moralès. He's the man lying here.'

Sébastien had to stifle a laugh at Lefebvre's star-struck enthusiasm, and Joaquin could see why the constable had been so keen to ask for a full checkup.

The doctor greeted Moralès and approached the side of the bed, placing a chart on the sheets as she leaned over to examine his injuries.

Lefebvre seized his chance to sneak up, grab the folder and peek inside.

The doctor raised an eyebrow. 'That's confidential.'

'I'm a police officer.'

Moralès shrugged. Lefebvre took that as permission and scanned the chart, giving a running commentary as the doctor proceeded with her examination. 'Nothing broken. A few bruises, and a mild concussion. What are you prescribing him? Valium? Dilaudid? Viagra?'

Dr Turcot smiled in spite of herself. 'Painkillers.'

Lefebvre gave Moralès a look of sympathy. 'Ah. Poor you. I bet that's disappointing, eh?'

'I'm discharging you, Mr Moralès. The nurse will be back in a moment to take you off the drip.'

The doctor took the chart back. 'Have a nice day, gentlemen.'

'Time for me to get going too, boss. Talk to you later.' Lefebvre's cowboy boots clacked on the floor as he hurried off in pursuit.

'Not so fast. I need you, Érik Lefebvre!' Moralès called.

The constable reluctantly turned on his heel as the door swung closed behind the fresh-faced doctor.

'Just as I was going to see about getting my blood pressure checked…'

'It's Angel's funeral this afternoon.' Moralès pulled the drip tube out of his own arm and used the dressing and tape holding it in place to cover the puncture in his skin.

He turned to Sébastien. 'Can you give me a lift back to the park, *chiquito*? I need to get my car.'

The detective pulled on yesterday's clothes. His coat was caked with mud, and his shoes were still wet.

'We've already been to pick it up. It's back at the auberge.'

'Is my case file still in there?'

'Er, I don't think so…'

'It was on the passenger seat.'

'I'll check.'

Sébastien accompanied his father out of the hospital, without managing to be of any real use. He walked ahead to open the doors, but they opened automatically; hurried to press the button for the lift, but it was already on its way; thought to retrieve Joaquin's health card from the front desk, but the doctor had already given it back to him.

'Érik, I have to stop by the auberge. I know it's Sunday, but I want to see you at the funeral, all right?'

The constable nodded. 'You can count on me being there. I'll get Jimmy Roberts and the Babin brothers to come in to the station.'

'It was light enough last night for Ti-Guy Babin to recognise me, you know.'

'I know, but he can still claim he didn't know it was you. Don't worry, we'll sort it out. They're going to spend the next few weeks being hauled in and out of interview rooms at all hours, and they'll be on our patrol officers' radar for the next year. If they drive fifty-one in a fifty zone, if their wood isn't strapped down right in their trailer, if their kids' car seats aren't bang up to code or if they raise their voices even once, we'll give them so many tickets they'll have to remortgage their houses. We've already slapped as many tickets on them as we could for their ATVs last night. And believe me, they'll never have blown into as many breathalysers in their lives. And we'll get in touch with the feds – the RCMP, I mean – to make sure all their firearms are properly registered. We've got it covered.'

As they approached Sébastien's car, Moralès turned again to his colleague. 'Ask the Babins what they were doing on the night of Angel's murder.'

'OK.'

'And I want to see Jimmy Roberts tomorrow.'

'He'll be there,' Lefebvre said, and sloped off.

Sébastien opened the passenger door for his father. Moralès stopped and turned to his son. Then he reached out and took Sébastien into his arms, pulled him close and kissed him on the cheek. Father and son stood face to face for a moment.

'How are your culinary experiments going?'

In the early hours of the morning, Sébastien had called his mother to let her know her husband had just been taken to hospital. She didn't answer her phone and she hadn't returned the call.

'I love you, Dad,' was all he said.

'I love you too, *chiquito*.'

The first unpleasant surprise Moralès ran into when they arrived at the auberge was Simone Lord, who was pacing up and down beside her truck. He should have expected this, he thought. She was so incensed, the auberge looked like it was quaking on its foundation.

'Go inside, Dad, I'll look for your file,' Sébastien said.

Joaquin nodded and got out of the car.

'You had no business meddling in my investigation, Moralès.'

'No, Officer Lord. Not today. We'll have this conversation tomorrow.'

He walked around her and into the dining room. His emerging migraine filled the whole space, but still she followed him.

'You went down to Grande-Grave in the middle of the night to intercept a gang of poachers, but that was not your investigation. It was mine!'

She was right. Moralès took off his wet shoes.

'Not only did you have no business being there, but you hid information from me…'

'I didn't hide a thing from you.'

'What were you doing there, then? Someone put a bug in your ear that the *Close Call II* was being used for poaching, did they? And did you think to tell me about that? No. You gave me hell the other day because you wanted me to respect your jurisdiction, but you didn't respect mine.'

'I would have been happy to respect your jurisdiction, but you chose to disappear for the last two days. I asked Constable Lefebvre where you were. Nowhere to be found.'

'All you had to do was call my office.'

'While we were busting a gut on a homicide investigation, Officer Lord, you decided to stop answering your phone and swan off on a little boat trip with your fishing friends.'

In her fury, she didn't see Sébastien come in, walk around her and disappear into the kitchen.

She took two steps towards Moralès and stabbed an accusing finger at him. 'Well, you just hit the nail on the head. You were supposed to be working on a homicide, not poking your nose into a poaching sting. You wrecked my whole bloody investigation because you want to control everything.'

Moralès opened his arms to the sky, desperate for someone or something to back him up. '*En la madre!* Look who's talking. How dare you throw control back in my face now?'

In the background, Sébastien put some music on so he could pretend he couldn't hear them.

'You knew from the very first day that Jimmy Roberts and the Babin brothers were poaching aboard the *Close Call II* and that might well be a motive for murder, And did you think to share that information with me, Officer Lord? No, because you were too busy keeping your own little investigation to yourself. A police officer was assaulted last night because you're too damned proud to work properly with a man. Now get out of my sight before I decide to share my version of the story with your superior!'

Sébastien had turned up the volume while his father made his point, and just as Simone Lord was about to lay into him again, she realised the cheeky so-and-so had chosen a tango number that echoed their back and forth. Moralès kept his mouth shut as it dawned on him how ridiculous his outburst had been. He was ashamed of the threat he had made.

Officer Lord let three bars of the music go by before delivering her parting shot calmly. 'You're an autocrat and a misogynist, Moralès. That beating you took, I wish I'd been the one to give it to you.'

With that, she turned on her heels and left. Sébastien came out of the kitchen and stood beside his father. Together, they watched her storm out of the auberge, get into her truck and slam the door shut.

'That neck of hers is something else,' Sébastien said.

'I know.'

'A hell of a temper, too.'

'She sets my head in a spin.'

'What vertebra is it that sticks out a bit when she leans her head forward?'

'I think it's the C3.'

Simone Lord's truck pulled out of the parking area.

Sébastien looked at his father and smiled softly. 'I couldn't find the case file. I looked everywhere.'

'*En la madre!*'

'Do you think someone might have stolen it?'

'I'll ask Lefebvre if someone at the station picked it up for safe keeping. Do you have my phone?'

'Yes. The battery's dead though, so I'll plug it in for you. Go have a shower. I'll rustle up a fish soup for us. Then I'll get some more groceries for dinner tonight.'

'OK. Thanks, *chiquito*.'

Joaquin headed upstairs. Sébastien returned to the kitchen and took stock of the fridge, then started preparing the soup. His father looked exhausted. He'd settle his differences and voice the reproaches he had come here to share with him another time. But he would never tell him that Sarah hadn't called back.

There was a strong turnout. Only creaks and sniffles broke the silence in the congregation. The sound of prayer echoed off the domed ceiling of the funeral home.

Leeroy Roberts was sitting to the right of the urn, with his son Bruce by his side. Even though there was space for two other people in the pew, Jimmy Roberts was sitting behind them. Alone. Neither his ex-wife, nor his children, who must obviously have known Angel, were there. The Babin brothers had chosen to sit a row or two behind, flanked by their wives and children. They seemed to be paying a great deal of attention to an elderly woman who was obviously their mother.

Moralès had arrived a little late and hadn't managed to find anywhere to sit, so he was standing at the back of the packed room with around twenty others. He took a step to the side for a clearer view.

To the left of the urn sat Clément Cyr, his shoulders shaking as he sobbed, seeing nothing but ghosts through the tears. In the pew beside him sat a petite, energetic-looking woman and a man with a similar build to Clément. Probably his mother and uncle Fernand.

Behind them was Jacques Forest, sitting beside a woman Moralès could barely make out through the crowd. Earlier, when he got out of the shower, the detective had listened to his voice messages. Apparently, Forest had been struggling to sleep last night, and he heard the ambulance drive past his house and turn off towards the national park. He got into his truck and went out to see what was going on, and noticed Moralès's car in the trees beside the road, he said. So he went over, noticed the doors were unlocked and saw the file was on the front seat. Worried the documents might fall into the wrong hands, he had taken them home with him.

The detective hadn't managed to get through to him earlier, since Forest was probably already on his way to the funeral service. Moralès didn't want to be insensitive, but he did want to get the file back that day. He especially wanted to make sure word didn't get out about what had happened. Jacques Forest obviously shouldn't have taken the file, but it had been a faux pas for the detective to leave it in plain view in his car.

The service was over now. People stood and waited while Leeroy Roberts stepped forward, picked up the urn and carried it down the aisle. A man weighing the gravity of his loss in his own hands. He held the whole life of his daughter – her first words, her hopes and dreams, her first bicycle, her lobster trawler – in that little container, and there was nothing to balance the other side of the scale.

Moralès thought about the Robertses and the Cyrs. The two clans couldn't stand the sight of each other, in spite of their shared grief. What could have caused so much bad blood between these families? The procession filed out through the double doors at the rear of the Langevin brothers' funeral home.

Moralès raised his eyebrows in surprise when he saw the woman walking by Jacques Forest's side. It was his boss, Marlène. The resemblance between them was striking. As he caught her eye, it dawned on the detective that Lieutenant Marlène Forest must be Angel's aunt – her late mother's sister. As his boss walked outside, Moralès wondered why she hadn't told him she was sending him to investigate the disappearance of her niece.

The crowd filed out in a procession of tiptoes, whispers, crumpled tissues, buttoning-up of coats and children happy to see long-lost friends and relatives again.

Moralès noticed Corine and Kimo in the corner of the room, waiting their turn to step out into the fresh air. Kimo's lips were pursed. She seemed to be using Corine as a screen – to protect herself from getting too close to other people. Corine caught Moralès's eye, gave him a nod of greeting, then whispered something in her friend's ear. Kimo's eyes were scanning the crowd. When her gaze landed on the detective, she nodded coldly and turned away. Seeing a gap open up in front of them, the two young women weaved their way through the others to a side door, clearly choosing not to say goodbye to the families. As Moralès crossed the threshold, he saw them striding away through a sea of parked cars.

Meanwhile, the tide of friends and family marched on towards the cemetery. Moralès chose not to join them. He had seen Érik Lefebvre and Simone Lord among the crowd. If anything of significance for the investigation happened, Lefebvre would let him know. A few people were waiting for the mourners to return from the cemetery on a small circular patio planted with perennials and dotted with benches. The funeral home was built on a hill, embracing a partial view of Gaspé Bay. The sun felt pleasantly warm, and Moralès decided to sit for a while too.

Jacques Forest arrived back from the cemetery with Annie Arsenault by his side. She was planning a fishing outing, by the sounds of it.

'Friday morning would be good for me. The tide should be right for us to make it to L'Anse-aux-Amérindiens,' she said.

'Good idea. Do you mind if I invite Sébastien? He's Mr Moralès's son.'

Angel Roberts' friend said hello to Joaquin.

'Not at all. You'd be welcome to join us too, detective.'

Joaquin gave the two Gaspesians a questioning look.

Annie smiled at him softly. 'I have a boat. It's not very big, but it's comfortable enough for four or five passengers. Jacques and I are going sea fishing on Friday. In the morning, because of the tide. You and your son would be welcome to join us. It might give you a bit of a break.'

'With pleasure; I love fishing.'

She gave them a sad, pained smile that struggled to light up her eyes, then went to join her husband and sons.

Marlène Forest finally came over to him. She had been chatting with Lefebvre and Lord, who had now stopped to have a word with the Langevin brothers. Moralès awkwardly offered her his condolences. He didn't like these stilted formalities. He felt like a vulture circling over other people's dramas. Arriving after the kill. Too late to change a thing.

'Was it you who sent the forensics team the day the boat was found?' he asked.

'Yes. And I was the one who asked for you to be assigned to this investigation.'

'Why didn't you tell me Angel was your niece?'

She shrugged and looked away. Her brother stood motionless by her side. 'I can't be seen to intervene in the investigation; I might be accused of a conflict of interest,' she explained. 'But if you don't mind, I'd like to finish reading your file tonight, at my brother's place.'

That was why Jacques Forest had been so keen to scoop up the case file: so his sister could read it.

'You can have it back tomorrow morning,' she continued. 'For once, I have to admit I'm not displeased to see you make a blunder.'

Moralès nodded uncomfortably. At the moment, the file was a mess. There were too many indecisive leads, no reliable witnesses, no motive for murder and the suggestion that the murderer managed to perform the impossible feat of returning to dry land without a boat.

'By all appearances, it looks like your niece might have taken her own life, Marlène.'

She took a deep breath. 'When a woman commits suicide, no one beats up the detective who's investigating.'

He didn't say anything.

'Listen, Moralès. I'm not supposed to stick my oar in, but I'm going to tell you something, strictly as the victim's aunt.'

He didn't move a muscle, just waited to hear what she was about to reveal.

She glanced at her brother. 'My sister, our sister, married Roberts, and we never understood why. My sister, my brother and I inherited a fair bit of money from our father, so we always thought Leeroy married Irène for the money. Right after the wedding, he went and bought himself a fancy boat in New Brunswick. He started showing off, saying French-Canadian fishermen had always played the poor card, but he was going to strike it rich with his fishing. He's worked hard, that's true, and my sister never wanted for anything, but that hasn't stopped him being a macho penny-pincher all his life.'

Moralès wasn't sure where she was going with this.

'When their kids grew up, they wanted their own boats. Leeroy stumped up the cash for his youngest to buy a scallop trawler, but don't get me wrong, he made it very clear that it was a loan and charged him every penny of interest he could. When Jimmy sold his boat, I think he realised his dad had fleeced him. I can't be sure, because our sister passed away right around that time.'

'And Angel?

'That's the thing. Leeroy never wanted her to have a boat, because she was a girl and fishing was a man's job. That was when my sister was sick. She told him, if he didn't get Angel a boat, she'd divorce him before she died, make him split all their assets down the middle and put her share of the inheritance in Angel's name. That gave Leeroy a fright; he wouldn't just feel it in his wallet, but his pride would take a dent as well. Can you imagine? The richest guy on the block getting shafted by his dying wife? So he said yes. He bought his daughter a lobster trawler, by which I mean he loaned her the money, of course, but we're pretty sure, Jacques and I, that he had her sign some sort of document. I haven't seen anything about that in your report, but we wouldn't be surprised if he's the one who inherits the boat.'

Moralès had a hard time believing it. 'Are you suggesting your brother-in-law had his daughter killed to get his hands on her boat?'

'We wouldn't know about that, but you might want to take a closer look at that lobster trawler.'

Jacques Forest shifted his weight from foot to foot, and Moralès saw him glance at Érik Lefebvre and Simone Lord, who were approaching their trio. 'We'll see you at my place tomorrow morning, then?' The fisherman was clearly keen to wrap up the conversation.

Moralès nodded as the constable and the fisheries officer joined them.

Lefebvre knew everyone and was soon shooting the breeze as freely as an insurance broker. 'Apparently the Langevin brothers have got branches all over the Gaspé Peninsula. Have any of you made arrangements? The older brother gave me his card. He's pushing the columbarium pretty hard. I have to admit it's tempting, because anyone who comes to visit won't get their feet dirty. He says it's better than the cemetery for visiting in the winter. I found him quite convincing. Truth be told, I do know the guy a bit. He used to be a car salesman, so he knows how to talk to customers.'

Marlène and Jacques Forest took advantage of the awkward silence that followed to say their goodbyes and slip away just as Leeroy Roberts and his sons approached. As Lefebvre and Lord offered their condolences, Moralès shook Jimmy's hand and kept hold of it as he took him aside.

'I want to see you down at the station tomorrow afternoon,' he said.

The young man glanced at his father, who was watching them with hard eyes. 'Listen, I'm sorry about last night, detective, but we were told there'd be no charges pressed because…'

Moralès twisted Jimmy's hand and cut him off, but lowered his voice so his father wouldn't hear. 'Where were you on the night your sister died?'

'I don't understand…'

'I hope you have a solid alibi, because I think you went down to the boat to go poaching. I think your sister was there when you arrived and she wanted to stop you taking her boat.'

'We Robertses have nothing to hide!' He raised his voice so his father would hear.

'What about those friends of yours – the Babins? Do they have something to hide? Did it happen like it did last night? You just stood by and let them hit her, and claimed you weren't part of it?'

Roberts junior gulped.

'You love being on the water? Well make the most of it while you can. Because there's no such thing as a waterfront jail cell, Jimmy boy,' Moralès said, releasing his hand.

Roberts senior muscled his way in, annoyed to have been sidelined from the conversation. 'We've organised a few nibbles for people, if you'd like to join us…'

Lefebvre was only too happy to accept the invitation, while Lord and Moralès politely declined. The detective stood and watched them walk away before he went back to his car.

'You can leave Jimmy Roberts alone. The Fisheries and Oceans Canada officers are already—'

Moralès whirled around to face Simone Lord. He'd had enough. 'I have to wonder why you keep swooping to the rescue of Jimmy Roberts, Officer Lord.'

That seemed to knock the wind from her sails. It took her a moment to find her voice.

'I'm not swooping to—'

'Do you have an interest in protecting these poachers?'

She paled.

'Officer Lord, you have two options. Either you assist this investigation by telling me what you know, or I will consider that you have been obstructing our enquiries by covering up the poachers' activities, which, in this particular case, might make you an accessory to murder.'

Simone Lord had turned as white as a sheet.

'I'll be expecting you to fill me in tomorrow. Don't stand me up.'

He left her there, speechless and motionless, and got into his car. He could feel his migraine coming back and hoped his son had kept his promise to make something for dinner.

Monday 1st October

Joaquin Moralès had slept enough to get back on his feet. But despite using painkillers, he was still struggling to control his persistent headache, so he was taking things slowly. He was looking at the photos on the walls in Jacques Forest's living room while Jacques made a pot of coffee.

The fisherman saw him peer at one of the frames for a closer look. 'Are you looking at the shark? That was a rare catch.'

'You've been shark fishing?'

'As little as possible.'

'But you still caught one?'

Forest poured the coffee and put their mugs on the table, by Moralès's case file.

'Only by chance. A couple of years ago, I went fishing for halibut around the Magdalen Islands. And we ended up hooking that little monster. At first we thought it was a seal, but it was fighting much too hard. It was the skipper who first realised it was a shark on the hook. Not a massive one, but still big enough to do some damage. When we came to land the sucker, he got really nasty. You should have seen the size of his mouth, full of razor-sharp teeth. We put a .22 bullet in his head. That'll calm a fish down fast, believe me.'

'Do all fisherman carry rifles on board?'

They sat at the table. The inside of Forest's home was a treasure trove of souvenirs from the sea, photos from his time working the lifeboats and snapshots of him and Angel aboard the *Close Call II*. They were a record of the various refits and upgrades –

from the practical to the cosmetic – the young fisherwoman had made to her lobster trawler over the years.

'Some do, but not all. We're allowed to shoot a seal if it's swum too close to the boat and got itself mangled up in the propeller, that kind of thing. To put an end to its suffering, you know. But that doesn't happen much anymore. On the shrimp trawlers, when the whole moratorium thing happened, all the fishermen had one. Well, almost all of them did.'

Moralès tasted the coffee. It was good. The house was well kept, too. This was a man who liked to keep things in order.

'Why?'

Forest took his time and chose his words carefully. The detective thought this must be an important story for him to tell.

'When the government closed the cod fishery, half the fishermen in the area lost their only source of income. The boat, the licence, the equipment, none of that comes cheap. When you work your socks off like your father, your grandfather and your great-grandfather did, and you've been poor for so many generations you can trace your misery back to the first boat that landed in North America, when you've just mortgaged your house to the hilt and your boat to the top of the rigging and your dog to the tip of his tail just to keep your livelihood afloat, you're desperate for the season to start. Just imagine, you're up to your eyes in debt, the bank's chasing you and all you're waiting for is the fishery to open. But then it doesn't.'

'What happened?'

'The fishermen asked the government for help. And do you know what the ministry of fisheries did? They gave them shrimp quotas instead.'

'So the cod fishermen had to change all their equipment?'

'That wasn't the biggest problem. There were boats fishing for cod, and others catching shrimp in the same fishing grounds. From one day to the next, you tell all them fishing for cod to start catching shrimp like the others, what do you think's going to happen on the water? The sea turned into the Wild West. I threw in the towel and went down to the States to work search and rescue. But there were plenty of others who took rifles aboard with them.'

'Was that when your brother-in-law bought himself a new boat?'

That seemed to strike a nerve for Forest. 'Like a bloody hypocrite!'

'Why do you say that? Because he was fishing on a boat paid for by his wife?'

'No, everyone knew about that.' Forest leaned back in his chair. Took a swig of coffee. 'You've met Roberts. He went down to work in the States because people here wanted nothing to do with him. When he came back, he said he knew how to fish better than everyone else. He married Irène, then used her money to buy himself a shiny new boat and said the sea was a gold mine, if you knew how to work it.

'It's true, he's always worked hard. But Roberts had an advantage. His brothers worked at the ministry and they gave him the inside scoop. He always knew which way the regulations were going before anyone else. And that gave him a head start. When he found out there was a moratorium coming, he kept it to himself and let all the others go out and spend money on new nets. Meanwhile, he was plotting his future. The summer before the moratorium came, he filled his wooden boat to the nines with fireworks and burnt it to a crisp out in the estuary. You're going to tell me that wasn't staged, and he could have just sold his boat to someone else. But who would have bought it? Leeroy knew that no one from the States all the way up to Labrador could have gone fishing with that gear anymore. And getting his hands on that insurance money a season early meant that he could get himself a fancy new shrimp trawler, built in New Brunswick. He found a naval architect to design a high-tech boat like nothing anyone here had ever seen, with a net that came back up over the stern on a winch that ran on engine power. Here, everyone still had nets that went out to the sides, and they had to haul them in by hand. So here was Leeroy, with a boat that could bring in more shrimp than all the others combined. He had a better boat, better gear, a better engine, and he had sonar. Can you imagine?'

Forest came up for breath.

'Then he went and cast his brand-new nets out at Firmin's spot.

'Firmin's spot?'

'Firmin Cyr.'

'Cyr?'

'Yes. Clément's father.'

Moralès was thunderstruck.

'Firmin was a shrimp fisherman. He was forced to split his fishing grounds with Leeroy Roberts.'

'And that caused friction, I presume?'

'No. Firmin had always said he'd never get worked up over money, and there were plenty of shrimp for everyone. Leeroy was lucky to end up with him and not someone else.'

'What happened to Firmin?'

'Drowned. Clément took over his dad's fishing operation. That was when I was in the States.'

'So, Leeroy Roberts and his son-in-law fish for shrimp in the same area?'

'They used to. Bruce took over his dad's licence. And he changed boats. Meanwhile, Leeroy, he bought all the cod licences that were still around, all those no one else wanted anymore. Believe me, if ever the ministry reopens the cod fishery, Roberts is going to sell those for a pretty penny.'

Moralès thought about what he had just found out. Forest's revelations may have cast Leeroy Roberts in a new light, but that didn't necessarily make the circumstances of Angel's death any clearer. He looked down at the case file, which Forest had kept close to hand. The man reached out and opened the file.

'I know I'm not supposed to, but this is my niece we're talking about, and the file was right there. So I had to have a look.'

He turned the file so the detective could see. One photo had been moved to the top of the pile: the one of the knot in the line used to tie Angel's legs.

'There was something about this photo that bothered me. I spent a long time looking at it and trying to put my finger on what it was. Then it jumped out at me.'

Forest stood and went to fetch a length of cord from the kitchen counter.

Moralès raised a hand. 'The forensics technicians have already filled me in. It's a bowline and sailors use it a lot because it's strong and it won't slip.'

Undeterred, Forest brought the rope over to Moralès. 'I know. I read that in their report. But I've been fishing with Angel for years, and she's always had a peculiar way of tying that knot. She always did it backwards. Every time I saw her do it, it made me smile. She made me think of a child who learned to always tie a double knot in her shoelaces and never lost the habit when she grew up.'

He held the rope behind his legs and sat down again.

'Now if I were to tie a bowline around my legs, I'd do it like this.' Forest showed Moralès what he meant. 'Then, when the trap pulled me overboard, the knot would end up at this angle, see?' He turned the end of the rope to face the floor.

Moralès compared the two knots. Could Angel have changed the way she tied that knot on the night of her death? Not likely, especially as her senses would have been dulled by the sedatives and it was dark. She would have done it instinctively. It would have been a reflex.

Forest pointed to the photo.

'She didn't tie that knot. Someone else did. Someone who thought that was the way a person sitting there would tie it – to make it look like a suicide. Someone who didn't know that Angel would never have tied that knot that way.'

All was calm at the water's edge. The sea lapped gently at his feet, then his ankles and calves. Soon it was up to his knees. He stopped before it reached the top of his thighs, though. The sand beneath his feet made for a comfortable platform to stand on. This was a sheltered spot, with the waves breaking more than a hundred metres offshore. It was his first time wearing fishing waders. He had Forest to thank for those, who had also given him a lure for striped bass and shown him this prime location.

It was turning out to be a beautiful afternoon, with the sun perched high and proud in the sky. There were eight of them on the shore in Barachois. Three teenagers skipping school, two retirees, two deckhands whose seasons were over, and him. Other than the youngsters, they had all found their own way there. They were all fishing in silence. One of the deckhands had brought a dog, who was now lying on the sand having dutifully inspected the contents of everyone's buckets. They were all wearing rubber waders, like him. Sébastien cast his line over the water, secretly imitating his companions' every move.

It was a truly exceptional spot. Rising from the sea to the south, like a secret the Gaspesians kept for themselves and a select few guests, was the hidden face of Percé Rock no one would ever see on a postcard. Sébastien reeled his line in.

If he were to build a life for himself in the Gaspé, Percé was where he'd choose to live. Maybe he could get work in a restaurant out here, find a little house. He cast it out again.

The others were swaying to the rhythm of the gentle shore-break. He looked down at his own body and realised he was naturally doing the same. The sea was coaxing him into its tranquil flow. Again, he reeled in.

Kimo's body had felt warm against his on Saturday night. He had buried his nose in her hair and taken a deep breath, filling his senses with the scent of her. How big a deal was infidelity for him, for Maude? He cast the line.

Suddenly, to Sébastien's left, one of the other anglers yelled, 'They're biting!' With a tug on his line, he set about winding in the spool. Sébastien could feel the adrenaline rising. He gave his own spool a turn and felt the line start to tighten.

He wasn't expecting to see her there. Sitting in the room beside the interview suite, Simone Lord didn't say a word. Moralès looked at Lefebvre, who shrugged. He didn't like to get involved in other people's squabbles.

The detective had briefly returned to the auberge for a bite to eat and another dose of painkillers, but the headache wouldn't go away. The end of this day couldn't come soon enough. He still had to catch up on his reports and was hoping to read everything over again that night.

He pushed the door open to find Jimmy Roberts, somewhat the worse for wear after recent events, waiting in a sky-blue plastic chair on one side of a table. An identical chair sat empty on the other side.

When he saw Moralès come in, the young man got up and stood with his arms by his sides and head slightly forward of his shoulders, in a posture resembling that of a schoolboy who had copied an assignment from the smartest kid in the class and was about to be given the just punishment he deserved.

'Are you doing better, detective?'

Moralès wasn't going to answer the question. He motioned for the man to sit down, then took a seat across the table, read him his rights and asked him if he understood them.

Jimmy Roberts nodded. 'What do you want to know?'

'Who put up the money for your scallop trawler?'

Caught off guard just the way the detective had hoped, young Roberts reacted without thinking. 'My old man.'

Realising he'd given away more than he'd planned, he let out a deep breath and shook his head. Moralès could see his shoulders slump. He had already laid down his arms.

'When I was sixteen, I got my first girlfriend, and, guess what? I got her pregnant. I loved her. We thought we were so mature, and we kept the baby. I got married when I was eighteen, and I asked my old man to lend me the money to buy a scallop boat I'd found for sale. You know, an arrangement just between me and him.'

He shifted in his chair. Moralès said nothing, just waited to see where the confession would lead.

'My dad didn't want to lend me the money, but my mum persuaded him. The thing is, he charged me a stupid amount of interest, way more than all the banks. But I wasn't in any position to be borrowing from a bank. At that age, you're clueless. You're just proud of your new boat and you've got no idea your old man's screwing you over royally. Even if it does cross your mind, you don't dare admit it. But me and my wife, we were living like paupers.'

He pulled out a pack of cigarettes, toyed with it and put it down on the table.

'When the lobster fishers' association offered me a deal for my boat, I couldn't believe it. The figure they gave me was more than enough to pay off my debt and all the interest. There was even money left over for me to go back to school and do my skipper's course so I could go work on the big commercial ships. You can't do anything without the right qualifications these days.' He shook his head. 'But at the same time, my wife told me she wanted a divorce. And since I'd bought that scallop boat while we were married, I was on the hook for giving her half the amount I sold it for, wasn't I? I told her, look, I'll pay my old man back, then we'll split the rest in two. Anyway, she wouldn't hear a word of that and dragged me through the courts. Since the money came from my old man and there were no papers anywhere that said the boat was full of debt, I had to give my ex-wife half of the entire amount. What I had left was only just enough to pay back my dad. He insisted on getting his hands on the full amount, with all the interest over ten years, even though I didn't keep the boat that long. The bloody shark even tried to get me to give him a percentage on the sale, but I said no. Ever since, he's treated me like I'm his employee, not his son. I don't think he's actually disinherited me, but he wouldn't think twice about doing it.'

The overhead light filled the room with a cold fluorescent glow and an annoying hum.

'When I was twenty years old, I had a father, a wife, three kids and a scallop boat. I was poor, but I was happy. And I was bloody naive. By the time I was twenty-six, I'd lost it all. My ex bought herself a semi-detached house in Rimouski with my money. Since she told the lawyers she was the one who'd always looked after the kids, she got full custody. Of course she was the one who'd always looked after them, because I was always out on the water so I could put food on the bloody table!

'I'm not sure if you know how child support works, but they calculate it based on your salary. The first year after the divorce, the lawyers calculated how much I had to pay based on my last year of fishing. No matter which way you looked at it, there was no way I could ever afford to go back to school now. So anyway, I scratched that out of my life and did what I could. I got a job at the fish plant and told everyone I was all right with that. I said I didn't want to go out to sea anymore, I just wanted to keep my head down and work indoors. I don't know who I was trying to fool.'

Jimmy Roberts bit the corner of his lips and drummed his fingers on the wooden table.

'I've never had a bloody cent of my own. My ex works under the table, waiting tables at her boyfriend's pub. I'm not saying she's happy, but she must be raking in the tips, and if she declared what she earned, I wouldn't be on the hook for as much child support. My kids are ten, eleven and thirteen now. I'm not done sticking my hand in my pocket yet, am I? But that's not the worst of it. The worst thing is, Rimouski is four and a half hours away. So that means I only get to see my kids a couple of times a year. They come here for two or three days at Christmas and then again in the summer holidays. And don't get me wrong, they never stay long, just twenty percent of the time. Their mum calculates it down to the minute so I can't claw back a cent of child support I pay her. Then off they go again, and I don't see them for another six months. It's not that we don't love each other, me and my kids, we just don't know how to talk to each other. We have to go camping, because my apartment's too small. I cook for them, we go off exploring in the park, but they've got nothing to say to me. Maybe it's normal at that age not to know what to say to your dad, but I don't know how to talk to them either. I can barely recognise them sometimes, they've changed so much.' He shrugged, as if resigning himself to something. 'And then, whenever some hot-headed young things come along and preach at us about feminism, they've got the gall to tell me I've got anger issues. For fuck's sake! I live in an apartment as big as a postage stamp, I barely ever see my kids, and every one of my pay cheques gets siphoned off by my ex who works for cash in hand and can afford to dress herself in bloody North Face.'

'So you started poaching, then?'

He smiled bitterly. 'It's true, we have used my sister's boat a few times. But last night was an accident. We didn't know it was you. When we parked the quads, we saw footprints in the mud. At night, we're not the only ones to … use the boats. And after what happened to Angel, we've all been a bit on edge. I never laid a finger on you, I want you to know that.' His voice was breaking up. 'To you, and to plenty of others, I'm just a lowlife. But I love my kids. I've never raised a hand to them. I've never raised a hand to anyone. And I swear I didn't lay a finger on you. If you slap an assault charge on me, they'll never let me see my kids, not even in the summer.'

Moralès could feel his ribs aching.

'It's true that I used my sister's boat on the sly. But Angel knew I was doing it. She wasn't the type to blow the whistle on me, though.'

'On the night your sister Angel disappeared, did you go into the national park to use her boat?'

Jimmy was struggling to breathe. He picked up his pack of cigarettes, opened it and closed it again mechanically. This admission might cost him dearly. Eventually, he put it down flat on the table again.

'Yes. Angel had told us we had to pull up our traps.'

'Why?'

Jimmy Roberts glanced uncertainly at the two-way mirror. Moralès wondered what he hoped to see in there.

'I don't know why, but she told us to. So I went down to the wharf with the Babin brothers.'

'Around what time?'

'About half past three.'

'Half past three? Are you sure?'

'Yes. The commercial fishing season was over. There was no one out on the water anymore. Other than a few crackpots who go out sport fishing at times they're not supposed to. You know what it's like: I'll keep my mouth shut if you keep yours shut too. We turn a blind eye to each other.' He wiped a hand across his brow. 'That night, the tide was high at half past one. Two hours after high tide, the current's running too strong for sport fishing. We knew we weren't going to run into anyone.'

It was a convincing explanation.

'What did you see when you got there?'

'Angel's car was parked down there and the *Close Call II* wasn't at the wharf.'

'Did you find that strange?'

'Yes I did. I tried to call her, but her phone was off. So I went up to Rivière-au-Renard to hang around the wharf. The Babin brothers took turns keeping me company. I was worried about her, and I knew my old man and Clément wouldn't bother letting me know if she turned up. So I just waited there and kept telling myself if Bruce and my old man went out looking for my sister, I'd go as well. I just had a feeling that something had happened. I was on tenterhooks, waiting for someone to get a search under way.'

'To find your sister, or the boat?'

Moralès almost regretted the question as the words passed his lips. He hated sarcasm. Jimmy Roberts sucked in a deep breath. Saltwater filled his eyes. He waited for a moment before he opened his mouth to answer.

'I know what you're thinking. You're wondering if I could have killed her. No way. Why would I kill her?' He looked Moralès square in the eye. 'Think about it, detective. I was free to use that boat as much as I wanted because my sister never said a word about it.'

'But she asked you to pull up your traps, didn't she?'

'Well, I'm not going to be poaching again, am I? Especially not with you lot watching my every move from now on. Either way, the boat's going to be sold now, I suppose.'

He shook his head energetically left and right as he toyed with his pack of cigarettes.

'Angel asked me if I wanted to work for her two years ago, but I said no. I should have said yes, but I didn't. What can I say? We tend to have a misplaced sense of pride in our family. But sometimes, I used to go along the coast and watch her sail past. I liked to see her with her captain's hat on, kitted out in her orange overalls and heavy deck boots, going to sea to set her traps in the spring, the boat sitting low and steady in the water, and I'd be lying if I said I didn't envy her. She used to head out in the roughest of seas to prove she was just as capable as the men. She used to sit at the helm and blast reggae out of her speakers. Reggae! People around here only listen to the local pop stars, or they just put the radio on. I suppose she wanted her deckhands to feel like they were on holiday, or something.'

Jimmy Roberts shook his head again.

'I had no reason to kill her. I loved Angel. I did envy her, because she was successful. She had guts, she had charm, and she had her head screwed on the right way. Everything I don't have. She was my little sister. I never told her, but I looked up to her. I'm no angel, but I'd never have done her any harm.'

He was driving, with the music shaking his car almost to bits, when his phone rang. He had caught as many fish as he was allowed to. A bucket full of fine striped bass was wedged tight in the backseat footwell, and he was salivating at the thought of cooking his catch.

'Hello?'

'It's Kimo.'

He braked and pulled over to the side of the road.

'Corine gave me your number. She's gone away for a couple of days, and she was worried I wouldn't know what to do with myself.'

Sébastien was stunned, and didn't know what to say.

'Is this a bad time?'

'Er … no. I'm just a bit surprised to … I'm on my way back from fishing.'

'Oh, really? Where?'

'Barachois.'

'Ah, you caught some striped bass, then?'

'Tons. A whole bucketful.'

'Do you fancy coming over to my place? We can clean and cut them down by the water and cook them up outside. I've got the perfect setup. It'll give you the chance to continue with your culinary experiments…'

He was hesitant, confused by these mixed messages.

As if she could hear the question he hadn't voiced, she hurried to add that she wanted to apologise about the other night. 'I know I've not been very nice to you. That's partly why I want to invite you over, to have a beer and make peace. If you don't want us to cook your bass together, it's not a big deal.'

He smiled. 'I love it when a woman tells me what to do in the kitchen. I'm on my way.'

He ended the call, turned the music up and put his foot down.

Joaquin closed the door to the observation room behind him. As Constable Lefebvre was escorting Jimmy Roberts out of the building, the detective had told his colleague he wouldn't be needing him for the rest of the day. Simone Lord was still sitting behind the two-way mirror. Now that the light in the interview room was off, the glass was opaque and reflected the image of a defeated woman.

'I need you, Officer Lord.'

She sighed as she saw his reflection approach. He found her reaction exasperating.

'And why is that?'

'To calculate how long it would have taken the *Close Call II* to travel from the Grande-Grave wharf to the place where Angel Roberts' body was found.'

'That's not exactly a taxing question for someone with my expertise, is it?'

'Sorry?'

'Any fisherman worth his salt can figure that out.'

'Very well. Don't bother. I'll ask a fisherman instead. And not only will I find out what I need to know, I won't have to put up with being called a moron because I came from the big city, a pensioner because I'm fifty-two years old, a misogynist because I'm a man, and every name under the sun because I arrived fourteen hours late to this investigation.'

She all but cut him off. 'About ten days ago, when I was out patrolling the inshore waters around the bay, it dawned on me that the *Close Call II* was being used by poachers.'

The words flooded out, as if she were delivering a practised spiel. Her gaze was floating in midair.

'I had the same instinct as you. I went down to Grande-Grave one night to see what was going on. Except I had the code to the barrier and the men didn't spot me. I saw what they were doing and I should have reported them straightaway. Fisheries and Oceans would have sent a boat, hauled up the traps, confiscated Angel's trawler and slapped her with a hefty fine. That's the procedure, and for any lowlife out there, I wouldn't have thought twice.'

She was struggling to catch her breath.

'But I've been immersed in these waters for a long time. I know what kind of guts it takes for a woman to hold her own in a sea of men. Angel and I were acquainted. I knew she worked hard and probably felt obliged to cut her brother some slack. So instead of calling in the cavalry, I went to see her.'

She lowered her head and Moralès, standing in the background, saw the alluring vertebra jut so prominently at the nape of her neck, it made him gasp.

'Angel took what I said to heart. She went to see her brother and gave him four days to take all of his traps out of the water. She told him that if he didn't, she'd report him and the Babin

brothers because she wasn't going to lose her livelihood for them.'
The rest was just a whisper. 'Two nights later, she was dead.'

Simone sat up straight and found Joaquin's gaze reflected in
the glass.

'I know I should have told you. But I'm a woman in a sea of
men too, Detective Moralès. If my team and I had caught them
red-handed out there on Saturday night, I would have come
clean about it all the next day, I swear. But then you stuck your
oar in and ended up pulling the plug on my plan. Don't you
worry, I'm going to get it in the neck for this. My boss is going
to tell me I should have been more careful and that my actions
led to the assault of a police officer. I'm sure he'll be only too
happy to throw the book at me and transfer me to somewhere
even more remote than here. If he learns from you that I gave
Angel a chance, he'll show me the door. No one is ever going to
see that I was standing up for another woman. They'll just
accuse me of protecting a poacher, like you did yesterday.'

Moralès was at a loss for words. He just looked at the sad,
beautiful woman before him in the two-way glass.

'Make of that what you will,' she said. She lowered her eyes.
'In any case, it's true that I didn't do my job properly. Angel is
dead and I can't forgive myself.'

Joaquin left the room in silence. He was exhausted, and the
migraine still wasn't letting up. He went out the back door of the
station to avoid running into the receptionist. He got into his car,
reached for his phone and dialled the number for Cyrille Bernard.
No answer. He started the engine and set off back to the auberge.
All he could think about were the women of the sea. Catherine,
who had turned his heart upside down and set sail for the horizon.
Angel, who had loved to cruise the coast. And Simone.

They could make love right here, he thought. Here on the shore.

She had been waiting for him when he got there. She had tied her hair up and slipped into a colourful jumpsuit that clung to her chest and showed off her taut tummy and toned hips. There was something almost unsettling or threatening about a firm, toned body like that for a man like him – who was in decent shape, but not exactly musclebound.

She had taken a knife and gutted the fish. He had tried to watch and learn from her technique, but his eyes had quickly wandered to her fingers, her hands, her wrists, lingering on the muscles of her forearms, rising past her elbows, to her shoulders, his gaze then falling almost naturally to her breasts, not that they were large, but they were suited to her athletic body. She wasn't wearing a bra.

He had thought about Maude. She cooked like that sometimes, without her bra on. Now he was sharing that kind of intimacy with another woman. He had knocked back his first glass of wine in order to shake the image from his mind, only to choke on it. Kimo had ended up having to slap him on the back and offer him a sip of water. This she had done with a certain proximity, coming so close as to brush one of her small breasts against his arm, and making him wonder whether she'd done it deliberately, whether she'd invited him here just to make him uncomfortable. If she had, her plan was working. He was certainly ill at ease.

So, he had poured himself more wine, taken it steadier with the second glass and gradually felt himself relax. The evening had gone on like that, with few words but plenty of proximity. Kimo had started a fire in her outdoor fireplace long before he arrived, and its warmth took the chill off the autumn air, which tended to set in as soon as the sun went down.

They had cooked the fish in the embers together, a touch too close. He had caught the occasional glimpse of her athlete's body through that jumpsuit of hers that seemed like it would be so easy to undo. He had caught himself thinking that the thin film of perspiration on her skin must smell – and taste – just like a campfire.

They had savoured the fish unseasoned with nothing on the side, their fingers touching as they ate from the same foil plate with a *here, taste this bit* here and an *oh, that's so good* there, him opening his mouth and her pressing the warm, sticky flesh of the fish and the tips of her fingers to his lips. 'Do you like it?' she had asked, and it had been all he could do to keep a lid on his urges as the lapping of the waves on the shore whispered that the sea was within reach, that the horizon could take shape in a woman's curves and murmur a breath of permission.

They had rinsed their hands, and she had told him she was going inside to fetch the dessert she had made. That had been his cue to put some more wood on the fire. When she returned with the chocolate mousse, he put a Celia Cruz song on. She handed him a bottle of rum, and he took a swig. She said she liked the music and asked him if it was time for a dance class. She turned her back and leaned into him, like she had the other night at the bar. She reached for his left arm and wrapped it around her shoulders and neck, so he would hold her tight. Then she took his right hand and slid it down her waist, until he could feel the hip bone, the place where, with the right pressure, he knew he could tip her forward. She snuggled her shoulder blades into his chest, and her buttocks into his crotch. There was no hiding his desire now.

'Dance with me, Sébastien,' she purred, and he dutifully obeyed.

He spun her around, in that jumpsuit that clung to her every curve, held in place by a knot, just a single knot that teased his hand and stoked his fire. He pulled away, pretending he'd had enough, and that was when she decided to stop playing and started to kiss him.

She tasted like chocolate, rum and a lick of salty sweat. Her tongue was supple and sultry, and she went easy with the teeth. Sébastien pulled her close and let his hands tease their way from her hips to her buttocks, then lower, grasping her by the tops of her inner thighs and lifting her onto him. She locked her legs around his waist, and all he could feel, all he could think about, as he kissed her, was her warmth, her wetness, pressing tantalisingly close to him.

On the shore behind them was a sun lounger as big as a bed, complete with a mattress-like cushion and ample pillows for him to raise her hips and enter her, smooth and deep. He wanted her. He lowered her feet to the ground. She guided his hand to the knot holding her jumpsuit together. He tugged the ends undone and watched the garment billow open around her lithe body in the fiery glow of the flames. He took a step back to feast his eyes on her toned muscles and gymnast's breasts, nipples dark in the starlight. *Sans* underwear, she was naked in a flash. As his eyes were drawn down to her small, velvety blonde triangle, Sébastien knew he was playing with fire.

He leaned closer, slid his hand between her thighs and heard her moan. Right there, right then, she was perfect, this was perfect, he told himself. The whole day, the fishing and now this woman offering herself to him. He could hear the sea pounding on the shore. He swallowed, buried his nose in Maude's neck – *no, Kimo's* – and inhaled the scent of her, teased a finger down her inner thigh, then up again. She clung to his shoulders and threw her mouth open with a gasp and a whimper that clashed with the music of the sea. It wasn't the same kind of moan as Maude's. Sébastien suddenly felt a shiver across his upper back.

He teased his hand away again, as he tried in vain to blink away the vision of Maude. Her legs, her stomach, her hips. Her laugh, her voice, her whole body. Her eyes, the scent of her. The other men.

Sébastien Moralès withdrew his hand and took a step away from Kimo. Clumsily, he tugged at the jumpsuit to cover her up, tried to close the flaps at the front and mumbled an apology. Then, leaving his chocolate mousse untouched, he abandoned his car outside her house and retreated to the auberge on foot.

Tuesday 2nd October

Sébastien's car wasn't parked outside when Joaquin got up that morning. He wondered where his son had spent the night. He had suspected for a while – since he'd seen him dancing with Joannie Robichaud – that Sébastien had cheated on Maude, but had been trying not to think about it.

Did that bother him?

Moralès took a sip of his coffee.

Yes, it did bother him. It wasn't so much his son's infidelity, but being an accessory to it. He didn't want to know about Sébastien's troubles or judge his behaviour, or have to lie to Maude if it came to it. And Lefebvre was right, anyway: when you loved a woman, you had to focus your gaze on her. As soon as your eye started to wander, it would never return.

That brought him back to Sarah. He'd been thinking about her less and less. The silence between them seemed to stretch on and on. Maybe it had been building for years. His friend Doiron had told him what was happening. A simple, subtle bit of private investigating was all it had taken for him to learn she'd bought a condo in Longueuil. Joaquin knew a divorce was coming. Before long, he'd be finding a lawyer, getting the papers drawn up, signing disclosures, dividing assets. The separation agreement would have to go down in writing, be signed four times over and filed with the court with dues paid for their story to be duly consigned to the official records with the letters E, N and D at the bottom of the page. Was that really how thirty years of a life together and two children had to end? Thirty years of everyday life, washed and hung out to dry time after time, the challenges they had tackled together, the emotions they had ridden out and the nights of passion they had shared – how could all that be eclipsed by sulking and resentment? What if he was overreacting, though, and she was simply intending the condo to be a *pied-à-terre* in the city? Perhaps she was still planning to come out here to join him.

He was suddenly struck by the curious impression he had lived his life on mute, silenced his youth in Mexico and only ever spoken in hushed tones about the crime scenes he had in-vestigated, stifling the inner turmoil that surfaced when he encountered the dead, washing away the blood before he went home so nothing would show, sheltering his family from what he had witnessed. Burying the seed of human suffering deep inside himself, only for it to sprout, take hold of the silence he'd created, and grow into a tree of solitude.

Again he looked out to the parking space where he was now accustomed to seeing his son's car. Was he envious of Sébastien? Of his freedom, his youth? Of him being in the arms of a woman other than his partner? Joaquin washed his breakfast dishes, then went back up to the apartment. No. That wasn't the issue. It was just that he had raised his sons with the values he believed in, and he was surprised by his eldest's disloyalty.

When he pushed the door open, he was startled to see his son standing there in the kitchenette, wearing jeans and rubbing his eyes.

'What are you doing here?'

Sébastien was just as startled to hear his father's voice and turned around. He thought Joaquin must have still been asleep, knocked out by the painkillers he'd been taking. He hadn't dared to make a sound for fear of waking him.

'I'm just getting up. Why?'

'Your car isn't parked out front.'

'I had a bit to drink last night. With a friend, next door. I walked back. You know, Dad, it's not a good idea to drive when you've had a drink or two.'

Sébastien tiptoed his way down her driveway. In shame. He didn't knock at the door. He wanted to steal away undetected. Now he turned onto the road towards Barachois, put his foot down and turned up the music. The sound of Macaco filled the car, the bass so loud he could feel the rhythm pounding into his back through the driver's seat.

What did it take to be happy?

Since he'd been out here on the Gaspé Peninsula, he had danced, drunk until he couldn't see straight, felt his body swaying in time with the waves – and last night, he had tugged a knot undone. The sun-kissed horizon of a woman's body had opened up before him like the secret space he had already entered with just his hand. But he had pulled away.

Why? What had happened? He couldn't wrap his head around it. If he had the words to express what he was feeling, surely he could set himself free. Something was burning in his throat. Suffocating him. The music kept pounding at his back.

He had come here with his hands full of resolutions. He had wanted to confront his father in order to find a sense of freedom, but he hadn't found the right time. Had he really tried, though? He yanked the wheel to the side as he saw the turnoff to Haldimand Beach coming up. This wasn't the place he'd been heading to, but he needed some air.

He had always hated discussions that went on for hours and explanations that dissolved into chit-chat. Still, he felt he had to express his discomfort – to himself at least – before he drowned in the sea of his confused emotions. Perhaps he could condense all his malaise into just one word, then pull it out of his mouth like an uprooted weed.

He drove to the end of the road and parked facing the sea. He turned off the engine and the music, and in the silence inside the car, he could hear the voice of his father. He no longer spoke Spanish. And Sébastien thought that perhaps he too was losing his tongue, his language, his ease of expression and his capacity to define himself and make sense of what he was feeling. He swallowed, and suddenly he felt the word rising in his chest, emerging at last in a bubble of bitterness on his lips.

Loyalty.

If there was one person Moralès had little desire to see again, it was the tall, forlorn Clément Cyr, a man haunted by his own ghosts, guilt and yearning to be held responsible. The widower was understandably confused and distressed, and even Moralès had sensed the shadows lurking in his messy shambles of a home.

He rang the doorbell. The giant of a man answered the door and invited him in. Moralès followed him and couldn't help but notice how much tidier the hallway, dining room and kitchen were. The house looked as if Angel had somehow ordered it to be kept spick and span. Moralès found this reassuring. Lefebvre had told him that social services had taken Cyr under their wing, but sometimes the damage caused by a violent death was irreparable. Now, though, even the man's voice was bright and shiny.

'The *Close Call II*? Leeroy's probably going to sell it. He's retired now, and Bruce has got his own fishing operation.'

'But you're the one who inherits all your wife's assets. The same goes for her fishing operation.'

Cyr turned his gaze to Moralès and the detective could see him slipping away again, drifting somewhere without an anchor, like an abandoned buoy bobbing atop the waves. But the man didn't let himself get swept out of his depth. He stood and walked over to a large desk in the corner of the living room and opened a drawer.

'I suppose it's inevitable for the husband to be considered a potential suspect in his wife's death.'

He plucked a document from a folder, returned to the dining area and slid it across the table to Moralès. 'I get everything, except the boat and the fishing licence.'

Moralès frowned as he peered at the paper in front of him.

Clément summarised the contents as he sat down again. 'It's an agreement entered into by Angel and her old man, witnessed by me and Bruce Roberts.'

As Moralès read the contract, Clément leaned back in his chair.

Angel's looking over the detective's shoulder now.

'Leeroy Roberts is a penny-pincher. That's common knowledge around here. He's got money. He was the one who stumped up the cash for Angel's fishing, you know. Fishing grounds, licences, boats and all that often come as a job lot, and it costs an arm and a leg. Angel never wanted to fish with me. She wanted her own boat. But the lobster trawler that came with her territory was a rustbucket. You'd have needed deep pockets to buy a money pit like that. Angel's old man agreed to bankroll the whole purchase, but on one condition.'

'Let me guess: that everything reverted to him if she died?'

'For ten years. For the first ten years of his loan, if anything happened to Angel, Leeroy Roberts would inherit all of it, as if she'd never paid him a penny of what she owed. After that, if she died, then it would go to her legal heirs.'

Moralès scanned the document, looking for the expiry date. 'And when would the ten years have been up?'

'The ten years was up on Wednesday last week, the day of our wedding anniversary. Angel insisted on signing the two biggest contracts of her life on the same day. As soon as he found out she'd died, in the early hours of Sunday morning, Leeroy filled out the paperwork for the deed of ownership – to be transferred immediately. The notary told me it'll be a done deal as soon as Angel's assets are released.'

The detective pondered why Leeroy Roberts hadn't volunteered this information.

'Do you plan to contest the validity of the contract?' he asked.

Clément Cyr's gaze grew distant. 'Why would I do that? I haven't set foot on my wife's boat since she died. I don't want anything to do with it. I inherited my old man's fishing operation, you know. I had to invest in another shrimp trawler, because his old one sank, but it feels like it's his boat I'm working on.'

'Why didn't you tell me this when I came to see you before?'

Cyr shrugged. 'My wife had just died, detective. You'll have to excuse me if I had other things on my mind.'

The man was right. Moralès should have thought to ask. After all, he was the one leading the investigation.

'Do you think Jimmy's going to want to buy the *Close Call II* now?'

'I haven't the foggiest. He's always been jealous of Angel. Plus, she was one of the lobster fishers who went around buying up all the scallop fishermen's licences. He thought he'd struck it rich when he sold, but he got screwed over. Angel ended up asking him if he wanted to work with her. He threw the offer right back in her face. She loved him, even though he wasn't the nicest to her. He was just unlucky, she used to say. I don't think Jimmy's old man would fall over himself to help Jimmy buy that boat. In fact, I'd be surprised if he did.'

'What happened between your father and your father-in-law when the moratorium was introduced?'

All the expression drained from Cyr's face. 'The same things as everywhere else up and down the coast. The rich got richer, and the poor kept their mouths shut.'

He sat for a long time on the beach, haunted by that word – loyalty – without knowing what to make of it. He stood and decided to stretch his legs a bit. It was a mild day, but he was cold. Hands stuffed into his pockets, he walked out along the point. Suddenly, his phone vibrated in his palm, and in a mechanical gesture he checked the message on the screen. There was no text, just a black-and-white photo. He didn't understand. So he unlocked the screen, zoomed in on the image – and had the wind knocked out of him.

In a heartbeat, the horizon vanished and everything in Sébastien's view turned monochrome. The sea, the sand, the sky, all turned to white in one static image that stood out from the black ultrasound screen. Ink welled in his throat. He couldn't breathe. Sébastien opened the attachment, closed it again, and opened it once more, hesitant both to delete and to save it. He really didn't know what to make of that photo of moving pixels in Maude's belly.

Leeroy Roberts opened the door warily and let him in, but kept him standing in the hallway. He wasn't going to invite the detective into the kitchen or the living room. He'd sailed the seas for long enough to know that time could turn a man into a traitor.

Moralès regretted not bringing Constable Lefebvre along, but, then again, his colleague's presence might have riled the man even more, and they may have had to take him down to the station. Anyway, it was too late now to backpedal. He was here now, and Roberts wasn't happy. The entryway was longer than it was wide. A closet with triple sliding doors occupied one entire wall. On the opposite side, two decorative chairs flanked a small round table topped with a Tiffany-style lamp. The French doors at the end of the hallway beckoned to an open-plan kitchen with dark wood cabinets, separated from the dining area by a marble counter.

Leeroy noticed the detective's eye wandering behind him as he outlined what he knew about the agreement he and Angel had signed when he funded the purchase of her boat.

He held his head high and folded his arms across his chest. 'I don't see what the problem is. Each party knew what they were signing.'

That moment had been the biggest affront of Leeroy's life. Talk about adding insult to injury, after his wife had forced him to pay for their daughter's studies at the marine institute in Rimouski. Plus the apartment, the car, and all the rest.

She had always hated fishing, had Irène, but she was the one who had put up the money for her husband's wooden boat, using her father's inheritance. She didn't approve, but she loved him and so she had said yes. When they gazed at the stars at night and she saw the light of the moon reflected in the sea, she used to say it was fool's silver, that it was drawn to a lure like a fish to a shiny spoon. That had always made him see red.

She had never set foot on any boat of his, and Leeroy had taken that to heart, so much so that he had sworn he would prove her wrong and show her how lucrative fishing could be. And he had done exactly that. When their children had each decided in turn to go into fishing, Leeroy was comfortably well off. He could afford to drive nice cars and trucks and strut around on the wharf.

But then one day, Irène had insisted he put up the money for the kids to buy their own boats. He didn't want to, but she reminded him that at first she herself had been reluctant to put her hand in her pocket for him to buy his wooden boat with her father's money. Then she had told him that he had believed in fool's silver, whether he would admit it or not, and he had no right to stop their children from chasing the lures he himself had dangled before their eyes. So yes, he had put his hand in his pocket, but he had reserved the right to draw up the contracts his way.

Leeroy Roberts looked at Detective Moralès. He had children, so there must be a wife. He must know how those kinds of thing could tear a man apart.

'I told Angel she should choose another way to make a living, that fishing wasn't a woman's job. It's sad to say, but I suppose she decided her own fate. Don't take that the wrong way. She was my daughter and I'm heartbroken. But sometimes I just wonder what young people get into their heads. We raise our kids to work hard so they won't want for anything. How come they end up making such crazy choices?'

'The other morning, when you were telling me about your children, you neglected to mention this contract,' Moralès said.

'I wasn't hiding anything from you. You asked me if I was the one who'd told Jimmy to bring the *Close Call II* back to her wharf, and I said yes.'

'But you didn't tell me the boat belonged to you.'

'You should have realised it; I'd never have touched someone else's boat.'

'I'm sure you'll agree that the contract you had your daughter sign was less than scrupulous. Talk about making her pay a heavy price…'

'Listen, Angel would never have had that lobster boat if I hadn't stumped up the cash.'

'Were you aware that your son Jimmy was using the *Close Call II* for poaching?'

If they had been outside, Leeroy would have spat on the ground. Instead, he stood tall and proud, arms folded, eyes boring deep into the Mexican's. 'The sea's not your jurisdiction.'

Moralès wished he had brought the man in to the station for proper questioning.

'As I understand, the cod-fishing grounds have been closed for a long time. You wouldn't get much now for all those licences you rounded up, would you? With that in mind, it seems to me that a lobster-fishing operation would be a nice thing to inherit.'

Leeroy Roberts paled with anger. 'Listen, detective, I've spent my life trying to prove I'm a good fisherman. When your wife pays for your first boat, that sticks to you like a port-wine stain on your face. Everyone in the bloody Gaspé knew I was sailing under her thumb. I looked like a profiteer, not a fisherman. So I worked my socks off to show them all, and especially my wife, that I could make my own money. When the fishing season ended in the gulf, I used to go down to the Magdalen Islands to boost my quota. I used to fish so late in the year, one time the fisheries officers even thought I was drug running. I've made my money honestly, and here you are accusing me of killing my own daughter? Do you know what it feels like to see your own child devoured by the fish in the sea? Get out of my house, detective. Go look for your murderer somewhere else.'

Moralès carried the weight of the last few days back to the auberge. He went up to his room, left the case file on his bed and stood for a moment in the kitchenette. Simone's little origami creation was still there, on the corner of the table. Right then, he realised he didn't feel like dining alone again. He hesitated at first, then called Lefebvre. The constable picked up on the second ring.

'Got any plans for dinner?'

'No, why?'

'Want to meet me at the Brise-Bise?'

'I'm on my way.'

Moralès hung up and called his son, but the line must have been busy because the call went straight to voicemail. He left Sébastien a message and drove off to meet Lefebvre at the pub.

The line was busy because Sébastien had had enough of this tide that kept sweeping him away. He picked up his phone and dialled the number. She answered, and as he heard the gentle hello on the other end of the line, at last he could breathe again.

'I'm calling to say I'm sorry.'

Lefebvre was already there and happily knocking back his first pint when Moralès walked into the Brise-Bise. His colleague was seated at the bar, in the same spot the detective had chosen both times he'd been here before, in front of the tap handles.

'I gather you've met Louis?'

Moralès said hello to the barman and ordered a beer. The pint glass was on the bar in front of him before he knew it.

'It's sad, what happened to Angel Roberts,' the man said.

Both police officers nodded. Moralès took off his jacket and sat down.

'It's not the first suicide we've seen around here, though…'

The investigators kept their mouths shut. That was the kind of bait they were thrown all too often, and they knew better not to take it. Seeing that his tactic to extract information from his customers wasn't going to deliver a result, the barman slipped away discreetly. He reached for the remote and put a baseball game on the TV, then went to enjoy the bohemian charm of the attractive young women sitting at the other end of the bar instead.

'Baseball, now that's a real sport!'

'You play baseball, Lefebvre?'

'Yessir, I certainly do. You're looking at the best pitcher in the whole of the Gaspé league. I'm a proud Sainte-Thérèse-de-Gaspé Mariner, I'll have you know.'

Moralès tried to imagine Lefebvre and his serious little moustache in a baseball cap and team uniform cinched at the waist, squinting from the pitcher's mound.

'It's just a friendly league, but other than jogging, what do you do to keep fit? Don't look at me like that. Everyone knows every-thing around here. You're staying at Corine's. Word gets out fast.' Lefebvre drained his first beer and waited for Joaquin to answer.

'I played a lot of football – soccer – when I was younger. Back in Mexico, with friends, but also in Montreal with colleagues.'

'Is that all?'

'Well, I used to ride horses, and I was pretty good with a lasso.'

Lefebvre's jaw dropped to the bar. 'Are you pulling my leg, Moralès?'

'My dad's brother had a ranch and I used to go there a lot to help him brand and herd the cattle.'

'That must have been a great way to get women into bed too.' Lefebvre pretended to twirl a lasso by his side, throw it far and pull a woman towards him. The barman misinterpreted the gesture and came over to see if they needed anything.

'Two more beers.' Lefebvre turned to Moralès. 'It's my round, cowboy. You do know we have Western festivals out here in the Gaspé, don't you?'

'I've hung up my lasso for good.'

Louis slid their pints across the bar and sidled back to the women. Moralès was yet to finish his first beer.

'Right, well, where are things at with the investigation?' Lefebvre said.

'I went to see Leeroy Roberts this afternoon. Did you know he's inheriting his daughter's boat?'

Lefebvre whistled between his teeth. 'That's not the way it's supposed to be, parents inheriting from their children...'

'Clément Cyr seemed completely indifferent about losing the lobster boat.'

Lefebvre picked up a pen from the bar and tried to make a note of something on his beer mat, but it was soggy and the ball wouldn't let the ink flow. He put the pen down again.

'Leeroy Roberts threw me out of his house. It's not like he needs the inheritance, but there was something that bothered me...'

Lefebvre reached over to grab an order pad from behind the bar and flipped through the scribbled pages as he swigged his second beer. 'There are cheapskates everywhere, you know.'

If Moralès had never seen the man work that way before, he would have sworn he wasn't listening.

'A decade ago Angel Roberts signed a ten-year contract to

borrow the money for her boat from her father,' the detective explained. 'She was paying him back in instalments, but the contract stipulated that if she died during the term of the loan, then her boat, her fishing licence and all her gear would go to him. I'm thinking that maybe she paid at the end of each fishing season. And this year's season has just ended, so perhaps she had already paid off the whole debt slightly early, and didn't owe her father another penny.'

'That sounds like a strange arrangement to me. So you're saying she'd paid back everything, but she died before the contract ended?'

'Three days before.'

Lefebvre stood, went over to the stage and plucked a wireless microphone from a shelf at the very back and returned to the bar.

'Can you check the amounts Angel paid her father in the last ten years?' Moralès asked.

Constable Lefebvre carefully inspected the microphone before placing it on the bar beside his soggy beer mat, the useless pen and the order pad.

'He pulled a similar financial trick on his youngest son as well. I'd like you to check the transactions between the father and his eldest too.'

'When Leeroy dies, it's his sons who'll inherit.'

'Just check Bruce's accounts, will you?'

Lefebvre caught the barman's eye. 'Would you bring us a menu?'

Louis sauntered to the till at the end of the bar, grabbed two menus and handed them over distractedly before going to greet some customers as they walked in the door. Without even glancing at it, Lefebvre put the menu down beside the soggy beer mat, the useless pen, the rough order book and the disconnected microphone.

'Do some digging into Clément's family as well, so we can get a sense of his mother's assets, and his stepfather's too. I want to know if Angel's insurance might benefit the extended family.'

There was no point giving Lefebvre a pen and paper, Moralès realised. He seemed to remember information by gathering assortments of random objects. It must be a mnemonic thing, he thought.

'I'm going to pay Clément Cyr's mother a visit tomorrow.'

The constable stood up again, but Moralès motioned for him to sit down. 'It's all right, Lefebvre, I'm done. We can order something to eat now.'

'I don't need the menu. I know it by heart.' Lefebvre sat and raised his glass to his lips.

Louis came over to take their orders. He seemed perplexed that his pad and pen weren't where they usually were. When he saw them on the bar in front of Lefebvre, he sighed the way a tired parent would after repeating simple instructions to a child, and pocketed the pad and pen, took the menus away and tucked the microphone behind the bar. Suddenly, Lefebvre's glass was half empty.

'Same as usual, Érik?'

He nodded. Moralès went for the catch of the day. The barman went to punch their orders in to the screen by the till.

'Speaking of the investigation, Moralès, I've got a personal question to ask you.' Lefebvre took a deep breath. 'Right, well, it's not my place to dictate who you sleep with, but your relationship with Simone Lord…'

'Relax, Lefebvre. I haven't slept with Simone.'

The constable was visibly relieved. 'Oh, good. I mean, it's no skin off my nose if you are sleeping together. I'm head over heels in love with my Teresita at the front desk and no one at work makes a song and dance about it. So long as there's no talk of abuse of power or authority, and there's consent and pleasure on both sides, it's all right. But when one's not floating the other's boat, if you know what I mean, then the waters start to get muddy.'

Moralès was lost for words.

'When you're both getting what you want, then it eases the atmosphere and the sexual tension.' Lefebvre nodded with self-assurance. 'Believe me, I've seen it for myself. I'm always more productive after a hard night's work.'

'So it's going well with your doctor friend, then?'

'Shush. She's married. Let's just say it's a mutually beneficial arrangement.'

Moralès burst out laughing. Louis brought their plates out, put some cutlery on the bar for them, and walked away. The detective realised he was ravenous, his migraine had disappeared and the salmon looked delicious.

This time, he didn't invite her to dance. The first time, a woman can forgive a pullback. But not the second. He knocked at her door; she invited him in. She was wearing a workout skirt, leggings and a camisole. *I'm sorry.* That was all he'd had to say on the phone. She backed up against the kitchen table, beckoning him closer. He locked eyes with her, slid her hands beneath her skirt and took off her leggings. On his knees in front of her, he held her skirt up with his left hand and used his right to part her thighs a touch. He moved his lips closer, murmuring a word of apology before he kissed the cream-coloured cotton-and-lace panties veiling a dome of soft, golden hair.

Lefebvre took a bite of an enormous hamburger and carried on talking with his mouth full. 'You haven't told me, is your son having a good time?'

'I don't think so. We haven't really had a chance to talk about it.'

'Did he come to the Gaspé to meet women?'

Moralès was wolfing his fish down without realising it. 'He's had the same girlfriend since he was fifteen years old.'

'That just means he's not single. And believe me, most couples don't have that much sex. That's why women are often unfaithful. The burden of sexual responsibility falls far more on men than it does on women, if you want my opinion. It's easy enough for men to get their rocks off. But it takes quite the touch to keep a woman happy in bed year after year. Do you think he's got what it takes? Come to think of it, where is he right now, that son of yours? You should give him a call and get him to come and join us.'

'My son was going fishing again today. He must be sitting in front of the TV with a plate full of fish.'

'You're kidding me. He sounds just as boring as his old man.'

Moralès pushed his empty plate aside and took a sip of his beer before he replied. 'Not boring, Lefebvre. Loyal.'

'That's an admirable quality for a dog, Moralès. Adventurous and sexy, those are a real man's qualities. Adventurous, I tell you.'

'Lefebvre, you can't even keep your own gun loaded, and here you are going on about being adventurous. Leave my son be and let him relax. That's what he came here for.'

This time there was no holding back. He started with his mouth as she stood upright, holding on to the kitchen table, and finished with his hand as she bent over the sofa. Then, he whispered for her to do what she wanted, so she had him lie on his back on the living-room carpet. Sébastien did as he was told. She undid his belt and pulled it off, unbuttoned his jeans and pulled those, and his boxers, down to his mid-thighs. Then she straddled him. Her skirt was keeping the scene under wraps, but he could feel the young woman's hand reaching beneath it. Then she lowered herself in one smooth, calculated movement.

'Is that Kimo?'

Lefebvre followed Moralès's finger to the photo on the wall. 'Yes, that's her.'

'Does she work here?' He leaned in for a closer look at the picture.

Louis made his way over to the two men, who were standing at the till waiting to pay. 'Is that Kimo you're wondering about? She used to work in the kitchen here before she opened her yoga studio. Now she teaches classes and she gives Corine a hand at her auberge. We were working together the other Saturday. The night Angel Roberts disappeared. That was the last time I saw her. Have you got any leads?'

Lefebvre passed his credit card to the barman. Moralès had tried to pay his way, but the constable had insisted on picking up the tab. Moralès suspected he'd be claiming it back from the Sûreté du Québec as investigation expenses.

'Where were you working? Here?'

Louis inserted the card into the payment machine and passed

it to Lefebvre. 'No. At Corine's place. She needed an extra pair of hands for the fishermen's party.'

Lefebvre pressed a few buttons on the machine and handed it back to the barman.

'So you and Kimo were both at the event at Corine's the other Saturday night?'

Louis tore off the receipt and handed it to Lefebvre, who drifted towards the door. 'That's what I just said. We were working for Corine that night.'

'What time did you and Kimo leave?'

'I don't know about Kimo. Around two o'clock, I think. Clément Cyr was pretty drunk, and he wouldn't leave her alone. At one point she got fed up of him making eyes at her. I said to Corine I'd go back the next day to finish cleaning up. I must have left around three.'

'Did Kimo have a particular kind of relationship with Clément Cyr?'

'I don't think so. If there was something going on, it would be none of my business anyway. Kimo likes men, that's obvious, but Cyr was married. It's up to him to stay out of trouble.'

Louis said goodbye to Moralès and made his way towards the kitchen.

Moralès went outside to find Érik Lefebvre fiddling with his phone.

'I'll see you tomorrow, OK? I've got a phone call to make, if that's all right with you.'

Moralès didn't mind at all. The night was pleasantly mild. He walked to his car and got behind the wheel. He wondered where Corine was. It had been two days since he'd seen her. Tomorrow, he'd like to have a word with her. He wanted to ask her why Louis and Kimo weren't on the list she gave him on his second day there.

Still straddling him, she arched her body, thrusting her chest forward and throwing her head back in pleasure. Sensing she was about to come, she straightened her neck and cast her gaze far away into the distance, out onto the shore and into the deep blue night.

Wednesday 3rd October

Gaétane Cloutier was standing at the kitchen counter, preparing sushi, as shimmers of sunlight reflecting off the sea danced across her face. She motioned to a stool for Moralès to perch on and poured him a cup of coffee. The fatigue from his concussion was still lingering, but the detective had taken his time and only left the auberge around mid-morning. Sébastien had still been in bed, and still there had been no sign of Corine's car outside.

Through the window, Moralès could see Fernand Cyr, the man who was both Clément's uncle and stepfather, doing some autumn tidying, putting sea kayaks and paddles away in the shed, rinsing wetsuits and hanging them to dry.

Gaétane Cloutier was sixty-two years old. She was thirty when she married Firmin, Clément's father. It had been a civil ceremony.

'We did it for Clément,' she said, slicing salmon into strips. 'Firmin and his brother inherited this house and my father-in-law's shrimp trawler when their parents died in a car accident, on their way back from a wedding. When I first met the boys, they were living here together, fishing for shrimp and partying hard. I suppose, after their parents died, they thought life was too short not to make the most of it and do what made them happy.'

She stacked the strips of salmon neatly and cleaned her hands and the knife. Then she reached for a generous piece of tuna and set about slicing it the same way.

'Those were the days of peace and love. I grew up in Quebec

City and had just come out of university there. I wanted to be a teacher and I'd found a job in a school in Limoilou, not far from downtown. I was going to be starting in August. I had the whole summer off, so I dipped into my savings and decided I'd hitch-hike my way around the Gaspé Peninsula before I settled down to start my teaching career. Those were the days, eh? Or perhaps you're too young to remember.'

Moralès chose not to answer. Those were the days when police opened fire on student protesters in Mexico City.

'When I met the Cyr brothers, I took a shine to them straight away. They invited me to stay here with them. I say "they" because I can't remember which one of them asked me, but I said yes, and I never left. When the end of the summer came around, I found a job at the school in Cap-aux-Os. I never did go and teach in Limoilou, and I've never regretted it.'

She set the strips of tuna to one side and washed her hands, then the knife, again.

'One day, I found out I was pregnant. The baby was Firmin's. I'm sure of that, because Fernand was away travelling.' She smiled and glanced at him through the window. 'One morning, Fernand got out of bed and decided he was going to travel the world. Just like that. We told him to go back to bed, he'd had too much to drink the night before, but once he'd got the idea in his head, there was no changing his mind. So he packed his bag, put his walking sandals on and off he went. He was gone more than twenty years. He came back for Firmin's funeral. You get the picture?'

Now she started to peel and slice a mango.

'Firmin was always very sociable. He had a loud voice and he made everyone laugh. When he died, I really felt it. Fernand came along and told me he was tired of travelling, so he moved in with me. In the beginning, it was for comfort and consolation. But now it's more than just a convenient arrangement. We really love each other.'

Moralès envied this ease of happiness and almost natural acceptance of fate. 'How old was Clément at the time of the accident?'

'Twenty. He got his share of the inheritance, bought a new boat and took over Firmin's fishing.'

She moved the slices of mango aside and laid a cucumber on the cutting board.

'Was the cod moratorium already in place around here?' Moralès asked.

For the first time since the beginning of their conversation, she held the blade in midair over the work surface. Either she was surprised he knew the story, or she hadn't been expecting that question.

'They brought it in the year before.'

'Did it have a big impact on you?'

'Well, Firmin had to share his fishing area, of course.'

'With Leeroy Roberts.'

'Yes. But the moratorium didn't really affect Firmin. He and Fernand didn't have any debts, and I was working. A little more or a little less money, that never really rocked the boat. You know, we've always planted a big garden on the point out back, and we've always fished. We've got a hunting camp as well. We do all right for ourselves. I've never wanted to travel. I'm already at the end of the road, aren't I? Where would I go? I never did make it all the way around the Gaspé Peninsula. We've never had big financial needs, and the fishing's always brought in enough money to keep the house in order. What else could we have wanted? A marble countertop in the kitchen? A heated floor in the bathroom? When we love the sea, doesn't that make us rich enough?'

'Does Clément share the same opinion?'

'No. Clément thought it was unfair because Leeroy was richer than us.'

It struck Moralès that she was the only person he had interviewed to have called Roberts by his first name, with a kind of friendly familiarity.

'Did your son go fishing with his father a lot?'

'Yes, but not on the day of the accident. He was sitting his captain's exam that day. He's always felt guilty he wasn't there.'

She reached for a bowl of tempura, a pot of lukewarm rice and a stack of nori – thin sheets of roasted seaweed – and put one of the sheets on a sushi mat before she continued.

'Twenty's a young age, no matter which way you look at it. Clément did his best to take it all in. He always thought Firmin was depressed after the moratorium came in, you see? I've told him a thousand times that his dad's death was an accident, that there was nothing to suggest suicide. Firmin wasn't depressed, and he wasn't suicidal. My Firmin was a happy man. But Clément wouldn't rest until he'd found someone to blame for his dad's death. So, he started to point the finger at Leeroy Roberts. In his mind, if it was suicide, then it had to be the rich guy who'd muscled his way in on his dad's shrimp fishing who was to blame, you see.'

She spread a thin layer of rice on the nori, added lines of fish, tempura and mango and rolled it together with the sushi mat.

'I've never understood all the fuss about finding the cause or the reason for something. Don't you get tired of having to weed out the bad guys from the good? Separating those who live in the light from those who dwell in the darkness?'

She took the sushi roll out of the mat, placed it on a cutting board and reached for her knife.

Moralès gave her a gentle smile. 'Nothing's black or white, I know that. There are plenty of grey areas.'

She shook her head. 'It's not all shades of grey, detective. There are thousands of colours out there. Prison guards are the only ones who see your shades of grey. In real life, Romeo and Juliet fell in love. Clément was infatuated with Angel, even though he hated the Roberts family. He's never liked Leeroy, but over time he's come to see colours other than red.'

She moistened the blade and sliced the sushi roll. One by one, the pieces rolled off the knife, falling flat on the cutting board to reveal an inner core of red tuna, yellow mango and golden tempura inside the outer layers of seaweed and rice.

Moralès strolled into the police station with a container of fresh sushi. Behind the bulletproof glass, Thérèse Roch pretended she hadn't seen him. He approached the front desk and leaned towards the intercom. She was still tapping away at her computer keyboard as if her life depended on it.

'Hello there, Ms Roch. I hope you're well. I'm doing much better, thank you. As you know, I was the victim of a violent assault on Saturday night. I know you know that, because Dotrice Percy paid me a visit at the hospital. Now, I wondered who might have shared confidential information and informed her of my whereabouts. Of course, a civilian should never be told that a law-enforcement officer is in hospital, because it might put that officer's life in danger. Then I remembered that you had personally passed me a note from Ms Percy and it had come to my attention that she was a friend of yours. Now, if I were the kind of detective inclined to file a complaint, such a breach of professional secrecy would surely lead to dismissal for the unfortunate person who…'

He heard the door click open.

'Ah, I'm glad to see that we can finally be cordial with each other, Ms Roch. And for your information, my name is pronounced Mo-ra-less. Not Moral-less. You have a nice day, now.'

He entered the bowels of the building, heading straight for Lefebvre's office. He had to move a box, close the door and shift two file folders before he could sit down.

Lefebvre smoothed his moustache as his printer spewed one sheet after the other. 'Don't touch those, they're for another case,' he said to Moralès, handing him a different file.

'Here are the financials for the Cyr and Roberts families. All in all, they're in good shape. Clément Cyr's mother is drawing a pension. She and her husband aren't rich, but they've got a little nest egg to keep them going in old age. And you were right about Angel's old man. He cashed a substantial cheque on the Thursday before his daughter died, which suggests she'd probably made her final loan payment. We already know that Jimmy works to pay his child-support payments. What I did find surprising was that Bruce, the eldest of the Roberts children, didn't have more money to his name. He's got a hefty loan at the credit union, which would tally with part of what his boat must be worth.'

'Part of it?'

'Yes. Going on the payments he's been making into his old man's account, I'd say Leeroy Roberts is bankrolling the *Ange-Irène* just like he did his other two kids' boats.'

'At an exorbitant rate of interest.'

'Not hard to believe, not easy to prove.'

'Is Bruce Roberts managing to make ends meet, then?'

'Well, he's paying his debts and I imagine he can afford to treat himself to sushi for dinner once in a while.'

Moralès smiled and opened the clear plastic container. His colleague jumped at the chance to grab three or four pieces and wolf them down.

'It could use a dash of soy sauce.'

'And I need you to look for something else.'

'I'm your man.'

'I'd like you to find me the report on the investigation into Firmin Cyr's death.'

'What year?'

'The year after the moratorium came in.'

'The nineties; all that's in the paper archives. You're just trying to butter me up, aren't you? I love digging around in there.'

'How long will that take you?'

Lefebvre looked at his watch. 'Those archives are in Rimouski. I'll get on the phone to a colleague and ask him to email me a photocopy of the file. If you've got half an hour now, I'm sure we can find a few newspaper articles about the accident.'

Without waiting for an answer, Lefebvre turned his screen for Moralès to see, and initiated a search in a media database. A series of titles and dates appeared.

'These are all local newspapers. Follow me.'

Érik Lefebvre got up and left the room without bothering to check that Moralès was behind him. It occurred to the detective that his colleague was acting with the same air of preoccupation as he did when he gathered random objects from his surroundings during their conversations. They went down the corridor and turned right into the open-plan area, where Lefebvre opened the door to the archives room. He went straight to the far corner and plucked eight newspapers from three different drawers, piled them into Moralès's arms and led the way to the photocopier, next to which an empty table was conveniently placed.

Lefebvre took the newspapers from Moralès one at a time and opened them in turn, flipping straight to the page pertaining to Firmin Cyr's accident, as if he had memorised the page numbers from his computer in the blink of an eye. Lefebvre spread the papers out on the table and scanned them all remarkably quickly. He turned to Moralès before the detective had even finished reading the first article.

'Firmin Cyr died by drowning. It was an accident. Witnesses stated that his boat had capsized after a sudden change of direction. It seems that the skipper of the shrimp trawler the *Midday Girl* was trapped inside the wheelhouse and drowned. The investigation report will tell us more about that. His two deckhands were Réginald Morin and Daniel Cotton, of Cloridorme, and – wait for it – Bruce Roberts, of Rivière-au-Renard. Neither Morin nor Cotton knew how to swim. Bruce Roberts was the only one who managed to make it back to shore.'

On his way back to the auberge, Moralès noticed Leeroy Roberts' truck parked outside the fish market. He turned off towards the wharf, parked his car a little further away and pretended he was surprised to see the old fisherman coming out of the building carrying a plastic bag. He waved and made his way over.

'Ah, Mr Roberts, I'm glad I've run into you. I wanted to apologise for yesterday. You see, we just can't leave anything to chance in a case like this.'

Leeroy pursed his lips. 'It's all right.'

'Can I ask you a question?'

The old fisherman wasn't the type to shy away. 'Go on.'

'I've been told that during the cod moratorium, you went shrimp fishing in Firmin Cyr's zone and he was reasonably tolerant.'

Leeroy hesitated. He should have smelled a rat. 'That's true.'

'I'm finding it hard to grasp why you seem to have harboured so much animosity…'

The silence left a long wake. Leeroy weighed up the pros and cons and concluded he had nothing to lose by telling the story. Since day one, he'd told himself the detective would understand, because he had children of his own.

'Ever since Bruce was a young lad, he always wanted to come fishing with me. The day my wooden boat burned, he was on board with us. He was twenty-two. He was studying marine biology at university, and he came home for the summer holidays. When the boat caught fire, it gave me the fright of my life. I was afraid for my boy, not for myself. After that, I never took any of my kids to sea again. But they wanted to stay on the water whatever the cost. The season was over, anyway, so you know what Bruce did? He went to see Firmin. They didn't need another deckhand on the *Midday Girl*, but her skipper still took my son aboard. In the autumn I said to Bruce, finish your studies, find a career for yourself and forget about fishing. He spent the winter in the city, but he came back here in the spring. And he went back aboard the *Midday Girl*.' Leeroy sneered in disgust, as if replaying the scene in his mind. 'I might have been taking away some of his shrimp, but Firmin Cyr took my boy away from me. And later on, his Clément married my Angel.'

He shook his head, as if that could erase the episode from his memory.

'I didn't want my kids to get caught up in a life of fishing. I did everything I could to discourage them. You can ask them yourself. They'll tell you I charged them a hefty whack of interest, but I told them they could go to university for free if they wanted to study something else. And after you've spoken to them, have a look at my will. All the money they gave me is going right back to them.'

He took a few steps towards his pickup. Moralès turned on his heel to follow. Leeroy Roberts rested a hand on the roof of the truck and rubbed at the metal absentmindedly.

'I don't trust Jimmy's ex-wife. If I gave my son his money back, she'd drag him back to court to make him hand it over. But she can't get her mitts on his inheritance; that's protected by law. I had my eye on Clément too. I wanted to make sure he didn't end up with Angel's boat.'

He opened the driver's door.

'When we found the *Close Call II*, I didn't go out to sea to find a boat. It was my daughter I was looking for. When it dawned on me I'd never see her alive again, I said to my boys, I don't want to see your names dragged through the mud. Because they don't deserve that, and I don't want either of them behind bars.'

Roberts senior got behind the wheel and put his bag on the passenger seat.

'I'm the one who gets to inherit my daughter's boat. I know what that looks like, but would you let her husband have it, if you were in my boots?'

Moralès didn't answer. Leeroy Roberts slammed the door, started the engine and lowered the window.

'I've never hated the Cyrs, but I've never liked them either,' he said, before shifting into gear and driving away from the fish market.

Before he went up to his room, Moralès took a moment to go into the kitchen and put the cod fillets he had just bought at the fish market in the fridge. He placed some green onions, a red cabbage, peppers and a jalapeño on the counter and pushed aside two kiwis Corine had left there. He had all the fixings for tacos, and everything he needed to make the dough for the tortillas too. He thought about Leeroy and his sons, Clément and his mother, the Babin brothers, the men who had cut Angel's lines and the women who envied her spirit of adventure. He took off his jacket and holster, and went up to his room. He had noticed Sébastien's car parked out front, so he thought he would invite his son to join him for dinner.

As he drew near the door of their holiday apartment, he could hear movement inside. Was Corine nosing around his things again? He tiptoed closer and opened the door a crack. The first thing he saw in the soft light was Simone's origami seabird lying on the floor a few steps away. He pushed the door wide open. Sébastien, who had his back to the door, turned his head sharply, flushed, and did his best to preserve the modesty of the woman whose naked posterior he was giving a good seeing-to over the kitchenette table.

Joaquin averted his eyes in a flush of embarrassment of his own and avoided looking at the woman, whom he certainly did not want to identify. He tried to make a hasty exit, but was encumbered by his jacket, holster and weapon. In one swift movement, he bent down, put it all on the floor – the revolver and its holster with the jacket over the top – and gently picked up the origami creation before leaving the room, closing behind him a door he would rather not have opened.

When Sébastien was a teenager, he used to tell everyone he wanted to be a police officer. Then one day, he changed his mind. One day, children start to talk about things their parents can't even begin to understand, embrace values different to their own and make choices that leave those of the older generation scratching their heads and feeling like strangers.

Joaquin was rinsing the vegetables when his son walked into the kitchen.

'Dad…'

'Is that what you call a culinary experiment?'

Moralès was clumsily trying to unwrap the fish. He walked out of the kitchen. He wasn't going to be able to cook in this state. He strode over to the bar and returned with a bottle of rum. Rum wouldn't have been his first choice, but the tequila wasn't up to his standards. He poured two glasses and put them on the counter. One he knocked straight back. He didn't touch the other, but didn't invite Sébastien to drink it either.

'When you choose a woman, you condense into her the beauty of all the others – all their delicate touches, all their sensual movements, all their perfection. That's the only way to love.'

Joaquin turned away, rinsed the fish, sliced the fillets. Sébastien drizzled oil into a pan and put it on the burner, then took the knife and cut the green onions and jalapeño and sent them sizzling into the hot oil. Behind them, Joaquin heard the front door open and close, and guessed his son's guest had just left. He took a generous pinch of spice and sprinkled it on top of the onions.

'And when you're cooking the sea, you put everything in the same pan – the onions, the salt, the flavours, the memories, the doubts, the good times and the bad, the strong spices and the ones that cost too much, the herbs and the fiery peppers.'

In a show of defiance, Sébastien grabbed a kiwi, sliced it in two and tossed it into the pan. He did the same with the second kiwi.

'Like that?'

Joaquin clenched his teeth. '*En la madre!*'

He wasn't sure what sickened him the most: his son's cheating

on his partner on his work surface, or his insistence on concoct-
ing dishes devoid of flavour. He felt guilty that he hadn't found
the right questions to ask Sébastien, and had to resort to using
other people's words to talk to him – Lefebvre's, and those of
the grandmother who taught Joaquin to cook when he was a
boy. Sébastien took the lid off the blender and poured the ques-
tionable contents of the pan right into it. Then he tossed in
everything else he could see on the counter – lime juice, fresh
coriander and hot sauce. He looked at his father with an air of
defiance.

'Maude's pregnant.'

Sébastien abruptly turned the blender on, invading the
kitchen with a noise as unbearable as a child's annoying toy.
Joaquin reclaimed the pan, put it back on the heat and gently
added two of the fillets with a drizzle of oil. Sébastien turned
off the blender.

'When your mother was pregnant with you, I left my country
to be with her. And you, when your partner's expecting your
child, what do you do? You act like a stroppy teenager and run
away!'

Joaquin left it at that. His words were leaving him short of
breath.

Sébastien grabbed the red cabbage, looked his father in the
eye and plunged the knife in deep. 'It's not mine.'

He pushed the blade down and made short work of chopping
the cabbage first into quarters, then fine strips. Joaquin could
feel his knees starting to give way. The fish was sizzling in the
oil, filling the kitchen with its aroma.

'The first time she cheated on me, we were eighteen.'

Sébastien picked up the tongs and turned the fish his father
had left sizzling in the pan. He put a cast-iron plate over another
burner and turned it on to heat, then set the cabbage to one side,

reached for the dough, gave it a quick knead, and divided it. He rolled out the first tortilla and placed it calmly on the hotplate.

'She's cheated on me a lot. With I don't know how many other guys. She does it all the time. I thought she'd get fed up of it. But she hasn't. And you know what? At some point, I just got used to it.'

The dough was swelling and writhing in the heat. Sébastien flipped the tortilla before it burned and transferred the chopped cabbage to a bowl. He rolled out more tortillas and cooked them one by one. Joaquin pulled himself together and went back to frying the fish. One by one. That was all he could bring himself to do, stack one fried fillet on top of the last. And he listened, because he couldn't not hear.

'When she told me she was pregnant, I didn't know if the baby was mine. Still, I told her if she wanted to keep it, I was willing to take responsibility. To be the father. She said she needed to think about it. So I got in the car and drove, to give us time to think. I didn't bring anything with me, just my pots and pans really, and most of those came from you anyway. I thought that talking to you would help me understand. But on the way here, I got drunk. Then I started to dance, I took up fishing, and I don't know why, but I…' He gestured upstairs, to where he had been with the other woman.

Joaquin took the last fillet out of the pan, put it with the others and turned off the stove.

'That's what you've always done – invested yourself in one thing and made everything fit around it,' Sébastien said. 'You live your life the same way you do your cooking. You throw everything into your investigations, your relationship and your kids. But sometimes, something's got to give, because you can't do it anymore. And that's what's happened to me. I can't do this anymore.'

Joaquin wished he were drinking tequila, listening to music too loud and fishing with Cyrille. He wanted to be able to console his son, but all he could manage to do was put the pan in the sink and fill it with soapy water. Sébastien flinched as he felt the phone vibrate in his jeans pocket. He grabbed it and handed it to his father.

'It's her. She won't stop texting me. She wants to know where I am, what I'm doing, if I've met another woman. She says she's going to make up her mind soon.'

Joaquin took the device, not so much to look at it as to take it off his son's hands while he finished cooking the tortillas.

'What's your code?'

Sébastien took the lid off the blender and poured the curious kiwi salsa into a bowl. 'Maude. The five letters of her name.'

Joaquin tapped them in.

'She had an ultrasound yesterday. At thirteen weeks and four days. She was at a conference in Dallas at the time of conception.'

Moralès couldn't stop the phone vibrating in his hand. It made him feel old. Old and ridiculous.

'There's just one thing that's been running through my mind since the day I left, though. Do you know what that is?' Distraught, he looked at his father. 'Your loyalty.'

'What are you talking about, *chiquito*?'

'When you fell in love with Mum, you turned your back on your country, your culture and your language. You rejected your whole identity for her.'

'No. That's not true. I didn't turn my back on anything.'

'You never listen to Latino music.'

'I listen to lots of different kinds of music.'

'You lost your accent for her.'

'No. I changed my accent for my job. I was a cop and I was

fresh off the boat from a country of drug traffickers. You get the picture?'

'You let her walk all over you and did everything she wanted.'

'Appearances can be deceiving, *chiquito*. You thought you saw something, but you didn't. It was just a figment of your imagination.'

Moralès had explained this theory dozens of times to his investigation teams – that people crafted their own fiction and convinced themselves it was the truth. Could his son have done precisely that – modelled his love life on a lie?

'That's what you taught me – to be submissive.'

'I never taught you that, or asked that of you. I was never submissive. I loved your mother.'

There it was. He'd done it. Joaquin had conjugated his love in the past tense. He knew his son had heard what he'd said. He held Sébastien's gaze. Then he walked over to the sink and dropped his son's phone into the dish water.

'*Chiquito…*'

Joaquin found two foil trays and put them on the counter. He took a moment to savour the aroma of the perfectly cooked meal. In each of the trays, he placed two tortillas and topped them with fish, yogurt, chopped cabbage, kiwi salsa and fresh coriander. He fitted the lids, stacked one dish on top of the other and put them in a plastic bag, which he held out for his son to take.

Some days you have to take it all, and others it's better to let it all go.

Sébastien looked at his father, reached for the glass of rum and downed the amber liquid in one. Then he snatched the bag and left the kitchen.

♈

There was enough food left to feed an entire family, grand-children and all, but Joaquin Moralès had lost his appetite.

'Right, well I wouldn't say no to fish tacos!'

Moralès jumped and turned around. Lefebvre must have slipped into the auberge as Sébastien was leaving.

'Help yourself.'

The constable wasn't going to wait to be asked twice. He grabbed a plate and filled it generously.

'I've got photocopies of the case file for Firmin's death,' he said, tasting a spoonful of salsa somewhat apprehensively. 'Mmm … This saucy little mix of yours is quite something. Is it a Mexican family recipe?'

'No. It's a culinary experiment.'

Moralès picked up a spoon, scooped up some of the salsa and tasted it with his eyes closed. It was the first time something concocted by his son had tasted so good.

'Aren't you having any yourself?'

'I'm not hungry.'

'You've got a face like a prison guard's, Moralès. Come and sit down.'

Holding his plate in one hand, with the other Lefebvre grabbed the bottle of rum, two clean glasses and cutlery and made his way over to a booth by the window, offering the sea as a backdrop. He sat down, poured the rum and tucked into his first taco with gusto.

'I saw your son hoofing it out of here like someone had lit a fire under his behind. What's been going on here?'

Joaquin sat down too, and took a swig of rum. 'Sébastien's angry at me.'

'It's every kid's prerogative to declare war on their parents. But yours is a bit old to be stomping around like an angry teenager.'

'He accused me of being submissive.'

'Are you a submissive man, Moralès?'

'I don't think so.'

'Listen, you know I wouldn't think twice to get down on one knee in front of a woman like my Teresita, but I suppose that's not the same thing.'

'He accused me of abandoning my Mexican roots.'

'Is that true?' Lefebvre struggled to ask through a mouth full of taco.

'I left Mexico in 1976. Five years after the paramilitaries opened fire on students in Mexico City. In June.'

Lefebvre stopped eating.

'I was studying to be a police officer in a country of drug traffickers then. If I'd stayed there, I'd have been dead before I turned thirty-five.'

Lefebvre leaned against the backrest of the booth, took a swig of rum and waited for the rest of the story.

'I met Sarah by chance. She had flown to Mexico to meet up with a guy, but she ended up at the wrong airport and didn't speak a word of Spanish. I was patrolling around the airport and found her in tears.'

'Ah, so you took it upon yourself to play the tour guide and show her a good time. I knew you were the type to do whatever it takes to serve and protect,' Lefebvre said with a wink, diving back into his plate.

Moralès smiled in spite of himself. 'Yes, but I got her pregnant.'

Érik Lefebvre nearly choked on his fish tacos.

'So I did the decent thing. I came up to Montreal and married her.'

Lefebvre stopped coughing and pulled himself together. 'How old were you?'

'Twenty-two.'

Joaquin Moralès turned his gaze to the window and contemplated the gulf as it disappeared into the evening shadows.

'One of Sarah's uncles was a police officer with the Sûreté du Québec. He pulled some strings and got me into police-training school here. I had to repeat what I'd already studied down south, and perfect my French.'

Lefebvre pushed away his empty plate, wiped his mouth with the back of his hand and took a swig of rum.

'In the early eighties, all the law-enforcement agencies – the Mounties, the SQ and the municipal forces – were waging war on the narcos of Latin America. So being a Mexican in the SQ back then was as sketchy as being undercover. After a while, I'd had enough.'

'Of being undercover?'

Moralès had lost sight of the sea. The moon was yet to rise, and in the window all he could see were the reflections of the lights in the dining room, the bottle of rum, and his hands cupping the empty glass.

'Of seeing the worst Latinos doing the worst things. Of feeling ashamed. Of listening to the same music as them, hailing from the same continent and hearing their accent on my lips.'

'So you decided the Quebec accent wouldn't be as bad? It's not often you hear that.'

Joaquin mustered a smile.

'So what's your son holding against you, exactly?'

'He thinks I sacrificed my Mexican identity to please my wife.'

'And if that were the case, how would that be a problem?'

'He says I've passed on the gene of male submissiveness to him.'

Lefebvre opened his eyes wide, whistled between his teeth

and poured two more shots of rum. 'And I thought my mum had her head in the clouds.' Lefebvre raised his glass to his lips and downed it in one. 'So where's that son of yours gone now?'

'To see a woman he's met.'

'Didn't you say he was living with someone?'

'Yes.'

Joaquin didn't tell him Maude was expecting another man's child.

'It's a good way to exercise his freedom from male submiss-iveness, I suppose. And who's the girl, anyway?'

'No idea.'

Lefebvre slipped his way out of the booth. 'We all take turns playing someone else's tourist here in the Gaspé. Do you miss Mexico?' he asked.

Moralès didn't answer. He just sipped his rum as Lefebvre cleared his dishes and took them to the kitchen. On his return, the constable picked up the file he had brought with him and slid it across the table to the detective.

'Here, read this while you're waiting for your submissive teenager to come back. It's your copy of the case file for the in-vestigation into Firmin Cyr's death. I'm going home now. I'll have a look at my copy before I go to bed.'

Lefebvre walked over to the door and stopped, as if he had just remembered something. 'Turns out one of the officers who worked that case is still floating around.'

'In Gaspé?'

'Yes. Maybe the two of you can chat tomorrow. I'll get in touch and see what I can do.'

'OK, thanks.'

Lefebvre retrieved his coat from the hallway and put it on.

'Mind if I leave you to do the washing-up?' he said, on his way out the door.

Thursday 4th October

Moralès was finishing his breakfast when Corine walked in the front door of the auberge with a spring in her step. He hadn't seen her since Angel's funeral.

'Corine? Where were you?'

She looked at him and seemed taken aback. 'Is there a problem, Joaquin?'

He realised he had come on a little strong. Maybe because he'd been waiting to interview her for the last few days and had started to suspect she was avoiding him. Or maybe because he hadn't seen Sébastien since yesterday and that was tugging at his paternal heart strings. Or perhaps because he'd imagined them together and that had set him ill at ease.

'No. No problem at all. I'm sorry. I was just worried because I hadn't seen you.'

She hung up her coat and switched her autumn boots for indoor shoes as Joaquin got up to wash his dishes.

'No one needed me here, and the grief felt like it was weighing me down, so I thought I'd go and spend three days at my boyfriend's place. I told your son I was going. And I left my mobile number here just in case.'

She went over to the reception desk and pointed to a board on the wall where a number had been scribbled. Moralès hadn't thought to ask Sébastien if he was aware of Corine's comings and goings.

'I didn't know you had a boyfriend.'

'Well, I do. He works at the microbrewery in L'Anse-à-Beaufils and he lives in Sainte-Thérèse. Oh, and he plays on the same baseball team as your colleague, Érik Lefebvre. The Sainte-Thérèse-de-Gaspé Mariners.' She said it with comic enthusiasm.

'I have a question to ask you, Corine.'

He returned to the breakfast table and reached into his file for the list of names she had given him the morning after his arrival at the auberge.

'Why isn't Kim Morin's name on this list?' he asked.

Corine frowned. 'You asked me for the list of fishermen who were there that night. So I just wrote the names of the fishermen.'

'Are there other people who were there that night whose names weren't on your list?'

'Yes. Louis Legrand, who's a barman at the Brise-Bise in town, my boyfriend Gabriel Sutton and me.'

Moralès picked up a pen and added these names to the list.

'I'm sorry, I misunderstood what you asked,' Corine said.

'What time did they all leave?'

'Kimo left around two. She's single and tends to get a lot of attention from men. She was getting fed up of them putting the moves on her. You know, the guys were letting their hair down at the end of the season, and they'd had a fair bit to drink…'

'Who was putting the moves on her?'

She hesitated for a moment, clearly unsure what to answer. 'Plenty of guys…'

Moralès stared at her, waiting for her to elaborate.

She took a deep breath. 'Oh, all right then. You know I don't really like answering those kinds of questions, but it seems to be important … Kimo spent all last week on an emotional roller coaster, and to be honest that's partly why I went away for a few days. I'm a friend, not a therapist. And sometimes I have a hard time wrapping my head around complex relationship stuff, so I tend to put my foot in it without meaning to.' She stood rigidly and spoke like a teacher reciting a lesson. 'Kimo's been single for a long time. Maybe men are intimidated by her athletic physique, I don't know. But back in the spring, she went out to watch the boats going back in the water after the winter, because she likes that kind of thing, especially the big shrimp trawlers. Anyway, Bruce Roberts soon invited her aboard, and they started to see each other. But not long after that, Clément Cyr invited her aboard his boat as well. It's almost like he was jealous of Bruce, you see?'

She waited for him to say yes before she continued.

'Bruce is a shy kind of guy, but the drink brings him out of his shell. So he had a few the other night to try and win Kimo back. But you know how men get when they've had a drink, and Clément was trying it on with Kimo too. He was as drunk as a skunk. It's creepy when you think about it, because right around the same time, his wife was taking her own life. So Kimo's ticked off at Clément, and she feels guilty for what happened. I mean, it's normal to be a bit shaken up, but it was a suicide. It's not like Kimo killed her.' She bit her lower lip. 'You know, Kimo wouldn't hurt a fly, but try and put yourself in her shoes. She's been single for three years, then out of the blue two guys come along and are all but ready to fight over her. Of course, you're going to say she should have just chosen Bruce, because he's single, but it's not as simple as that.'

She toyed nervously with a salt shaker and pepper mill that were minding their own business. So many words were pouring from Corine's mouth, standing there in the dining room at the auberge, she could power an electric turbine, Moralès thought.

'Kimo's an athlete. She's competitive by nature, and winning competitions and medals isn't just something she wants, it's something she needs. And she's very physical, if you know what I mean. Angel Roberts was like a superwoman around here.

Even I have to admit I admired her. It took some guts to be a woman fishing in a man's world.'

It struck Moralès that she must have been wrestling with her conscience in the last few days, and that her boyfriend had likely encouraged her to tell the police everything.

'I think that in Kimo's mind, Angel was probably the stiffest competition she could find in the whole of the Gaspé. It was a pride thing. The woman who's a model of strength, the one we all aspire to be, is right there, and you've got the chance to get your rocks off with her husband. Talk about a trophy to hang on your bedpost.'

Her eyes widened in horror at what she'd just said.

'I know that sounds brutal. It's not the kind of competition that deserves a trophy, but who are we to judge Kimo? She's not a bad person. She's just a single woman in a man's world. Are you with me?'

Corine sighed deeply, as if she were squeezing a beach ball against her chest to get all the air out. Revealing everything and navigating a maze of explanations to get to the bottom of it all had left her exhausted. She pulled out a chair and collapsed into it.

'Louis Legrand left around three in the morning. My boyfriend stayed the night here with me. We tidied up the next day. Louis was supposed to come back and lend a hand, but we called him and said not to bother.'

Moralès gave her a gentle smile. 'Is there anything else I should know about that evening, Corine?'

She looked at him, sorry to have kept him in the dark for so long, and shook her head.

'Did Kimo go up to see Clément Cyr in his room?'

'No. I'd tell you if that had happened. Kimo found it insulting when drunk men came on to her. She might have slept with him, but only if he was sober. It would have been humiliating for her if he'd been on the sauce. Otherwise she might have ended up in bed with Bruce, but he was drunk as well. Eventually she just got fed up and left. By that point, things were just about wrapping up anyway, and I didn't really need her here anymore.'

'Had Bruce Roberts left by then?'

She thought for a moment. 'No, he left right after her. You asking me that, it's reminded me that I was surprised to see him stay so late. He's not usually a party animal. I did wonder if he was sticking around to try it on with Kimo, or to keep an eye on his brother-in-law.'

'Keep an eye on him?'

'Yes, to see if Kimo was going up to Clément's room.'

Joaquin thanked her.

'Don't hesitate if you have any more questions. You know, I liked Angel Roberts. I can't believe a woman like her took her own life.'

Moralès picked up his file and went up to his room to grab his jacket and his holster.

His legs were aching, and it was painful to breathe, but Sébastien kept on running. He had woken up with the taste of another woman on his lips. The taste of adultery, he mused cynically, before correcting himself. No, a half-hearted nibble of freedom.

Leaving her place in the middle of the night, he had been reluctant to go back to the auberge. He hadn't wanted to run into his father. So, he had got behind the wheel and driven out to the national park. Finding the barrier locked, he had turned around and parked off the main road in the waste-disposal area for motorhomes, where he had come to retrieve Joaquin's car a few days earlier. He had taken his sleeping bag from the boot, found a space to stretch out on the backseat and dozed there uncomfortably until dawn.

When he heard the park rangers' truck go by, he had hurried to get up. Not wanting to look like a ruffian who had spent the night sleeping in his car in a waste-disposal area at a national park, he had driven up to the barrier and told the park staff he had been waiting for the park to open to go fishing. The guy in the booth had barely given him a second glance. He himself looked like he'd just spent the night on his mum's sofa.

Sébastien felt silly for having lied for no reason.

As he approached the turnoff for Grande-Grave, he slowed down, but didn't go down into the parking area, towards the boat that belonged to the woman in the wedding dress, towards the wharf where the anglers might soon be setting up.

Instead, he continued straight on, feeling compelled to keep driving on the gravel road ahead, towards the tip of the park he knew wasn't too far away.

What do we inherit from our parents? He couldn't stop turning the question over in his mind. Some genetics were easily discernible: silky hair, perfect vision, broad shoulders, heart disease.

When he reached the end of the road at L'Anse-aux-Amérindiens – Indigenous Cove – he couldn't bring himself to turn around and go back. He parked by the picnic area and got out of the car.

Other things weren't so easy to see, like loyalty. But he was sure that kind of thing was hereditary. If Sébastien had loved and accepted Maude in spite of her whims, it was in obedience to a silent order, a sort of paternal injunction that dictated he should be submissive to his partner, like his father had been, in order to be a worthy Moralès son.

From the picnic area, he saw there was a path leading down to the water and along the shore. He set off at a jog, driven only by his own momentum, by what he had set in motion when he left Maude, drove away from Montreal, travelled all that distance along Highway 20, then further as it narrowed into Highway 132, had one drink too many, danced from bar to bar, tried his hand at fishing and slept with another woman.

He had prepared his arguments in anticipation of yesterday's confrontation. Strong words about the power of a sense of belonging, and accusations too. That confrontation had to happen for him to be able to put the past behind him. He had been expecting his father to feel hurt, and also to acknowledge the truth in Sébastien's revelations. But all Joaquin had said was that appearances can be deceiving, and he was deceived. But how could he have been mistaken? He was there all along, growing up in the family home. How many times had he heard his mother telling his father that such and such a word was pronounced such and such a way in Quebec French? She even used to tease Joaquin when he had difficulty wrapping his tongue around something.

As he ran through the brush, the ocean opened up before him, shining calm and bright beyond the shore, so near and yet so far-reaching, its surface only broken by the powerful breathing and graceful breaching of the whales offshore.

How did his father react? He used to laugh. They were happy together. Sébastien shook his head firmly. No, that was just a facade. Like with him and Maude, things were not what they seemed.

The further he ran, the closer he got to the end of the path. Before long he found himself at the Cap Gaspé lighthouse, at the very peak of the headland. His legs were aching, and his lungs were burning. A sign pointing to Land's End beckoned him further still, down the cliff side, to the end of the world, it seemed.

His mind flashed to Maude, crying, admitting she'd cheated on him. She was eighteen, and she'd kissed another guy at a party. He had laughed it off. And then? Flash forward to the ultrasound, twelve years later. You thought you were suffocating, but you weren't. It was just a figment of your imagination. The white pixels of the image against the black background.

Sébastien set off down the steep staircase and continued along the boardwalk amidst the excited chattering of the songbirds and the cruel cries of the gulls.

He turned his focus to the last few days, to the fishing, and thought about the bass biting the hook. That flooded his mind with images of Kimo's body and a feeling of relief or unease, he wasn't sure which. He thought about the mackerel that had twisted and writhed at the end of his fishing line. *I was fresh off the boat from a country of drug traffickers.* That's what his father had said.

Sébastien caught a glimpse of the sea emerging between the tree branches. There, off this point, was where they had pulled up the body of the drowned woman the other day. Sébastien could still see her floating there, her dress fanning out like coral around her. A bride in her wedding dress. And her husband, kneeling over her, paralysed by pain.

A sign proclaimed that Land's End – the end of the world, if the sign in French were to be translated literally – was just a few steps further. He slowed his pace and stopped to catch his breath before he stepped onto the wooden viewing platform. Beads of sweat trickled into his eyes. He cast his gaze around the cliffs surrounding the crow's nest of a lookout. Then he let his head become heavy and his hands hang down by his sides.

He allowed himself to be lulled by the gentle murmuring of the waves below as they lapped over the rocks that lurked just beneath the water's surface. A sudden splash jolted him out of his trance. It sounded like the divers had when they went overboard to free the woman in the wedding dress. The coral bride. *Did you too dream of the horizon?* The vision of her came to him again. Her head held high, her arms wide open, before the endless ocean. *Were you too a slave to an illusion? Did you follow orders that were never voiced?*

He took a step out onto the lookout platform. And saw a seal cavorting in the water below. *I never asked that of you.* The early-morning light splintered on the swell like a golden carpet shimmering from the rising sun to the shore. Sébastien was astonished. This was like seeing something for the very first time. He had noticed the birds, the seals and the fish, he had watched the fishing line and he had admired the Percé Rock. But only now did he really see the sea and understand what Cyrille had meant.

Sébastien Moralès was transfixed by the sight. He was overwhelmed by something welling up inside him. A desire to be swallowed up by the horizon. The clouds scudded away, the sky turned blue and the entire Atlantic Ocean opened up before his eyes. It took his breath away. As Sébastien ventured to the handrail, a wisp of cloud veiled the sun and cast a shadow on the shimmering swell. It wasn't a carpet, and there was nothing golden about it, he realised. With a pounding heart, he backed sharply away from the edge to the safety of the path. The ocean was making his head spin.

Walking up to the *Ange-Irène*, the detective was impressed by the sheer size of her hull. She cut an imposing silhouette above the waterline, but loomed even taller and broader in her winter cradle. A pickup truck was parked alongside. Moralès deduced that Bruce Roberts was inside this behemoth of the seas. Reluctantly he set foot on the stepladder on wheels the crew had installed when they took the boat out of the water. Even though the steps were securely attached to the deck, Moralès found the vibrations beneath his feet disquieting. The ladder wasn't just steep, it must have been at least ten metres high. At last, he was standing on the deck.

He hated these kinds of heights at the best of times, but especially now, with the mild dizziness he had been experiencing since his Saturday-night concussion. Looking over the railing of the shrimp trawler, he couldn't see a thing below, other than the hard ground his body would smash into if he were to fall. He had seen that sort of thing before, men who had fallen or been pushed from heights lower than this and ended up as flat as a pancake with their skull caved in. Sights like that were enough to make you want to keep your feet firmly on the ground.

He ducked into the wheelhouse. Had it really been ten days since he was last here? There was no one in sight. He descended the steep, narrow staircase at the centre of the wheelhouse into the bowels of the boat. For a second, it occurred to him that he should call Lefebvre, then he thought better of it. This was just going to be an informal chat. Plus, even if he did reach out, his colleague would probably find an excuse not to leave his office.

The stairs turned ninety degrees, releasing Moralès on the port side. He ventured towards the bow and found a kitchenette equipped with a fridge, one of those pivoting stoves that were made to stay upright at sea, and built-in bench seating around a table, all awash with fluorescent light. Further still, a door opened into a six-berth forecabin, three bunks stacked on either side of the bow. There were still sleeping bags in the bunks, and coats hanging from hooks on the wall. Between the kitchenette and the forecabin, two doors stood across from one another, one revealing a toilet, and the other, a shower. There was no one there either.

Moralès retraced his steps to the bottom of the stairs and hesitated, unsure which way to turn. A strong smell of oil, melted ice, fish guts and salt hung in the air. He turned towards the stern and saw a corridor leading to the tween deck. Suddenly he heard a noise beneath his feet. He made his way to the starboard side and discovered another flight of stairs below those he had followed a moment ago. Setting foot on the first step, he was struck by the uncomfortable sense that this mechanical beast could swallow him whole as he descended into its belly. A glass globe on the ceiling cast a harsh light around the steel-girder-framed space, exposing all its flaking paint, salt residue and muddy boot prints.

Unlike the first, this staircase descended in a straight line across the entire width of the trawler. Again, Moralès emerged on the port side. He sneaked a glance towards the stern. The layout looked similar to the level above, with closed doors at the end of a narrow corridor that probably opened onto a shrimp-loading area.

A bright-yellow electrical cable ran down the stairs and snaked through a door located at the bow. A red metal toolbox plastered with stickers from Newfoundland sat open on the threshold. The top layer of tools had been removed and placed on the floor alongside. Moralès walked slowly towards the open door. As he approached, he could see an engine, or generator – he couldn't tell – under a fluorescent strip light just like the one in the kitchenette. To the left of the engine, he saw a pair of boots. There was a man there, on the floor. Moralès froze in alarm, reached a hand to his holster and glanced around warily.

Bruce Roberts straightened himself up and turned his head. He was wearing overalls and holding a blue rag. He looked at Moralès and seeing the detective's palm resting on his revolver, he slowly raised his hands in the air.

'Easy there, I'm just doing an oil change.'

Feeling like he'd overreacted, Moralès let his guard down and tried to relax. 'I'm sorry. I didn't realise you were kneeling down. I thought you were in trouble. Can't be too careful.'

'These contraptions aren't exactly designed to be ergonomically accessible for mechanics. If you don't mind, I just have to put a plug back in. I'd rather you didn't shoot me.'

Moralès nodded and backed his way out into the corridor to leave the man to finish his job. He stood outside the door for a moment, feeling nauseous and ill at ease, then realised he didn't have to stay right there.

'I'll wait upstairs, all right?' he called.

'OK.' Bruce Roberts' voice was barely audible amidst the metallic tapping of the tools against the engine.

Moralès went up the first flight of stairs, hesitated, then continued all the way up to the wheelhouse. He avoided going too close to the windows and looking down at the ground far below. Being up here did nothing to ease his discomfort. He sat on the bench that stretched along the port side of the bow, with his back to the window. Staring at the floor, he waited, mulling over what he was going to ask the fisherman.

Minutes later, Bruce Roberts tramped up the stairs. He stopped two steps from the top and rested his forearms on the wooden handrail, using the rag in one hand to rub the grease off his fingers. He didn't look particularly happy to see the detective.

'What do you want from me?'

'About fifteen years ago, you were a deckhand for Firmin Cyr, aboard the *Midday Girl*,' Moralès said.

Bruce Roberts took the statement like a punch in the face. He recoiled, then recovered quickly from the blow, but didn't answer. It wasn't technically a question.

'With Réginald Morin and Daniel Cotton,' Moralès pressed.

Still the man expressed no acknowledgement of these affirmations.

Moralès changed tack. 'Have you been working aboard this boat for long?'

'Two years, more or less.'

'Didn't you want to go fishing with your father?'

'He never hired his own kids. He preferred to take on strangers.'

Moralès nodded. 'What happened that day, when the shrimp boat went down?'

Bruce Roberts was really on his guard now. Moralès wouldn't have been surprised if the man asked him to leave. Roberts pressed his lips together and squinted like he was looking for a buoy on the water, a speck on the horizon. Then, as if he'd found the answer out there, he turned his gaze back to the detective.

'All you have to do is read the investigation report.'

'I've read it.'

'How come you're here asking me questions, then? Why are you stirring all this up? Isn't it enough that my sister's dead?'

He paused, took a step backward on the second-to-last step of the stairs and leaned against the handrail behind him. Then he hung his head in his hands and started to rub his fingers again absentmindedly.

'What do you want me to say? Firmin was drunk. He was always hitting the bottle. He'd filled the starboard ballast tanks and forgotten to empty them. That's why the boat capsized. The boat had paravanes for stabilisers. You must have seen those before. They're like two big triangular ladders with anchors on the ends. You lift them upright when you're docked and lower them at sea to keep the boat level. He hadn't lowered them. So anyway, when he turned the wheel sharply, the weight of the ballast heeled us to starboard and the weight of the stabilisers tipped us over. We weren't even that far out. Around Cap-des-Rosiers. I was thrown into the water. I lost my boots. I took off my overalls and I swam. It was so fucking cold out there. The waves washed me ashore and I went into hypothermia just before the ambulance arrived.

'Usually I was more on the ball. I knew we had to keep an eye on Firmin. He was drinking too much. And I should've seen this coming. Reg and Dan weren't strong enough swimmers to make it to shore. Later, I found out that the wheelhouse door had slid shut and trapped Firmin inside. Firmin – what a bloody idiot. He'd had a patio door put in on the wheelhouse because he wanted to look out and see everything, all the shoals of fish, everything we caught and any storms that were coming in. And he capsized on a sunny day with an east wind blowing. Sometimes I think about that patio door of his sliding shut and the metal bar locking into place on the outside. Then the water rising all around and him knowing he was going to die, with his bottle of Jack Daniel's in his hand.' The fisherman looked up suddenly, his eyes filled with turmoil, not wariness. 'This whole thing is a fucking human tragedy! The Cyrs had a gripe with my grandfather way back because he would never barter on anything when he worked at the old Hyman general store; my old man was pissed off at the Cyrs because Firmin took me on board; the Cyrs were up in arms at my old man because he muscled his way into their fishing grounds; Clément's obviously got a grudge against me because he said I'd killed his old man; my old man was irked that Firmin's son married his Angel … There's no bloody end to the madness!'

'The Cyrs think you killed Firmin?'

'At one point, that's what Fernand and Clément came out with. I was twenty-four years old, for fuck's sake. Jeez, you'd have to be wrong in the head to think a young deckhand would want to bump off his crew over a few measly shrimp.'

He hung his head once more.

'The Cyrs are a bunch of lunatics. All except Miss Gaétane; she was a good teacher when I was at school.' He stopped rubbing his hands, though, leaving the imperfections the way they were.

'Now look at me, dredging all that up again for you. Sometimes I wonder why the hell I went into fishing. They've all got me over a bloody barrel – the government that tells me what to do, the buyers who won't put their hands in their pockets, the Cyrs who are still hot under the collar over a handful of measly shrimp, my old man, who won't stop harping on about his bloody cod fifteen years after they shut the fishery down, my brother and all his secrets, poaching with those Babin lowlifes, and then my sister goes and kills herself! Look at me. I've got a degree in marine biology, but I'm swimming in debt like my ancestors and up to my elbows in grease, standing in front of a squeaky-clean detective who's asking me how life made my hands so dirty.'

Now he turned to the horizon.

'I'm in up to my neck, like the damned of the sea.'

Moralès climbed down the ladder very carefully and stood by his car for a long while, thinking about the net of misery this all seemed to be. Not wanting to rock the boat, so to speak, he hadn't asked Bruce Roberts whether he was envious of his sister, who used to blast out reggae when she went to sea. He had also refrained from asking whether he had been keeping tabs on his brother-in-law that night at the bar, or followed Kimo home or somewhere else. The fisherman had stood there in silence for a moment before he turned his back and the stairs swallowed him into the belly of the hull again. That had suited Moralès. He'd had enough of their discussion, of the sense of confinement on board that made his head spin.

Now he was back on solid ground, he turned his thoughts to Gaétane Cloutier. She had said that Firmin's death was an accident and insisted that never – not ever – had the father of her son harboured any frustration at sharing his fishing grounds. Bruce Roberts had stated precisely the opposite. Not just once, but twice.

Sébastien drove back to the auberge and was relieved to see Joaquin's car wasn't there. He didn't want to run into him. He had come here to the Gaspé Peninsula to confront him, but he kept putting it off. It was slowly dawning on him that he was a younger version of his father, whether he liked it or not. He was about to turn the shower on when he heard the landline ringing in the room. It was Kimo.

'My family's got a little cabin by the river,' she said. 'If you feel like it, I could show you how to fly fish later this afternoon. The season's over, but we can just pinch the hook closed and practise casting the line.'

He said yes without thinking, relieved to have something else to do, a project to look forward to, an escape from his own thoughts.

'Would you like me to bring something to eat?' he found himself asking.

'Er … yes. All right.'

He hung up and hesitated for a second, then dialled the number for his voicemail. The handset wasn't working since Joaquin had tossed it in the dishwater, but the line was still active and he could still receive messages. He entered his code and heard that he had two new messages. The first was from Maude.

'Hi.' She paused. 'It's all right, if you want to be the father.'

Sébastien bent double as if he had been punched in the stomach, and held the phone away from his ear. He didn't listen to the rest of the message. He deleted it so he'd never have to hear it again. And took a deep breath. He straightened up and leaned on the bathroom sink for support. The second message played automatically.

'Ah! Mr Sébastien, this is Renaud Boissonneau, calling to ask for help.' An octave higher than usual, the voice was overflowing with tears and drama. 'You'll never believe it, but let me tell you, we're all of a flummox here because of Cyrille Bernard.' Renaud sounded breathless, as if he were trying to choke back the emotion. 'He's gone. Gone, let me tell you. He's gone off in his boat, because it's not at the wharf and his sister came and said he wasn't in his room and now everyone's wondering why he's not come back.' Renaud burst out sobbing. 'Mr Sébastien, you have to tell your father to come home and investigate.'

Sébastien deleted the message and stepped into the shower.

Through the window of her dining room, Gaétane Cloutier watched the detective walk up to the house with her empty Tupperware container in one hand, and it occurred to her that she should have told him to keep it. She had given Moralès an excuse to come back, stick his foot in the door, and ask her to clarify this and that, and rub at the discoloured stains in the fabric of her memory.

She opened the door and forced a smile of resignation. Moralès nodded. He knew she hadn't told him everything. She let him come in. There was no point resisting the rising tide.

'Can I pour you a coffee?' she asked.

'Not today.'

She took that to mean that this would be a brief visit and pulled a chair out from the table, sitting down and inviting him to do the same with a wave of the hand. Moralès took a seat at the end of the table. He didn't want to sit across from her and make her feel like she was in the interview room.

'What do you want to know?'

He chose his words carefully. 'Yesterday, I was led to believe that Leeroy Roberts bringing his shrimp trawler into the fishing grounds of your late husband, Firmin Cyr, hadn't stirred up any trouble.'

She sighed. 'You've talked to Bruce, haven't you?'

'And his father.'

She took a deep breath, as if that would help her decide where to begin her admissions. 'After his boat caught fire, Leeroy didn't want his kids to go into fishing. So Firmin took Bruce on board for the rest of the season. Truth be told, maybe it was to get Leeroy's back up. After that, winter came and Bruce went back to finish his studies. Then, in the spring, they announced the cod moratorium, and Leeroy showed up with his shiny new shrimp trawler. If you ask me, when he was younger, Leeroy must have thought fishing was the finest way in the world to make a living. And maybe it was … until it wasn't. The moratorium sent him into depression. Financially, he bounced back with the shrimp he caught, but he was only killing time until they opened up the cod fishery again. He's still waiting, and he's going to carry those worthless licences with him to his death bed.'

'Did Bruce work for your husband for a long time?'

She regarded the detective pensively. 'Two years. The first time Firmin took him aboard, it was because Leeroy's boat had gone up in smoke. The next year Bruce came back from the city saying he wanted to be a fisherman. Leeroy was incensed. Bruce went back aboard the *Midday Girl* because his own father wouldn't have him. That broke Bruce's heart, you know.'

'And your son Clément, what did he make of Bruce being on his father's boat?'

'He said that Bruce was spying and was going to tell Leeroy where all the best fishing spots were. Bruce was what, twenty-three or twenty-four? Clément was twenty. For lads that age it's all about showing bravado and seeing who's the alpha male. When Firmin tried to tell him to keep his mouth shut, Clément took it the wrong way and thought he was siding with the shrimp poachers, as he called them. My Firmin liked Bruce, you know. He felt sorry for him, because his own father wanted nothing of him and Clément kept badmouthing him.'

'And when the accident happened…' Moralès prompted.

She nodded and continued with a heavy voice, filled with things that got stuck, encumbered by the harsh words her son had said about the Roberts lad she, like her husband, had taken a shine to.

'Clément wasn't on the boat that day. He had an exam at the Maritime Institute. He went overboard, if you'll pardon the pun, like any hot-headed young male who can't keep a lid on his pain.'

'And he accused Bruce of killing his father for a handful of shrimp?'

She glanced up at him. 'Was it Bruce who said that – a handful of shrimp?' She puckered her face into the expression of a school teacher telling off a pupil for swearing in class. 'We're talking about a quota of fifty thousand kilos of shrimp! That was worth a fortune, especially back then. The skippers used to carry guns on board, you know. That wasn't to protect a couple of measly rings of frozen shrimp, like the ones you buy in the supermarket. These trawlers aren't poor men's boats, Mr Moralès; they're commercial vessels. Fishing is an industry, and it's big business…'

She let those words drift into silence.

'I'm not saying that to point the finger at Bruce. No matter how many shrimp were at stake, he wasn't the one who killed Firmin.'

'Who, then?'

She forced the shadow of a smile, reluctant to reveal the love of her life once again. Her Firmin. She was fond of Fernand, of course. There was a certain comfort in their familiarity, and she wouldn't throw that away. But he had none of the sparkle, joy and exuberance of the man she had loved, the man who had given her a son.

'It's just like I said yesterday, you're trying to pin the guilt on someone.' Her voice was shaking. 'You're going to tell me Firmin had drunk too much to go on the water. Réginald Morin was on board that day and he lost his life too. Go see his brother if you want. He'll only get mad at you if you tell him it was Firmin's fault. That's not how things work among mariners around here. Reg, Dan and Bruce, they all knew Firmin was drinking on the job, but they still went aboard with him that morning.'

She took a painful breath that seemed to eat away at her inside.

'That's the way my Firmin was. He had a sense of humour, he was a people magnet, and he was always the life of the party. He used to welcome anyone on board, and he'd even give fish to the tourists. Once he found out Dan Cotton's brother didn't have two pennies to rub together to buy himself a fridge. Do you know what he did? He arranged for a brand-new one to be delivered right to the man's door. Generous of heart and spirit, he was. And he literally died in the drink, locked into his boat and watching the sea rise up around him.'

Gaétane Cloutier sat up and turned a severe eye on Moralès.

'When I saw you walk in here earlier, I had a feeling you were going to say you'd opened up the investigation file and had come to tell me it wasn't just an accident, to make me point the finger and admit my Firmin was a criminal because he'd taken the boat out under the influence, that he was the one who killed Reg Morin and Dan Cotton. You must be wondering why I didn't tell you all this yesterday.'

The question had certainly crossed the detective's mind.

'But why would I have told you? So that you would judge him, a man you never even knew? And what are you going to do with this precious snippet of information, anyway? You're going to dig up a bunch of reports that reek of damnation, melancholy and yellowed paper. And after that? Are you going to dig up his remains and put his coffin in prison? How long for? Just let him rest in peace, all right!'

As she finished her sentence, Moralès heard a door slam behind him. A man almost as tall as Clément Cyr, but older and with a knee affliction that gave him a slight limp, entered the room.

He looked at his partner, then at Joaquin. 'Are you the detective?'

Moralès nodded.

'Please get out of our home now. Leave us in peace. We've suffered enough as it is. We've never understood why Clément married that girl, but we've come to love her, in spite of her father. We're sad and sorry she's dead, but we've got nothing more to say about it.'

Moralès hesitated. He wanted to ask Fernard Cyr a question or two, but the man glared at him before looking past him to the front door, and the detective understood this conversation was over.

He had neglected to tell his father about Cyrille Bernard's departure. Well, technically, it had slipped his mind, but that wouldn't change anything. He had gone to buy wine and food on autopilot, without thinking. He had filled the shopping basket with too much wine and too much food, as it happened; as if he were going away for a week. Maybe that was what he wanted – to get away from it all, even from himself.

He arrived at Kimo's place. The hatchback of her car was open and loaded with fishing gear. Sébastien made some space for his bags, then returned to grab his jacket from his car as Kimo emerged from the house with a wave and walked towards the open tailgate. She looked at the bags, tried to find somewhere to stash her boots and ended up putting them in the rear footwell.

'How are you doing?' he asked.

'What about you?' she replied. 'Ready for your big adventure?'

He swallowed uncomfortably. For the first time, he noticed something distant in the young woman's smile. He found himself wondering what she saw in him and why she was inviting him to her cabin. But those were questions he couldn't bring himself to ask. He went with her without knowing the answers because he didn't want to go back to the auberge.

Moralès went directly to the Grande-Grave wharf from Gaétane Cloutier's house and it seemed like a pilgrimage of sorts. The *Close Call II* was out of the water now. On a metal cradle in a corner of the parking area, the orphaned lobster trawler sat facing the same body of water that had taken the life of her young skipper. Leeroy Roberts must have had the boat put in dry dock to outsmart the poachers.

Moralès couldn't shake the sense he was going around in circles. He turned back and drove out of the national park again, hesitated about which way to turn when he got to the main road and ended up heading towards the cemetery in Gaspé. That was where Angel Roberts' ashes had been interred.

He thought about his boss, Marlène Forest, who suspected her brother-in-law would be spending the rest of his life behind bars. Moralès had acted on her suggestion and looked into the inheritance as a potential motive. It was true that Leeroy Roberts would gain ownership of Angel's lobster trawler, and the Roberts sons would one day inherit from their father, but there was nothing to suggest that any of these men, acting alone or together, had made an attempt on Angel's life. It was also true that there was a history of bad blood between these men and the Cyr family, but nothing, at least in the detective's eyes, that would warrant the murder of the fisherwoman.

Even if one of them had decided to kill Angel Roberts, how they had done it remained a complete mystery. The young skipper had been dragged into the water seventeen kilometres offshore, after three in the morning, with no marks suggesting she'd put up a fight. Even assuming she had been sufficiently drugged to remain unconscious while the murderer or murderers tied her up and sent her overboard without leaving any prints, how would they have made it back to shore?

Moralès parked in the street, got out of the car and walked towards the cemetery gate. He was hoping to find the right spot by looking for fresh flowers. As he made his way down the path between the grass verges, he noticed a man trudging towards him. A sad giant of a man.

Moralès said hello; Clément simply nodded.

'Still haven't found the killer, eh?'

Moralès cleared his throat, reluctant to voice the conclusion he might have to draw in this case. 'I don't think it was murder,' he replied.

The giant of a man was trying to stop the images in his mind from losing their colour. If the memories turned to sepia, they would never come back to life. He remembered how happy they had been, camping together. She was going for a swim in the river. She was coming out of the water in her red swimsuit, her feet sinking into the sand. She was laughing as she walked towards him. The water was dripping from her body. Later that night, she was sitting by the fire and he saw her face lit up by the flickering glow of the flames. Every move she made was a grace and a blessing. Her laugh was a string of pearls in her throat.

He shook his head. 'Angel didn't commit suicide. She was far too happy a woman for that.'

He could see her running towards him now, a streak of light across the dreary autumn grass, only to lose her smile, fade to grey, dissolve before his eyes, disappear.

'You miss her, I can tell,' Moralès said.

'So much, it's making my head spin.'

The sea was a treasure chest for those who fished, brimming with the promise of full nets, heavy traps and sequins of sunlight shimmering on the water. For Clément Cyr, the sea was more than a source of wealth; it was a thing of beauty too, because when he raised his head, he would often see his wife's boat on the horizon.

'I was just at your mother's house,' Moralès added.

'Oh, really?' There was a hint of concern in Cyr's voice.

'Everything's all right. I just had a few questions to ask her about your father's death. You see, two deaths from drowning in the same family – I found that intriguing.'

'You should have talked to me. I could have answered your questions. It was a stupid accident. The starboard ballast tanks didn't empty and the boat capsized when my dad turned the wheel. According to the investigation, Bruce Roberts wasn't to blame, even though he was the only one who survived.'

It wasn't the first time Moralès had seen people deny the evidence. Clearly, Clément Cyr was struggling with his grief. As if someone were waiting for him, the man waved dismissively at Moralès. He was obviously in a hurry to leave, to flee the cemetery where he had just buried his wife.

Moralès took three steps forward, then stopped. Could the reason Bruce Roberts had stayed longer at the bar that night have been to make sure Clément didn't go home too soon, while someone else was busy killing Angel? The *Close Call II* was full of Jimmy Roberts' and the Babin brothers' fingerprints, but because Jean-Paul Babin worked for Angel and the two others were using the lobster trawler for poaching, that wasn't unusual. But still, the question remained: how would the killer or killers have made their way back to shore? If they had use of another vessel, they wouldn't have needed Angel's to go poaching,

Moralès figured. He carried on along the path that led down the middle of the cemetery.

'Oh, hello, Mr Moralès. Don't be alarmed, we've met before, over Caplan way. Langevin Brothers. We've got branches all around the Gaspé Peninsula.'

It was the undertaker, the chatty one. Moralès said hello.

'Are you here to visit Angel Roberts? Be careful not to get your feet dirty. Our columbarium in Gaspé is under construction. It'll be far more practical for people who want to pay their loved ones a visit without getting their feet dirty. I said to Clément Cyr we could keep Angel's ashes in storage until the columbarium's finished, then he could put her in there afterwards. He wouldn't hear of it. Oh, well. He still came to do his rounds.'

Standing on a small rectangle of freshly turned earth, he was busy tidying the flowers around a headstone which, Moralès read, bore Angel Roberts' name.

'His rounds?' the detective asked.

'Yes, he came to visit his wife's grave and his father's, just over there. Well, his wife's is an urn in the ground, not a grave, but that sounds nicer than calling it a plot, doesn't it?'

As he finished arranging the bouquets, the undertaker remarked that she'd received a lot of flowers. 'This one here, in the shape of a boat, it's nice and original, don't you think? It's one of our local florist's specialities. She makes arrangements to order, you know. If ever you have the urge to send a lady flowers, just pick up the phone and I'll give you her number.'

Moralès looked at the headstone, wishing it could tell him more than the dates carved in the granite: 1975–2007.

'Still, it's nicer when it's the old folks who die, isn't it? Seeing the young ones pass just tears our hearts out. I don't know why, come to think of it, because we don't know them as well as the old folks.'

The granite echoed the detective's stony silence.

'Mind you, the old folks do get some strange ideas in their heads sometimes. Did you know the old fisherman in Caplan, Cyrille Bernard, just went out to die at sea?'

Suddenly, it was as if something had knocked the wind out of Moralès's chest.

'What?' he gasped, staggering back a couple of steps.

'I know what you mean, that rubbed me up the wrong way too.' the undertaker scoffed. 'It's not good for business and it's not good for the loved ones, that kind of attitude. He went out to sea, threw himself overboard and made sure only his boat would drift back in on the tide. Crazy, isn't it? Truth be told, I don't know if it was just the tide. But word has it, his boat was back at the wharf this morning. Must be the sea that brought it back. No sign of the body, though. Strange thing is, Mr Bernard had a family plot in the cemetery right next door to his house; and I checked – there's still plenty of room. Funny how some folks choose to die, isn't it? I'd be surprised if he ever resurfaces. When fishermen decide to kill themselves, they know exactly where to go so their body won't be carried back to shore.'

At last the undertaker stopped talking and stepped off the mound of earth. He wiped his hands on a handkerchief, then reached into his jacket pocket.

'Let me give you a couple of business cards. You're a police sergeant, so you never know, eh? Feel free to hand one out, or even both of them. I've got plenty more, and if I get the chance, I'll bring some down to the station, just in case.'

Moralès left the cemetery on autopilot. He drove to the super-market and wandered through the aisles looking for products he couldn't find. After going around in circles for a while, he went to the fish market then headed back to the auberge. He dropped the groceries in the kitchen and went up to his room. Something caught his eye on the way in. It was the origami seabird – he had no idea what kind it was – the intricately folded paper Simone Lord had left on the kitchenette table a few days earlier. Moralès had picked it up off the floor and kept for some reason. He took some painkillers and went back downstairs, turning on the ceiling lights in the dining room, then turning them off again, opting for the little lamps on the tables instead. They gave a more muted light.

He hadn't looked at the sea at all.

Cyrille was dead. The ocean would make coral of him. Coral that might one day be turned into jewellery a bride would wear on her wedding day.

He unpacked the groceries, then picked up a measuring cup, opened the bag of flour and heaped two cupfuls into a mound on the counter. The wind must be blowing from the north. He could hear the waves crashing on the rocks behind the auberge. No. It wasn't that. It was just the sound of the fridge compressor. He was hearing the sea everywhere he turned. He added oil and salt, then started to knead the mixture with his hands, adding water, little by little, turning the flour into dough.

'Hi there.' It was Simone Lord's voice, so near and yet so far.

Moralès peered into the dining room and saw she was standing just inside the front door. By the looks of it, she'd just been on a boat. She bent down and took off her boots. Her socks got caught on the rubber and came off too. Moralès couldn't resist stealing a glance at the delicate yet disconcerting curve of her heels. Simone pulled her socks on again, straightened up and came into the dining room.

'I've done the calculations you asked me for – about how

Angel's boat would have drifted,' she said. 'From the dock at the Grande-Grave wharf, the lobster trawler has to be manoeuvred carefully for about a hundred and fifty metres to get out of the channel.'

She let her hair down, and her lively locks cascaded messily over her shoulders as she shook out all the tension of the day – like a warrior resting at last, Moralès mused.

'That night, the tide was high around midnight. Angel's death occurred in the morning hours, so the tide was going out. If the engine was off, it would have taken about two hours for the boat to get to where we found the body. Since the estimated time of death was after four in the morning, the killer would have had to have been at Grande-Grave around two o'clock.'

She stopped at the corner of the kitchen counter and made a clumsy attempt to smooth the wrinkles from her clothes. She looked uncomfortable. She lowered her voice. It wasn't quite a whisper, but almost.

'This morning, the coast guard brought a lobster boat back to shore that belonged to a fisherman in Caplan who, in all likelihood, went out to sea to die.'

Joaquin drifted to the bar, selected a bottle of wine and two glasses, and brought them into the dining room. He put the bottle and glasses down on a table. His body was aching. It wasn't just the pain in his ribs. There was a stiffness in his shoulder and his head felt heavy. Not surprising, given the beating he'd taken.

'Cyrille Bernard,' Simone continued softly. 'Someone at the station in Bonaventure told us he was a friend of yours.'

Last night there had been a magnificent full moon, perfect to pave the way for the ageing, ailing man. Moralès was aching in a place beyond the physical, a place the fisherman's death had hit far harder than all the blows he had suffered the other night.

'I'm sorry, Detective Moralès.'

He turned away from her and moved towards the kitchen counter. He draped a damp towel over the ball of dough, then picked up a bowl and reached for the tomatoes, mango, basil and a knife.

'I'd like to offer my deepest condolences for your friend.'

He set about dicing the fruit. Behind him, Simone Lord's voice had faded to silence. Joaquin swept the chunks of tomato and mango into the bowl and tore the basil.

'I'll leave you be, then…'

He drizzled some oil and squeezed a lime into the bowl, added the basil and pushed the salsa to the end of the counter so he could wipe the work surface clean. Leaning back against a kitchen unit, Simone Lord showed no signs of going anywhere. Moralès turned, looked her way without seeing her, found what he was looking for and moved towards her. She gulped. He reached a hand towards her, plucked a rolling pin from the shelf behind her, carried it back to the counter and placed it beside the ball of dough.

Simone straightened up and was getting ready to leave, when he started talking. Softly. She wasn't sure if he was even talking to her.

'When I was young, I used to go to Puerto Morelos for the school holidays. Both my parents worked, so I spent summers with my grandparents, who had a restaurant by the sea.'

Simone felt uncomfortable about staying, and about leaving too. He unwrapped the fish from their wax paper wrapping and put them on the counter.

'It wasn't really a restaurant. There were no signs, no tables and no menus. But my grandmother would always cook for people there.'

He reached for a slender, sharp knife and sliced the fillets, then put them on a plate beside the stove and wiped the counter clean.

'It was my grandfather's idea. He was a fisherman and, since he was afraid of dying at sea and leaving my grandmother destitute, he set her up with a little business so she could stand on her own two feet. She wasn't the kind of woman to refuse an offer like that.'

He floured the work surface, heated the hotplate, pulled the damp towel away and kneaded the ball of dough for a few strokes before breaking a chunk off.

'They had a house by the beach, across from the wharf. My grandfather built a brick oven into a wall that could be heated from inside or outside the house. There was a huge baking stone in there, and just beside it was a little window with a tiled sill that made a good hatch to pass dishes through.'

Moralès rolled the pinch of dough into a circle.

'My grandfather used to go out fishing every day. There were four of them on board. My grandmother and I, we would watch them until they were a blur on the horizon.'

He placed the flattened circle on the hotplate and started to roll another. The dough puffed up in the heat as if it were breathing.

'Then, she'd light the fire from the inside in the middle of the day, and once it got going all the local kids would come around and add more wood. She used to give them little sweet pancakes in exchange. In the summer, I was in charge of the fire – me and my friends.'

He flipped the tortilla. It was golden brown on one side.

'We used to pick up driftwood on the beach and put it out to dry in the sun. By the side of the river was where we put the dampest wood. The drier stuff went under the palm tree and we stacked the wood that was ready to burn beside the house.

When we saw the embers were dying, we would grab some of the wood that was ready to burn and toss it onto the fire.'

He took the first tortilla off the heat and slid it onto a warming plate, put the second one on to cook and rolled out a third. Then he reached for a frying pan, put it on the stove and turned the burner on.

'My grandmother always kept the baking stone clean as a whistle. When my grandfather came back ashore, he used to pick up a shell and blow into it like a foghorn. That meant he'd got fresh fish. There was a bench outside the local market and he and his men would gut the fish and sell them right there. He would always prepare some for my grandmother and give them to me wrapped in newspaper so I could take them to her.'

He placed a fillet in the pan and flipped the second tortilla.

'I had my own little part of the stone, where I was in charge of cooking the tortillas. On her side of the stone, she used to cook the fish. She always said it was a job to do together. I thought she meant the tortillas and the fish and the spices all had to be cooked at the same time, but it wasn't that. What she meant was that it was a job for the two of us. Her and me.'

Or him and his son. He continued to flip the fish and the tortillas, one after the other, like he and Sébastien had done the evening before.

'They weren't the same kind of tortillas as these. My grandmother used *masa harina* – corn flour – and she kneaded her dough on a big butcher-block worktop that my grandfather put in the kitchen for her. She used to make bread too, and she baked that on one side of the oven. She had to turn it three times so it would bake evenly and wouldn't burn.'

Joaquin finished frying the fish, opened the wine, poured two glasses and put one beside Simone without making eye contact, then slid another circle of dough onto the hotplate. Simone looked at the wheat tortillas breathing on the heat, then turned her gaze to the stack Moralès was building on the warming plate. An aroma of warm flour, like freshly baked bread, filled the air.

'When my tortillas were ready, I had to push them to her side of the oven. Then she would take the tongs and put the hot, flaky fish right inside. When people heard the sound of the foghorn shell, some would go down to the market, and others would come straight to my grandmother's place and stand in line. When the tacos were ready, she would put them on a sheet of newspaper on the sill of the open window, straight on the tiles. People would just put the money in a pot and walk away with their tacos.'

The stack of tortillas now complete, he slid them from the warming plate into a serving dish.

'My grandmother had a little wooden stool that her father had built. She always said it would be more comfortable to sit on that than to cook standing, but she hardly ever used it. She was always on her feet when she was kneading the dough and cooking the fish. But it was her special stool and we all knew it. My mother always reminded me every summer she drove me there. Sometimes, when it was just the two of us, my grandmother would look at the stool and say '*Sientate*, Joaquin' – sit down – with a nod of her chin.'

Methodically, Moralès scraped the floured work surface clean with the blunt edge of the knife.

'And so, I would go and sit on that wooden stool. I barely dared to breathe. It felt like I was sitting on something fragile, so precious and mysterious. I never stayed for long, because when you're eight, even twelve years old, that kind of fragility doesn't sit well with you, and besides, there was so much more to do than sit on my backside – fishing by the river mouth, chasing after lizards, swimming in the ocean, collecting driftwood.'

He looked at the tortillas without really seeing them.

'When my grandmother passed away, my mother sold every-thing the old lady owned, because she herself had no use for any of it. The only thing she kept was the wooden stool. She held it on her knees in the car all the way back to our house. She couldn't stop crying.'

He carried the tortillas, the fish and the salsa to a table by the window. Then he returned to the kitchen for the plates. He could see the sea in the window.

'One day, Cyrille Bernard told me the past was made up of dried, hardened memories worn into the grain of the kitchen counter. Those moments, diluted in the saltwater of our sorrow, he said, would rise up again, flaying everything to shreds as they shoot to the surface of our minds. Since I've been here in the Gaspé, it's not just the saltwater of sorrow that's been welling inside me, but the seawater I've swallowed in spite of myself. It brings everything surging back to the surface.'

He went back to the kitchen and turned to Simone Lord, observing the delicate crow's feet at the corners of her eyes, the soft lines on her cheeks that deepened her gaze, and everything else she must be harbouring that made her beautiful.

'What do I have left of my parents now? A wooden stool? A flayed accent when I speak? What do we really pass down to our children? Clumsy gestures, and hurtful words? A desire to be swallowed up by the horizon? A special way to slice fish and cook tortillas?'

Dumbstruck by his outpouring, Simone reached for her glass of wine and drank half of it in one go, only to choke a little and turn away slightly. As she lowered her head to cough discreetly, Joaquin saw the beguiling vertebra protrude ever so gently at the nape of her neck, so close it was unbearable. Could it be that the many images of beauty that had splintered into fragments in the last few weeks were condensing into this woman right here, right now? With a swallow, he glanced at the counter where he had just prepared, alone, the same meal he had made with Sébastien just yesterday, the same meal he prepared once upon a time in Mexico. Could it be that our own life stories, just like our perception of beauty, was a collection of fragments that were forever shattering and rearranging themselves?

Visibly ill at ease, Simone took a sip of wine to calm and collect herself, or at least try.

'It was Érik Lefebvre who asked me to come here,' she blurted. 'He said you wanted to speak to someone from the coast guard who was on the rescue team when Firmin Cyr's shrimp trawler went down – someone who saw Bruce Roberts. I was there.'

He plunged into her deep, green eyes and gave her the signal.

'Come and eat while it's still hot.'

Friday 5th October

The previous night, Jacques Forest had called the auberge to remind Moralès of the plan to take him and Sébastien fishing aboard Annie Arsenault's boat. Just dress warmly, Forest had said, he'd take care of lunch and all the gear. Moralès hadn't had the heart to turn the invitation down, even though the idea of a jaunt at sea didn't exactly fill him with enthusiasm.

Last night, he had talked a lot. Simone had been there, but it wasn't for her that he had spoken those words. Moralès took a sip of coffee. Who was he kidding? Of course she was the one he had been speaking to. If she hadn't been there, he wouldn't have told that story aloud, not to himself. He couldn't remember having opened up to anyone like that. Except to Cyrille Bernard, these last few months.

Sébastien hadn't come back to sleep at the auberge. As he had thrown Sébastien's phone in the dish water, Joaquin had no way of knowing whether his son had even remembered the invitation. At five in the morning, Joaquin scribbled a note to Sébastien and left the auberge. He was hoping his son would be waiting for him down at the wharf. But he wasn't. Disappointed and irked, he parked and got out of the car.

Jacques Forest and Annie Arsenault were already aboard the little fishing boat and they waved as they saw him approach. The detective had expected they'd be going aboard something resembling a glorified rowboat, but this vessel had a decent outboard motor and an aluminium hull, sat deeper in the water and looked altogether far more seaworthy than he would have thought.

'I brought you some waterproofs. I thought you might not have any at the auberge.'

Moralès gladly accepted the protective gear from Jacques Forest and pulled it on over his clothes.

'Have you heard anything from my Sébastien?' he asked. 'He didn't come back last night.'

Forest shook his head. 'I tried to call him last night, but he didn't answer.'

'His phone's dead.'

Annie Arsenault chimed in. She took her fishing seriously. 'I don't want to put a damper on your father-and-son fishing trip, but we can't hang around and wait, because we're going to L'Anse-aux-Amérindiens. It's already half past five, so we'll get there about half an hour before high tide. Then after high water we'll only have about half a knot behind us for three hours or so. We'll have to pack up and be on our way by half past nine though, because two and a half hours before low tide, the rip will be running.'

Forest nodded. Moralès had barely understood a word besides the fact they wouldn't be able to wait for Sébastien. He nodded, all the same. Jacques unhooked the mooring lines and Annie guided the boat away from the dock. It struck Moralès how quiet the engine was, then he realised it was an electric outboard motor.

The sun was just beginning to rise over Forillon Point. There was a refreshing chill to the air. None of them spoke for a while, as if the sea were demanding a certain silence. A solitary gull cried as the boat passed. None of the others in the flock bothered to look their way; these seafarers were none of their concern. Cormorants flew by so low, they seemed to skim the surface of the water.

To the north, Moralès saw the road he had driven so many

times in recent days, snaking along the shore. As the village of Cap-aux-Os came into view, it reminded Moralès of Caplan, the village along the coast he now called home. He thought about Cyrille, who had gone to sea one last time. Last night, he had happened upon a voicemail message the old fisherman had left for him on the same evening he and his son had cooked dinner together. Cyrille had always said the stormiest seas made the strongest sailors. Sitting on his bed, Joaquin had listened to the sound of his friend's voice and cried the tears of a child. He had saved the message not only because he couldn't bring himself to listen all the way to the end, but also because he sensed that if he deleted the voice of Cyrille Bernard, it would strip all the salt out of the Gaspé. As they passed the cove at Petit-Gaspé, the cold tickled his eyes and he had to blink to keep the tears at bay.

They were in the national park now, and Annie Arsenault was hugging the coast. Moralès looked up at the cliffs and recalled how, not so long ago, he had been walking there in the dead of night and heard Simone Lord's voice carrying over the water. Just before he'd taken a beating by the wharf at Grande-Grave, where the *Close Call II* now sat in her winter cradle, guarding her secret.

He turned away and scanned the horizon, looking out to sea, where they had found Angel. Then his gaze crossed Gaspé Bay and landed on Haldimand Beach on the opposite shore. It was like pulling a plug in places like these, when summer ended and drained the tourists away, shuttering the souvenir shops and seaside snack bars for the winter. Moralès thought about the happy places to which people flocked that he had seen stained with blood. On that beach, next summer, would people look out to sea, right where the sun dazzled the eye, and say that was where they found the body of a young lobster fisherwoman just last autumn?

The sand would be filled with colourful parasols, folding chairs, tousled beach blankets, gleeful children, sunburned teenagers, boys and girls hunting for crabs and building palatial sandcastles for the sea to consume with just a few careless waves. Hordes of hardy youngsters would run shrieking with joy into the chilly water and emerge with shivering smiles on their faces. Through their veils of lavender- and coconut-scented sun cream, lulled by their faith in the summer sun, they would cast a fleeting glance to the horizon and remember that the waiter at the restaurant last night had said the woman was wearing her wedding dress when they found her.

'This is the best spot for fishing.' Annie all but whispered the words.

The boat had stopped moving, but Moralès hadn't noticed. It had also escaped his attention that Annie Arsenault had turned off the engine and Jacques Forest was now holding a fishing rod out to him. He took the rod quickly, embarrassed to have drifted away.

Angel's deckhand gave him a wink that suggested he had been following the detective's train of thought. 'Welcome to L'Anse-aux-Amérindiens,' he said.

'I love it here,' Annie added. 'You won't find a calmer spot than this.'

They were alarmingly close to shore. The sand seemed almost within their reach.

'It's quite a deep pool we're in,' she explained, as if reading his mind. 'We're protected by the coast. We're not going anywhere for a while.' She glanced at her watch. 'The water's so slack for the next half an hour, there's no need to drop anchor.'

Joaquin cast his line and took his time reeling it in. The boat rocked gently beneath their feet. It suddenly dawned on him that these were Angel Roberts' fishing grounds. Perhaps this was one of the places where year after year, around this time of day, she and Jacques Forest would haul up her traps to harvest the lobster and dump out the mud before lowering them back down to the seabed. It was a cold morning, but there was a peaceful air blanketing this cove. Was this what Angel searched for when she went to sea? He reeled the line in all the way and cast it out again.

'Everything was hard, that first summer. Do you remember, Annie? You were so pregnant, we thought you were having triplets.' Jacques Forest's voice was a hoarse whisper, no louder than it had to be on a boat in this place, at this tranquil time.

'You can say that again!' Annie chuckled.

'There was that one day at the beginning of July when there was a storm forecast to blow in.'

The three of them reeled and cast their lines with the calm, gentle cadence this place seemed to command, as if commemorating something unspoken.

'The other guy who was fishing these grounds didn't come to pull up his traps that morning. He just let us get on with our fishing, and didn't say a word. We just thought he was taking it easy that morning. So we headed out here, pulled up our traps, brought the lobster on board and dropped the traps again, and back to shore we went. That day, he waited until after sunset to go out and pull his own traps up, and we thought that was strange. You know why he did that? Because about four the next morning, that's when it started to blow, and it was a hell of a storm. It was gusting seventy knots. The seas were so bad, we couldn't go out for two days. We drove out here to check on Angel's traps from the shore, and they were all smashed on the rocks. Then we understood why the other guy had gone out after dark, so we wouldn't see him hauling up his traps and dropping them a kilometre and a half offshore. He knew the waves here would tear them loose and smash them all up. If he'd come out fishing that morning at the same time he always did, we'd have seen what he was doing and done the same. He went out of his way to keep us in the dark. He made Angel learn the hard way and have to pick up the pieces.'

As time slipped by, the boat glided slowly out of the cove and the rising sun peeked over the cliffs. Cyrille often used to talk about the beauty of the sunrise, how it captured the eyes while they were pure and fresh from the night, whereas the sunset flooded pupils already filled with a day's worth of images. The air felt milder now, and Moralès was enjoying the warmth on his face and his hands. Annie opened a flask of coffee and filled a travel mug for each of them.

'When the capelin are rolling, sometimes they're in shoals so dense they wash right up on the beaches. Near the shore, the water's thick with mud for a good two weeks. So you have to drop your traps further out to sea then as well. But no one told us that, either. Again, Angel had to figure that out on her own. She didn't just have to learn the ways of the sea, she had to learn to be wary of the men of the sea as well.'

'I've got one!'

Annie laughed and Jacques snapped out of his trip down memory lane to see Joaquin's line go tight. 'Just after high water is when they're the easiest to catch, the bass and the mackerel,' he said.

The three anglers were in their element for the next couple of hours, gleefully landing one catch after another as the boat drifted lazily out into Gaspé Bay. By the time mid-morning rolled around, Annie called it a day for the fishing. They had to head back before the ebb tide started to race and carried them out to sea. Moralès reeled in his line and put his rod down. Skipper Annie started the motor and turned back to shore. This time, fighting against the current, the boat was struggling to make headway. Joaquin's thoughts turned again to Cyrille Bernard, who had taken his boat out to sea for the very last time. He wondered if the old fisherman had lectured Sébastien and told him to stop staring at the hook, open his eyes and look out to sea. Standing up straight, he turned his gaze to the horizon and spent a long time speaking silent words to his departed friend.

There was still no sign of Sébastien when they docked at the wharf. They tied up the boat and carried their rods and their catches ashore, along with what was left of the lunch Jacques Forest had made for them. Forest suggested they take care of the fish at the public cleaning station while Annie washed the boat down with fresh water from the hose on the dock. Moralès started to accompany him, but suddenly stopped.

'Are you all right?' Forest asked.

The detective nodded. 'I need a word with Annie.'

Forest gestured for him to go ahead and said he would take care of cleaning their respective catches. Moralès made his way back to the dock. Annie had made short work of rinsing off the boat and was just turning off the hose tap.

'Annie, could you tell me more about the tidal current you calculated earlier?' he asked.

Winding the hose back onto its reel, she raised a confused eyebrow. 'I didn't calculate anything.'

'Yes, you did. You said we'd get there by high tide and the water was so slack for a while, there was no need to drop anchor.'

'Oh, that! That wasn't a calculation, it's just a natural phe-nomenon.'

Now the hose was back in its place, she stood and turned to the detective. 'Half an hour before high water, the tide stops rising. That means there's no current. The water is nice and slack for a good hour. After that, the tide is on the ebb, but it takes an hour and a half or so for the current to start flowing. L'Anse-aux-Amérindiens is a sheltered cove in a sheltered bay, so it takes longer – about three hours after high water – to really feel the current there. It'll carry you slowly towards the tip of Gaspé Bay, and the current runs much faster there.'

'Is that what you meant when you said the rip would be running?'

'Yes. If you're not careful, it'll carry you a long way out. Once you get past the point, you're in the open sea. I've got a decent engine on this boat, but I don't want to run out of juice fighting a current like that. That's why I wanted to get out of there by quarter past ten at the very latest.'

Moralès thought for a moment. 'And the tide times – and currents – aren't exactly the same every day, are they?'

The smile vanished from Annie's face. 'No. They get later from one day to the next. There are two high and two low tides every twenty-four hours and fifty minutes. I've got a tide table on the boat if you want to have a look.'

'Can you tell me what time the current would have been stable on the night when...'

He hesitated for a moment, then looked her straight in the eye. She knew what he was thinking and met his gaze with determination.

'You can bet your life I'll calculate that for you, Detective Moralès.'

Sébastien Moralès woke with a brutal migraine. It pained him to sit up on the uncomfortable camp bed, and he was perilously close to throwing up. He could barely think. On the wall in front of him, the face of a dead deer stared at him with its black beady eyes. The room was damp and smelled fusty. A shiver ran through him.

He was starting to remember things in dribs and drabs.

Kimo had brought him here yesterday. But where was here exactly? He didn't really know. They had driven to Gaspé and taken the road inland towards Murdochville from there. That much he remembered. Then, she had turned onto one gravel road and forked off onto another. She had prepared two travel mugs of gin and tonic for them to drink on the road.

'Don't worry, you'll never see a police car this deep in the woods,' she had said.

That had taken him aback. 'We're not going somewhere by the sea?'

She shook her head and kept her eyes on the road. 'No. But don't worry, it's a fishing camp in the woods, by a salmon river. You'll see, the place is to die for.'

As the alcohol and conversation flowed, he lost track of where they were going. He had to admit, he'd never had a strong sense of direction, especially in the forest. He stood up. His head was spinning. Through the tiny window, he could see nothing but trees. They had arrived in the late afternoon. There had been a moment of awkwardness when Sébastien unloaded the car and put the bags of food on the table.

'I should have told you, there's no electricity at the cabin,' Kimo said.

She had made some more cocktails while he sealed all the perishables in plastic bags and put them in the river to stay cool. She had pulled out the fly-fishing rods and shown him the ropes, but the alcohol soon went to their heads. Well, to his, at least. He had to admit, he hadn't slept much the night before.

He was exhausted from the jogging and the flood of emotions that morning, and he hadn't eaten a thing all day.

Then, they had put the fishing rods away and she had demanded sex before supper. That much he remembered. She had even barked something assertive and slightly vulgar that had both caught him off guard and turned him on. She had made him strip off from the waist down, sat him on a little wooden chair in the kitchen and straddled him with nothing in the way of foreplay, simply helping herself to what she wanted. She had made them both come.

Only then did she light a fire in the woodstove. He had gone to fetch the food bags from the river and rustled up a bite to eat while she poured the wine. That had opened the door for their first real conversation. Sébastien felt a lump in his throat. What had they said to each other? They had talked about submissiveness. Who had broached the topic?

'I always end up with dominant men.'

'I think I'm more submissive with women.'

She had been chopping the vegetables while he seasoned the meat.

'Not with me, you're not.'

'Oh come on. You've just played the dominatrix.'

'Because you asked me to.'

'I never asked for that…'

'Yes, you did. You said you were fantasising about a kinky dominatrix having her wicked way with you in a cabin deep in the woods…'

'I was only joking.'

'You had this defiant, sarcastic look on your face and I don't know … I didn't feel I had to, but I suppose I'm so eager to please that I always end up taking that kind of thing as a challenge. Sometimes I think I picked that up from all my sports training. When my coach used to say things like "prove to me you've got what it takes", I always felt I had to live up to the expectation…'

'Stop it, Kimo. I've always been a submissive man.' He had thrown the words in her face, adamant he was going to assert himself for once.

'You're deluding yourself, Sébastien. When I danced with you, you twirled me around like a puppet. And you're the one who calls the shots in bed too.'

Suddenly, he felt a surge of anxiety. He took a deep breath and walked towards the bedroom door.

'Sûreté du Québec, Gaspé police station.'

Thérèse Roch wasn't the type to sugar-coat the simple answering of a telephone with cheery hellos and cursory how-are-yous. She had done a diploma in office administration, got her first aid and CPR certificate, taken fencing and self-defence lessons and completed a firearms safety course, but the powers that be had stuck her on the reception desk. She could be helping the detectives with real investigations. She would be a far better field officer than Constable Lefebvre and could make a real difference in law enforcement, but she was confined to a chair behind a bulletproof screen. Why? Male chauvinism, most likely. Didn't they know it was illegal to discriminate against lesbians? She had filed an anonymous complaint, but no one had followed up on it. She'd have to write to the government about it. She'd been thinking about doing that for the last four years. One day she was going to report them all.

'Ms Roch, it's Detective Sergeant Joaquin Moralès.'

She wrote his name in big capital letters on her notepad. He was going to be one of the first she'd report.

'Your friend, Dotrice Percy, has some important information about the murder of Angel Roberts. Now that I've finished interviewing the immediate family, I'd like to meet this key witness.'

Thérèse Roch was quick to object. 'She came to see you at the hospital, but you sent her packing. Given how rude you were, she might not be inclined to talk to you anymore.'

'First of all, I had just woken up with a concussion and I was heavily medicated.'

Thérèse Roch was reluctant to believe him.

'Second, I would never have taken such an important statement in a public place. You've worked in law enforcement for long enough to know that if the identity of a key witness in a murder case were to be publicly known, it may put that person's own life in danger.'

Thérèse Roch drew a question mark besides Moralès's name. She hadn't considered that might be a concern.

'It was risky for her to even come to the hospital. You do know a police officer should never, ever put the life of a civilian in danger, don't you?'

'Yes.' She admitted it with a sigh, embarrassed that this hadn't occurred to her earlier.

'Finally, she will tell you herself that it wasn't me who strong-armed her out the door, because I was on my back in a hospital bed attached to an IV line.'

That was true, Thérèse had to admit. Dotrice had said it was a young man, perhaps a security guard, who had arrived at the same time as the nurse.

'I'll get straight to the point, Ms Roch. I need to know where I can find Dotrice Percy right now so I can take her statement.'

Thérèse Roch was more than just a receptionist stuck on the front desk. She had her CPR certificate, her firearms safety course and her self-defence training, and she had taken fencing lessons. The powers that be had entrusted her with this position because she could be counted on to act in the interests of public safety and relay confidential information between sergeants who respected her. She tore the top sheet off her notepad and raised her voice to cover the sound of the paper shredder as she gave the detective her home address.

Moralès hesitated for a moment when he got out of the car. As he walked up the steps to the front porch, he noticed his ribs were still aching and wondered if it was a wise idea to have come here alone. He thought about what Lefebvre had told him about slipping his handcuffs countless times onto consenting wrists, and shook his head with a smile as he rang the doorbell. Even in handcuffs, Dotrice Percy would be a dangerous woman. Plus, she'd probably refuse to talk to him.

She opened the door. Her shock of hair was held back by a bright-purple headband paired with a lilac, skin-tight bodysuit, over which she had slipped what looked like a yellow one-piece swimsuit and a neon orange belt. She wore a pair of leg warmers in just as loud a shade of orange, which were rumpled around her ankles and the tops of her high-heeled shoes. In spite of the gravity of the case and the seriousness of the situation, Moralès couldn't help but think that Lefebvre would be cracking a joke that the seer must have really wanted to make sure she was seen.

'Thérèse said you were on your way. Better late than never. What do you want?'

Thrown off by her clipped tone and the acute observation –

he really should have made time to see her before now – Moralès was momentarily lost for words. He could hear the sound of a television coming from inside the house, the voice of a fitness trainer barking instructions for some sort of home workout. He hurriedly strung his question together.

'The other day, at the hospital, you said that on the night Angel Roberts died, you had seen—'

She cut him off, impatient for him to finish the question. 'A naked monster, with a transparent appendage and a shrivelled phallus. What's it to you?'

The door creaked open a touch behind her to reveal a peppy home-fitness instructor on the screen, isolating the triceps, a muscle group that just dangles until you flex it, said the voice. Dotrice was getting antsy. She was missing her workout.

'What time was that?'

'Quarter past midnight.'

'Are you sure?'

'Yes. At midnight exactly, I heard the sound of an engine on the water. I know that for a fact because it was a time of alignment.'

She didn't elaborate, but Moralès gathered she must be talking about stars and energy rather than hands on a clock.

'The sound of an engine arriving or leaving?'

'Arriving and being turned off. Fifteen minutes later, the naked monster passed right by me.'

The triceps were pumping hard on the TV screen, by the sounds of it.

'Where, exactly, was your meditation taking place?'

She gave a sigh of exasperation. 'You're not very good at listening, are you? I told you all that the other day.'

'You said something about red land, as I recall.'

'The land of our red ancestors – though I know it's not very

PC to say that kind of thing these days – where the all-powerful breath of the whales meets the earth. It's not that hard to understand.'

'Perhaps, but I didn't grow up around here…'

She looked him up and down and gave a curt nod that suggested she admitted this fact might have been an impediment to his understanding of the blindingly obvious.

'L'Anse-aux-Amérindiens. It's a popular whale-watching spot. There's a little cabin on the right. You'll see it when you get there. I was sitting just behind it, so I'd be out of the north wind.'

Moralès thanked her.

'If you do happen to have any other questions, I'd rather you come back at a different time.' She closed the door.

Moralès dashed to his car and set off in a hurry for Forillon Park – the end of the road.

He grasped the door knob, turned it one way, then the next, and gave it a pull. The door wouldn't budge. It must have warped with time and damp. The knob threatened to come off in his hand. A surge of nausea made him feel dizzy for a second. His heart was pounding. He tried again. Was he swaying, or was it the room? Then he pushed the door, and realised that it opened outwards, not inwards. He felt like an idiot to have panicked like that for nothing.

He was glad to get out of the room. Everything in the little camp kitchen was spotless. All the dishes had been washed, dried and put away. He went over to a cupboard and opened it. Dishes. He opened another one. And kept going until he found what he was looking for. Tools. Towels. Spare rain jackets. Eventually he found a cabinet filled with containers bearing pharmaceutical labels. He swallowed a couple of tablets. They scraped their way down his throat and his mouth felt like it was full of cotton wool.

He stepped outside into the fresh air. Kimo's car was still parked there, but she was nowhere to be seen.

It took Detective Sergeant Moralès barely twenty minutes to cover the distance from Cap-des-Rosiers to L'Anse-aux-Amérindiens. He parked and walked into the observation area the wildlife officers had set up for visitors. A rustic-looking wooden fence surrounded the broad grassy promontory that perched on the cliff top, dominating the shore below. There were three picnic tables near the cliff's edge. To the east, a gravel slope led down to a small rocky beach, at the far end of which was a wooden staircase.

Making his way towards it, Moralès could see the spot just offshore where he, Annie Arsenault and Jacques Forest had been fishing that morning. He could also see the little cabin on the cliff edge that Dotrice Percy had mentioned. It was more of a wooden box.

The clairvoyant must have been sitting on the other side of it, looking out to sea in the lee of the wind, when the monster with the atrophied member came up the stairs at the far end of the beach. He ventured off the path for a closer look at the small wooden structure, to get a sense of what it might be used for. He had no idea. It was narrow and about a metre and a half high. There was a small padlocked door on one side, to which a faded notice was stapled, warning curious passersby not to touch. Whoever had built the structure had left a gap of about ten centimetres between the planks on the side that faced the sea.

Moralès turned on his phone's torch function and looked inside. It was empty. He backed away and turned towards the path again, and that was when he noticed another box to his right, further east, on the other side of the stairs that led down to the shore, and another one a little further away. Moralès made his way back to the parking area and looked for a path that might lead to the second wooden box. He couldn't see one. From the parking area, there was only one path, the main one that led to the viewpoint at Land's End. He set off in that direction, keeping his eyes peeled for a way to get to one or other of the boxes. There was no obvious path, so he ended up forging his own way through two thickets of bushes to where he figured the boxes must be. It was slow going, and after a while he still couldn't see either of the boxes. They must be camouflaged – designed to be visible only from the sea, he thought.

Moralès kept inching his way forward until he reached the edge of the cliff. When he turned around, he saw one of the two boxes not far away and went over for a closer look. It was the same kind of structure. On the padlocked door, there was a notice similar to the one on the first box, but this one wasn't as weathered. *Do Not Open*, it read. At the bottom of the notice, there was a printed logo bearing the letters MLI.

Moralès walked around the structure, turned his phone torch on again and peered inside through the gap at the front. What he saw made him gasp and take a step back. Now he understood why these boxes were so well hidden. He looked out to sea, turned off his torch and dialled Lefebvre's number.

'Hi, Moralès. Where the heck are you, you and that son of yours? I stopped by the auberge at lunchtime and—'

'I need your help, Lefebvre. A company called MLI – does that ring any bells?'

Silence. Then: 'Not off the top of my head, no.'

'Look into it and get back to me, will you?'

Moralès hung up. There was no point hiking over to the other box. He walked back to the parking area. Eager to hear what Lefebvre had managed to find out, he checked his phone as he approached his car – and saw he had missed several calls that morning. He had turned off the ringer when they were out fishing and forgotten to turn it on again. He must have been too preoccupied to see the notifications when he used the torch function earlier. As if on cue, the phone vibrated in his hand. He picked up right away.

'MLI could refer to a packaging company near the Ontario border, a company in the Eastern Townships that makes plastic wrappers for the agrifood industry, a label design business in the suburbs of Montreal – or the Maurice Lamontagne Institute near Rimouski.'

'What is the Maurice Lamontagne Institute, exactly?'

Moralès could hear Lefebvre tapping away at his computer keyboard.

'Right, well, here's what the website says – "The Maurice Lamontagne Institute is a marine-science research institute located in Mont Joli, Quebec and is part of the Canadian department of Fisheries and Oceans..." – is that what you're looking for?'

'Fisheries and Oceans Canada, you said?'

'Yes.'

Moralès leaned against his car for a moment to wrap his head around this information. Why hadn't Simone Lord told him about these boxes?

'Listen, Moralès, I want to make myself useful – that's what I'm being paid to do – but you're going to have to help me help you by telling me what you're looking for exactly.'

'What's the link between the Maurice Lamontagne Institute and the Fisheries and Oceans administration?'

He heard Lefebvre's fingers flying across the keyboard.

'It's part of a network of research centres that are all connected to Fisheries and Oceans Canada, by the looks of it. I don't know what it is you've found, but if you're wondering why Simone didn't tell you about it, maybe she wasn't aware of it. It says here there are more than three hundred people who work in independent research centres like this. They're funded by the federal government, and they specialise in ocean science and aquatic ecosystems management.'

Moralès finally understood and breathed a sigh of relief. 'Lefebvre, I want you to call Simone Lord and tell her to contact the Maurice Lamontagne Institute.'

'And what is she supposed to ask these whale scientists? '

'She needs to ask for the video recordings from the camera they set up at L'Anse-aux-Amérindiens.'

'At L'Anse-aux-Amérindiens?'

'There might be two cameras. Maybe more. I want her to get the recordings from the night Angel went missing, and all those from the previous week. Then I need you to go through all that footage, Lefebvre.'

'Me?'

'And you call me as soon as you see anything resembling a naked monster, with a transparent appendage and a shrivelled phallus, emerging from the water, all right?'

'I hope you're buying the popcorn.'

'I can do better than that. I'm also tasking you with a mission to call that charming doctor of yours.'

'Now you're talking, boss. It's nice to see you know what I'm good at.'

Moralès hung up and turned the phone ringer on again.

𝚿

Sébastien Moralès was suffocating. He turned to his left and ran as fast as he could, but after just a few metres he fell to his knees and vomited profusely. His body shook with spasms. His skin was drenched in sweat. Tears streamed down his cheeks. His throat was on fire. He struggled to his feet and leaned back against a tree, trying to catch his breath. Water, he needed water. Feeling steadier on his feet, he made his way to the river.

There he saw Kimo, sitting in the lotus position on a large flat rock. She was barefoot and had pulled her leggings up to her knees.

'Are you all right?' she asked.

Appearances can be deceiving. That was what his father had said. He moved towards her, crouched at the water's edge and rinsed his hands.

She rose and stretched. 'Want to borrow a towel? There are plenty in the cabin.'

Kimo's body was firm and athletic, much more toned than his. 'It might do you good to go for a dip, or at least dunk your head in the water.'

He was ashamed to be sick in front of this alluring young woman who was full of energy and had offered him her body again just last night. He was suffocating again. Just like he had with Maude. He wanted to run away. Not because he was paying the price for a night of drunkenness, with his stomach turned upside down and his head feeling like it was about to explode. Because he had just admitted to himself that he had erred, that he had been the author of his own misfortune with Maude. Of their misfortune.

The images scrolled through his mind like a horror film he couldn't bear to watch. She was eighteen, and she'd got drunk and kissed another guy at a party the night before. The silly kind of thing that happens when you're young and just starting to

have regrets. She did regret it, he remembered that. In his mind's
eye, he could see his girlfriend timidly asking him to forgive her.
And, more importantly, he could see himself. Mocking her,
scoffing at her lack of commitment, both to him and to what
she'd just done. He had laughed in her face and told her she was
as shy as a mouse in love and infidelity alike. 'If you're going to
cheat on me, you might as well do it for real!' That was what he
had said. He had done it on purpose. His arrogance and
apparent indifference were intended to hurt her. But his words
had been a challenge, and she had risen to it.

A few weeks later, tired of all his mocking, she had gone out
and slept with someone else just to prove to him that she could
'do it for real'. She had been hoping he would tell her to stop,
tell her he loved her and wanted her all to himself. But he had
been hurt, and had shrugged it off to protect himself. And so
the game had continued. 'Do you want me to cheat on you
tonight?' she would tease. 'Maybe it'd turn me on,' he would
laugh, even though he didn't mean it. Again and again she had
done it, and he had taken it upon himself to get his own back
by making love to her with words that, in the cruellest of
ironies, echoed a pain he couldn't bring himself to acknowledge.

She had cheated on him out of resentment because they were
barely twenty years old and that was the way they were learning
to love each other, by tearing each other apart. As time had gone
by, they had settled into a certain rhythm and crafted a narrative
they both believed. The rhythm had become a rut, and they
would only rarely make love, fuelled by alcohol, turmoil and
nostalgia. Last year, when she had announced she wanted to
have a baby, he had told her to go and pick a father from her
crowd of lovers. She had simply nodded, out of habit more than
anything.

Lying on the ground, he looked up at the sky. A ray of sun was emerging from the clouds. There was a warmth to the air, but he couldn't feel it. He took a deep breath and plunged his head below the water's surface. It was bracing, to say the least. Slowly he released the air from his lungs in a string of bubbles and opened his eyes. On the shallow river bed, he saw the faint moving shadow of Kim Morin looming over him. With a knot in his throat he realised that he had let the situation get out of hand, and a shiver ran down his spine.

Moralès drove out of the national park as quickly as the bends in the road would allow. When he got back to the auberge, Sébastien's car wasn't there. He looked at his watch and went into the dining room. Corine came out of the kitchen to say hello, wearing a headscarf like a vintage housewife's. She seemed happy to see him.

'You just missed Jacques Forest,' she said. 'He left a bag full of fish for you. Looks like a decent catch. Should I fry up a few fillets for lunch?'

'Absolutely.'

'Feel free to work if you like, I'll bring it out when it's ready.'

Corine disappeared into the kitchen. Moralès went up to his holiday apartment, saw that Sébastien hadn't been back, went into his room to retrieve his copy of the case file from the back of the drawer where he had hidden it, under a pile of clothes, and returned to the dining room. He would have preferred to work at his kitchenette table, but he didn't want to seem rude by shutting himself away while Corine was making lunch.

He sat at a table by the window, opened the file and went over the timeline of the night Angel Roberts died. That afternoon, the young couple put their wedding outfits on and went to Gaétane Cloutier and Fernand Cyr's for a drink.

Corine poked her head out of the kitchen. 'Ah, you're here already. Perfect. I'm going to make us a little salad to go with the fish.'

Next, around six that evening, the couple went to Leeroy Roberts' house to have dinner with him and Angel's brothers, Bruce and Jimmy. Angel took what she thought were her allergy pills. They all ate a meal that had been catered by Corine and Kimo.

'Jacques did a good job with the fillets, they look beautiful,' Corine called from the kitchen.

Then, around ten o'clock, Angel and her husband made their way to the bar here, at Corine's auberge, for the party to celebrate the end of the fishing season. Besides Corine, her boyfriend, Kimo and Louis Legrand, the barman from the Brise-Bise, some sixty fishermen and deckhands from the local area were present. Leeroy put in an appearance, but Jimmy Roberts didn't come, because he wasn't fishing anymore.

'I'm just rustling up a quick tartar sauce, then I'll be with you.'

Around eleven-thirty, Angel complained she was feeling dizzy and nauseous. Her husband drove her home. There, they had an argument, because Angel didn't want Clément to go back to the bar. But he insisted he was going back to the party, and left his wife at home around half past midnight after changing into some more comfortable clothes.

'It's ready. Close that file for a minute or two, Joaquin, so I've got somewhere to put your plate.'

Moralès tidied his papers and pushed them to the end of the table. Corine slid a hearty plate of food in front of him and sat at the table beside him. That wasn't going to help his concentration.

'I think I prefer bass to mackerel. I'm quite partial to river salmon as well, but the fishing regulations are strict, so…'

Moralès tried to tune out her chitchat. He could sense he was close to a breakthrough, but something was still eluding him.

Angel was lured aboard the *Close Call II*.

'She's a good angler too. And she's got a little fishing camp in the woods, a cabin right beside a salmon river.'

What time had Annie said the water was slack that night, at L'Anse-aux-Amérindiens?

'I reckon that's where they must have gone. I wouldn't be surprised, especially as Sébastien's left his car in her driveway.'

Moralès looked up in alarm. 'In whose driveway?'

Corine's mouthful of fish went down the wrong way. She coughed and took a sip of water. 'Kimo's. Weren't you listening?'

'My son is with Kimo? I'm sorry, Corine, I didn't catch everything you said, I was a bit distracted.'

She smiled. 'It's all right, I could tell you were absorbed in your investigation. I said I was happy to see that Kimo and Sébastien were having a fling.'

Was that her – the woman he had seen bent over the table upstairs?

'I'm surprised your son didn't tell you, because the two of you seem so close. It's obvious he looks up to you.'

Moralès put his fork down, He thought back to the morning Sébastien had washed up at his place in Caplan, hiding behind his box of pots and pans.

'Perhaps I shouldn't have said anything, but in a place like the Gaspé, secrets are hard to keep.'

What was it that his son had spoken about the other night? Loyalty. To whom? Joaquin Moralès felt uncomfortable. The way everything had happened suggested that Sébastien had come to see his father to ask for some sort of permission. What for, though? There was something he wasn't seeing.

'This is a breath of fresh air for Kimo. It'll do her good. She needs to see that love has nothing to do with jealousy and competition.'

They had made fish tacos together. A family tradition. But what had they really talked about? The relationships we choose. He could picture Sébastien's phone sitting on the kitchenette table upstairs. His son was trying to get something off his chest. But what? He couldn't quite put his finger on it.

Detective Sergeant Moralès stared at Corine without seeing her. Suddenly he had lost his appetite.

'Aren't you finishing your plate, Joaquin? Where are you going? Was it something I said?'

'Fast-forward the video,' Simone Lord insisted.

'Why, are you in a hurry?'

Lefebvre took his feet off the conference-room table with a sigh and reached for the mouse. The fisheries officer had been granted access to a link to view the recording from the camera online. The technician from the marine research institute had explained to Simone that they always set up three wooden boxes at their video-recording sites. Two were located in places that were not difficult to access and were left empty to deter vandalism and theft. The idea was that if any criminally minded individuals saw that two of the boxes were empty, they wouldn't bother trying to access the third. It was a cost-effective strategy that had saved countless cameras.

The numbers at the bottom of the screen scrolled by rapidly, with the occasional pause in playback while the video was buffering. Night fell over L'Anse-aux-Amérindiens and the sea was bathed in moonlight.

'There, look!' Lefebvre paused the video, rewound the recording and resumed playing at normal speed, then pointed to the screen. 'Look at that whale's spout. It's breathtaking.'

Simone Lord sighed. 'Yes, but that's not what we're looking for.'

'I'm just being thorough,' Lefebvre protested.

'Put it back on fast-forward.'

Reluctantly, he did as she said and the numbers scrolled by against the background of a calm moonlit sea broken only by the occasional spouts of whales surging up without warning, like geysers in the night.

'There!' This time, Lefebvre had made the right call.

He paused the video, rewound the recording and played it back again. A lobster trawler glided onto the screen. Even in the half-light and the shadows, it was easy to identify the contours of the *Close Call II*. Suddenly, a silhouette emerged at the bow. The figure approached the anchor well, crouched or knelt down for a moment, then moved away from the front of the boat. A few moments later, the silhouette reappeared at the very stern of the vessel. It was impossible to see exactly what was happening. Whatever it was, it took a while. Next, the figure dived into the water and quickly swam ashore, pushing something. It looked like some sort of package, floating on the surface. The angle of the camera didn't show the figure emerging from the water.

The officers craned their necks towards the screen.

'Who is it?'

'I don't know.'

Lefebvre's phone rang, but he didn't answer. He was too focused on the screen. Eventually the figure reappeared. It moved closer to the camera and retrieved something from the bushes.

'It's a bicycle,' Lefebvre said.

The figure moved out of the camera's field of vision before they could see any real detail.

Simone Lord turned to look at Érik Lefebvre just as he was peering at his phone to see who had called. 'Did you see the time?' she asked.

He nodded. 'Yes, I saw.'

For a moment, she seemed to come completely undone. Then she pulled herself together. 'We have to check the previous days' recordings. That bike didn't get there all by itself.'

Lefebvre nodded again. 'We need to find out who put it there. You take care of that. I have to call my doctor back.'

He stood and left the room.

Moralès went outside, walked to the far end of the parking area and looked over to the neighbouring property to the west. A few hundred metres away, on the other side of Kimo's house, he saw the rear of what looked like Sébastien's car. He walked back to his own car and got into the driver's seat.

That night, the killer had sailed the *Close Call II* to L'Anse-aux-Amérindiens half an hour before high tide. The place had been deserted, the sea a millpond. They'd killed the engine and gone to the bow. Cut the anchor line and removed the anchor from its chain. Carried the chain and line across the deck and bound the legs of Angel Roberts, who was drugged and left slumped against the wheelhouse. Then the killer had gone inside the cabin of the trawler, found the old wooden lobster trap, stuffed it with blankets, grabbed a length of cord and gone to the stern. There that person had attached the trap to the chain, then opened the tailgate, taken the cord and tied one end to the trap and the other to the boat, so the trap filled with blankets would be suspended over the water from the stern. Finally, the 'monster', as Dotrice Percy had described the killer, had undressed, stuffed those clothes into a plastic bag, dived into the sea and swum ashore. The water was frigid, but it hadn't taken long for the killer to make it to the shore, because the slack water had held the trawler completely immobile just metres from the beach.

As he drove, Moralès played out the scenario in his mind. He pictured the gentle curve Annie Arsenault's boat had followed that morning, when the current had started to flow along the coast. Angel Roberts' lobster trawler must have drifted the same way, very slowly, for more than two hours. Then, two and a half hours before low tide, before the dawn, the *Close Call II* was caught in what Annie had called a rip, a powerful current that had carried the boat out of Gaspé Bay and into the open sea.

Moralès turned off the road and onto the gravel driveway. He was amazed how meticulously the whole thing had been planned. The further out to sea the boat drifted, the choppier the water became. As the waves began to crest, the blankets in the lobster trap soaked up the spray. The heavier the trap became, the closer the cord suspending it from the stern came to snapping. When it did, the trap plunged into the sea and sank, dragging the chain and line overboard – and carrying Angel Roberts to her watery demise. The current had swept the *Close Call II* out to sea without her, until the vessel was dis-covered some seventeen kilometres offshore.

While Sébastien dunked his head in the river, Kimo went inside to make him some breakfast. Then she came back to fetch him with a mug of coffee in her hand. Could it be that he had led her, like Maude, in a direction other than her own? And had he perhaps unjustly accused his father as a means to justify his own behaviour? Sébastien Moralès took the coffee from the young woman's hand. He felt ashamed. He wished he could shed this skin of his, delete this whole narrative of clinking pots and pans.

'Did you plan for us to spend last night here?' he asked.

'No,' she replied.

'But when you saw how drunk I was getting, you felt obligated to stay here with me.'

'It's all right, it's good for me too to take a bit of a break.'

He took an embarrassed sip of coffee. 'The day we met, you asked me if I was a decent man, a loyal man, and I didn't give you an answer.'

She turned away from him. She'd had enough of men who didn't care about her, who courted her only to engage in cock-fights on the wharves and indulge in petty acts of vengeance. A craving for liberation was what had drawn her to him. She wanted to be free to think of nothing but her own desire.

'I invented a way to love that wasn't right. I'm sorry,' Sébastien continued.

She felt awkward as she led him back to the cabin. She had never liked that kind of conversation. 'Come and eat while it's still hot.'

He kept on talking as they walked, as if he needed to vent all his frustrations at once. 'My dad always says criminals make up their own truths to believe in.'

'We all do that to some extent. Don't beat yourself up about it.'

They went inside and she sat beside him.

'You were right the other day when you said I manipulated people.'

'That's not what I said.' She reached for her coffee.

'I did exactly that with my dad. The other day, I told him I was all messed up because of him. I accused him of ruining my life.'

Suddenly, she frowned. 'What do you mean by that?'

'I did some stupid things. Cruel things that messed up my relationship. And I found it hard to admit to myself what I'd done, so I pointed the finger at my dad instead. I told him I had acted the way I did because of him and the way he always behaved.'

Sébastien leaned over his plate of scrambled eggs and picked up his fork. He took a mouthful and turned to Kimo. She was staring at him.

'Out of loyalty to him?'

'Yes. That was exactly the word I used. But it's not true. What I'm trying to say is, I'm sorry, Kimo.'

She wasn't listening to him anymore.

'Are you all right?' he asked.

'It's just that when you brought up loyalty, it reminded me of a conversation I had…' She froze and slowly shook her head as her words tapered into an eerie silence, as if she had just seen a ghost.

'What's wrong?'

Kimo sprang to her feet.

'I know who killed Angel!'

At the winter mooring yard, the detective wove his way between the shrimp trawlers and pickup trucks, found a spot to park and got out of his car.

The *Close Call II*, relieved of her skipper and engine power, had glided away towards the horizon. Twenty-four hours later, Leeroy Roberts and his sons, Bruce and Jimmy, had found the boat by following an approximate trajectory Bruce had calculated based on the current and the tide.

Moralès hated these rickety metal stairs. He climbed up to the deck, very carefully. He was kicking himself for not having given more thought to the currents earlier in the investigation. When he had first gone aboard the *Ange-Irène*, Leeroy Roberts had mentioned his son's calculations and the detective should have caught on that this was a key clue.

Instead of feeling relief when he set foot on the deck, he felt an unpleasant sensation of dizziness and nausea. He opened the door to the wheelhouse and stepped over the threshold, trying to focus on putting one foot in front of the other. Did all shrimp trawlers have a similar layout? he wondered as he descended the interior staircase that turned ninety degrees and released him on the port side of the vessel.

He continued into the kitchenette with its harsh overhead lights and cast a glance into the berth at the bow. This part of the boat was eerily silent. He retraced his steps, turned left at the staircase and continued down the starboard side of the vessel. His eyes fell on the gaping mouth descending to the deck below, and he paused. He should really go back above deck, call Lefebvre and wait for backup. No, there was no danger, he reasoned with himself. The fisherman had never shown himself to be threatening, so there was no cause for concern. Besides, he had no proof to support his theory, not yet. Before making any formal accusations, he would have to wait until Lefebvre had checked what he had asked him to.

Moralès descended the second staircase in silence. The overheads cast a severe light on the rust-streaked walls and the salt-encrusted treads of the metal steps. The doors leading to the hold were closed, and the lights along this side of the vessel were off. He shivered. It was damp and cold down here. Turning towards the bow he saw the door to the engine room was ajar. He was drawn towards it like a moth to a flame. As he inched closer, he heard the fisherman's voice ring out through the silence.

'It's all right, Dad. It's all taken care of now. Let's just think about next season.'

Moralès froze. He could feel the hairs standing up on the back of his neck. He shuffled two steps back towards the stairs.

Simone Lord backtracked the video recording as quickly as she could. If the figure they had seen was who she thought it was, that person would have gone there early in the morning, or the previous evening, at a time when no one would have been around to see. When the recording from the early hours of Saturday morning appeared on the screen, she pressed the play button.

It wasn't long before a figure appeared in the camera's field of vision. On the screen, Simone saw a man pushing the bike, then casting a furtive glance around. She froze the image when the camera captured his face.

'I know who it is!' Lefebvre cried, barrelling into the room.

Simone one-upped him. 'I've got him on video.'

'Let me see.'

'Here…'

He peered at the screen and gave a nod. 'My doctor's just confirmed there's a history of mental illness in his family.' He reached for his phone. 'We have to let Moralès know!'

He entered the digits to unlock the screen, his fingers poised over each of the keys as if they formed a secret code to remote-detonate an explosive device.

Moralès froze as the ringtone erupted in his pocket. He gulped. He knew the fisherman had heard the phone too, because he had stopped talking.

'Who's there?' the fisherman called.

Moralès grabbed his phone and turned the ringer off. When he saw the name flashing on the screen, he drew his weapon. The fisherman emerged from the engine room and stood in the doorway. He squinted, then frowned.

'What are you doing here, Detective Moralès?'

Before he could reply, the man saw the weapon in his hand and understood. He nodded and went back into the engine room. Moralès followed him towards the open door.

Sébastien and Kimo threw open the car doors and started running. They had been trying to call Joaquin, but he hadn't picked up. They dashed into the police station and came to a standstill in front of the receptionist, whose hands were flying across the computer keyboard so quickly, she couldn't possibly risk a glance in their direction.

'Excuse me, officer, we need to speak urgently with Detective Sergeant Moralès … Please,' Sébastien added.

The sentry threw them a scathing glance. 'And who informed you of the presence of DS Moralès in this police station, may I ask?'

'Please, I have to speak to him. I'm his son, Sébastien Moralès.'

'Can you prove it?

He pulled his wallet from his pocket, deftly plucked out his driver's licence and passed it to Thérèse Roch through the slot at the bottom of the bulletproof screen. She scrutinised it carefully and looked him up and down.

'I'm afraid I can't tell you whether DS Moralès is or is not at the station at the moment. It's a question of making sure the life of a superior officer is not put in danger.'

She eventually returned his driver's licence and turned back to her computer screen. Sébastien was stunned, and stood there for a moment in silence.

'If my father isn't here, could you please let Constable Lefebvre know that Sébastien Moralès is at the door wanting to see him? It's urgent.'

She didn't bother to answer, but Sébastien and Kimo saw her sigh and press a button, and heard her reluctantly announce their presence to Lefebvre.

'Opening the door is not in my job description,' she added.

The giant of a man was hunkered over an engine. He was busy changing the oil now the season was over, just as Bruce Roberts had been doing on his own shrimp trawler the other day. Moralès took in his surroundings. His head was spinning. Clément Cyr looked up. There was a figure lurking in the shadows beside the tool box, but this time it wasn't Angel. It was Firmin, drinking a beer in silence as he watched his son work.

'My old man died because of a conspiracy between Leeroy Roberts and his son Bruce.'

If Moralès told the fisherman to get down on his knees so he could slap the cuffs on him, he would be right beside the tool box, and that would give the man an opportunity to grab a weapon. Ideally, he'd get him to back up, but there wasn't enough space. If he told him to move forward, it was the detective who would end up cramped between the wall and the stairs.

'When I found out what had happened, I knew I had to find a way to avenge his death. Because I'm a loyal son, you understand?'

The giant of a man unscrewed a filter and dirty oil began to flow into a metal drum.

'I didn't know Angel at that point. I didn't meet her until a year later. And when that day came, I fell hopelessly in love with her. Head over heels. I couldn't believe she was the Robertses' daughter.'

He drew himself upright and stared into space. In the shadows, his father motioned for him to line the drum up properly, otherwise the oil might spill. You couldn't be too careful.

Moralès was seeing stars. He found the enclosed space, the smell of the oil and the fisherman's delirium dizzying.

'What would you have done if you were in my shoes, eh? I put it off. I said to myself, one day I'll kill her, I'll do what I have to do, but I'm going to let myself love her a little first. I'm going to fill myself up with her – my body, my head and my eyes. I'll fill myself up with her so much, I'll empty her out and there'll be nothing left of her, that's what I said. But it never happened. Every day I said to myself, I'm just going to take a little bit more, then tomorrow, I'm going to kill her. But then at some point, I came to see she'd never be empty. Because every day she was more beautiful than the last. That was when I understood I'd never see the end of it.'

The oil had stopped dripping. Clément Cyr put the plug back in and opened a container of fresh engine oil. His eyes flicked to the figure in the shadows, then he poured the oil into the engine. He could hear his old man laughing. He was in a good mood, as always.

'So I said to myself, I had to bite the bullet and just do it, so Leeroy Roberts would pay the price once and for all.'

'There's a marine research camera at L'Anse-aux-Amérindiens. We have the murder on video.'

Clément Cyr turned his head. He seemed surprised to see the detective was still there. Moralès shouldn't have come down here. He was suffocating. This place felt like a trap.

'Clément Cyr, you are under arrest for the murder of Angel Roberts. You have the right to remain silent. Anything you do say may be—'

'Yes, I understand.'

'I want you to turn around, get down on your knees and slowly raise your hands above your head.'

Moralès took a step closer, but Clément Cyr didn't step back. He took the time to screw the cap back on the oil reservoir, tidy his tools away and put the empty oil container in the bin. A man of his stature was a particularly imposing figure in a space as cramped as this. He turned to his shadow of a father figure for a second, seeking his gaze, then noticed the detective was pointing his revolver at his chest.

'No, detective. That's not how this is going to end. The boat might not be on the water, but you know full well you're in a fisherman's territory here.'

Thérèse Roch was proud of herself. Not only had she protected her superior officer and ensured professional secrecy, but she had also played a role in accelerating a key intervention. When Constable Érik Lefebvre and fisheries officer Simone Lord had come out to the reception area, they had understood right away that this was an emergency, raced to their vehicles and hurried to the rescue of Detective Sergeant Moralès, targeting the most likely ambush points. Thérèse Roch knew this because she had tuned in to the police emergency-response radio frequency and was listening as the events played out. The Fisheries and Oceans Canada officer had waited for nearby patrol officers to arrive and taken them as backup to Clément Cyr's house, while Constable Lefebvre, who wasn't cut out for field work, decided to make sure everything was all right down at the wharf.

Moralès could pull the trigger and be done with Clément Cyr once and for all. But he knew he would always feel sickened by what he'd done.

'I came to the station ready to turn myself in, you know,' the fisherman said.

Moralès realised he had been too quick to dismiss Cyr's confession-of-sorts nearly a week ago. He had thought the man was simply blaming himself for what had happened to his wife.

Cyr tightened the cap on the oil reservoir and wiped his hands. 'I'll still go willingly, but not in handcuffs, and not with that gun pointed at me. This is probably the last time I'll be aboard this boat of mine. I don't want to walk off it like a criminal. So either we play it like that, or you're going to have to shoot me. I'd rather die on board here than be carted off in shame.'

Moralès opted to negotiate. 'Here's how we'll play it. You're going to put your hands behind your head and walk past me. I'm going to keep my gun pointed at you as long as we're inside. If I get the slightest inkling you're changing your mind, I shoot. If everything goes calmly and smoothly, I'll let you put your hands down when we get outside.'

'And you'll lower your weapon?'

'Yes. I'll lower my weapon.'

Cyr raised his arms and interlaced his hands behind his head. Moralès pressed himself against the wall across from the stairs and the giant of a man walked past him.

'Could you turn off the lights behind us?' the fisherman asked, as he moved towards the stairs.

Moralès followed and flicked the light switch as they went up the first flight of stairs. He still felt queasy, but relieved to have talked his way out of the tricky situation. They arrived on the deck above and Moralès turned off the light over the stairs they had just climbed.

'Does my mother know?' Cyr asked as he led the way down the corridor between the two flights of stairs.

'I think she has her suspicions.'

'Why do you say that?'

They started up the second flight of stairs.

'When I spoke to her, she asked me why everyone was looking for someone to blame. I came to understand she was talking about you.'

'What do you mean?'

The men arrived in the wheelhouse. Clément Cyr lowered his arms without turning around, pushed the door open and stepped out onto the deck. Moralès followed him.

'You're a loyal man. You were looking for someone to blame for your father's death, because you wanted to avenge him, but it was an accident.'

'No. It wasn't an accident.'

Moralès lowered his weapon. He was a man of his word.

'Your father was drunk and he made a mistake. That's why the boat capsized.'

'My old man wasn't drunk!'

Moralès immediately realised his error and raised his arm to shoot, but he wasn't quick enough. Clément Cyr whirled around in a flash and lunged at him. He tackled him so hard, Joaquin was thrown against the wall of the wheelhouse. In the impact, he let go of his weapon and heard it clattering across the deck towards the hold. Before he had time to react, the giant of a man grabbed him by the collar and dragged him towards the edge of the boat. Moralès extended his arms, grappling for something to hold on to. In vain. He could feel the wall of the wheelhouse sliding away beneath his fingers.

'You just don't get it, do you? My old man was murdered by the Robertses!'

Moralès could feel the guardrail of the trawler pressing into his back. Clément Cyr lifted him off his feet. Moralès saw three storeys of thin air out of the corner of his eye. *En la madre!* The giant was going to throw him overboard, and it wouldn't be a splash landing.

'Hands up, Clément Cyr. You put him down now, or I shoot!'

The fisherman froze and turned his head. Moralès tried to grab hold of something as Érik Lefebvre advanced across the deck with his gun pointed at Clément Cyr.

The fisherman laughed. 'Give it a rest, Lefebvre, everyone knows there aren't any bullets in that toy gun of yours.'

'Maybe not in his, but believe me, I've got plenty of lead for you in mine.'

Clément Cyr turned to see where the voice was coming from. Standing aboard the neighbouring shrimp trawler was Bruce Roberts, pointing a rifle right at him.

'Oh come on Roberts, you don't want to shoot a cop in the back, do you?'

'Maybe not, but I'll be blowing a hole in the face of the man who murdered my sister.'

Clément Cyr was about to retaliate when Moralès heard the clinking of Lefebvre's boot spurs on the metal deck. The next thing he knew, the giant was crumpling to the ground, as if he'd been knocked out cold. He heard a sound similar to the one his weapon had made moments earlier when it went clattering across the tween deck.

Lefebvre swaggered over to Moralès pumping his fists. 'Ladies and gentlemen, he's down for the count.'

Moralès realised that Lefebvre had thrown his revolver at Clément Cyr and hit him square on the head.

'Strikeout for the Mariners!' Lefebvre cheered, happy to have put his baseball training to good use.

Bruce Roberts unloaded and put his rifle down, while Moralès pushed the unconscious giant away from him and sat against the edge of the boat to catch his breath.

'Cuff him before he comes around, will you?' he said.

Lefebvre was only too happy to turn the man over onto his stomach and cuff his wrists behind his back.

'I've never used it like that before. What a thrill.'

Moralès sat in silence. Through the dining-room window, he saw a sliver of a crescent lazing in the night sky. The moon was waning, casting the pale glow of a tired streetlamp on the autumn water. Somewhere out there, Joaquin thought, Cyrille was slowly turning to coral. In just a few days, it would be pitch-dark out there. A sudden eruption broke the surface before his eyes. It was a seal, launching itself into the air as if trying to snatch a shimmering of silver, then plunging back into the sea like a stone.

'I have to say, I'm mighty proud of you, Moralès.' Érik

Lefebvre strode into the auberge and hung his jacket at the entrance.

Sébastien and Kimo had come down to the winter mooring yards to check on him, but Joaquin had been busy explaining to his colleagues from the Gaspé station what had happened, so he hadn't had the chance to talk to them. His son had hugged him tight, then left him to it. When he had finally prised himself away, he had invited Érik Lefebvre and Simone Lord to join him for supper at the auberge.

'How about a beer?' Lefebvre sidled over to the bar, pulled two bottles from the fridge and went over to join Moralès, who had just closed his case file, in the dining room.

SQ patrol officers had rapidly descended on the winter-mooring yard after Lefebvre had intervened, and taken Clément Cyr away. Moralès and Lefebvre had followed the patrol cars to the station, given their statements and promised to deliver their reports that week. Moralès had called his boss, Lieutenant Marlène Forest, from the road.

In the early morning of Saturday 22nd September, Clément Cyr had gone to hide his bike in the bushes at L'Anse-aux-Amérindiens. Next, he had gone home and switched his wife's antihistamines for sleeping pills. At the end of the afternoon, the couple had begun their wedding anniversary celebrations, starting with a drink at his mother's place, followed by dinner at her father's. Angel was allergic to dogs, and her father had two of them, so she took an antihistamine pill. It didn't seem to be working, so she took another one. The alcohol and sleeping pills had made her feel so ill that around eleven that night, she had asked her husband to drive her home.

Clément Cyr had lied to the investigators. He hadn't taken the road the locals called La Radoune, but the coast road that skirted the national park. His wife didn't know – she didn't like driving that way at night – because she'd closed her eyes and fallen asleep. He had driven her to the wharf at Grande-Grave. They had taken her car that night, and he had only touched the bottom of the steering wheel to leave as few fingerprints as possible. He knew the code for the barrier at the entrance to the park, because he had often gone with his wife to her boat in the middle of the night.

When they arrived at the wharf, he had put gloves on and carried Angel aboard the *Close Call II*. Then he had pushed away from the dock and driven the trawler to L'Anse-aux-Amérindiens. There, he had brought the boat to a standstill, killed the engine and tied Angel's legs to the lobster trap. The entire manoeuvre had taken about half an hour. He had undressed, stuffed his clothes into a transparent plastic bag, dived into the water and swam ashore, pushing the bag of clothes, which in the light of the moon the clairvoyant had perceived to be a 'transparent appendage'. The frigid water certainly explained why she had thought the 'monster' had a 'shrivelled phallus'.

The men sipped their beers in silence. Sébastien's car pulled into the parking area. Moralès junior got out of the driver's seat, opened the hatchback and took out the fishing rod, lures and other paraphernalia Corine had loaned him, walked to the shed by the shore and returned without them.

All told, Cyr was away from the party at the bar for an hour and a half. Because fishing had been a common topic of conversation for him and his wife, he knew that the slack water at L'Anse-aux-Amérindiens at that stage of the tide would keep the boat in place for at least two hours. When he returned to the bar, he had drunk to get drunk. Not just to forget the chain of events he had set in motion, and perhaps to flee from his demons, but also to have an excuse to stay the night at the auberge, which would give him an alibi.

Sébastien walked into the dining room carrying some plastic bags. Earlier that day, their discussion about loyalty had jogged Kimo's memory about a conversation she had had with Clément Cyr at the bar on the night Angel went missing. The man was haunted by a devastating and fateful sense of loyalty. It had dawned on her that he had been drinking heavily and coming on strong to her that night, not to make Bruce Roberts jealous, but to strengthen his own alibi. Deeply shaken by what she had realised, she had gone with Sébastien to the police station and asked him to drive her home afterwards. She just wanted to be alone now, she had said; she'd call him later.

Sébastien had picked up his own car from her driveway and gone back to the auberge to phone Maude and end their toxic relationship. Feeling both saddened and relieved, he had driven down to the fish market; it was about time he started those culinary experiments of his.

'How about lobster for dinner?'

Érik Lefebvre was certainly on board with that idea. Joaquin watched his son carry the bags to the kitchen, then return with a bottle of tequila and three glasses. He put the glasses on the table, opened the bottle and poured three generous measures. Sébastien raised one of the glasses to his father, who had already raised his. Lefebvre followed suit, grabbing the third and clinking glasses with Moralès senior and junior.

'Yuck! Call that a drink? It's gross.'

The detective looked at his son, his eyes filled with emotion. 'Why don't you put some music on for us, *chiquito*?'

Sébastien nodded while Lefebvre rinsed his mouth out with beer.

Clément Cyr knew that Jimmy Roberts and the Babin brothers were poaching with Angel's boat. He knew they'd be hanging around the wharf like a bad smell and their prints would be all over the lobster trawler. That was probably why the three of them had been so insistent to join the search efforts – otherwise, how else would they explain the marks of their presence aboard the *Close Call II*?

But Leeroy Roberts was the man the murderer wanted to cast under suspicion. He wanted to make sure the finger was pointed at his father-in-law, and the inheritance clause in the loan contract he had made Angel sign would do the job nicely. Clément knew that if he waited another week before putting his plan into action, he himself would naturally fall under suspicion, because he would have been accused of killing his wife to inherit her boat. So he had decided to strike as soon as Angel had finished paying off her loan, but before the contract technically expired. He had calculated everything, from the tides and currents to the note Angel had left for him a few weeks earlier, which he had tucked away somewhere and brought out to show the investigators when his wife was reported missing.

The men drank in silent contemplation.

'Do you think she woke up – Angel – when she heard the splash of the old wooden trap hitting the water?' Lefebvre asked.

'I don't know,' Moralès replied.

Had she opened her eyes? Had she looked at the sea and the rope tied around her legs and known she was going to die?

'Well I suppose if she had, she would have put up a fight, eh?'

Moralès cringed. Some couples went strange ways. They might seem like a solidly built house, but at their very founda-tion they were destroying one another, oblivious to the devastation unfolding before their eyes. Some were a train wreck happening in slow motion, never realising they could turn onto a different track before they went off the rails. Had Angel been one of those people who resigned themselves to their fate? Had she known her husband was both head over heels in love with her and obsessed by the idea of killing her?

The detective wanted to say no. But he had his doubts. Because Angel Roberts had chosen her destiny. She had chosen a life at sea, and she'd had the guts to dive to the frigid depths and retrieve her traps when her lines were cut. Because she loved her brother enough to turn a blind eye to him using her boat for poaching. He looked at his son, who had filled the air with music and brought the sea into the kitchen. Because she was loyal.

Outside, they heard the sound of a car door closing.

'It's Simone.' Lefebvre got up, not so much to greet her as to get more drinks.

Moralès turned to the window again and gazed out to sea. The voice of Celia Cruz piped louder from the kitchen.

Perhaps that was why Angel had celebrated their wedding anniversaries with such gusto – to mark one more year of overcoming her husband's delusions. And she had stayed with him, in spite of the ever-present threat, blinded by the mirage of her love, by those photos of their travels and camping trips she had clung to like fool's silver.

Simone made her entrance, Érik brought more beers over and Sébastien emerged from the kitchen. For a fleeting moment, Joaquin's thoughts flashed to Sarah.

Angel had known her husband was up to something. Moralès was sure of it. Because after a certain amount of time with someone, you come to sense what's hidden in their silence. You can sense when love becomes nothing more than an illusion that scatters and dissolves like the shimmering sequins of the moon on the water. You can sense when your life partner isn't going to come out and join you, not on the Gaspé Peninsula and not anywhere else. You know when there's no sense in spinning yarns to one another anymore. You know when the condo isn't just a *pied-à-terre* in the city. You know when the time has come to sign the divorce papers.

Moralès moved the case file to the window sill to make room for the others to gather around his table.

'Hey, Simone. One of the guys at the wharf told me you'd got a transfer to the Magdalen Islands. Is it true?' Lefebvre asked.

Moralès felt his jaw drop to the floor.

'Yes. For the winter.'

'Oh, are you going to join the seal hunt?'

She threw him a look of horror. 'I hope not…'

'Ah, but you're not sure.'

Suddenly, a phone rang. Lefebvre gave a start, thinking it was his. 'I thought it might be my doctor. I asked her for an urgent medical consultation. You can't take any chances. What if the star pitcher for the Sainte-Thérèse Mariners suffered a serious injury in his act of daring heroism?'

He sulked while Sébastien went to pick up the cordless phone at the reception desk.

'Mr Sébastien? Let me tell you, this is Renaud Boissonneau on the line.' The waiter from the bistro in Caplan could barely contain his excitement.

'Renaud? How did you know I was here?'

'You told me yourself, you'd be at the Auberge Le Noroît. Now let me tell you, I've got big news for you.'

Sébastien took the phone into the kitchen to see if the water was close to boiling.

'I'm all ears, Renaud.'

'Well, Cyrille Bernard's sister went to see the notary, and it looks like it's Inspector Moralès who gets to inherit his boat!'

Sébastien was flabbergasted. He turned to look at his father through the porthole in the kitchen door. Joaquin saw him staring at him, saw the look on his face, and went into the kitchen to see what was going on.

'Ah, and let me tell you, I've got an idea. If you like, the three of us could run it as a floating snack bar – the inspector at the helm, you in the kitchen, and me taking people's orders. What do you think?'

'But where would we find the customers, Renaud? Would we just pluck them out of the water?'

'Ah, yes. I didn't think about that.'

Sébastien heard the phone being muffled and Renaud's voice addressing the people around him in the bistro. 'Where would we find the customers?' Laughter erupted in the background on the other end of the line.

'Renaud, if it sets your mind at ease, I'll come by the bistro next week to give you a dance class, all right?'

'Ah, well let me tell you just one thing, now that's a good idea.'

As he heard Renaud announcing the good news to the others in the background, Sébastien hung up. His father was standing by his side, in the kitchen.

'Are you all right?' he asked.

'Yes. I called Maude. I told her I wasn't going back. She thinks it's better that way too.'

He let a moment of silence float by.

'Listen, I have to tell you something about Mum…'

Joaquin shook his head.

'She's not coming to the Gaspé.'

'I know.'

'Are you getting a divorce?'

The water was starting to boil. Sébastien moved closer to the pot.

'If it's all right with you, I'd like to stay at yours for a while … Corine says her boyfriend might have a job for me at the microbrewery.'

'You're always welcome, *chiquito*.'

Sébastien picked up the lobsters and dropped them into the boiling water.

'That was Renaud Boissonneau on the phone. He was calling about Cyrille Bernard … He said you've inherited his boat.'

Joaquin blinked away a tear.

Sébastien turned away, feeling uncomfortable. 'When I went to see your friend, I tried to describe the sea, like you asked me. I told him I'd seen two container ships…'

'Did he say you were watching the sea like an accountant?'

Sébastien gave his father a look of relief. 'He said the same thing to you, didn't he?'

Joaquin laughed and pulled his son close. Sébastien leaned into the hug, letting his father's arms envelop him the way they used to when he was a boy. As he held his son tight, Joaquin saw Lefebvre through the porthole in the door, stretching his right arm with a windmill-like motion, and his eye was drawn to the graceful little vertebra of Simone's that teased at her skin as she leaned over the table to look at something on her phone. A sad smile melted Joaquin's lips.

Beyond the windows, the sea scattered incalculable shards of moonlight, their illusory fragments of silver shimmering on the surface as the horizon stretched into the night.

Acknowledgements

Thank you to my friend O'Neil Poirier, and to Gaétane Cloutier, Jimmy Lepage, Leroy Roberts, Réginald and Dan Cotton for all the fishing stories.

Thank you to Simon Bujold for the images, to Annie Arsenault for taking me fishing for striped bass, and to Michaël Lecours for his detecting advice.

Thank you to Ghislain Taschereau for providing Sébastien Moralès's soundtrack.

Thank you to Annie Landreville, whose keen reading eye cast doubt on the suspects, and to Dominique Corneillier for putting Moralès on a diet.

Thank you to Marianne and Fred Pellerin for the ice fishing and our chilling conversations about crime fiction.

Special thanks to my English publisher, Karen Sullivan, who opened the door for me to write this crime series. It's a privilege to be a part of Team Orenda. Thanks to West Camel for the editing, and to Mark Swan (kid-ethic) for the cover art.

Thank you to my one and only Pierre Luc, who makes the tortillas, turns up the music, breaks out the dance moves and pours the rum when I'm writing. *Je t'aime.*

And thank you, dear readers, again and always. You can reach me at roxannebouchard.com. I'm always happy to hear from you.